Sacrifice of the
SISTERS
LOT

CHRIS KURIATA

Palimpsest Press
1171 Eastlawn Ave.
Windsor, Ontario. N8S 3J1
www.palimpsestpress.ca

Printed and bound in Canada
Cover design and book typography by Ellie Hastings
Edited by Aimée Parent Dunn
Copyedited by Sohini Ghose

Palimpsest Press would like to thank the Canada Council for the Arts and the Ontario Arts Council for their support of our publishing program. We also acknowledge the assistance of the Government of Ontario through the Ontario Book Publishing Tax Credit.

LIBRARY AND ARCHIVES CANADA CATALOGUING IN PUBLICATION

TITLE: Sacrifice of the sisters lot / Chris Kuriata.
NAMES: Kuriata, Chris, author.
IDENTIFIERS: Canadiana (print) 20230489133
               Canadiana (ebook) 20230489192

ISBN 9781990293566 (SOFTCOVER)
ISBN 9781990293573 (EPUB)
CLASSIFICATION: LCC PS8621.U75 S23 2023 | DDC C813/.6—DC23

Sacrifice of the Sisters Lot

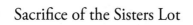

To the great, and dearly missed Adam Dale, whose years of creativity and encouragement made this book possible.

1988

My sisters and I wrote to Auntie Linda, begging her to come to our rescue.

She did the best she could.

Auntie Linda ignored our pleas to fly, figuring with delays and layovers she would be just as fast coming by car as she would by air. She never flew because she hated the view from the plane window, barely moving, just nudging through the clouds. Planes were full of nervous people, and they made dangerous company. Get too many scaredy-cats on the same flight, and their bad energy crashed the plane every time. She'd rather take her thumb to the highway any old day. Cars always stopped to give Auntie Linda a lift. She'd sit on the edge of the passenger seat, surrounded by the scent of air freshener, loving the blur of rocks and trees shooting past as she smacked the dashboard, commanding her driver to go *Faster! Faster!*

Now that she was coming to our rescue, her once friendly highways grew treacherous. Auntie Linda hadn't co-piloted a vehicle into an accident yet, but sudden rains and sloping roads repeatedly swept the car into the wrong lane. Blinded by the light of an approaching tractor-trailer, her driver froze with panic, and only Auntie Linda saved them from a head-on collision, reaching across the dashboard to take the wheel herself. During traffic jams she made up for lost time by hopping guard rails and sprinting between the cars, taking every foot closer to us she could steal.

In defiance of the force trying to stop her, Auntie Linda kept moving.

The average hitchhike from Thunder Bay to our home could be accomplished in seventeen pickups. This time she did fifty-eight, often in the car for just the length of a tunnel. A true people person, she could recall the name and at least one detail about everyone who picked her up; from Colin, the depressed woodwind salesman, to Paula, who'd been run out of town after she'd inadvertently forgotten to put the G-46 ball into the Bingo tumbler, thus running a crooked game, to Jay, the dour young man who claimed to have stolen his car during a bank robbery outside of Sarnia, but when Auntie Linda looked in the glove box she found the registration in Jay's name and a photograph of him in a classroom surrounded by children. She remembered every face, good joke, and close call during her twenty-hour journey, which felt like two months of travel balled into one frantic hop from car to car.

And she beat the first available flight from the Thunder Bay Airport, which had been forced to shut down after a glitch in their instrumentation nearly sent a landing plane off the end of the runway.

She arrived on our street at noon, cupping a palm over her eyebrows to protect against the glare of the sun and the grit in the smoky air. Wooden sawhorses and yellow police lines prevented her from getting any closer. Auntie Linda waved her arms to summon the officers guarding the barricades, offering the letter my sisters and I had written as proof she'd been invited and should be allowed to pass. The police wouldn't even read our letter. All they wanted from Auntie Linda was a phone number in case she was needed to make identifications. She tried sweet-talking the officers, suggesting she brew up big pots of coffee. "Maybe I could make you all sandwiches, depending on what groceries my sister has in the house." The police refused her generous offer, hiding behind their sunglasses.

Without birds or dogs or traffic, our entire neighbour-hood remained quiet as a closet, all the way from the General Hospital to the canal locks past Victoria Lawn Cemetery. The only sound came from the sky, the chopping blades of a hovering news helicopter that took the famous photos of the hundreds of dead bodies laid out on all the front lawns—each mummified family in their own neat column, like the bone-yard in a game of dominoes. There weren't enough sheets to cover all the bodies. Many of them lay exposed; no privacy. Thankfully, their eyes were closed. The shame of looking at them would have been unbearable otherwise.

Days passed before the police found me and my sisters, the only ones left standing. Our rescuers scowled at us, un-able to disguise their anger over what we had done. One at a time, my sisters and I were marched out of the house, our battered and burnt bodies paraded before the news cameras, where we were assigned the blame for each terrible thing that had happened.

*

Decades later, Niagara remains bitter over the Great Catastrophe.

The ghosts of missing parents and children will forever pollute the atmosphere—all that lost potential for happiness clogs up the sky like smog, so even on a clear day, you can barely see further than the end of the street. My sisters and I hide indoors, but when we venture out for supplies (always early morning, under the cover of dark for maximum ano-nymity), we sense the uncharitable thoughts from the store clerks and hobos who cross our path.

Unbelievable. Thousands dead because those brats wanted a goddam cat.

Let it be known the cat was my idea. That's on me.

ONE

The sidewalk burned brimstone-hot on the soles of my feet. I'd idiotically kicked off my flip-flops to run faster, not realizing the streets were paved with hot coals. The heat of the noon sun scattered my family. Cold weather draws everyone closer—sharing a fire, sharing body heat. Hot weather does the opposite. You want to be alone, and if you find a cool spot, the last thing you want is to get crowded.

My older sister shielded her eyes with cucumber slices when she sunbathed in the backyard. She'd learned this trick from pictures in her favourite magazines, the ones piled under her bed, their perfume inserts stinking up the whole room. Her skin glistened with oil and perspiration. The dedicated hours she'd endured beneath the sun concerned me. I couldn't help but imagine biting her leg and having a whole sheet of her skin tear off, like a piece of fried chicken.

I came bearing news I expected would make her jump up and hug me.

"Free kittens!"

"Where?"

"Mr. Bruinanski's garage sale."

She didn't even lift a cucumber slice to look me in the eye.

"Oh. Good luck with that."

My sisters and I had lived our entire lives without a pet.

Going to school taught us this was not normal. Every class-mate had a dog or a cat; sometimes both. Even kids from broken homes who lived in grimy downtown apartments took care of gerbils or parakeets. The more adventurous kept lizards or hermit crabs. Meanwhile, Mom wouldn't so much as let us set out a lousy bowl of milk for strays. She thought pets were for pirates and blind people.

"Pets are exhausting," Mom said. "You take them to the vets, you keep them fed... Who's going to look after them when you're at school all day? You think a dog wants to sit around the house sad and lonely?"

She overexaggerated. Animals spent most of their time sleeping. The ones who didn't were happy to have the TV left on to keep them company. It sure beat rotting away at the pet shop, where shitty boys disturbed your nap by rapping quarters against the glass and if the building ever caught fire, you'd be roasted alive, helpless.

"Pets die," Mom said. "If they don't get hit in the road, they get old and sick. Who needs that sadness?"

And this was Mom's true objection to pets. Not the mess or the expense, but the fear of unnecessary sadness.

In the garden, my older sister didn't notice the plump ant crawling up her cheek, perhaps mistaking the tickle of its feet for a drop of sweat. I saved her by flicking the ant away before it reached the cucumber over her eyes. "We're getting a kit-ten"—I promised her—"I have a plan."

Mom was bunkered down inside, hunched over a fan in the kitchen. She listened to the weather report on the radio, hop-ing for a cold front to come in and slay this heat wave, just long enough for her and Dad to get a night's rest. She longed for one of those mythical June snowstorms Grandma claimed came all the time in her youth.

"Guess what I saw at Mr. Bruinanski's garage sale?"

Mom wore a bag of frozen peas on the back of her neck. The plastic sagged, the insides gone mushy. She flung the de-frosted vegetables into the sink where they'd sit for days, until they became smelly enough for the trash. Mom never turned the stove on in this temperature. We ate peanut butter for dinner or we went hungry.

"He's got ice cube trays."

I knew Mom longed for more ice cube trays. She envisioned a fleet of them stacked in the freezer, making enough ice to fill the sink for her to dunk her head. Homemade arctic water would cool her off in a big hurry, cool her off so fast she might even pass out. She found the thought delicious, so she grabbed her purse and followed me out the door.

I led the way with my hands above my head, to shield my eyes from the blazing sun. "Hurry! Someone else might buy them if we don't get there in time."

Mom suspected she'd been set up the moment she stepped into the cool dankness of Mr. Bruinanski's garage. The concrete floor smelled of oil and water from his boat, on which he often promised to take us out to the lake but never followed through. Mom pulled the neck of her damp shirt over her mouth to filter the offensive odour. Tufts of cat hair floated past her face, and she swatted the soft fluff away as though they were disease-filled mosquitoes.

My younger sisters, the twins, sat where I'd placed them, next to a collection of push mowers. The girls crouched on their knees, peering into a cardboard box filled with fresh, mewling kittens. My younger sisters giggled as the kittens crawled up their arms. The baby claws weren't sharp enough to puncture their skin. The twins chattered away in the low voices they used when they wanted to shut out the rest of the world. I cleared my throat and the twins looked up, pretending to be surprised to see Mom in Mr. Bruinanski's garage. *Why, fancy meeting you here.*

Mom swatted the back of my head. I'd dragged her away from her comfortable kitchen for dumb kittens?

"You girls. Always scheming something."

We wanted one of those kittens desperately. That they were free seemed to clear the only logistical roadblock to bringing one home. If a kitten cost hundreds of dollars, sure, we may have pouted and offered to forgo this year's birthday and Christmas gifts, but we'd have accepted Mom's excuse they were too expensive. But free? How often does one luck into a deal of this magnitude? Hell, we should take them all!

Mom plucked a fresh cigarette from the pack beneath the shoulder of her shirt. The corners of her mouth lifted into a sarcastic *you'll-have-to-do-better-than-that* smirk. Unlike Dad, who got carried away, Mom prided herself on her ability to say "No" and mean it.

On cue, Mr. Bruinanski waddled over to our begging circle and delivered the lines I'd suggested to him earlier.

"Shame I can't keep the little things much longer."

The twins and I whipped around to face Mr. Bruinanski. Whatever did he mean?

"Tonight it's off to the vets for a sniff of gas. I've already got another cat about to drop a litter. It's too much."

Ignoring Mr. Bruinanski's irresponsibility for failing to get his cats spayed (didn't he listen to Bob Barker?), the twins and I grabbed Mom's arms, scratching her worse than any cat.

"Mom, you can't let that happen!"

"Poor little things!"

"We have to save at least one!"

The twins wrapped their arms around one another. Tears dripped from their cheeks to the oily garage floor. Mr. Bruinanski had sentenced our new playmates to a cruel, frightening execution. That's the power of kittens. Not even ours, and already they were creating unnecessary sadness.

Mom lost all patience. She made sure to blow her cigarette smoke away from the kittens, exhaling right into my face— punishment for upsetting the twins.

"The crying you girls are doing now is nothing compared to the crying a kitten will make you do one day. You should be grateful to go home empty-handed."

Of all Mom's strengths, an optimistic outlook was not one of them.

She tossed her cigarette to the floor, not even bothering to stamp it out. She hoped the next time Mr. Bruinanski took his stinking boat onto the lake he crashed into a reef and got stuck for a few days to think about what he'd done. Denied her ice cube trays, she walked home alone. She specifically said, "Don't follow me."

The twins and I returned to the litter of kittens to say good-bye. We hung our arms into the box. Their fur tickled our arms and their teeth nipped at our skin, but we didn't giggle or smile. I hope we didn't get the kittens' hope up too much.

A surprise visit from Grandma always brought joy.

I opened the front door, having no idea she'd be standing on the other side, smiling broadly, unashamed of her rotten teeth, holding both hands behind her back. My sisters all gathered in the hall, and together we whooped and danced, celebrating Grandma's arrival. She basked in our admiration.

"I heard some lonely girls live here who need someone to hug."

From behind her back, Grandma produced a beautiful kitten, its four paws waving in the air like octopus tentacles, eager to be placed on the floor. The kitten's green eyes and shimmering blue fur took our breath away. She looked precious. Worth abandoning the ones in Mr. Bruinanski's garage for.

Mom fumed at the sight of the new kitten, already brushing itself along the hallway baseboards, leaving behind fur. "Uninvited guest brings unwanted companion," she announced like an anchorman reading the headline. Grandma laughed. Mom hadn't been joking. She was dead serious.

"Please take your shoes off when you're coming into my house."

"Why? Don't you vacuum? Don't you wash the floors?"

Later, I overheard Mom telling Dad, "If I'd known she was coming, I would have waxed all the floors and watched her slip and fall on her rump."

During dinner, Grandma told us the kitten already had a special name. She made us guess and, in between bites of our Kentucky Fried Chicken, we interrupted the grown-up's conversation with names that increasingly became shots in the dark.

"Sadie!"

"Princess Leia!"

"Thunder Paws!"

"Featherhead!"

"For Christ's sake!" Mom snapped, turning her knife on Grandma. "Either tell the kids the damn name or I'll pick a new one."

But Grandma refused to say. Imitating the voice on late-night radio, she preferred to keep us all in…SUSPENSE!

While we ate, New Kitten settled in by exploring the wide-open frontier of our house. Her tiny paws echoed over the hardwood floor as she scampered back and forth, waiting for us to guess her secret name. My sisters and I abandoned our ice cream to resume playing with her. We followed the sound of her pattering feet into the front hallway, so we could scoop her up and smother her with our affection, but when we arrived, New Kitten was nowhere to be seen.

"Where is she?"

Thinking she must have tuckered herself out, we went on the hunt, expecting to find her sleeping under the couch or curled up in one of Dad's smelly old work boots. Soon, we were peeking under chairs, lifting sofa cushions, and calling "Kitty, kitty, kitty!" and cursing ourselves for not being clever enough to guess the secret name Grandma withheld from us.

Our hysteria amused the grown-ups. Dad popped the tab on his beer can and hollered helpful advice.

"Better check under the sink in the kitchen. Make sure she's not drinking bleach!"

The four of us scrambled to the kitchen, threw open the cupboard doors, but found only water pipes and bottles of cleanser.

"Oh my God! Check the bathroom. She might be drowning in the toilet!" Dad cackled.

An hour later, Mom's annoyance turned to concern. She'd been counting on Grandma taking the cat away with her.

She didn't care that we'd hate her for sending "our" cat away. Didn't care that for the next two days all of her daughters would be sullen, thinking, *Oh, we have the meanest mother in the world. She ruins everything good in our life.*

By nightfall, Mom grew frantic, shaking down each of our house's many nooks and crannies looking for New Kitten. She threw open closet doors, and made Dad pull the TV cabinet away from the wall, but all they found were stray cigarette butts and dead bugs. She continued to look even as Grandma stood in the door making her goodbyes.

"There's no reason to worry—she found a comfy spot to rest in private. Open a can of tuna and watch her come flying if you don't believe me."

At bedtime, Mom called off our search. We could resume in the morning. Without much enthusiasm, she asked if we knew how long cats lived.

"I'll still be looking after this cat when the last of you leaves home for college," she muttered.

Surprisingly, not even my older sister demanded the right to stay up until New Kitten resurfaced safe and sound. We dutifully marched upstairs and began our bedtime ritual. We brushed our teeth and changed into pyjamas without a word. Already, our hope of finding New Kitten was dashed.

Mom's estimation of the feline lifespan was tragically inaccurate. For starters, none of her daughters have left home, despite us being well past college age. Each of us smelled trouble in the air. We intuitively understood New Kitten was not coming back.

Of all the ways to be awakened—loud noises, heavy shaking, splashed with water—the worse by far is having your hair pulled.

Two hands tugged my pigtails, nearly dragging me out of bed by my scalp.

"Leave me alone."

The twins often visited in the night, demanding I fix small problems such as a burnt-out night light or empty water glass, things they could either do themselves or that could wait until morning. They never pestered our older sister the same way. She'd laid down the law, making her bedroom off-limits, and the twins respected that.

They tugged my hands, leading me down the hall to their room. The captain's bed they shared stood pushed away from the wall, revealing a rectangle of wallpaper still vibrant and clean from having been covered up for so long.

The twins knelt and pressed their ears flat against the wallpaper. I yawned and tugged the hem of my night shirt closer to my knees. The twins put fingers to their lips and shushed me.

"Listen."

Skeptical of this game, I placed my ear to the wall, half expecting to find something sticky smeared there as a practical joke. From the other side, I heard movement. Scratches and bumps. Something tiny squeezed between the rivets and clawed through puffs of insulation. New Kitten! I tapped the wall, and she purred loudly in response. Unbelievable. All was not lost.

"Everyone! Wake up! Come quick!"

The whole family gathered in the twin's bedroom; my older sister in her long silk nightie, Mom in her black kimono, and Dad bare-chested, showing off the first threads of grey in the black swirl between his breasts. My sisters and I crowded around the purring wall, jostling like piglets for their turn at a nipple.

We spoke soothing words to New Kitten.

"We're here."

"We'll save you."

I strummed my fingers along the wallpaper, imagining I stroked her furry, whiskered chin. Mom and Dad ought to be ecstatic. New Kitten was saved; we were delivered from unnecessary sadness. I waved my hand, inviting them closer to the wall to share this happy moment.

Mom and Dad did not celebrate. They looked worried. They traded whispers.

"What are you waiting for?" I asked Dad. "Get her out of there!"

Dad hesitated, which surprised me. He loved home repairs. The sound of his drills and saws sometimes beat the first chirps of the morning birds. I thought he'd be running to the basement to fetch his hammer to punch open the wall. New projects excited him. The destructive parts were his favourite. Knocking down walls and tearing out kitchen counters interested him more than the process of building them back up. Here was the perfect opportunity to grab his sledgehammer, yet he stood down.

"Cats have phenomenal memories," Dad said. "Some cats you can drive fifty miles into the country, toss out the window, and they still find their damn way home. If the cat got in the wall, she'll get out."

Back in bed, I hoped New Kitten wasn't frightened being trapped in the wall. Maybe Dad was right about her finding her own way out once she got bored. She was still under our roof, it wasn't as though she'd been buried alive, or trapped at sea on a sinking ship.

Mom and Dad's voices chattered in the living room below. Smoke from a dozen cigarettes chugged up the stairs, accompanied by snatches of worried conversation.

"I'm writing Linda tomorrow and telling her this is it— Mother is not welcome in this house ever again."

"Your mother meant well…"

"No. Horseshit. As soon as my back is turned, she's upstairs snooping through the girls' rooms looking for you-know-what."

"We've kept it under control this long. We've got things organized."

"It's not even her I'm worried about, but Todd."

Dad's voice turned serious.

"Yeah, for God's sake, don't breathe a word of this to your brother."

As usual, the twins awoke first. Before getting dressed, the two of them were back at the same spot near the wall where we'd last heard New Kitten. They wished her a good morning and asked if she'd had pleasant dreams. No scratching noises came from behind the wall. The twins pounded the surface, telling her to wake up, it was time to rise and shine, but they got no response. She'd moved on to another part of the house.

Helping them search, I went room to room listening to the walls, but heard no movement either. No more scuffling in the hollows. In my room, I patted the wall and spoke in a gentle voice, hoping to call her close.

Mom grabbed my hand and jerked it away. I hadn't even heard her come upstairs.

"Stop touching the walls."

I lifted my palms, showing her that they were all clean. I'd washed thoroughly. My hands wouldn't mark up the wallpaper.

"Leave the cat be. She's probably resting. Cats are nocturnal. All her exploring last night tuckered her out."

"But it's dark inside the walls. How does she know if it's day or night?"

"Animals have their own internal clocks. When I was a young girl on the farm, your grandmother had a rooster who liked to bully other animals. When the chickens got sick of his bullshit they ganged up and pecked out his eyes. But even blind, he knew how to crow each morning at the crack of dawn, never a minute late."

School lasted an excruciatingly long time. Concentration was impossible. The teacher wrote math questions on the board, but all I thought about was New Kitten trapped behind the wall. Was she lonely? Was she hungry? When the final bell rang, I collected the twins and hurried them across the busy roads without waiting for the crossing guard. They were as eager as I was to check on our missing baby.

Positive thoughts are important. I told the twins when we got home we'd find New Kitten waiting for us, grooming the wall dust from her coat. She'd purr, and we'd pet her together, until her secret name became obvious.

We came in the front door and found Mom and Dad waiting for us with solemn faces. Our older sister sat on the living room couch, arms crossed sulkily over her chest. She got caught sneaking out of her last period at high school to come search for New Kitten. She'd been crying. She already knew.

I took a deep breath, bracing for the worst. The twins grabbed my hands.

"I'm sorry girls. New Kitten's not here anymore. She left."

"How to do you know?" My voice cracked.

Dad bent down and hugged the three of us. The twins crawled into his arms, but I squirmed away. I didn't accept what he was telling us yet.

"I checked every opening, honey. The cat's not in the walls."

"She must have crawled out in the middle of the night," Mom said. "Filled her belly with scraps from the sink and headed after Grandma. You remember what your father said about cat's homing sense. Just you wait. In a week or two my mother will open her front door and find New Kitten sitting on her doorstep, swishing her tail and asking, *What's for supper, boss?*"

That night, I dreamed of New Kitten's trip to Grandma's house out in the country. She caught rides along the highway with lonely truck drivers, making new friends, and sleeping on their warm dashboards. Charmed truck stop waitresses fed her bowls of milk and old hamburger ends.

"Mom and Dad are lying."

My older sister bent over my bed, her lips tracing the outline of my ear as she whispered. Ignoring her, I rolled over, but she wouldn't allow me to go back to sleep.

"Mom and Dad would rather tell us a made-up story, because it's easier to believe than the truth."

She linked her arm with mine and pulled me out of bed. We crept down the dark hallway into her room. I took her seriously now that she'd brought me into her inner sanctum. My older sister guarded her privacy ferociously. She constantly asked Mom and Dad for a lock for her door, even though she didn't have anything the twins or I were interested in stealing. Mom always refused. Family didn't lock one another out.

Inside, her reading lamp cast a spotlight onto the wall

beside her headboard. I put my hand in the light. The wallpaper felt warm, almost melted. As soon as my fingers made contact, fresh purring came from the other side of the wall. Life remained in there yet.

My older sister looked proud. "See, who's the one who's got us a kitten now?"

I shouted with joy, prompting my older sister to clamp her hand over my mouth.

"Are you crazy? Do you want to wake everyone up?"

I felt ashamed. She trusted me enough to share her discovery, treating me like an equal, and I nearly blew it by alerting Mom and Dad.

"Mom and Dad are no help," my older sister said. "They don't care if she dies in there. We'll have to get her out ourselves."

I tapped the wall, and New Kitten tapped back. Her little paws were inches from my fingers, separated only by wooden planks and plaster. *I'm still here,* she told us. I sang softly and stroked the wall, asking New Kitten to be brave. We would come for her. The wall vibrated against my hand, a steady pulsing as New Kitten purred.

"Maybe she found bugs or a mouse to keep her alive," my older sister said. "But she must be nearly starved to death by now."

The thought frightened me. Very soon, New Kitten would be a curled mound of bones for a work crew to find. Work crews found secrets in the wall all the time. I once overheard Dad telling Mom about finding a cloth sack inside the wall of a house he'd been repairing. Wrapped in the sack was a mummified baby, as much as fifty years old. I thought about that baby for a long time. Was she put in the wall out of shame, having been born to a young girl whose family name couldn't suffer her existence? I wondered if she'd been born dead, or if someone stitched her into that cloth casket while she was still breathing. I made the mistake of asking Dad, and he roared like I'd pressed my finger into a gaping wound, telling me he didn't want to hear about it.

"This is awful," I said.

"No, dummy, this is our big chance to lure her out of the wall."

After carefully reconnoitring the house, my older sister felt certain she knew where New Kitten slipped into the walls.

"Beneath the dishwasher."

Last year, Dad had cut open the kitchen floor to reroute water pipes from the basement to Mom's new dishwasher. With the heavy appliance (which Dad had bought from a mysterious truck parked down by the canal) in place, he saw no sense in sealing the floor back up. For fun, my sisters and I took turns shooting marbles underneath the dishwasher, listening to them ping against the pipes as they tumbled through the hole into the basement. We played in shifts, one of us waiting down below in the basement to catch the marbles as they fell out of the ceiling.

The longer we played, the less marbles came back. Mom and Dad were furious. Our marbles might have ruined the pipes, cracking them open and flooding the house. We were forbidden from messing around beneath the dishwasher ever again.

Mom went outside to water the garden, and my older sister and I took the opportunity to invade the empty kitchen. I grabbed a can of tuna from the cupboard and ran it beneath the electric can opener. The gears spun, peeling the lid off and perfuming the air with a fishy aroma. My older sister flapped her skirt to fan the smell. We peered into the darkness beneath the dishwasher but heard no sign of New Kitten.

"Huh," my older sister said. She'd honestly believed this would work. "Open another can."

I followed her instructions, though it occurred to me New Kitten wouldn't know what the sound of a can opener meant. We never had a chance to feed her from one.

"She's too far away to smell anything," my older sister said.

I grabbed a wad of wet tuna and stuffed it beneath the dishwasher, putting the food right at the edge of the hole leading into the basement. Air blew onto my fingers, the draft chilled, as though the hole ran all the way to the arctic.

"Put more. If the scent is strong, she'll come."

My older sister ran the can opener, feeding me a steady supply of tuna fish to pack beneath the dishwasher. A bounty of manna piled high and deep, calling for New Kitten to crawl into the light and relieve her hunger.

New Kitten didn't take the bait. She stayed hidden, sleeping.

We tossed the cans in the garbage, burying them deep so Mom wouldn't find them and punish us for making such a waste of good food.

Angry curses erupted from the kitchen. Mom shrieked like she'd suffered a bad burn or chopped off a finger. I sat in front of a whirling fan in the living room, speaking into the churning blades to hear my voice echo like a robot. I hoped Mom's accident was a burn instead of blood.

My older sister and I found the kitchen in utter pandemonium. New Kitten may have ignored our tuna offering but the mice hadn't. They swarmed from the hole to gobble the tuna. Unaware of our rescue efforts, Mom had switched the dishwasher on and the rumble sent a flurry of frightened mice scrambling into the kitchen. My older sister and I watched as dozens of grey rodents surged from beneath the dishwasher, like water from a backed-up drain. They scrambled and bumped into one another, running across the floor in a blind panic.

Mom grabbed a broom and tried sweeping the mice back under, but more kept coming. They squeaked in unison, cursing her attempts to swat them away. Basement mice scurried everywhere; along the edge of the counter, into the sink, beneath the fridge.

She knew to blame us immediately.

"What did you girls do?"

My older sister felt too old to be intimidated by Mom, so she took a heroic pose, placing one hand on her hip. "You told us to leave the walls alone. Well, we didn't touch the walls. We touched the floor. So there!" Her brashness impressed me. I'd never dare speak to Mom that way.

Our rodent troubles weren't over yet. When the dishwasher's cycle ended, Mom opened the door and found our clean plates and glasses surrounded by dead mice. Drowned in scalding water, their cooked bodies dangled from the plastic grate and clogged the cutlery basket, their tails intertwined through fork tines. Mom issued us yellow gloves and stood watching, chain-smoking while we plucked the corpses from the machine and rewashed every last plate and fork in bleach.

My older sister worked mute, seemingly traumatized. I, however, took the multitude of mice as a positive sign.

"That's why she didn't come for the tuna," I whispered as I scrubbed a handful of knives beneath the faucet. "The walls are so full of mice she's pigging out. She's too fat to move."

At dinner, Mom laid down the law. "Today is the end of this nonsense. As far as all of you are concerned, New Kitten is gone. Finito. There will be no more searching, no more luring, in the walls *or the floors*. In fact, there will be no more mention of her again. Please."

Suppressed grief only intensifies. I lost my composure first, overwhelmed by the reality of beautiful New Kitten forever trapped in our walls, her last moments certain to be of fear and suffering. My tears rained into the scalloped potatoes before anyone got a chance to be served. My older sister cried next, then the twins. Mom tried to be stoic, ignoring our tears, but soon her own eyes burst. The five of us soaked the tablecloth, and our salt stained the fabric so bad Mom had to throw it away after two failed washings.

Dad couldn't live with a household of unhappy women. He loved coming home to the cacophony of our joy; girls playing, Mom singing, the five of us running to pepper him with hugs and kisses. Our laughter fulfilled him, and our sorrow made his life unbearable.

"All right," Dad said, chugging the last of his beer as he pushed off from the table. "Let's look under that goddam floor."

In the kitchen, Dad wrapped his arms around the dishwasher and wrenched the machine from the wall. Cords jangled and metal strips gouged the floor. He kicked aside our tuna mound, the pink flesh dotted with dozens of black mouse droppings. The hole in the floor looked no bigger than a baseball, just room enough to allow passage of the pipe.

"We need to make that hole bigger," Dad said. He turned to my older sister. "Rebecca, get my sledgehammer."

As soon as my older sister retrieved his trusty tool from the basement, Dad raised the hammer over his shoulder and smashed into the floor. The pounding tickled the bottoms of my feet. Mom winced at the unnecessary surgery to the house, but I saw excitement perking up the corners of Dad's mouth. He was in his element, expanding the hole until his arm fit inside all the way up to his shoulder.

"Be careful," Mom said. She grabbed Dad's forearm, squeezing his muscles. "There's mice down there." Mom worried the mice would latch onto his bare arm, nibbling off whole chunks. Perhaps he'd draw back a stump.

Dad's arm emerged dusty but unscathed. Next, he used the "snake", a large canister holding a hundred feet of metal rod for plunging down pipes to clear blockages. He shot the snake into the enlarged hole, unwinding foot after foot.

"Everyone needs to be quiet."

More than quiet, Dad needed a complete absence of sound to follow the scrapes and pings the snake made as it burrowed through the walls, allowing him to mentally chart its progress. With his eyes closed, Dad visualized the snake's journey. *Past the kitchen, into the hall, up behind the stairs...* Mom unplugged the refrigerator to kill the electric hum, and my older sister and I wadded paper around the ticking pendulum of the hallway clock.

Dad spent ages with the snake, unfurling it deeper into the house, using all his concentration to keep track of where the rod travelled. He stopped every now and then, reeling a length back in and re-sending it in a different direction. Unlike a toilet pipe, the walls offered multiple paths of travel, and he methodically snaked each one. He kept one hand on the rod, his sensitive fingers reading the resistance it occasionally ran into. He learned to tell the difference between the snake hitting a corner or punching into insulation. He searched for a resistance different from either of those.

We all jumped out of our skins when the snake bumped into what Dad searched for. New Kitten cried out like a colicky baby, a surprisingly energetic burst of pain, like weeks of bottled up torment being released all at once. Her dreadful howl echoed from the heating ducts. She was in so much pain, for a moment, I wished we hadn't found her.

Dad nodded, sweat cascading off his face.

"Upstairs."

Without waiting for us, Dad hustled, his hammer swinging off his hip, coming dangerously close to smashing the face of anyone following too closely behind. He charged into our playroom, knocking the paint station and dollhouse away from the wall. Mom tried to stop him as he un-holstered his hammer.

"Jack! Wait!"

SMASH! White chunks of plaster skidded across the floor. Mom covered her eyes. Quickly, Dad broke into the hollow behind the wall. A cold draft blasted the room, lifting the pages of our scattered colouring books. A foul odour followed, and those of us with a free hand plugged our noses. The smell settled into our sinuses, and for weeks afterwards, every time I blew my nose, I tasted a mix of rotten meat and cat piss. The smell clung to poor Dad so badly he washed his hair in tomato juice and shaved his beard.

Putting our arms around one another, my sisters and I clumped together, watching Dad as he plunged his entire body into the wall. He cursed and stretched while Mom grabbed hold of his belt, anchoring him to shore. My sisters and I tried to help, but she told us to stay back. I held my breath, remembering Mom's warning when Dad stuck his hand into the floor, afraid the mice would chew him to bits, and she would pull back a skeleton.

Dad emerged with New Kitten in his arms. We barely recognized her. During her time in the wall, she had transformed into Old Kitten. She'd lost most of her hair. The delicate details of her joints and the knot of each vertebra were visible, like a teaching model at veterinarian school. Her thin skin looked painted on. Her paws had withered to nothing, leaving yellowed claws exposed. Her ears were gone, nibbled to ribbons. Her eyes were open, but the pupils hadn't the strength to dilate in the fresh light. Her lungs could barely inflate beneath her tight skin. Each breath wheezed through her teeth, half of them missing.

I reached for her, but Dad pulled away.

"No, Emery," he said. "I'm sorry. Go downstairs with your sisters."

He joined us a few minutes later, bearing New Kitten wrapped in a small quilt from a doll's cradle. She was gone, and we didn't want to speculate whether she left on her own or with the help of Dad's mercy. He'd done his best to arrange her like she was sleeping (her hind legs tucked underneath her body, her chin resting across her front paws) but I thought she looked like an animal ready for the oven, only needing an apple shoved in her mouth.

We ran our hands over her cold body, feeling not only the absence of her tiny life force, but the potential years of happiness stolen from us. Dad pulled the edge of the quilt over her gnarled face and carried her to the backyard. Mom cried too, but she still made us line up in the bathroom to dip our hands in bleach and wash in painfully hot water.

In the days that followed, we piled New Kitten's funeral mound with yellow dandelions and turned the dirt to mud with our tears. The twins lobbied Dad to build a proper tombstone, better than the two sticks we pathetically strung together to mark her plot, but Mom felt New Kitten preferred an anonymous grave.

"She was a quiet cat and wants to rest without a lot of hoopla."

That sounded right, but deep down, I think Mom just didn't want the morbid distraction in her garden.

Dad's work didn't end with the removal of New Kitten's body. After tucking us into bed, kissing us goodnight, and smearing our cheeks with his tears, he set to work repairing the holes he'd made in the house. These gaps couldn't wait until morning. We fell asleep to the sound of his table saw in the basement cutting drywall to fit over his punctures. Rather than being a distraction, the banging and grunting of Dad's labour was our favourite lullaby. The noise assured us our strong father stood nearby.

The smell of Dad's cigarettes poured from the playroom. Mom kept him company as he worked. They spoke quietly. The tone of their conversation difficult to decipher. Were they angry? Afraid?

"Maybe we should send the girls to stay at my mother's for a bit."

"Your mother? God, no! We might as well feed them to wild animals."

Mom laughed at Dad's joke, and I breathed a sigh of relief. Once a beer top popped, I felt confident the family ship had righted course. Everything would be alright. I rolled over, and for the first time since New Kitten's disappearance, I fell into a peaceful night's sleep.

In my bed, I believed we were safe, that my sisters and I were too big to ever lose our way and become trapped on the other side of the wall, between the rivets and insulation where New Kitten suffered and perished.

We had no reason to fear the wall.

TWO

Leaking chemicals have poisoned the ground beneath the wreckage of the General Hospital. Today, university students from outside the region sometimes sneak over the fence to collect samples, but the readings from a simple field test frighten them so much they leave behind their muddy shoes and jeans, choosing to drive barefoot in their underwear, back to the lab for a decontamination shower. Dozens of old boots and pants line the fence along what used to be the General, but the hobos know better than to try any of them on for size. Not even animals will take them for nesting.

The ground didn't poison overnight. When Dad landed himself in the hospital shortly after New Kitten's funeral, he wanted out as quickly as possible. Even all those years back, he knew sickness radiated from the General's foundation.

I pounded the Coke machine next to the elevators, ignoring the dirty looks thrown at me by the nurse at the front desk. She knew what I was up to, pushing buttons and jiggling the coin return, hoping to trigger a malfunction that would result in a free pop. The soda wasn't for me, but the twins, who were thirsty and cranky. All the coins in Mom's purse went into the cigarette machine. She smoked one after another outside the emergency room, while Grandma made her explain again and again how Dad got injured.

"He slipped over the side and landed in a pile of pipes. Thankfully, he wasn't higher up."

"Humph. Maybe if he'd been higher up, Jack would have paid more attention to where he stepped."

Dad wasn't dying, only busted up and bruised, so the nurses wouldn't let us see him. We would have to come back tomorrow during visiting hours. In protest, Mom spent the night in the hospital anyway, sleeping on the plastic benches in the emergency room, striking up conversations with the late-night drunks coming in to get patched up after a bar fight.

Grandma took us home. Instead of sending us straight to bed, she turned on the TV and let us watch Johnny Carson. We saw an old lady with a collection of potato chips that looked like famous movie stars. She had a potato chip that looked like John Wayne, and another that looked like Alfred Hitchcock. When the old lady looked away, Johnny Carson ate a regular chip and the crunching sound almost gave her a heart attack, thinking it was one of her precious celebrity chips. That was mean.

Noises in the kitchen stirred Grandma from her snoozing. She told us not to move and grabbed an umbrella with a great metal spike at the end, something you could harpoon a walrus with.

Grandma flicked on the kitchen light, catching the intruder, who turned out to be Dad's best friend, Roman, as he used his boot to wedge a two-four of Dad's favourite beer into the fridge. The cardboard groaned and the bottles clanged together, but Roman was determined to get that son-of-a-bitch in there.

Mom didn't like Roman. She told Dad, "You and Roman can get boozed up in the garage all you want, but stay out of the house." It wasn't that she thought Roman was so untrustworthy he'd steal our ashtrays and snoop through the medicine cabinet, but she feared Roman making himself comfortable and never wanting to leave. Mom was always on the defensive against a Roman infestation.

"Such a thoughtful gift," Grandma cooed to Roman, patting

his back, which was covered in dirt from work. I heard small clumps break off and hit the kitchen floor. "You're a good friend."

After Grandma showed Roman to the door, my sisters and I heard a series of pops and fizzes. We peeked into the kitchen, catching Grandma as she opened all twenty-four bottles of beer one by one and dumped them into the sink. The drain was a mess of white foam.

"He won't be needing this," Grandma said. She shook the last bottle, flinging drops of amber liquid onto the counter. She grabbed a sponge and mopped up, humming the whole time, aware we were watching her. "People don't get better by sitting drunk in front of the TV all day."

I knew Dad would be pretty disappointed if he came home from the hospital and there wasn't anything in the kitchen to relieve his thirst. Lucky for him, Roman had him covered. I got up in the middle of the night to use the bathroom. Someone tapped outside the window above the toilet. It was Roman. I lifted the window, and he handed me two brown bottles.

"Hide 'em for your dad," Roman said. As usual, he spoke way too loudly, so I flushed the toilet to mask the sound of his voice.

"Be careful," I said. Nobody wanted Roman falling off the side of our house and landing in the hospital bed next to Dad's. All the doctors would quit if they had to put up with that pair's shenanigans all day.

Roman laughed. "You worry like your mother." His hand came through the window and mussed up my hair before he jumped from the side of the house, disappearing into the darkness. He didn't grunt, so wherever he landed, he did so safely.

The beers nestled comfortably under Dad's pillow, hidden away like two fossilized babies dug out of the wall, so old their skin had turned to glass. Only this time, Dad would be happy to find them.

Dad returned on crutches, his knees swaddled and his back aching. With a groan, he settled into his favourite chair. I ran to fetch the one item I knew would cheer him up—the TV Guide.

"Thank you." He licked his fingers and flipped through the pages. "Time to work out my church schedule."

Dad abhorred Sunday morning service. He and Roman banged up their Saturday nights real good, racking up empties and blaring music in the garage, or driving around, looking for action. Rising early Sunday morning disagreed with him.

"The last thing I want to hear is a sermon about how I'm going to hell."

To prove she could be reasonable, Mom cut a deal. If a good movie came on the Channel 11 Sunday Morning Matinee, she excused Dad from worship. Each week, when the new TV Guide arrived, Dad took a pencil and shaded the listing of any movie good enough to warrant staying home for. He kept a whole box of Guides in the basement, a diary of his TV viewing. The pencil shading told us what Dad was doing between 10 and 12 on any given Sunday. He didn't watch musicals or anything geared towards children, so while *Funny Girl* or *Herbie* went un-pencilled, he put a light charcoal shading over:

(CH 11) 10 am Abbott and Costello Meet Frankenstein (1948)
The comedic duo match wits with Dracula and the Wolf Man in a battle for Lou's brain. B&W.

I wasn't so lucky. Each week, Mom marched me and my sisters to Queenston Cathedral, a red brick building intended to be a small-scale replica of Westminster Abbey. A sinister gargoyle squatted overhead, wings draped across his shoulders like a stone cape, pointing to the arched doors with the stub of a tail that had once been longer before crumbling under the elements. I always looked at my shoes when entering the church, afraid of the gargoyle's judgement. My older sister thought this hilarious and blew the stone monster kisses, calling him "Mr. Cheapo." According to her, during construction, the builders were promised a significant bonus if they completed the church by a certain date. Although they met this goal, the church reneged, refusing to pay. In retaliation, the stone masons added the gargoyle, crafting the scaley, winged demon in the likeness of the head minister.

"If that's true, why doesn't the church knock it down?"

My older sister rolled her eyes. "It's stuck up there with cement. You can't knock it down with a broom like a hornet's nest."

After his accident, I overheard Dad on the phone with the television station. The Sunday Morning Matinee had been suspended to make way for the summer Olympics. Dad put forth several passionate arguments to have this decision reversed, but the station eventually hung up on him.

"So I'll be seeing you at church tomorrow, then?" Mom asked.

Dad upheld their bargain, showering, shaving, squeezing into his suit, and hobbling down the street on his crutches. The gargoyle over the door amused him, and he solemnly crossed himself beneath its gaze before flashing me a wicked grin. I didn't dare mock the gargoyle.

Dad didn't belong in that stuffy church. Seeing him squeezed into the pews reminded me of a bear riding a little motorcycle around the circus ring. There is something obscene about taking a majestic animal out of its natural habitat and making it perform against its nature.

Church bored me. Every week, the same routine. A couple of off-key hymns, then the children were herded downstairs for Youth Bible Lessons. They split us into two groups: the older kids and the younger kids.

No matter how many times I insisted I belonged with the big kids, the church forced me in with the babies.

"What happened in the basement today?" Dad asked on the walk home, squeaking his crutches against the hot pavement.

"Ecch! Colouring."

Our religious education came down to the teacher dumping a bucket of broken crayons across the table, like a farmer filling a hog's slop trough, and instructing us to colour in countless ditto sheets. How insulting. I graduated from this baby colouring years ago.

"Why can't I stay upstairs?"

"Children don't know how to be quiet during grown-up talk," Mom said. "You'd be bored."

"Grown-up talk about what?" Did the minister tell dirty stories? What's the big hairy deal?

She sighed. "It's grown-up talk about the great calamities coming soon and how afterwards there will be paradise on Earth." She counted off the benefits on her fingers. "Everyone loving one another, the lion lying down with the lamb... Y'know, all that nonsense."

The first time Dad heard the minister use the line about the lion and the lamb he shouted out, "That'll be the day!" The congregation bristled but the minister took Dad's heckle in stride, smiling and saying, "Yes, Jack. That will be the day indeed."

Truthfully, Mom and Dad chose our church not for reasons of ideology, but convenience. The gargoyle church did nothing for our souls but provided us with an excellent excuse for why we could never attend our Uncle Todd's church.

The kids at school called Uncle Todd a faith healer. They'd seen him on TV.

Uncle Todd insisted he did not "faith heal", a title he rejected for its negative connotations. Faith healers were crooks and charlatans, putting on late-night monkey shows where they pushed people down and asked for money. I watched him on TV once, late at night, holding the volume knob at one while Dad slumbered in his favourite chair. In snowy black-and-white, Uncle Todd prayed for someone, pushed them down, and then asked for money.

At his church, Uncle Todd boasted of dramatic healings.

He claimed one person grew their entire arm back. I wondered what that must have felt like. Did the man have complete control over his new arm right away or was there a learning curve? I pictured the new arm sprouting from his stump pink, glistening, the new skin too sensitive to touch.

Uncle Todd called himself a "Spiritual Anointer", swearing everyone he pushed down, from sweaty GM workers to little old ladies draped in pearls, were miraculously cured by his healing hands. He stated this with such confidence you felt like a fool to contradict him.

Dad delighted in contradicting Uncle Todd. He read the obituaries aloud. "Look at this, honey. After Todd cured Olga Hollander's cancer, she developed an entirely new case. One aggressive enough to kill her in less than a week. What you figure the odds of that? Some people have no luck."

"Poor Olga," Mom said.

Whenever Auntie Linda visited, she loved to regale us with stories about the olden days, happy to whisper all of Uncle Todd's secrets into our ears with the dramatic gravity of a fortune teller.

"He drank bad. Right from high school. He'd get bombed in the parking lot, drinking some cheap bathtub liquor the stores sold under the counter to hobos and teenagers. It's a miracle no one ever went blind. The janitor used to haul Todd home in the back of his pickup. Your grandma would return from a friend's house, sometimes with her friends in tow, and find Todd dumped on the front lawn like a load of manure. Puke coming out of his mouth, his pants half off. A real embarrassment."

Auntie Linda invited Mom to join in the shaming of their troublesome brother. "Do you remember when Todd crashed the car?"

Mom nodded. "He split it right in half. Like something out of a *Herbie* movie."

"He went through the windshield headfirst, so he didn't get any scars on his face, but the day he goes bald people are going to see the ugliest, nastiest scalp. He's gonna need to buy ten wigs."

Mom disagreed. "Daddy kept his hair right 'til the end. Todd's hair isn't going any place."

"Right. And even if it did, all he's gotta do is run his 'healing hands' over the bald spot and PRESTO! God'll grow him new hair." Auntie Linda broke up laughing. Mom only sighed and cinched her lips, wanting to set a good example for us little ones. She believed in children respecting their elders, even the abhorrent ones.

When Uncle Todd announced he was going to university, Grandpa called him crazy. Because of his drinking he'd surely flunk out. All that money wasted. Back then, Uncle Todd had a lot of money. He did odd jobs for odd men, requiring tense trips back and forth over the border. Auntie Linda asked Mom to speculate what Uncle Todd had been transporting.

"Oh, I don't know," Mom said. "Booze, cigarettes, who cares?"

Auntie Linda said, "I like to think it was birds. Rare tropical birds with beautiful plumages of colours I've never seen before. The birds came off a ship in Port and weren't allowed in North America because of disease, so Todd wrapped a rubber band around their beaks to keep them from squawking and stuffed them all over his body. Two under each arm, one in each pant leg, three or four around his belt. I bet the feathers tickled and he had some close calls talking to the border guards, trying to keep from laughing." My sisters and I thrilled to the idea of Uncle Todd as a bird smuggler. Auntie Linda gave the story an extra pinch of credibility by saying, "One time while doing laundry, I found some strange looking feathers clinging to his underpants."

After one too many glasses of wine, Auntie Linda's mood turned dour. "Sometimes I think it was women he smuggled over the border. Young girls snatched up from somewhere."

"That's enough," Mom said. "The girls don't need to hear it."

Uncle Todd invited us to his church constantly. He promised, "Miracles. Signs and wonders. People being cured; people being set free." Grandma pestered Mom to bring us girls, "You can leave Jack at home."

Mom smiled politely, skilled at keeping peace in the family by saying, "Thank you for being so thoughtful, but we're very happy with our current church."

Back home, Dad asked to see our colouring pages.

"Is that Adam and Eve?"

I nodded.

"You made her a red head."

The church's yellow crayons were all filthy, smeared with chunks of blue and brown, so I coloured Eve's head in a heavy layer of red wax. I wanted her to look like Cyndi Lauper.

"Don't you girls know red hair is the result of a genetic mutation? The first two people on Earth can't have red hair. That's a fate for their children's children."

He next examined the twin's colouring work, which he found even more historically inaccurate than mine.

"Adam needs a beard. Maybe on *The Flintstones* you can trap some bumble bees in a clam shell for your morning shave, but not in the goddam garden of Eden."

He put us back to work, supervising while we gave Adam a good long beard. Since Adam was older, his beard needed to be longer than Eve's hair, which cascaded strategically over her breasts.

Dad set down his beer and pointed to the green leaves covering their crotches. "How do those stay in place? With Scotch tape?" We scratched away the green wax and re-crayoned Adam and Eve's crotches the same colour as their hair, giving them thick, full bushes. Dad looked forward to us showing these revisions to the teacher next Sunday, but Mom put a stop to the hilarity.

My older sister loved church. In the older kid's basement group, their discussions concentrated on dating, a subject of great interest to her. There, she learned all the pitfalls awaiting undiscerning young girls. The most dangerous date was allowing a boy to take you to the movies, because you got bored not talking to one another and started kissing. To prevent this, the church recommended going on group dates, all the girls and boys together, enjoying wholesome fun and Christian comradery. My older sister closed her eyes and imagined how exciting that would be.

"Best of all," she told me, "There's no reason you and your date can't sneak off somewhere for a little kissing. In fact, there's no reason you couldn't sneak off for kissing with more than one. It's like being on a date with ten boys at once."

The final Olympic medal got handed out, and Dad returned to shading in Sunday movies in the TV Guide. Unfortunately, during this time, Mom grew used to his company in the pews, and insisted Dad continue coming to church, even when the TV Guide promised:

(CH 11) 10 am Ghost of Frankenstein
(1942)
Sinister hunchback Ygor (Bela Lugosi) resurrects
the Frankenstein monster, putting the village
under siege. B&W.

"You've seen the Frankenstein monster a hundred times," Mom said. *Ghost of Frankenstein* wasn't even one of the good ones. Instead of Boris Karloff, the monster was played by the guy who's supposed to be the Wolf Man.

Dad refused to put on his suit. When Sunday morning came, he walked to church clad only in his bathrobe, carrying a thermos of orange juice to replenish his liquids after a long night in the garage with Roman. Mom's ability to be embarrassed had eroded long ago. Seeing no need for husband and wife to be mismatched, she put on jeans and a men's flannel shirt she last wore while painting the garage. My older sister looked mortified. No boy would ever ask her out if she went to church with hillbillies for parents.

The church pews were crowded that week, crawling with new parishioners. Like Dad, most of them wore bathrobes. One man was tethered to an IV bag. All the sick men wore hospital bracelets. An usher came forward and took Dad's arm, trying to corral him with the rest of the infirmed.

"Get your hands off me! I'm sitting with my family."

The sick men were there to receive a special blessing. The minister beseeched the spirit of the Lord to move through the men and cleanse their souls. Prepare them for eternity. Mom thought the whole situation was a riot. She whispered into Dad's ear, asking him if he felt healed yet. Dad seethed and tried to stow his crutches under the pew, not wanting anyone to see them. He felt this was too close to the kind of stuff that happened at Uncle Todd's church. Wasn't the whole reason for coming here to get away from that kind of malarkey?

A metallic jiggling sound rolled down the aisle, approaching our family. One of the sick men, his face gaunt and his cheeks hollow enough to hold a hardboiled egg, wheeled a clanging IV stand with one hand while the other grabbed the triangular points of each pew to steady himself. Dad tensed up. He looked around the church, signalling for one of the ushers. Couldn't they see this man should not be on his feet? Someone ought to wheel him back with the rest of the dying before he slipped and fell.

The IV Man squeezed into our pew, grabbed Dad's hand, and whispered, "So wonderful to see you again! Look at the pair of us, turned into grown men!" He gestured his shaking hands towards Mom and my sisters. "And look at the beautiful flowers sitting here. Haven't we been blessed?"

Dad's eyes travelled from the man's stained gown to his withered face. "Jesus, Jerzy, you look like shit."

The IV Man's chest gurgled, the sloshing in his lungs either a suppressed cough or a forced laugh. "Good to see you've still got your sharp wit. So sharp, a joke from Jack and you don't know if you're laughing or bleeding." His gnarled yellow fingers rubbed the fabric of Dad's bathrobe. "Are you sick too, Jack? Please say you're alright."

"Work injury," Dad said. I'm glad I let him answer. I almost said, "Hangover."

Dad ignored the IV Man. He watched the minister intently, giving the sermon a concentration he normally reserved for a football game he had twenty bucks riding on. The IV Man couldn't take a hint. He scootched closer, whispering into Dad's ear like a lover. "What a blessing to see each other again. Grown men now. The last time we were together you had just bought the house. Remember?"

Dad nodded. Following the minister's lead, he bowed his head for prayer.

The IV Man shuffled back to his hospice pew. I saw a plastic cord running from between his legs to a piss-filled bag strapped to his shin. A few drops of pee remained on the bench beside Dad, catching the sunlight like stained glass.

"Who's your friend?" Mom asked.

Dad slung an arm over her shoulders. His fingers came to rest at the top button of her flannel shirt. He must have thought they were at the drive-in. "Jerzy used to work at GM back in the day. I remember one time he chased our supervisor waving a metal rod. No shit, he would have killed him, only he ran headfirst into one of the car bodies being lifted and knocked himself out."

Loud, brassy notes blasted from the organ, calling the congregation to their feet for the first hymn. Dad and Mom remained seated. When everyone buried their faces in their song book, Dad took the opportunity to snap open the top buttons of Mom's shirt. I pretended not to notice them, but the twins gaped unashamed. My older sister hid her face behind a hymn book, praying none of the boys looked our way.

Mom closed her eyes as Dad rubbed his face against the smooth skin of her neck.

"I don't think you have to worry about seeing him ever again," she said. "People give off a very specific odour when they're close to the end. I remember from my father. The same smell is pouring off that guy."

Dad hobbled home quickly, distancing himself from the ringing church bells, hoping to catch the closing moments of the Channel 11 matinee. He arrived in time to see the Frankenstein monster burn up in flames. Moments later, someone knocked at our door.

"Aw, Christ."

The IV Man hadn't come empty-handed. He brought his wife and two teenage daughters. If he'd arrived alone, Dad would have grabbed a metal rod and chased the IV Man down the street, just like the old days in the GM plant, but surrounded by his family, we had no choice but to invite them inside.

Mom put on coffee and asked me to bring out the cookies we baked last night. I hoped our guests would be conservative, not wanting to spoil their appetites, but the IV Man's daughters plowed through the cookies two at a time, eating like they didn't know the meaning of the word embarrassed.

Dad sat in his chair, keeping the injured legs up and letting his old workmate do the talking. How strange to think this man once terrorized the assembly line at GM, and now he leaked into a bag between his legs. No one in his family urged him to save his strength. I'm sure they preferred his energy be spent talking. The remnants of bruises marred each woman's face, the last proof of the IV Man's strength, and in another month or so those too would be gone forever.

The IV Man talked about big plans. A return to the old country. "Take the girls, show them where they came from." His mother had brought him over on a boat, eight miserable days tossing and turning, puking into a cardboard mug. Now he'd return in style, in a silver airplane. His girls were pure beauties; they'd drive every boy crazy. The boys would dream of them for years. It was a gift he wanted to give the old country, a thousand sweet dreams of his two beauties. They would call them Jerzy's Girls, and through them he would be remembered forever.

"I'm sure you'll make it there, Jerz," Dad said.

"It's not the money; it's the time. Every morning I reach into my pockets, looking for an extra year or two, but I come up short. I hope you can help me out."

"I'll do what I can, but it won't be much," Dad said. "Just a spit in a bucket, but if enough people contributed a few dollars, it'll soon be enough to get you on that airplane." He snapped his fingers. "Rebecca! Fetch my wallet."

My older sister played dumb. "Where is it?"

"You know exactly where it is, young lady."

The IV Man slammed his cup of watery coffee onto the table, nearly toppling his metal stand. "Hey! Don't insult me. I told you already I don't need money. Open your jackass ears."

My older sister stood rooted to the spot, her search for Dad's wallet suspended. We both anticipated a good show. No one spoke to Dad like that. Even on crutches, Dad could toss this bum out onto the street, snapping his arms like a scarecrow's.

Dad pinched the bridge of his nose. "How am I supposed to give you time? What, you think I can snap off a couple of weekends and slip them into your pocket?"

The IV Man gulped his coffee like a shot of whisky. His body no longer required alcohol to trigger his rage, any liquid thrown down his throat fast enough would do. His family scooted down the couch, away from him, clearly veterans of his warning signs.

"You never invited a goddam person over here your entire life. Not when Walter had his accident. Not when Freddie's son twisted in agony, his spine leaking poison. You never offered to help anyone. And now that I'm asking, you're pretending you got shit up your ears."

I'd never seen Dad so patient. "Listen, Jerz, believe it or not, I have no idea what you think I could do to help you."

"You think you're keeping a big secret, but smart people know. We've kept our mouths shut over these years, so maybe it's time you start repaying that goddam favour, before we realize it don't benefit us to keep quiet."

Dad knew to leave before the IV Man angered him further. He grabbed his crutches and hoisted himself out of his chair. The IV Man flinched, expecting a fight, but Dad thumped into the basement.

"Fine, Jerz. Do whatever baloney you want and get the hell out." The heels of his crutches squeaked down the basement steps. A moment later, his table saw roared to life.

Left alone with our guests, Mom didn't know how to proceed. Offer more coffee? Send us into the kitchen to bake another batch of cookies for Jerzy's Girls?

The IV Man shuffled around the living room, pointing his nose in the air, sniffing, searching for something. He looked lost, like a housewife holding an electrical cord with no idea where to plug it in.

All at once, he began doing a fine impression of the Frankenstein monster, growling and swinging his arms. He knocked his IV stand over. The plastic cord tore from his arm with a sound like a drumstick coming off a turkey. Fluid dribbled onto the floor and lines of blood streaked down his arm. He pressed himself flat against the wall, his palms over his head, nose squashed. He rubbed his body against the wallpaper, sobbing. Jerzy's Girls looked away, unable to take the sight of what appeared to be their dying father having a nervous breakdown.

"Go to the backyard," Mom ordered us. "Now."

Was she kidding? Not on your life! Entertainment of this calibre didn't come along every day. It almost made up for Dad not punching his lights out. We watched the IV Man furiously rub the wallpaper like his hands were hot scrapers working to get down to the original paint. He cried as he embraced the flat surface, but the wall did not return his affection. The wall remained quiet, waiting patiently for the IV Man to tire himself out.

When he finished, he sobered up instantly and tried to play the part of the pleasant house guest, thanking Mom for the coffee. "So nice to see you again. It's been too many years. Look at us—how much we've changed. Too many years."

His wife picked the IV stand off the floor and did her best to stick the cord back in his arm.

"Oh, leave it, honey pie. We'll get a nurse to take care of that. It needs to be cleaned anyhow."

Lastly, he called goodbye down the basement stairs, but if Dad heard him over the whirls of his band saw, he did not answer.

After closing the door on our departing guests, Mom said, "I think we're done with church for now."

Next to my head, inside the bedroom wall, familiar vibrations purred. I sat up, expecting the sound to be the remnant of a dream that would fade away once I fully awoke.

But the purring persisted. It grew louder as it moved across my room. Did New Kitten leave a litter of babies in the wall? Did her ghost roam the hollows, purring like a shrieking banshee? Either option horrified me.

The sound made me uneasy. The strength of the echo inside the wall suggested a bottomless pit. I imagined the wallpaper and plaster crumbling away and myself tumbling out of bed into the infinite darkness. I'd fall and fall forever, dying not when I hit the bottom, but when my body gave out from lack of food and water.

Fed up, I leapt out of bed and slapped the wall.

"Be quiet! It's late!"

The entire house went dead, as if my command had knocked out all the electricity, throwing everything into silence. This peace only lasted a moment, broken by my older sister's taunting giggle. The purr resumed, but quieter, further away, coming from the wall in her bedroom now.

Good for her, I thought. She wants to deal with that nuisance all night long, have at it.

We never saw the IV Man again. I'm doubtful he made that trip back to the old country. Those poor boys were deprived of the dream of Jerzy's Girls, and now he would die in obscurity.

During a trip to the supermarket, I spotted one of his daughters. The butcher, who usually monitored the magazine stand to keep kids from dog-earing the comic books, was occupied with a customer, allowing me to catch up with Archie and the Gang until an older girl tapped me on the shoulder.

"I liked your cookies."

I didn't recognize her at first, distracted by the purple ring around her eye and the fresh bloody scab over her cheekbone. I couldn't believe it. This is what the IV Man so desperately wanted extra time for? Making his family miserable? I wanted to roll the comic into a pointed cone. I'd use it to poke out both of his eyes.

My older sister stood in the produce aisle, sneaking green grapes, not caring that they were covered with chemical spray. I told her what I'd seen—the marks of the IV Man's angry hands across his daughter's face. I expected her to fall into a deep malaise, but instead she yawned, unable to stop snapping grapes off their stems and popping them into her mouth.

"What a creep. No wonder Dad didn't want to help him."

How was Dad supposed to help him? Did the IV Man want an introduction to Uncle Todd so he could jump to the head of the line for his miracle cure? Dad called that healing stuff a bunch of bullshit.

Stunned, my older sister let the final grape tumble from her lips and land on the Miracle Mart linoleum, waiting to be crushed by a buggy wheel. Excitement spread across her face. She grinned.

"You mean, you haven't figured it out?"

I'd seen this grin before. My older sister loved sharing her knowledge with me, because when it came to being cruel and frightening, nothing surpassed the truth. She'd already tortured me with the excruciating details of how babies were made, but the sadistic grin on her face suggested this new information of hers would be even more upsetting than the invasive nature of procreation.

I braced for the worst, but she decided to hold on to her secret a while longer, enjoying the power she held over me. My repeated failures to guess made her giggle. All she would say was, "When you're older, your fingers will figure it out on their own. I promise, you are going to love it."

THREE

I don't miss the orchards. Before the Great Catastrophe, this used to be wine country, dozens of wineries bearing the same family name for generations. I don't imbibe alcohol, so the loss goes unnoticed by me.

Nothing grows in the razed soil outside the city, so all our fruits and vegetables are imported. Expensive, rubbery fakes. They look genuine, I'll give them that, but I can taste the lack of nutrition. I wouldn't be surprised if they came out of a 3-D printer, everything made from the same generic substance. I'll stick to canned goods. All these years later, I still find the occasional aluminum can in the backyard, and feast on the delicacies inside.

My sisters have suggested we make a trip into the ruined countryside. They've saved seeds, hundreds of them, and we'll plant them into the ashy ground. The gesture will be more symbolic than practical. Nothing will take root in our lifetime, but my sisters feel it is important to behave as if you have hope, because if you fake being hopeful long enough, you may wake up one morning and find yourself transformed into the real thing.

But I have no desire to return to the orchards, not even to see their ruin firsthand, and so my sisters' seeds continue to accumulate, drying out until they are no longer fit for the ground or the birds.

*

"Your sister found herself a summer job," Mom announced, blissfully unaware of the catastrophic events being set into motion.

I sat on top of the toilet tank, playing lifeguard for the twins in the bathtub. They wanted to run through the sprinkler, but Mom couldn't abide the expense of wasted water, so she dressed them in their swimsuits and dropped them into five inches of cold water, where they splashed around with all the enthusiasm of captive dolphins.

"She'll be helping the farmers in the orchard. Just for the harvest. Why don't you join her?"

"Doing what? Farming?"

"Sure! They're always looking for workers. Why not roll up your sleeves and get your hands dirty. Get a head start on the other kids your age and learn some work ethic."

Mom's concern for my well-rounded upbringing aside, she figured the twenty minutes it took to drive my older sister to the orchard would be better amortized if she brought two daughters instead of just one. Also, she expected me to keep my older sister out of trouble.

Mostly, Mom needed two hands bringing in extra money. Dad needed more recovery time for his injury than first expected, which meant keeping him off the job site. During her last visit, Grandma wondered how we'd support ourselves, suggesting with a great deal of glee that Mom would soon be forced to come begging for handouts. Mom told Grandma we had so much money saved up the bank hardly knew where to stack it all. Once Grandma left, Mom phoned a friend and pleaded for her old job back at the Stokes Seeds factory.

"It's only for a few of weeks," Mom said.

In the orchard, my older sister and I picked peaches from morning until noon, breaking for an hour during the sun's apex. I struggled the first day. Too much orange juice at breakfast. I had to wait until lunch to walk a discreet distance to relieve myself behind a wall of grape vines. I jealousy observed the orchard men were on no such schedule. Whenever the urge struck, they'd sling out their tool and blast the base of whatever tree they were working on, leaving a wide, foamy trail in the dirt. The orchard men peed so often I felt like they were marking territory, warning others not to pick from trees with wet bark.

The longer I worked, the more I resented the ease with which the orchard men relieved themselves. They flaunted their advantage, whooping and hollering like children, play-fully shooting a stream at a friend's back. Sometimes two men faced off, interweaving their pee streams while making the clanking sounds of a sword fight.

My older sister noticed me watching them.

"Stop staring! Holy cow, you're sick."

I stuck out my tongue. She had a gutter mind. I couldn't see anything, anyway. The fruit sacks slung over each hip shielded the men's soft parts from view, which suited me fine. Mom told me men don't wipe after they pee. They must look disgusting down there.

Although lesser in number, there were women pickers. The orchard women did their picking wearing skirts, which I initially thought terribly impractical. I pitied them coming from a country where women were not allowed to wear blue jeans like me. But the longer I watched, the clearer it became their skirts presented no difficulty. They climbed tree trunks to reach the highest bough. Despite my earlier assumption, their skirts were actually advantageous. When I needed to pee, I had to trudge half a mile to a private spot where I could drop trou, exposing my entire front and behind to whatever lecherous bird might be swooping overhead, but the orchard women squatted with the same regularity the men unzipped their flies, their private's shielded beneath their skirt's tent. This struck me as unfair.

I renounced the shame surrounding my waterworks. Why be so modest? Who did I think was looking at me? The need to pee struck again, and this time, I didn't even break the song I sang. I undid my jeans, squatted at the base of the tree and let nature take her course. The other pickers around me were amused by the way I shook my behind and kicked dirt over the puddle. My older sister, however, was mortified.

"Oh my God, Emery! I can't believe you did that."

Her priceless reaction kept my energy up, and I picked faster, more efficiently, perfectly happy to play free-spirited Ramona to her stuffy Beezus.

Mom still wore her factory overalls when she picked us up. The car windows were foggy from a cooling bucket of chicken. My older sister immediately told her what I'd done. Naturally, she exaggerated, claiming I'd stripped my pants right off, blinding the orchard with my naked flesh, before leaning my bare ass into the tree and unleashing a stream loud and long enough to scare the birds and drown a mole hill.

"People are going to think I was raised the same as her. Now they're all expecting me to do something disgusting." Her voice carried the subliminal message: *Punish her! Punish her!*

Exhausted by her own day, Mom was incapable of being scandalized. "Rebecca, when a person has to go, they have to go. Some of those people you're working with come from countries without running water. Nobody is looking down on you 'cause your little sister went piddle in the grass."

Dad gave my older sister the reaction she wanted. After dinner, he called me into the basement for a private talk.

"Young lady, I don't ever want to hear about you exposing yourself in front of those men again. Do you understand me?"

Even at my young age, I understood the volatile mix of prejudice and pride colouring Dad's reaction. Number one: he distrusted the foreign men who came to this country during the harvest. Number two: he was embarrassed to be out of work while his wife and two daughters earned a day's salary. Sitting at home all day depressed him. While us women glowed with the justified sweat of a day's honest labour, he lounged in his chair, seeing how many empty beer cans he could balance on his knee. He used this opportunity to vent his frustration.

"All I did was pee. Those men pee every five seconds. How come when I have to—"

"I don't want to hear about it!"

My older sister had harsh words for me at bedtime.

"You nearly blew it today. Dad got so mad he doesn't want us going back to the orchard."

"You're the one who got him upset in the first place, opening your big mouth."

"Keep your pants on tomorrow, Miss Piggy."

The early morning condensation splashed our knees as we crossed the field. The guts of an old Cadillac (no doors or hood, just an exposed engine, one seat and two rusted fins) carried a dozen workers, all squished together. The orchard men held a hand for me and my older sister to leap aboard, and they cradled us like daughters, their arms making sure we didn't slip beneath the missing floorboard. By their smiles, I knew they welcomed us as one of them.

The men came to the orchard to earn as much money as they could, and that meant filling those bags as fast as possible. Without the same motivation, I picked at my own leisurely pace. No one wanted to pick alongside me. I'd have only got in the way, slowed them down. The men picked furiously, some nearly as quick as the mechanical harvesters that would eventually replace them. Some men worked in teams, one climbing into the top boughs and tossing peaches to their partner below. They could fill a bag by the time I snapped my first stem.

Something changed. Suddenly, I attracted attention.

One of the orchard men migrated to my tree. He picked quickly. Every few peaches, he would drop one into my bag. A gift. Each time he did this, he flashed a smile, nearly all gums. I wasn't sure what to say. I didn't expect his generosity to last all morning, but soon, without lifting my own arms, my bag drooped heavy, full of peaches.

I knew better than to allow the orchard man to do my work for me, but I didn't know how to make him stop. When someone wants to do you a favour, they get mighty insulted if you tell them "No." So I learned to anticipate when a peach was about to be dropped into my bag and say, "Trick or Treat!" to make his gift feel natural.

Smiling, the orchard man pointed to the top of the tree and lifted his hands, like he meant to toss me up there. I shrugged my shoulders, using my body language as best I could to say, "I don't understand you."

He doffed his shoes and scrambled to the top bough, singing in his own language as he rained peaches down on me. Too embarrassed to take more and already feeling greedy, I deposited each one into his sacks.

When I emptied my bag and collected my chit, I felt the eyes of the whole damn orchard on me, and I knew I'd made a mistake. The men looked at me with stern faces, their lips pressed tight. All had seen my new friend and knew how much of my bag I'd picked myself. I flung the chit away, not wanting to be seen as a little girl who took advantage of foolish grown men.

My new friend couldn't have been a day over twenty-five, but to my young eyes he appeared ancient. His skin was tattered and stained with the wear of a tough life, the wrinkles spreading around his eyes to the rough burns on his cheeks from years working outdoors. His hands were covered in scars I imagined came from his dramatic slog through whatever civil war raged in his home country.

He continued to shower me with peaches, grabbing the plump, golden ones sitting too high for me to reach. In return I gave him my smile, a friendly face to carry him through the day. Perhaps I reminded him of a daughter. I imagined myself a recurring character in the letters he wrote home. I was his sole source of comfort in this new country. My friend slept with the other orchard men in the bunkhouse, where I'm sure nights were dark and scary, and I was happy to be a firefly in his loneliness.

"He's a creep," my older sister said. "Always buzzing around you like a fly on a turd."

"Maybe if you were nicer, you'd have a friend, too."

"You're lucky we're working outdoors in the wide open, because there's no telling what those people might try in private."

It saddened me to hear my older sister share Dad's prejudice. I recognized the unfair way these foreign men were treated. The farmer spoke to them like they were children, as if proper respect would only be wasted. The condescension the farmers showed the orchard men made me angry.

The town bigots feared the orchard men, imagining every last one a criminal. A weakness for liquor might lead to thieving or taking lascivious liberties with innocent young women.

I wished the so-called decent folk, whose minds were stained with such wicked thoughts, could spend a day working alongside my friend. They would learn a lot. He had a wife and daughter back home, anxiously awaiting not just the money he sent, but tales of his adventures in this new country, too. He worked hard, a family man. When I went to bed at night, I slept with my conscience free from the prejudice infecting the older generation. I saw who my friend really was.

And he turned out to be, just as my older sister warned, a creep.

He started smelling my hair. Frequently. Every few minutes, he'd poke his nose through my locks, rubbing his snout against the back of my neck, trying to tickle me as he inhaled my scent. Why did he enjoy it so? All that sweat and skull grease.

He placed a hand on my hip as he sniffed me. I moved away, leaving him at a tree too laden with fruit to abandon. He needed to fill his bags more than I did and couldn't afford to pass up easy picking. I put three ripe trees between us, an impossible distance to catch up. Yet he did. He didn't like being separated from me. He worked with a speed unmatched by anyone in the orchard. His arms turned into the blur of a bee's flapping wings. The leaves rattled in his breeze, and the branches swayed until some of them cracked.

No one in the orchard could bear to watch him work. They averted their eyes. The unnatural speed frightened them. Even I couldn't look. I turned my back, shivering in his breeze, dreading the moment when the wind ceased and he'd be on top of me, his nose sucking up the scent of my hair. As he breathed me in, I felt the pounding of his heart against my back, as forceful as a hammer against a wall.

Soon, smelling me no longer satisfied him. He began pinching my sides. The first time he did this I really let him have it. I spun around and smacked him. I told him to keep his hands to himself. Pinch the peach stems, not me.

Everyone in the orchard stopped picking and watched us. I felt vindicated. I thought he would turn red, lower his head and slink away, ashamed to be called out publicly. Instead, he laughed, smacking his knees and doubling over, as though I'd said the most precocious thing imaginable. He used his laughter to tell everyone he had done nothing wrong, that I was childishly overreacting to some gentle teasing.

For a while, I thought I'd won. He kept his distance. I thought, *Good. I'll fill my own bag. I don't need your help.*

My bladder killed me, begging to be drained, but circumstances had me trapped. I didn't dare pee in the open like before. Such boldness had attracted my pinching friend's attention in the first place. Still, I knew better than to walk into the distance for privacy. That would have looked like I was retreating. Seeing me slink off with my tail between my legs would have given the Pincher a sense of victory. I might as well have cried in front of the schoolyard bully. No way would I do that.

I concentrated on redirecting the pain in my bladder. Avoiding the shade, I worked directly in the sun, feeling the tip of my ears and nose reddening. I tossed my hat away and worked my arms rapidly in a pathetic parody of the Pincher's superior speed. I worked up a sweat, hoping to empty my bladder through the pores on my forehead and under my arms. It didn't help. I only got woozy. I was lucky I didn't get heat stroke.

Taking advantage of my weakened state, the orchard man came out of nowhere to pinch my sides again. This time, there was no mistaking his maliciousness. He laughed when I yelped in pain. He made a game of my torment. Ages would pass, long enough that I began to believe he'd lost interest in me, and then he'd be at my back again, his pinchers squeezing my narrow sides, sometimes digging deep enough to grasp a rib between his fingers. The pinches were calculated. Precise. Each one saying, "Take that."

I tried returning his earlier generosity, dropping a peach into one of his hip sacks, my way of calling a truce. Big mistake. Looking insulted, he removed the peach and took a bite, sucking the juice and spitting the wad of flesh at my feet before tossing the chomped peach to the ground. Unfit for either of our bags now.

The day wore on. I lost a squirt of pee each time he pinched me. Hot water rushed into my jeans with such force the whole orchard heard it drumming against the denim. A few of the other orchard men decided my torture had gone on long enough. They tried to help by surrounding my tree, acting as a buffer between me and the Pincher. A kind thought, but ineffectual. The Pincher used his speed to combat their presence. Each time one of the orchard men reached for a peach, the Pincher plucked it first. In a blast of wind, the fruit was gone and his interlopers grasped at empty branches. The wind from his arms raised clouds of dust from the ground, filling our eyes with grit and making it difficult to breathe. The orchard men's bags went empty for so long they had no choice but to drift away, leaving me at the Pincher's mercy.

My older sister hates when I tell this story, demanding to know why she is nearly absent from the narrative. *"I was there, why don't you remember?"* she once wrote from the hospital. *"I saw every minute of the horrible way you were treated, and I fought for you. Admittedly ineffectively, for which I feel tremendous guilt, but it hurts when you talk as if I left you thrown to the wolves."*

I will be generous and say neither of us likely remembers exactly what happened in the orchard. There is no shame in that. Faulty memory is a universal affliction. But I maintain my older sister spent less time trying to protect me than she did chatting up the orchard women, teaching them English phrases and angling for invitations to join them on Saturday nights, when they wore newly sewn dresses and danced with the American teens visiting from over the border.

At home, I undressed for a bath, looking forward to scrubbing away the stickiness clinging to my hands. The tree sap soaked through my work gloves and absorbed into my skin. When I saw my sides in the mirror, I broke down sobbing. Both my left and right ribs were marred with blotchy, yellow bruises, like the nicotine stains on Dad's fingers. The markings shamed me. People can call me names, insult my family, ridicule where we came from, that's fine. I can rise above that. But attacks on my body, ones that cause a physical mark? Only someone with a low opinion of themselves would permit such abuse. I felt like I'd failed myself and my entire family.

The shame prevented me from telling Dad. I was afraid of what he'd do. One look at my splotchy yellow sides (already turning brown, then purple—odd how bruises look worse the more they heal) and Dad would be on the hunt, flushing every bar and after-hours spot until his hands were wrapped around the Pincher's neck. Dad would have killed him. No doubt.

Once the Pincher's corpse lay at Dad's feet, he wouldn't be finished, not by a damned stretch. If Dad was going to jail, he was going large. Dad and Roman would drive to the orchard, grab hold of our employer, and beat him senseless. Then, drunk on these gulps of violence, Dad would turn his anger on the bunkhouse, swinging his fists at the sleeping men in their rusted cots, cursing all those who allowed his daughter to be battered and bruised. Not even the trees would be deemed innocent. Dad's rampage wouldn't stop until he uprooted every tree in the orchard, returning home with bloodied paws Mom would spend hours drawing splinters from.

Dad would never know what I endured to keep him safe from rage and prison. I remained quiet for his sake.

The bedroom door creaked and my mattress bounced as my older sister crawled into bed beside me. She brushed the hair away from my ear and whispered, "We can make him stop if we want."

The gentle pressure of her body against mine made my bruised side sear. I panicked, afraid the pain would always be there. Never again could someone hug me, not even family.

"Don't be afraid. Close your eyes and think about that creep from the orchard. Think of his face. Think of his claws."

While the image of the Pincher's sunburnt face and sickening leer polluted my mind's eye, my older sister gently massaged my hand. She circled the knuckles, making them feel loose and cool.

"He's not going to hurt you again," she whispered, kissing my ear. "Believe that."

She lifted my hand and guided it to the wall. The moment I connected with the cool, flat surface instinct took over. My fingers stiffened and worked their way along the creases and grooves of the wallpaper, finding the correct pressure and rhythm. The wall began to purr, vibrating like a plucked piano string.

As gentle as a lover, my older sister urged me to keep thinking about the Pincher. She slipped from my bed, leaving me to strum the wall in private.

Purring poured from the wall and soaked into my fingertips, spreading up my arms and surrounding my chest, until every part of my body vibrated. If you'd pressed a quarter against me, the coin would have buzzed. The feeling was ecstasy, so encompassing I had no idea if it lasted seconds or hours.

When I drifted off to sleep, I did so comforted by the knowledge that I was still capable of experiencing joy. The days ahead could still be better than the ones left behind.

I leapt out of bed, eager to face the orchard. At breakfast, I guzzled glass after glass of orange juice. Let my bladder fill to the brim—I wasn't afraid of having to urinate.

Mom woke to a different disposition. She shuffled into the kitchen. The steaming eggs my older sister shovelled onto Mom's plate disgusted her. Mom pushed them away and put her head down, causing great offence to my older sister, who would use this poor treatment as an excuse the next time it was her turn to cook breakfast.

In the car, Mom drove with one hand on the wheel and the other clutching her stomach. Something toxic brewed inside her, contained under pressure. Hitting a bump in the road could release it. Mom tried to distract herself by singing along to one of her old songs on the radio (the one about the boy who dies in a motorcycle accident and spends his last breath crooning for his stupid girlfriend), but she couldn't get out all the words.

"What's the matter, Mom?"

"Ohh...I need to keep breathing." She sounded like a midwife talking themselves through their own delivery. I reached over the seat to pat her shoulder.

At the orchard, I hoped the fresh country air would revive her. Mom rolled down the window and regurgitated a foul, bilious mess. I'm not weak stomached, brave enough to face road kill and dirty diapers, but I couldn't watch. I turned away, clamping a hand over my mouth before I copied Mom's involuntary muscle contractions.

"Disgusting," my older sister said. "Get out of the car!"

Mom unleashed another torrent. She bent over too far and twin streams of black goo dribbled from her nostrils. We ran to find her water.

"Why couldn't I get sick before leaving the house?" Mom asked in her best *Woe is me* voice before driving away. "You realize I'm going to be late for work now?"

Despite all the taunting and pinching I'd endured, I felt comfortable being back in the orchard. Between the blue sky and the lush trees, I felt armoured. Protected. For the first time, I concentrated on filling my bags quickly. I waved to the other orchard men, singing as I picked. The air stood still. No wind came from the Pincher's arms, filling our mouths and eyes with tree grit. He was nowhere to be seen. His twin bags were left hanging on the railing outside the bunkhouse, flat as empty sock puppets. The orchard men said the Pincher had been sick all night long. They pantomimed lifting a bottle to their mouths and laughed.

"How's today's picking?" Farmer Gamble asked when I turned in my first bag of the day.

I lifted my arms and flexed like the Incredible Hulk.

A mighty wind beat against my bedroom window, rattling the glass in its pane. I climbed out of bed and turned the latch. Outside, stillness pervaded the moonlit neighbourhood. The clouds sat motionless in the sky and the tree branches were at rest. Odd. Where had this fierce wind battering my window come from?

I spotted the Pincher in our backyard, fanning his arms to knock at my window the way a boy might toss rocks for a late-night visit with his sweetheart. Upon seeing me, the Pincher humbled himself, touching the top of his head and bowing.

For the first time, I understood when he spoke. "A mistake has been made. I came to apologize."

I considered walking to the backyard to deal with him privately, but I heard the click of my older sister's lamp coming on. If I went outside, she would certainly follow, bringing trouble where none was needed.

"I don't want to talk to you!"

There came the sound of his arms flapping, and in a blink he was on the roof, hanging upside down from the eaves trough, his pinchers grasping the trim for support. Hanging upside down put a great strain on his voice. He whispered, "I didn't understand who you were. I never would have teased you if I knew. Please believe me."

I believed him but wasn't sure why his mistaking me for a helpless victim was supposed to make me empathetic. If anything, that made my having got the better of him all the sweeter. The fly now caught the spider.

"Go away!"

I wanted him off the roof before someone heard us talking. The hallway floor creaked from my older sister's approach. She'd be here soon.

"I promise never to speak to you after tonight. I will never disturb you again if you make everything stop."

I slid the window shut, flipping the latch with a self-assured swat. Of course, he'd never talk to me again. He wouldn't dare.

The sun threw a diamond shape onto the rug, the silhouette of a photograph the Pincher left in my bedroom window, pasted in place with his spit. The picture showed a young woman holding a swaddled newborn.

I guessed the picture to be of his wife and baby, mailed to give him comfort on the long, lonely nights in the orchard bunkhouse. A reminder of what he worked for. I thought about how he betrayed them, drinking in the scent of my hair, probably dreaming of snatching me up and keeping me beside him in his bunkhouse cot.

The woman in the photo looked the same age as my older sister. I thought her very pretty and envied the natural curl of her long, dark hair. Then I noticed the sadness in her eyes. She overflowed with maternal love for the baby in her arms, no doubt about that, but her pupils were coloured by disappointment. She looked like she wanted to apologize to the child, as if by giving birth she had doomed the baby to a terrible fate. I wondered who took the photo. A brother? A cousin of the Pincher? She had been forced in front of the camera, ordered to smile for her husband. The face in the picture did not say "I miss you" or "Come home soon." I wondered how badly he pinched her sides. I imagined them scabbed over. A baby meant he'd got intimate enough with her to draw blood.

True to his word, the Pincher didn't speak to me. He stayed inside the bunkhouse. I heard from the other men that the Pincher had suffered an even worse night than the one before. He kept them awake by tossing and moaning, clutching his stomach as if it boiled over with poison. They told me this coldly, wanting me to know any satisfaction I earned came at the price of their own peace.

This lack of sleep killed productivity in the orchard. The men picked slowly, moving their arms as if underwater. During lunch break, they snoozed beneath the trees, their sacks floppy and half empty.

My older sister no longer laughed and joked with the other women she'd worked so hard to make her friends. The women's sympathies lay with the exhausted men. She and I were forever outsiders now.

Mr. Gamble scorned the day's take, which fell far below an acceptable quota. He called us together to mourn the pitiful load of peaches we'd amassed. He threatened that if we didn't return to form, we would be gone. Tomorrow's take better improve to top standard or else he would slash the pay rate by twenty-five cents a bag. I felt the glare of the other pickers. They blamed me for ruining everything.

The next day, the orchard men carried the Pincher out of the bunkhouse and propped him up in the field, forcing him to work. He looked weak and fragile. The speed in his arms had been vanquished by his illness. He picked slowly, falling behind even the old men. The air grew sticky and we would have died for a good breeze off his arms.

The day's take barely improved over yesterday. Mr. Gamble fumed, cursing and spitting on the ground. He didn't dock the wages but accused us of having things too good. While this may be just a job to us, one of a dozen ways we might earn some money, to him the harvest represented the security of his whole family. He'd spent the year planting and raising his crop. The money was only there at the end. If we couldn't pick every peach in a timely manner, what did it matter to us? We could always find more work. He'd be stuck with his entire year wasted.

Harsh words to disband on. None of us looked forward to reuniting in the morning.

"Will he get better?" I asked my older sister.

"You don't feel sorry for him, do you?"

"He apologized."

"Listen, he wanted to do a lot worse than pinch you. I saw him strutting around, like the king of everyone. He never once felt sorry for you."

I knew she was right, but I regretted crippling the other orchard workers. The Pincher carried the harvest. Hurting him meant hurting everyone else.

The Pincher disappeared from the orchard completely, confined to the bunkhouse with grief. A letter had arrived. A short report of the death of his wife. Or his baby. Maybe both.

One of the men from the bunkhouse approached me.

"Your friend wants permission to break his promise." He wanted to speak to me one last time.

I visited the bunkhouse, getting my first look at where the men slept. A converted stable with bad insulation, liveable only in the summer months. Each cot had some personalized dressing on top of it: a Bible, a deck of cards, an intricate whittling project. At the far end lay the Pincher's bed, sequestered behind pinned-up sheets. At first, I thought the men put up those sheets for the Pincher's privacy, but then I got a whiff of his terrible odour.

Heavy sweat glazed the Pincher's skin. He looked ancient, a much older man than the one who'd flirted with me, so confident in his charm. He reeked of gum disease. His entire jaw was swollen, pulsing with infection. Even to speak was painful.

The skin of his once chiselled arms pooled on the bed, like his special muscles had melted into fat. Even if he got better, he would never move them so fast again.

I reached the bedside, and his nostrils flared. He inhaled deeply, his lungs wheezing like a punctured accordion.

"You're here," he said, and inhaled again. His nostrils searched desperately for one last journey through the scent of my hair.

He looked finished, no longer in control of any part of his body. Believing him to be harmless, I softened, remembering condemned men were always offered a last meal, the chance to enjoy a moment of happiness before being snuffed out. It seemed the humane thing to do, so I leaned over the bed, allowing my hair to pool over his chin. Go ahead, take one last drink of the scent that drove you to the state you now lie.

Big mistake.

I bet the sneaky bastard saved his final bits of strength for days, anticipating such an opportunity. His floppy arms wrapped around my neck, the loose skin enveloping me like an ant in a Venus flytrap. He yanked me right out of my shoes into his bed. His arms smothered me. I couldn't breathe. Stupid stupid stupid!

Once he had me immobile, his pinchers went right for my bruises, groping for a rib. He still had the anger but none of the strength, so instead of hurting me, his pinches tickled. I giggled beneath the fat of his arms, inadvertently making fart sounds. This made me laugh harder and harder until the Pincher's arms slid off me and he lay still, the last of his foul breath wafting between his scabbed lips. Within seconds, dust from the filthy air covered his dead eyes.

I crawled from under his embrace, thankful to have survived. Two orchard men leaned their heads into the bunkhouse. They looked horrified. Both saw me laughing over the body of a dead man, mistaking my being tickled for gloating. They thought they saw one monster celebrating victory over the corpse of another.

The photograph of the Pincher's wife and baby stayed in my possession. I rewrote a different fate for them, deciding she hadn't died but met a new man. A happy, caring gentleman, who loved her child and made her laugh. Together, they had faked the letter of her demise, knowing the Pincher would never come back. The new family lived in a cabin on the beach, learning a new language every year, raising horses, and their child grew to be a happy little girl who never felt chilled by a threatening wind.

*

My bruised sides ran through seasons of colour, melding from purple to blue, before settling on a permanent grey, the colour of refrigerated hardboiled egg yolk.

Years afterwards, I had my bruises covered by a tattoo, a bright bouquet of roses, winding in and out of each other. A million needle pricks built a wall of flowers so thick and thorny no one could ever pull them open and see the ugly markings underneath.

The tattoo artist asked me if I didn't want to wait for my sides to heal up first, but I told him my bruises stopped hurting ages ago and that I was tired of waiting for them to fade away.

FOUR

To this day, my older sister still puts on makeup. She's always in the bathroom refurbishing herself, as though she's expecting a hot date. I guess the ritual soothes her.

She hasn't bought any new makeup since the Great Catastrophe. Apparently, she's stocked up enough tubes and powders to last her until the sun burns out. She has shoe boxes stacked to the roof of our closet, each one crammed full of fruity lipstick, smutty mascara, and enough nail polish to paint the house crimson rouge.

Makeup doesn't keep like wine. The older it gets the more its compounds break down. Some mornings I can hear her spitting into her blush so the crumbling powder will hold together. She uses matches to warm her withered lipstick so it will melt enough to spread across her lips. Painting her face takes effort, but she knows all the tricks to resurrect her vintage makeup.

She offers to make up my face but I always decline. I never wear makeup. The parody of femininity she trowels across her face kills my desire to start. I'll keep my natural face, thank you. Wrinkled and crowfooted, the time has long since passed when makeup might have enhanced my appearance.

*

Mom never bought makeup for my older sister. There was no way to justify the expense when Mom's piddly salary from Stokes Seeds barely paid to keep water coming out of the taps. The entire family balanced on thin ice. Any day, a bounced cheque could plunge us into poverty.

"What about the money I earned in the orchard?" my older sister demanded. She lost a chunk of her summer toiling in the sun, coming home with blistered fingers stinking of tree sap. Surely, her labour deserved some reward.

I knew where the orchard money went. Those picked peaches afforded Dad the cases of beer he worked his way through while watching the Frankenstein monster on TV for the one-hundredth time. No one resented Dad his sloth. Each time he used his teeth to wrench the cap off a bottle, you could tell he yearned to be strong enough to return to the job site to haul bricks and shear lumber and earn a good goddam living for his family.

During a shopping trip to the Drug Mart for "necessities," my older sister lingered at the cosmetic counter, insisting the frustrated clerk spray her wrist with every sample of perfume and smear the back of her hand with each beauty ointment on display. She threw a tantrum when Mom refused to buy her makeup for the first day of school. She flailed her arms and cried. Even the twins were embarrassed for her. She was about to start her second year of high school—what if one of her classmates saw her like that?

Mom didn't break. After checkout, she thrust a small white box into my older sister's chest. "Be happy with this, which believe me is a luxury, because there will be other girls at school who'll have to make do with wadded up toilet paper."

Back home, my older sister sulked. Dad fell asleep early, leaving the TV open for whatever we wanted to watch, but my older sister wouldn't leave her bedroom. She stared at the wall with red and puffy eyes.

"What pisses me off is you don't know how easy you have things," she said.

Did she think she was the only one who desired luxuries? When I walked through the toy aisle dozens of beautifully packaged items called out to me. Action men and games I felt I deserved after enduring the horrors of the orchard, but you didn't see me crying to Mom. I understood the family was a unit, and none of us suffered individually.

My older sister shook her head. "I'm not talking about that." She tapped me between the legs with the small white box Mom had bought her. "You don't even know you're supposed to want that going on down there. Mom and Dad baby you too much."

On TV, a crack commando unit was sent to prison for a crime they didn't commit, before promptly escaping from a maximum-security stockade to the Los Angeles underground. Upstairs in my older sister's bedroom, the wall purred, and the vibrations shook the TV's rabbit ears, so the twins and I took turns holding them steady to keep the picture from fuzzing out.

My older sister came home the next day with two Drug Mart bags, each one bulging with the weight of her purchases.

"How did you get all this?" I imagined a handkerchief covering the bottom of her face and a gun pointed at the clerk.

My older sister cracked the first tube of lipstick and applied a thick, crimson layer to her smile. "You're still in baby school with the twins. I have to be glamorous for high school, with or without Mom's help."

First day back at school, I lost the twins.

We were supposed to meet after dismissal to walk home together, but when I went outside after the final bell, the twins were nowhere to be seen. Had I taken too long in the bathroom, so impatiently my sisters set out for home without me? I worried about them navigating the busy roads, as well as the unfriendly dogs who barked and snarled from the front lawns of our less reputable neighbours. I ran up and down the block searching for them. When the police came to investigate their disappearance, the officers would shake their heads, astounded by my failure to look out for my younger sisters.

"Emery! Emery!"

The sound of their voices rang over the rumble of departing kids. What a relief. I hustled across the hopscotch grid towards them, happy to know nothing awful had happened.

The bottom dropped out once I spotted the twins, who waved their thin arms from the passenger window of Uncle Todd's truck.

"Hey there, slow-poke," Uncle Todd greeted me. "Let's rock!"

Before I could ask what he thought he was doing, Uncle Todd scooped me up and dropped me into the bed of his pickup. There wasn't room up front, so I had to ride in the back. One of the school's teachers walked by and, for a moment, I expected her to intercede, but she only smiled and waved at Uncle Todd, excited like he was a movie star.

"We have to go home," I said, gesturing for the twins to get out of the truck. "Mom's waiting for us." Truthfully, Mom was more likely to be surprised by our arrival home ("What, is school finished already?") and would make us play outside for another few hours, but Uncle Todd wasn't entitled to that information.

He looked hurt. "I wanted to spend some time with my favourite nieces."

Our home sat a mere five blocks from the school. Such a short drive would hardly give Uncle Todd the quality time he desired. I suspected driving us home was only a ruse. He wanted to come inside the house. Mom would be annoyed to see Uncle Todd pull up uninvited. Put on the spot, she would ask him in for coffee. He'd stay for dinner, and afterwards, guess who Mom would scold for bringing the bum home?

"First, let's get your older sister," Uncle Todd said, leaving a trail of exhaust as he squealed out of the parking lot. The backend of his truck fishtailed, nearly clipping a few of my schoolmates.

At the high school, my older sister had the right idea. Uncle Todd honked the horn and waved his arm above his head, calling to my older sister, who tried hiding behind a tree in the hope of going unnoticed.

"Rebecca! Hop in! We'll take you home!"

She wasn't falling for that. Instead, she turned heel and started running. We watched her hop the fence and scramble across the football field, kicking up tufts of grass and never once looking back as she disappeared beyond the goal posts. I wish I'd thought of that.

Instead of being offended, Uncle Todd chuckled. "Look at her go. Running off to her boyfriend, no doubt."

"She doesn't have a boyfriend."

"Yes sir, they'll be holding hands and smooching in no time."

Uncle Todd let up on the clutch and we rumbled through unfamiliar neighbourhoods, places too far for our bikes to reach. Before the intersection leading to our street, he pulled a wide U-turn, cruising past Victoria Lawn Cemetery and onto the skyway. Looking over the side of his truck into the canal a hundred feet below, I cursed myself for being so stupid. Mom counted on me to see my younger sisters home safely, and now I'd let Uncle Todd snatch us up like those kids who get into a stranger's car and are never seen again, no matter how many MISSING posters the police hand out.

"Hey! We're going the wrong way!" I banged on the cab's back window, but Uncle Todd couldn't hear me over the rush of highway wind. I tried pulling the window open, but he made a sharp swerve to the right, and I took a hard fall.

At the Peace Bridge, we waited for permission to cross the border. Mom and Dad took us over the border lots of times, so we knew how to behave. When the border guard leaned in the car window, everyone had to state their citizenship, even children, before he would wave you across. Americans happily invited us into their country, knowing we came to shop. The Canadian border guards on re-entry were less friendly. They put you under scrutiny, looking for purchases to charge duty on. Dad always stuffed cartons of cigarettes into the tire well, and Mom made us tramp along the side of the road, getting a good coat of dust on our new shoes. She told us not to worry—American mud washed right off.

I pounded against the window until Uncle Todd slid the glass partition open.

"We're supposed to be home. We have chores and homework."

"Homework at your age? I don't believe it. Don't you want to come to the fair?"

This piqued the twin's curiosity. "Fair?"

"You'll have a blast. There'll be a barbeque and balloons and lots more children."

The twins were agreeable, but I remained skeptical. This promise of a fair sounded like a scheme a stranger would use to lure kids into their car, but then again, Uncle Todd already had us in his vehicle, so I wasn't sure what he had to gain by lying.

"Do Mom and Dad say it's okay?"

"Sure. Your parents told me they wanted you guys out of the house. Give 'em some time to themselves."

That sure sounded like Mom and Dad. They hated when we sat around and always encouraged us to go outside. They said, "Play in the neighbourhood, just not too far, and don't get run over." Maybe I had this situation wrong, and my older sister would be the one in a heap of trouble when she came home, Mom yelling at her for not joining us, her evening alone with Dad ruined.

The border guard came around to the back of the truck.

"Who's driving this vehicle, young lady?"

"My uncle."

"Uh ha. And do your parents know where you're going?"

I shrugged. "I guess so?"

If the border guard noticed a problem, he'd leave it for the guards on the Canadian side to deal with when we returned. He nodded and waved Uncle Todd across into America.

After a clunky ride through overcast Buffalo, we arrived at a small building surrounded by a busted wire fence. The building had once been devoted to auto-mechanic repairs, and still reeked of spilled oil. A graveyard of engine blocks and tire piles cluttered the front. A few kids played amongst the ruins, tossing a hubcap back and forth like a Frisbee. If these were the kids Uncle Todd thought we'd have fun playing with, we were going to have a disappointing afternoon. I doubted these kids wanted to waste their time with a bunch of girls.

A hand-painted sign hung over the open door of the brick building, reading SUNRISE MINISTRY CHURCH OF LIFE. Due to poor planning, the letters in LIFE were crammed together to fit on the sign. Still, Uncle Todd pointed and said, "Would you look at that," impressed as all get out.

Back at the border, Uncle Todd had promised us a fair, which I took to mean in a park, not a car-part graveyard stinking of motor oil. Where was the barbeque grill? How dare he call this a fair?

"Alright girls, get out and stretch those legs."

No sense looking around for help. We were trapped. Stranded across the border, we might as well have been on the other side of the ocean. The twins and I couldn't walk home. Such a journey would take days. I wished my older sister was here. She would have grabbed Uncle Todd by his neck and made him drive us home. Actually, she wouldn't have let him bring us here in the first place. She'd have made him treat us to ice cream and then straight home.

Sometimes, I wished I could be more like my older sister. Stubborn. Insistent. Incapable of compromise. This was definitely one of those times.

I hopped out of the truck, and by the time my feet hit the ground, the twins had vanished. Stupid Uncle Todd hadn't given them a moment's thought. They could have wandered into a dark cave for all he cared. I started weaving through the piles of junk stacked on the asphalt lot, calling their names. If anything happened to them, Mom would hold me responsible. As the older sister, I was supposed to make sure we got home from school safe.

I peeked inside the soot-stained building, where all kinds of bustle was happening. Men set up chairs, microphones were connected to speakers, and singers warmed up their voices. A choir of women wearing purple robes over blue jeans clapped their hands and tried to outdo one another's sustaining high notes. No sign of the twins.

Avoiding the stares from the hubcap-flinging kids, I explored the yard. I peered into a stack of tires, and a man grabbed my arm, jerking me away from the black rubber tower.

"Bats and squirrels sleep in the rims. You'll catch a snootfull of a nasty surprise if you stick your face in there."

I continued searching, but now I kicked each stack of tires before looking inside. Neither bats nor the twins popped out.

A noisy scene played out around back, where a group of teenage boys and girls stood in the shadow of a school bus so covered by scorch marks and graffiti you couldn't see a remaining inch of yellow. Half of the teens imitated gibbering maniacs. They flailed their arms and convulsed violently, muttering in a foreign tongue. I kept my distance. This looked dangerous.

The other teenagers weren't afraid. Wearing compassionate expressions, they wrapped their arms around the loud, troublesome teens and held them in a tight embrace. These were loving hugs. Heads were pushed to breasts and backs were gently rubbed. Quickly, the wild, gibbering teens were soothed back to normalcy. Seeing such a display of heartfelt caring moved me. Not what I expected from surly teenagers.

Someone blew a whistle, and all the teenagers switched places. Now the huggers turned wild; rocking back and forth, gnashing their teeth and weeping while the former maniacs hugged them to quiet them down. What a confusing game.

In the midst of this chaos, I spotted the twins. They played along, both wrapping their arms around the waist of a convulsing young man.

"Give me your hands."

The twins dodged me, as though I were a stranger trying to haul them off. I needed cooperation. Out of options, I grabbed the back of their shirts and steered them towards the parking lot.

"Don't disappear. We don't know where we are."

People treated Uncle Todd like royalty. He leaned against his truck, enjoying a soda, revelling in the attention. I couldn't believe people got excited to meet him, but I guess that's what happens when you're on TV. Even if you're just the weatherman at 4:30 in the morning, people want to say hello. I used to feel proud of Uncle Todd's celebrity, until my older sister laughed and said, "He pays the TV channel to put him on. Anybody can do it. If Dad wanted, he could have a show right after Uncle Todd of him and Roman sitting around in their underwear, blowing songs across beer bottles."

Uncle Todd smiled his big grin, asking each well-wisher their name, but refusing to shake hands.

"Not a good idea to shake hands with someone like me. You don't know what's gonna happen!"

Like Bruce Lee, whose hands had to be registered as deadly weapons, Uncle Todd claimed his were too powerful to be swinging around naked. If he accidently made contact with someone, a waitress, a supermarket checker, his healing hands might send the unsuspecting woman crashing to the floor, overcome with the Holy Spirit.

But if he was being honest, he'd admit he just didn't want to get his hands germy.

While Uncle Todd loafed, an industrious crew transformed the empty warehouse into a theatre. Plastic chairs were lined into neat rows. Heavy black speakers were perched along the edge of a stage made from wooden blocks. The musicians pressed themselves against the wall to accommodate the choir, who had about five members too many for the available space. By the time everyone stood in place, there was barely room for a mosquito to fly. I got crushed between two hairy men in overalls, smelling nothing but armpits. The twins took advantage of my immobility and took off into the crowd.

"No, you guys. Get back here!"

They didn't listen. No matter how hard I pretended, I had no authority.

Outside, vehicles parked haphazardly on the street, blocking one another in. The plastic chairs filled quickly, and latecomers packed the aisles. Should the building be struck by lightning and the roof catch on fire, no one would make it out alive.

On the busy floor, the twins were in danger of getting stepped on. They threaded through the crowd, slipping between people's legs until they reached the front. Without asking for permission, they grabbed the edge of the stage and hauled themselves aboard. I was impressed to see them willingly stand before a couple hundred people and not feel self-conscious. They swung their arms and smiled, leaning over to speak into one another's ear, enjoying some private joke.

People didn't part for me so easily. I got nothing but dirty looks and sarcastic "Well, excuse you!" as I wedged my way through the crowd. I hated being up on stage, feeling like the whole room could see my underwear.

"Let's go. We need to stay together." I held out my hand, planning to haul them back to the truck. The truck would be cooler than this stifling warehouse, and once I locked the doors, the twins couldn't get away again.

The twins pretended not to hear me over the babble of voices. They didn't move. Before I could grab them, one of the choir members thrust a tambourine into my hand.

"When the music starts, rattle that thing. Promise me you'll rattle it hard."

Behind me, a musician pulled a pick from between his teeth. He tapped the strings of his electric guitar gently, barely touching them, yet a monstrous chord roared from the speaker, punching me right in the eardrums.

The evening got loud. Unlike the gargoyle church, where the minister sometimes invited an old man to play folk hymns on his guitar while his granddaughter sang, the musicians here played rock 'n' roll. Speaker vibrations pummelled my chest until I could no longer feel the beating of my heart. It might have stopped for all I knew.

The crowd embraced the volume. They stood up in their seats, lifted their hands, and swayed to the music. Even the old folk. I didn't think old people liked rock 'n' roll, only those big band records our teacher played for us to show the kind of music people danced to during the war. Good on them for being open-minded.

By the second song, I was giddy. A smile split my face from cheek-to-cheek. The music had a seductive effect even as the decibels ravaged my ears.

My body begged to dance. The purple-robed women in the choir waved me into their midst. Encouraged, I jumped between them, sweat lashing off my brow and splattering their gowns. They didn't mind being rained on. The choir women clapped their hands, cooling me with the breeze of their airy sleeves.

I wouldn't have believed it possible an hour ago, but I was having the time of my life. Incredibly, Uncle Todd had told the truth. This was fun. This was a blast! I forgot all about home as I twirled and whooped, banging the tambourine against my chest. The tiny cymbals jangled prettier than a princess's jewellery. No one banged as enthusiastically as I did. I was responsible for conjuring the enthusiastic response from the crowd. Their excitement was purely because of me.

Strange that Mom preferred to make us suffocate at the dead, gargoyle church when we could be having a wild party with Uncle Todd. Even Dad would enjoy this. He loved a good time. Before the accident, he and Mom always danced together, spinning in their socks on the kitchen floor until the record needle skipped.

By the time the music finished, the cement floor was slick with a river of sweat. I heard people's feet sliding.

The time had come for Uncle Todd to make his big entrance.

Coming from the cool outdoors, he strutted through the crowd, bouncing his fists up and down like a boxer entering the stadium. He soaked in their thunderous applause, nourishing himself on their positive energy. I swear, people clapped so hard you heard their knuckles crack. He charged onto the stage, pausing before taking the microphone to hand me the empty glass bottle of the soda pop he'd been drinking. Thanks, I thought, for giving me your garbage.

Supremely confident, his hair neat and face dry, Uncle Todd raised a hand for silence and spoke into the mic, "Don't panic, but there's an evil spirit in this building."

People murmured. They sounded nervous.

"Don't look around trying to figure out who it is. Whoever brought this terrible presence may not even be aware it's sticking to them. They have no idea this foul spirit is the cause of their illness, or the cause of their unexplained anger, or the cause of their lustful fantasies. Something unholy has taken advantage of their weakness, but all of you will witness the Lord cleaning this demon out tonight."

That got the crowd excited. They peppered the room with shouts of AMEN!

Ushers squeezed through the aisles, each carrying a box full of black masks to pass out to the crowd. Nothing fancy, just a strip of construction paper with two eye holes and a string stapled to the back. Everyone on stage got a mask too.

"These are your safety goggles. With your faces covered, the evil spirit won't be able to see you," Uncle Todd assured us.

Not everyone in the crowd put their mask on. Some men were like Dad. Clearly, they'd been dragged to this service by concerned wives. These men believed Uncle Todd to be a big phony. They weren't afraid of letting an "evil spirit" see their face. The twins didn't put their masks on either, but one of the choir women leaned over and strapped the black paper over their faces.

The band resumed playing. They looked unfriendly now, hidden behind burglar masks. Their mouths were grim as they strummed their instruments, making a low, percussive beat. No melody, only the same hypnotic chord over and over. Uncle Todd prowled the stage, sifting through the audience, hunting for the evil spirit. If he was as good as he claimed to be, he ought to have spotted the demon immediately. I bet he just wanted to make drama, like a magician who pretends to mess up their trick before the big reveal.

75

"I want everyone on this side of the room to stand up."

Fifty chair legs scraped the floor. Uncle Todd scrunched his face, concentrating hard.

"Okay, I want the first three rows and the last two rows to sit back down."

He paced some more, rubbing his chin as he studied the group of potential demons with deadly concentration.

"Now, the first three people at the end of each row... sit down."

This left seven folks standing. Some of them placed their hands in front of themselves, girding their loins.

Uncle Todd stopped pacing.

"Be not afraid. If you have faith, you'll be protected. Now, step closer please."

While the chosen seven approached the stage, Uncle Todd beckoned me to stand beside him. I didn't like being at the centre of attention, with a couple hundred eyes watching me through cardboard masks as though I were an eclipse, only observable with protection. My knees trembled, wobbling fiercely like I was holding in a pee, and for some reason this made a few more women shout PRAISE THE LORD!

"There's someone special here tonight," Uncle Todd told the crowd. "These are my nieces, who came to share this evening of miracles and healing."

He gestured towards me, sweeping his arm like I was the showcase prize on *The Price Is Right*. I held a hand over my eyes to block the glaring light, but the twins smiled and waved, basking in the adoration of the crowd. We must have seemed cute, which surprised me, as back home our reputation was well known for being dirty children. Mom and Dad often got letters from the school.

"Lift it up," Uncle Todd said, not into the microphone, but out the side of his mouth in our direction.

What, was he talking to me?

"Go on, up high."

I looked for someone onstage to offer a translation. Tired of waiting, Uncle Todd grabbed my arms and jerked them into the air, so the cheap, ten-cent-deposit pop bottle he'd handed me sparkled in the stage lights like a jewelled crown about to be auctioned off.

"Concentrate hard," Uncle Todd told me. "Just like you did in the orchard."

I nearly dropped the bottle. Looking back, I wish I had. What in the holy living hell did Uncle Todd know about the orchard? Who'd been whispering my secrets?

"Hold tight and concentrate on healing. Good energy."

In my foul mood? Fat chance.

Uncle Todd rolled up his sleeves. His arms were weak, all flab, not like Dad, who didn't even need to roll up his sleeves to show some turkey he meant business. When Dad flexed, his muscles bulged through the fabric.

A funny language bubbled out of Uncle Todd, coming in spurts like the first dribbles of foam from a baking soda volcano, before erupting into a rhyming babble, similar to the gibberish Sylvester the cat muttered after getting smashed over the head with a wooden mallet. He sounded silly, but, incredibly, people in the crowd began imitating Uncle Todd, speaking the same gibberish. His foreign tongue impressed me. I thought he spoke a real language. I wouldn't have guessed him to be bilingual.

A new sound filled the warehouse. One of the men Uncle Todd had called to the front of the stage made noises you'd expect to hear from someone locked in a coffin full of tarantulas. The fear in his cries sounded like an animal being devoured. Everyone around him leapt back, as if he exhaled poisonous breath. His black mask flew off; the eyes underneath red with hate.

The foulest words rushed from the unmasked man's mouth, words no one in the crowd expected to hear at a church meeting. If this had happened on Uncle Todd's TV show he would have been thrown off the air in two seconds.

Uncle Todd remained unfazed by the profanity. He took advantage of his higher ground and grabbed the unmasked man by his ears. The unmasked man twisted his head, gnawing at Uncle Todd's wrists, but Uncle Todd didn't let go. He lifted the unmasked man off the ground, pulling him onto the stage. I expected his ears to break off, so I looked away to save myself the gruesome sight.

I knew crazy men weren't to be trifled with. I once saw Dad wrestle a homeless man who'd sat on our lawn, waking us up with his woeful howling, as if the love of his life were imprisoned inside the house. When Dad tried to make him leave, the man went wild. My sisters and I knew Dad was good in a fight. We'd heard all the stories from his bar-room victories of youth. Dad had his hands up in the right spots to defend himself, but the man didn't fight like a normal person or even a drunk. He was faster and unpredictable. Trying to get him under control was like fighting two dogs in a sack.

Uncle Todd may have been larger and beefier, but he didn't have the moves of a fighter. Fortunately, two black-masked ushers arrived and lent some much-needed reinforcement. The yammering maniac showered their coats with spit. The black-masked ushers grabbed him, not like violent enforcers, but caring brothers-in-arms. They pushed his head to their breast and ran loving fingers through his hair while speaking gently. The wild man remained in the throes of aggression, his legs jerking, leaving the mark of violence scuffed across the stage.

"I command you, impure being, to leave this body. Your deceit and manipulation are over. Unclean spirits, be gone! Loose!"

Uncle Todd tapped the unmasked man's head. After one final spasm, his limbs went limp.

The band changed their tune to an uplifting melody. Victorious music.

"Take off your masks! Behold!"

As the unmasked man carefully got to his feet, Uncle Todd snatched the pop bottle out of my hands and threaded on the cap. Holding the bottle excited him. I could tell by the way his fingers trembled.

"It's heavier, isn't it?" he whispered to me. I nodded.

Holding the bottle over my head for so long made my arms sore. By the end, the bottle felt like it weighed a ton.

Uncle Todd patted the top of my head. "Good girl."

The unmasked man scrubbed his sweaty face with a handkerchief and smoothed down his hair. Being healed of his demon may have exhausted him, but he otherwise seemed back to normal.

The audience went wild. Some women had tears running down their cheeks. For a moment, I expected everyone to fall to their knees in awe of Uncle's Todd's power.

I was less impressed, having now recognized the unmasked man. I'd seen him earlier— one of the teenagers who'd been pretending to twist and jabber like a madman. Someone had dressed him differently, given him a suit jacket and tie to make him look more grown-up, but I saw through his disguise.

Wait until Dad hears about this, I thought, and resumed banging the tambourine until one of the choir ladies snatched it away. She looked annoyed, like I was being disrespectful. Didn't I know what was happening next?

Now we came to the part of the evening where Uncle Todd pushed people down and asked for money.

"Is there anyone here tonight who has cancer? That's terminal?"

Invigorated by the "miracle" of curing the possessed man, Uncle Todd began inviting sick people on stage to be touched by his healing hands.

Uncle Todd received a stack of blue cards from an usher. He sorted through them, calling out the names scribbled down.

"Althea? Where are you, darling? Is there an Althea who has pains in her leg?"

Two shrivelled men wearing veteran's hats helped a tiny woman hunched over a walker towards the stage. Each man held her by an elbow, helping her lift the walker. I imagined the three of them years ago, back before the war, dancing together. The men's rivalry for her affection had never been resolved, still they clung to her, waiting for her to make up her mind about which of the two she preferred.

The elderly woman and her two suitors arrived at the top of the stage ramp. The journey took a lot out of them. I tried to read the old woman's face to glean what had brought her to this strange place. Was she a true believer, or simply desperate, willing to try anything to relieve her pains? The bangs on her crooked wig obscured her eyes. I stood on tiptoe and adjusted her wig for her. I smiled, letting her know it was okay, no need to be embarrassed, but she looked right through me. In her eyes I saw the old bird was completely dotty. The two suitors were fighting over an empty shell at this point. I doubt she knew where she was.

While the usher held the microphone for him, Uncle Todd placed one hand an inch from the woman's temples, hovering in midair, vibrating like a kung-fu master charging up for a powerful karate chop.

In his other hand, he gripped the empty pop bottle.

"I can hear the Lord. He's watching over you tonight, Althea. He wants me to heal you."

Dad had explained Uncle Todd to us on many occasions. He made sure my sisters and I weren't confused on the matter. "God does not speak to your uncle. Todd doesn't hear anything. He lies."

On stage, Uncle Todd grabbed the old woman's head. For all his talk about blessings and energy beaming down from the Lord, I felt nothing special happening. Nothing rumbled and roared inside Uncle Todd, not the way the walls of our house did. Uncle Todd had all the energy of a stalled elevator. So it came as no surprise to me that the old woman remained normal under his touch. She did not shake, or speak in tongues, or roll her eyes, or give any of the other visual cues signifying a miracle took place. She was kind of blowing the whole show.

The power of suggestion can't work on her when she doesn't even know where she is.

Sometimes I wonder if Uncle Todd really believed he heard

the voice of God. Maybe after pretending to be a faith healer for so long, having so many people tell him he had cured their pains and their diseases, Uncle Todd now believed the lie.

That explains why he would do such a stupid thing as yank the walker out of the old woman's hands.

She fell. Hard. The two suitors propping her up fell too. They crashed on top of her withered, brittle body. The veterans' hats flew off and slid across the stage, coming to rest at the foot of the choir, who ridiculously kicked the hats away as though they were fresh bloodied scalps.

The crack of the old woman's head against the stage floor echoed through the hushed warehouse like a bowling alley strike. Now the old woman began to speak.

"Oh, ohhhhhh..."

Feeling terrible, I knelt and helped the two suitors roll off the old woman. Tears poured from her empty eyes. Her confusion made the situation worse. She had no idea who she was anymore, only that she was now in pain, and helpless.

Desperate, wanting to divert attention from the old woman he'd nearly killed, Uncle Todd hurried down the stage ramp to the next parishioner, a middle-aged woman holding a crooked, rickety arm. Uncle Todd seized her elbow, and she fell to her knees, howling in pain. I saw her arm collapse as the bones shattered beneath Uncle Todd's grip.

Having lost complete control of the room put Uncle Todd into a panic. He rushed into the crowd, grabbing anyone he could lay his hands on, too disoriented to know if he held a man or woman or child. Repeatedly, the Lord failed to deliver healings through Uncle Todd's hands. Instead of AMEN!, the warehouse filled with the sound of suffering.

Uncle Todd stayed quiet during our long drive home. He hunched over the steering wheel, concentrating on the beam of his single working headlight, following the yellow highway line reeling us back to the border. The twins voiced their hunger, disappointed the food Uncle Todd had promised never materialized. I helpfully pointed out drive-through restaurants, but Uncle Todd wouldn't slow down to see if they were open.

The only time he spoke was to say, "I'm very disappointed in you, Emery." As though I'd purposely done him wrong.

It had taken some effort to leave the church meeting. The people who initially welcomed Uncle Todd so graciously now didn't want to let him leave. They surrounded his truck, banging on the body. A few of them picked up rocks. All four of us squeezed into the cab; the back bed was too covered in spit. Uncle Todd tried waiting the crowd out. He switched on the radio, playing us some Bobby Bare while we rocked back and forth in the shaken truck. Only after the sound of shattered glass did Uncle Todd rev up the engine and start creeping forward, pushing people out of the way.

The empty pop bottle sat on the dashboard. The glass rattled whenever we drove over rough road. I wondered why Uncle Todd kept it. Maybe as a reminder of his evening, to teach himself better, and to not make the same foolish mistake again.

Flashing red lights on our street welcomed us back home. An ambulance idled, the revolving rooftop lights piercing bedroom windows and waking the neighbours. Along the street, men and women stood on their front porches, wrapped in bedsheets, looking concerned.

Uncle Todd swung carefully around the ambulance to park on our boulevard. He kept the engine running. He planned to zoom away as soon as we jumped out, taking no responsibility for swiping us.

A familiar green Chevy blocked our driveway. Grandma's car.

Before the twins and I could climb from the truck, our porch door swung open. Grandma flew outside, her face raging. She'd been waiting for quite some time.

"Todd, oh Todd, how could you?"

This looked grim. If Grandma was upset with Uncle Todd, the golden boy of the family, there was no telling how mad Mom would be. He must be a dead man.

Jumping from the truck, Uncle Todd was all smiles,

hugging Grandma and saying, "Mom, what are you doing up so late?" He lost the smile real quick when Dad thumped his way outside, balancing on his crutches while cracking his knuckles. Uncle Todd slipped on a penitent expression and Grandma smacked his shoulder.

"Your sister wanted to call the police! What in God's name were you thinking?"

Before any excuse could be offered, drama unfolded a few doors down. Two ambulance attendants rolled a stretcher out of the house. Mr. Bruinanski lay strapped aboard, his skin a disgusting pallor. Mrs. Bruinanski trailed dumbly out of the house, not even wearing a bathrobe, only a towel and tattered white underwear. One of our neighbours took her by the arm and led her back inside to get dressed before following her husband to the hospital. The ambulance doors slammed shut and the siren roared as they sped down the street. I watched the swirling red lights shrink into the horizon. A few blocks later, the siren crudely cut off, and in the overwhelming silence we heard Mrs. Bruinanski grieve from the bottom of her soul. She sounded like a thousand voices, the amount of pain too much for one person, so others spoke up to help carry her burden.

The chaos of the ambulance allowed Uncle Todd to drive away unnoticed. Just him and his empty pop bottle. Disappointing. I wanted to see him get yelled at more. Inside the house, my older sister waited, ready to give us hell.

"I ought'a slug you one for what you put Mom and Dad through."

Nearly a hundred percent of Mom's exasperation came from my older sister. Rich of her to cast me as the troublemaker.

Mom sat in the living room beneath a cloud of cigarette smoke. She was too angry to look at us and kept her head turned to the side, fixated on the wall. Ash covered her shirt and spent cigarettes had been butted against the wall and flung to a pile on the carpet.

Dad remained outside. He was long popular with the neighbours, always the first to help cut down a tree or to have the joke of the day. The other neighbour men, shocked to have witnessed the death of one of their own, migrated to our porch, happy to have Dad, counting on him to find the words to put tonight in perspective. Dad broke open some cold ones, and the men stood around getting philosophical until the sun rose. The next morning, half the men on our street went to work with beer on their breath.

While Dad consoled the neighbours, Mom questioned me. "What happened? What did your uncle do?"

I tried to explain, to make her understand that I'd been duped into following Uncle Todd to the United States. The twins and I had no more choice in the matter than a handful of cloth dolls scooped up and carried away.

"I don't care about that right now," Mom interrupted. She crumpled an empty package of cigarettes and flung it across the room. "Where did your uncle bring you?"

"Well, you know how Uncle Todd always asked us to come to church?"

"Goddammit."

The twins yawned. They were up well past their bedtime. I felt like they were still my responsibility. If I couldn't bring them home from school when I was supposed to, I could at least put them to bed.

Without getting off the couch, Mom reached over her shoulder to part the curtains an inch, spying on Dad drinking outside with the neighbours.

"Emery, I need you to go into the basement. Under your father's work bench, there's a green metal box. Bring it upstairs."

My older sister tried to follow, but Mom barked at her: "You stay put."

"What are you yelling at me for? I'm the only one smart enough to come home when Uncle Todd comes creeping around."

"Maybe you should have done something instead of running away like a scaredy-cat," I said.

"Emery. The basement. Before your father gets back."

I didn't like going to the basement alone. At school, they taught us any house with a dirt floor in the basement likely has bodies buried down there, from the time before the local cemetery. I felt vulnerable in my bare feet and imagined skeletal hands rising from the ground and wrapping their cold bones around my ankles. I found the green box, an army container that once held strings of bullets to feed into a machine gun. It felt heavy, the lone item inside shifting as I ran up the basement stairs.

"Take it to the playroom and hide it," Mom said. "Quick, before your father sees."

My older sister made to follow behind me.

"You! Stay put!"

Inside the playroom, the wall purred. Vibrations tickled the floor beneath my feet, so I raced for a hiding place. I chose the closet, putting the green box on the top shelf behind a papier-mâché pig.

"You girls might as well stay up all night," Mom said when I returned. "Because you're going to school tomorrow. I don't care how tired you are."

"Uh, excuse me," my older sister said. "I didn't ask to stay up late, worrying about these three blockheads. If anyone deserves a day off school it's me."

"Listen, if you were so concerned about your sisters' welfare, you wouldn't have let them disappear in the first place."

"You'd rather I'd been kidnapped too? That's nice!"

Dad came in from the porch, making a run to the fridge for more refreshments. "Calm down you two. No one has been kidnapped, and I don't want to hear that word again. This stays within the family. It is not to be discussed with anyone, understand?"

I didn't think to look inside the green box. It's all conjecture now, but I'm guessing Dad kept a gun in there. Mom wanted it hidden because she knew Dad would come off the porch all boozed up, ready to strap on and go out blasting. I visualized the aftermath at Uncle Todd's house. Hot shell casings melting into the carpet like cigarette butts. Dad unsteadily waving the gun, too drunk to hold it straight. He'd hit the wall more times than his intended target, who would choke on his last breath, bleeding out.

Thankfully, Mom prevented this violent scene. No matter the offence, family never turned against family. Gunning down her brother wouldn't be something Mom could forgive, and Dad would have found himself pushed from her life and subsequently ours forever.

*

Assuming there even was a gun. All these years later, my sisters and I have yet to find any evidence of a weapon. There are no ammo boxes in the basement. No holster strap hanging in Dad's closet. I never saw the green army box again. Maybe Mom buried it in the garden. If I wanted to know, I could put an ad in the paper, offering to hire someone with one of those metal detectors to scan our yard and see if anything is down there. I bet everyone's garden has a few pieces of mystery buried beneath the azaleas, and I'm not talking about missing trowels or jars of pennies from a child's pirate games. Dig long enough anywhere, and you'll always find the remains of something nasty.

FIVE

Just as Mom promised, she woke me and my sisters bright and early for school. She wouldn't allow us a day off because of the late night. Dad thumped his crutches into my room, shaking the bed frame and yanking away the sheets. He looked unrecognizable. Only the familiar hands convinced me it was him.

"Ta da!" Dad proclaimed, pivoting on his crutches to give me an all-around view of his new look.

His Samson-length locks were gone; only stubble and white scalp remained.

At the breakfast table, the sight of Dad's bald dome shocked my older sister. She stared at her lap, too ashamed to look at Dad's naked scalp, as though he were sitting there with his bathrobe wide open.

The twins ran their hands over his new crown, counting the red patches where the razor blade had nicked him.

"How did you cut your hair off?" they asked.

"I didn't. Mom did it for me. Tit for tat."

My older sister choked on her milk. "Please don't tell me that means—"

On cue, Mom skipped merrily into the kitchen, her own head swathed in an elegant cloth like an Egyptian princess. Beneath the patterned dressing, her head was as bare as Dad's, though I bet her scalp bore fewer cuts considering Dad had more experience with a razor to do her nicely.

"I like this," Mom said. "So much more comfortable."

"Safer too," Dad said, running his hand over his head. "Nothing to get caught in any machinery."

I wanted to ask when was the last time he operated any machinery but stopped myself. Rubbing his unemployment in his face would be cruel. Perhaps it was better to enjoy this moment of good cheer from Mom and Dad, so welcome after the events of last night.

Outside, Grandma's car pulled into the driveway. She let herself in, her arms laden with trays of McDonald's pancakes for us, still warm beneath their Styrofoam shells. Grandma knew this would be a real treat because Mom refused to acknowledge the existence of McDonald's. When my older sister was small, Mom told her the Golden Arches sold tractor wheels and other mechanical parts for farmers, not hamburgers like her increasingly frustrated kindergarten classmates insisted. When my older sister finally saw a McDonald's commercial on TV, she grabbed Mom by the hair, shouting, "You lie!"

Grandma stopped dead in her tracks as soon as she saw Mom and Dad. She slammed the pancakes onto the counter. I heard the Styrofoam shells crush. Warm syrup dribbled from the wreckage.

"I can't believe the two of you! You look as stupid as you're acting!"

Dad popped the top on his morning beer. Usually, Dad respected Grandma by not drinking in her presence, but losing his hair made him giddy, and he flaunted his beer, taking long, loud gulps.

"Would you like a trim too?"

Grandma sighed. She approached the kitchen table, holding her palms up to assure Mom and Dad she meant no harm. She spoke gently, like she was trying to talk a suicidal stranger off a building ledge.

"I know I'm just a grandmother with no say in how you

raise these children, but I beg you to reconsider. Remember, they still have to go to school. People are going to think the bunch of you joined a religious cult."

"Why not?" Dad joshed. "You and Todd have been begging us to join your religious cult for years." He cracked himself up with that one.

Grandma hugged us all before she left, grabbing the back of our heads to run her hand through our hair one last time. She left defeated, powerless to stop what was happening.

"Follow me," Mom said. She swept the pancakes into the garbage, denying us even that small treat. "I have to get you girls ready for school."

"This isn't fair! I'm never going to get a boyfriend now!"

Inside the bathroom, Mom wrapped a sheet around my older sister's neck and pushed her onto the toilet. Mounds of hair surrounded the bottom of the porcelain throne, hair that only hours earlier had been growing strong on Mom's and Dad's heads.

"I'm giving you a light trim." The scissors in Mom's hands clanked, and my older sister's long hair tumbled into her lap. The falling strands grazed her cheek for a goodbye kiss.

I was surprised my older sister didn't mount a more vicious defence; crying, pleading, wrestling the scissors from Mom. Instead, she sat completely submissive, as though she'd already plotted the chessboard and verified every move resulted in eventual checkmate. She might stall for a turn or two, but the end game was inevitable. Might as well get it over with.

"My hair's going to look like it got chewed off by a dog."

My older sister's description of Mom's work wasn't far off. The scissors were dull, so Mom's cut was uneven and patchy. All over my older sister's head, her pale scalp shone through.

My turn came next. Mom cut close, getting no better with practice. The cold metal blades nipped my scalp. Every clip made me wince.

My older sister scowled at me. "What the hell difference does it make how long your hair is? I'm the one with the whole world to impress. You can still wear jeans and play in the mud. I have to be a lady!"

"I'm a lady too."

"Bullshit. You could get fat if you wanted. Your belly will even out when you hit a growth spurt."

I asked Mom if we were saving our hair to sell to a wig-maker or to donate to those poor children who went bald from cancer medicine.

Mom shook her head. "Your guys' hair is no good to any-one; it's too dirty."

I scooped a handful of my stray locks from the floor and gave them a sniff. My hair reeked of Dad's cigarettes. I saw why a little cancer child might prefer to remain bald than to strap my smelly cuttings onto their head.

Mom cut from oldest to youngest. After me, she lifted both twins onto the toilet and chopped all the hair from the first born. Squeezed beside her younger-by-five-minutes sister, the two made a bizarre before-and-after poster you might see hanging in the world's worst barber shop.

"There we are—all done."

"What do you mean *all done*? What about Mary?"

My older sister pointed to the youngest, her legs dangling over the toilet seat, her hair still long and fine, seeming to mock us with its beauty.

"Oh, for Pete's sake," Mom said, snatching the scissors from the sink, and giving a few light trims to her bangs. "Happy now?"

I rubbed my hands over my scalp, listening to the *brtzz* sound of the short bristles.

"Emery, get the girls dressed for school," Mom said, lifting a cigarette to her mouth. "Not you, Rebecca. Stay here a moment."

The door closed on our faces before locking. Curious, we lingered outside, pressing our ears to the door, feeling entitled to know what our older sister had left to endure. Her giggling gave us no clue, neither did the hissing of the shaving cream can. Only our older sister's shrieks, somewhere between amusement and fright, convinced us to disappear outside before Mom changed her mind and forced the same mystery treatment on us.

The new haircuts made me dread the thought of school. Dad did his best to assuage my fear as I headed out the door hand-in-hand with my younger sisters.

"It's no big deal. Back in my day, kids got their heads shaved all the time."

"Really?"

"Sure. Everyone got lice and ringworm. Sometimes the whole school stank of kerosene."

He was right. No one at school said anything, which seemed worse than the put-downs and laughter I'd been expecting. I could have showed up with a fat lip and two blackened eyes and the reaction would have been the same: *What do you expect from that family?*

Robbie Clattenburg, a red-haired boy who routinely got sent into the cloakroom when the teacher had enough of his shenanigans, passed my desk on the way to the pencil sharpener, catching me off guard with a hard smack to the head. He licked his palm first, leaving my bare scalp stinging and wet.

The teacher pretended not to notice. She isolated herself behind her desk, unwilling to enter the murky, troubled waters surrounding me.

On the back of my arithmetic page, I wrote a note to Robbie: *Touch me again and you'll be sorry*, but I crumpled it up instead of passing it to him. Robbie would take my warning as a challenge. Next time, he'd smack my head with both hands, enjoying the game, unaware I could hit him back much more severely.

"There's going to be changes around here," Mom promised, sounding so dire I expected her to announce we were moving far away. The thought of packing up and having to meet all-new people frightened me.

Mom insisted from now on we cease referring to our younger sisters as "the twins."

"Your sisters are unique individuals and they deserve to be addressed as such. I know I have only myself to blame for allowing your grandmother to buy them so many matching outfits, but the shared name ends here."

From now on, we'd be celebrating my younger sisters' birthdays a month apart.

"We've been doing their birthdays all wrong," Mom explained. "Your younger sister should have been born on September nineteenth, but she decided to stick around a few weeks longer to keep your other younger sister company, until she was ready to be born on October twentieth. Wasn't that thoughtful? We ought to celebrate their real birthday, not the day they just happened to come out."

"That sounds like such bullshit," my older sister said.

"Oh Rebecca, no one wants to share a birthday. You know how kids born on December twenty-fifth grow up? Miserable."

Separate birthday celebrations suited me fine. Cake on two days instead of one.

Upstairs, a heavy padlock dangled from the playroom door. The cold steel made the house feel smaller and less hospitable. How could our home have rooms where we were unwelcome?

"The playroom is dirty and dangerous right now," Mom said. "Thanks to all the crumbs you girls left behind, there's squirrels and skunks and God knows what else nesting inside."

Dad attached more locks, sealing off each of our bedrooms save for mine, which happened to be the biggest.

"You four will sleep together for the next little while."

"Why are you doing this?" My older sister hurried to grab her clothing and makeup before the doors closed permanently.

"Cool weather is coming," Mom said. "And I don't want to pay to heat four rooms when we can just heat one."

"That sounds like such bullshit."

Mom sighed. "Rebecca, when everything starts sounding like bullshit, it's time to get your hearing checked."

The two extra beds filled my room to the brim. You couldn't run or leap in there anymore. There went my morning summersaults routine.

My younger sisters carried nothing from their old rooms. They appeared happy with this new arrangement but weren't about to say so in front of their older sister. They knew better than to poke the bear.

"What's the big deal? All you girls need your room for is sleeping. You have the whole rest of the house to do whatever you like."

My older sister got snotty. "You mean like the playroom?"

"Oh for—I never see you in there. You're the last person I want to hear complaining."

"I'm supposed to be a grown-up. And you're putting me right back with the babies."

"Young lady, you are nowhere near being a grown-up." As much as Mom wanted that to be true, she knew my older sister was right—adulthood stood around the corner, and that surely frightened Mom.

Our first night together felt like camping. With the beds pushed close, I could roll over and bump my older sister, who busied herself reading magazines, occasionally ripping out the perfume samples, wetting them with her spit and rubbing them on her neck until she stank like the detergent aisle. When I knocked into her a second time, she rolled up the magazine to swat me over the head, telling me to stay in my own bed, but smirking, clearly enjoying herself. She kept watch from over the edge of her magazine, daring me to return.

Mom came around at lights-out to say goodnight.

"Why do I have to go to bed the same time as them?"

Mom sighed. "It's after midnight. You're not going to bed early; they're going to bed late."

"Lucky."

Mom removed the patterned cloth from her head, giving us our first look at her baldness. She still looked beautiful. She wore large hoop earrings and had a clean, smooth skull;

no bumps or divots. Her head looked like an exquisite bust carved out of marble. I wanted to run my hand over her.

"You girls need to remember closeness is good. Your father and I can't always keep an eye on you, so it's up to you to protect each other from straying where you shouldn't. If Uncle Todd ever approaches you again, run. Scream. Tell people he's a stranger if you have to."

After Mom left, my older sister rolled into my bed and nudged my ribs. Although the orchard seemed a lifetime away, my bruised sides were still sensitive. She cupped a hand around my ear and whispered, "Listen."

It seemed I wasn't the only one who thought Mom retained her beauty under a bald head. The groaning of Mom and Dad's mattress a storey below was audible. Our bedroom wall purred to their rhythm. I tried to fall asleep, uncomfortable overhearing our parents in their privacy. My older sister balled two fists between her legs and shook the bed.

"Do you ever think about your first time with a boy?"

I told her never. Besides, I'd expect her to be first. Once she had her first time with a boy, then I'd start worrying about my own.

"You don't know that's true. Maybe you'll be with a boy first."

I told her I wouldn't dare. For one, she would kill me. Second, everything I'd been told about this docking process sounded disgusting. I needed my older sister to do it first before I'd know if I could ever go through with it.

"You're lying, Em. You think about it all the time. Right now, you're shaking the bed thinking about it."

I smacked her leg, telling her she was the one doing all the bumping and jittering, and to stop talking about this in front of our younger sisters. She rattled the bed violently, finishing herself off.

"Stop pretending to be so perfect, trying to make the rest of us feel dirty."

The vibration pouring off the purring wall tickled my cheeks. I rolled away, waiting patiently for the irritating sound to die down. The mattress shifted as my older sister reached for the active wall, her fingers strumming the air. I caught her by the wrist and gently lowered her hand to the sheets. "Don't."

At first, she seemed amused. "Don't?"

Making sure our younger sisters were asleep, their ears plugged with one another's dreams, I whispered, "If you had seen the Pincher in that bunkhouse, smelled his rotten insides, you wouldn't be so eager to touch the wall again."

She sat up.

"I sleep on my hands now," I told her. "Until they go numb. It keeps me from touching the wall at night, even accidently."

How could we trust something capable of creating horrific suffering such as the Pincher's final days? The best thing we could do was leave the wall alone.

"After a while, it'll forget us."

My older sister leaned in close, squashing her nose against mine. Our eyelashes tangled together.

"You're really stupid, you know that?" She tried reaching around me, but I grabbed her wrist again, less gentle this time. It surprised me to discover our physical strengths had caught up to one another.

"Who knows what happened to that pervert? Maybe he got food poisoning. Jeesus-peesus."

The Pincher deserved a good smack on his hand for what he had done to me, but I still felt sorry for him. Sometimes, his death on a cot in that filthy bunkhouse seemed like a dream, and I felt shattered the moment I remembered, *No, that really did happen.*

When you're a child, you imagine what your life will be like. Will I travel? Will my husband be handsome? Will our children be happy? You never wonder about the bad things. Will I grow up to hate other people? Will I steal? Will I kill? Here I was, not even a teenager, already sentenced for the rest of my life to carry the knowledge that I once hurt someone so bad they died.

The purring increased. Waves came off the wall, tickling the skin between my shoulder blades. The vibrations crept down my sides, inching closer and closer to the rough patch where the Pincher grabbed and pulled me until my skin nearly came off. My older sister tried again to reach around me, but I succeeded in keeping her from the wall. I won't lie—it felt good to be the one making the rules.

For a moment, I thought I'd convinced her. She respected not only my strength, but my maturity. At last, she accepted me as an equal. From now on, maybe we'd confide in one another better. Some day in the coming years, she'd tell me all about her first boy, and I would be happy for her, just as a loving sister should.

I loosened my grip on her wrist, setting her free. She rubbed her sore skin, red from my twisting.

"Who made you the big sheriff of the house, telling people what they can do?"

In the darkness of our new crowded bedroom, her hand sprung like a coiled snake, its fangs biting into my sore sides, her fingers pinching me where I hurt most.

"I`m the one who got you idiots home safe. If I listened to you and didn't touch the wall, you'd still be stuck out there with Uncle Todd. Remember that."

The purring ceased. The room fell so silent I could hear the blades of grass rustling in the wind outside. Ignoring the searing pain in my side from where my older sister had pinched me, I pretended to sleep, even though drifting off under these circumstances was impossible. She yanked the sheet from my body, leaving me shivering all night long, vibrating the bed worse than the wall ever did.

SIX

Early morning, before the flickering static on the living room TV resumed its broadcasting day, my older sister fished our hair clippings out of the garbage. Locked in the bathroom, she used glue and a skull cap cut from a plastic bag to fashion a wig.

She began the project with high hopes but the final results were disappointing. Wearing her new creation to school was out of the question; she knew it wouldn't fool anyone. The wig's dirty locks were different lengths, like something the Bride of Frankenstein would wear, stitched together from multiple scalps of dead hair.

Bravely, she wore the wig to breakfast, daring Mom to say something about it. Knowing my older sister wanted her to feel guilty, Mom refused to address the wig, even as it littered our plates with stray floating hairs.

Wanting to offer an olive branch to my older sister, I told her she looked pretty and wished my hair were as long and healthy as hers. She tore a hunk from the wig and threw it across my French toast, the blonde and brown hairs soaking up syrup.

"There you go. Make yourself beautiful."

Still locked out of her bedroom, my older sister took to spending hours in the bathroom, posing in front of the mirror, wearing the wig while she coated her face with lipstick and mascara. On her own, she pretended the wig looked real. She played records on the turntable in our communal bedroom with the volume maxed so she could dance without having to leave the privacy of her fantasy chamber. My younger sisters didn't mind the loud music, but I found it impossible to read. The windowpanes rattled whenever heavy bass farted from the speakers.

"Why don't you find someplace else to read," Mom suggested.

I refused. The bedroom had been mine first. My older sister had no right to move in, uninvited, and expect me to change all my routines just to accommodate her. Every ten minutes, I banged on the bathroom door, clamouring to use the toilet. My older sister tolerated these interruptions at first, but soon she insisted on watching me sit on the toilet and prove I needed to use it. I cried wolf one time too many, and she refused to open the door after that.

I tried Mom again.

This should have been my moment to cry on her shoulder but Mom took the side of my older sister, asking me to take things easy on her for a bit.

"Your father and I got lazy and we waited too long between the two of you. Rebecca is a teenager. She doesn't want her little sisters around. She wants to be a grown-up and you only remind her of all the things she hates about herself."

Our age disparity wasn't my fault. Had I been in Mom's shoes, I would have demanded my older sister open that bathroom door, wipe that paint off her face, and start playing with dolls again. She could act like a grown-up when I was ready to.

For once, Mom blew smoke out the corner of her mouth to avoid my eyes. "Rebecca won't stay this way forever. The only people who'll know you from cradle to grave will be your sisters. She'll realize one day that you're more important to her than anyone else." She puffed on her cigarette and quickly added, "You and the twins, together."

I'd been foolish to expect satisfaction. The middle child's concerns never carry the weight of their siblings. Everything my older sister does will be happening for the first time (first to be a teenager, first to graduate, first to drive) while everything my younger sisters do will be happening for the last time (last delivery, last diaper change, last kindergarten class). First times and last times are emotional, memorable. Everything that happens in the middle is mundane.

"Can I have some money to go to the store for a Coke?"

"No."

The middle child isn't worth fifty fucking cents to cheer up.

Black ants crawled along the sidewalk—the perfect target for my anger. I liked pressing my foot on them lightly, so they didn't die right away, and their bodies shook and jittered. A wild explosion of nerves. You can do that, because ants don't feel pain. They're too tiny to add suffering to the world, so you don't have to feel guilty about dripping gasoline down an ant hill and firebombing them by the thousands.

Roman stood across the street, scratching his back against a telephone pole like an old tomcat. I waved and he disappeared into the neighbour's bushes, confirming my suspicion he had been spying on me.

Dad claimed he never sent Roman to spy on any of us, but not even Mom believed him. Too many times she caught sight of Roman in the supermarket or outside the hair salon or in her rearview mirror. One time too many, Dad returned from the construction site knowing things he shouldn't, like how Mom had stopped to chat at Flo and Eddie's flower shop or bought her cigarettes from the vending machine in the lobby of the Lenard Hotel. Since Dad's accident, there had been an increase in Roman sightings. I always caught him ducking behind corners and crawling under bushes. All this, Dad claimed, was simple coincidence.

"Roman is a decoy," my older sister said. Dad knew the oaf couldn't sneak around for beans. We were supposed to see Roman to distract us from the real person watching us. Ever since she told me that I felt vulnerable and cold whenever I caught a glimpse of Roman standing outside the school window, peering in at me. I wondered where the second man, Dad's true spy, hid when he watched us.

"WOU WOU!"

A familiar whooping sound broke the lazy afternoon calm, diverting my attention from Roman.

"WOU WOU WOUUUUUUUUU!"

Normally, I stayed clear of Ricky Castle. He was the same age as my older sister but didn't go to high school. He still came to my school, but only one day a week, where he was taught in a special room down in the basement that had lots of toys but no books. I detested his favourite hobby, throwing pinecones at bird nests. For someone who walked with such an uncoordinated body, Ricky threw with incredible accuracy. When he hucked a pinecone at a bird's nest, he hit it dead on, creating an explosion of twigs and leaves, tumbling tiny eggs, or more gruesomely, baby birds to the boulevard. After each successful hit, Ricky lifted his arms and jumped up and down, whooping and hollering. Because of him, our neighbourhood was home to the most depressed birds in the nation. They returned to the trees with a mouthful of worms only to find their homes destroyed and their children gasping in the tall grass or being feasted on by neighbourhood cats. The devastated birds circled the trees, squawking their grief before flying to Port Dalhousie and committing suicide by diving into the lake.

Ricky couldn't understand the severity of his bird bombings. His celebrations were innocent, bearing no resemblance to a person revelling in wickedness. I'd seen boys press frogs under sticks until guts spilled from their mouths or shoot bottle rockets at stray cats. The delight they expressed had a vicious edge Ricky lacked.

Normally, I tolerated his bird slaughter, but watching Ricky pick up a pinecone and knock a bird off the eaves trough of Mrs. Bruinanski's lonely little house aggravated my already foul mood. I decided to teach him a lesson. Mom lined her garden with shiny, mineral-encrusted rocks, and I let one fly at Ricky as he danced happily. I wanted to hit his arm or leg, but my aim went off and the jagged rock smacked the side of Ricky's head, opening a flap that gushed blood like a punctured tin of tomato juice. He ran away shrieking, and I spotted my older sister watching the violent scene from the bathroom window. She mouthed the words: *I'm telling*, before jerking the curtains shut.

Mom didn't want to hear about provocation and faulty aim. "That's shameful you would do such a cruel thing."

She assumed I threw a rock at Ricky because he was different, that I wouldn't have thrown a rock at someone who might fight back. I hated her for being so eager to attribute an ugly motive. Did she not know me? When Mom left for work, I refused to hug her goodbye. A light rain fell, and I hoped the seed dust on her work overalls would get wet and sprout long, thorny vines that would curl around her neck like a python and choke her.

To redeem our family name, my older sister attempted to befriend Ricky.

Winning Ricky's friendship wasn't easy. Like a wounded animal hiding under the porch, my older sister first had to win his trust with food before being allowed close enough to pet him. She used a plate of marshmallow cookies to lure Ricky into our yard. He gobbled them down, smearing chocolate around the corners of his mouth, and once his belly filled up, he ran down the street making his loud whooping noise.

"What happened to all the cookies?" Mom wanted to know when she got home. I expected my older sister to suggest Dad had eaten them during *Frankenstein Meets the Wolf Man*, but she admitted she fed the cookies to a guest.

"Hmmm, well, I better call Ricky's mother and make sure that's okay. I think he might be diabetic."

Ricky wasn't, but Mom told my older sister to break the cookies into smaller pieces next time so Ricky thought he got generous, multiple servings without cleaning us out.

When my older sister needed more cookies to lure Ricky into the house, she turned to her younger sisters for assistance.

"Let me have your cookies."

"What will you give us?"

She thought for a moment. Then, excitedly, "I'll make up your faces!"

My younger sisters and I sat along the edge of the bathtub while our older sister shared her bounty of cosmetics. She troweled on ruby lipstick and enough eye shadow to make us look like raccoons. We looked in the mirror and shrieked with delight. We rushed outside to parade her exquisite work. Lined up like cheerleaders, we danced along the boulevard, directing our marvellous faces towards traffic for everyone to see.

Honking car horns woke Dad from his nap. He got up on his crutches and thumped onto the porch, confused by the sight of our newfound beauty.

He pulled us away from the road. Once we were safely on the porch, he pressed his fingers against each of our necks, checking for a pulse. He became cross we had grown into teenagers without his permission.

"Get inside and scrub your faces before I turn the hose on the lot of you."

We asked our older sister for our cookies back, feeling Dad's forced washing nullified our contract. She said no.

My older sister continued to make progress. At first, Ricky wouldn't set foot on our porch. He didn't trust the house any more than a crumbling bridge you'd feel too nervous to put your full weight on. After a week of eating cookies, he overcame his reticence and travelled further and further across our yard. He'd come to count on those cookies.

"He's going to knock on the door tomorrow," my older sister predicted.

"No way."

"Come sit at the top of the stairs with me, you'll see."

Late afternoon, after school, Ricky arrived right on schedule. He looked for my older sister, but she wasn't in the yard waiting for him. After a few minutes of shuffling around, he made his way to the front door.

It astonished me to see Ricky breaking his patterns. My older sister clapped her hands, proud to have won him over with her cunning and perseverance.

Ricky's knocking woke Dad from his nap. Groggy-eyed, he opened the front door and placed his fingers on Ricky's neck. After finding his pulse, Dad tucked a dollar into Ricky's shirt pocket, thinking he had come by to collect for UNICEF.

My older sister grabbed Ricky by the hand and brought him upstairs to our bedroom. I trailed behind, curious what game the three of us would play, only to have the door slammed in my face. Before I could force my way in, my older sister pushed my bed to barricade the door. The caster wheels squeaked across the floor, sounding like a mouse being strangled.

"She's locked us out of our room!"

I tried getting my younger sisters outraged, but they paid no mind. Unless they were sleeping, they stayed out of the bedroom, preferring the coolness of the basement where they played with an old phone.

I went back upstairs and kicked the door.

"Go away."

"Rebecca, the room isn't yours."

"We're supposed to share it. You can have the room all to yourself later."

I rattled the doorknob but couldn't move the weight blocking the other side. "There's never a later!"

The same routine happened each day. Ricky arrived and my older sister forcibly removed me from the bedroom. I tried hiding under the bed or in the closet, but she'd pick me up and drop me into the hall like I weighed nothing.

While my older sister entertained Ricky in our bedroom, I sat outside the door, unwilling to give them privacy. Listening to them play Monopoly day after day bored the hell out of me. Ricky barely knew the rules. He rolled the dice, but my older sister moved his piece for him and read off the names of where he landed. She took advantage of his inexperience, advising him not to buy any of the utilities or Boardwalk, and she landed on Free Parking way more than an honest player would have.

Ricky spoke very little. The few words he did utter weren't questions or thoughts, but simple statements of fact, as if he were trying to figure out the world by compiling information. He only said things like:

"You got a Band-Aid on your leg, you cut yourself."

Or:

"It rained yesterday, it rained, all wet."

I tried aping his style of communication, telling him, "Your sneakers are tied," or pointing to the road and saying, "That's a red car," but none of these conversational gambits interested him. The only thing I really wanted to say was, "Sorry for throwing a rock at your head."

The bedroom door always opened promptly at five o'clock, when Ricky's mother finished work and he went home for the day. My older sister walked him down the stairs. She didn't see me squatting behind the bathroom door, but Ricky pointed and said, "You were spying." As much as I hated being caught, I was impressed that Ricky was astute enough to sense me when my older sister couldn't. I'd misjudged his abilities.

I waited up for Mom to return from the seed factory.

"Ricky is making himself too much at home," I said. "He's going to be another Roman."

Mom stood in the kitchen, placing her hands on the table to keep her balance. Working the evening shift exhausted her. Dark stains marked the collar of her overalls, like she'd been sick on herself.

"Your sister is doing something nice. Ricky probably lives a very lonely life."

Dad laughed, calling Ricky my older sister's boyfriend, comforted by the knowledge his daughter's paramour had only the purest of intentions.

His daughter's intentions were more suspect. Late into the night, the wall purred for much longer than it normally did.

She couldn't keep her hands under the covers. When the wall finally went silent, I believe that was only because my older sister finally tired it out.

A two-toned Coupé de Ville pulled into our driveway. Ricky had the radio turned way up so the whole block heard his music, a rock 'n' roll oldies station. A cigarette flew out the driver's window, rolling across the front walk and coming to a rest at my foot.

"You're driving a car," I said, in the same patronizing tone I might have used to compliment his sweater.

"Tell your sister I'm here."

Before the running engine could wake Dad from his nap, my older sister barrelled out the front door. The long hair of her wig flew behind her like a bridal train. She jumped in the car and the pair sped away. For one terrible moment I feared her hair would get caught in the back wheel, like the scarf that ripped the head off that actress.

Their road trip didn't last long, only as far as Port Dalhousie. It sounded very romantic. They walked hand-in-hand to the end of the concrete pier, where one could squint and see the grey ghost of the Toronto skyline. Ricky bought ice cream, using money my older sister gave him (because the boy should always pay). Afterwards they rode the carousel, until they were kicked off for necking.

The police brought my older sister home, wrapped in a blanket to protect her from the night chill. I wondered if they'd used the same blanket to lay over dead bodies at traffic accidents and if it had been washed recently.

Ricky was driving a stolen car. He had swiped the idling de Ville from in front of the drugstore. Ricky didn't get into too much trouble; the police reasoned it was a crime of opportunity. If Ricky had mugged someone for their keys or ripped open the dashboard to hot-wire the ignition, the police would have crushed him, but because he drove off in a car left running unattended, the cops treated it as an unfortunate, rash decision.

I couldn't help but feel proud of Ricky, who went from an aimless, shouting boy who little girls throw rocks at, to a full-fledged juvenile delinquent. The subject of a police manhunt! Ricky was cool.

Mom and Dad took the news much calmer than I expected, as though they figured my older sister would be brought home by the police regularly and they wanted to get off on the right foot. Mom and Dad invited the police into our house. One officer stood in the hallway, arms folded over his chest, while the other took a seat in the living room and flipped open a leather notebook. I saw him glance at the teetering stacks of Dad's empty beers.

They wanted to ask my older sister questions. Mom and Dad nodded, gesturing for her to cooperate.

All she said was "I didn't know the car was stolen."

The police said she must have known someone like Ricky didn't have a car, that, of course, it was stolen.

"Never occurred to me. Maybe someone lent Ricky the car. Maybe he won it in a contest."

The police reminded her that it was dangerous to get into a car with someone without a licence. Ricky didn't know how to drive; there could have been an accident.

"Ricky drives as good as everyone else. Better."

This was demonstratively false. Ricky was not a good driver. Only the reflexes of other drivers prevented a fatal collision. Ricky drove fast and sloppy, unable or unwilling to commit to a lane. He drove worse than Roman.

The police told my older sister she was lucky to be under the age of majority, otherwise she would have been arrested too. Unfair when you think about it. She's more mature than Ricky, yet had to shoulder none of the consequences.

"Where is Ricky now?" my parents asked.

After surrendering, the police took him to the station to wait for his mother.

"She works."

I didn't like the way the police said that, as though having a working mother explained everything. I expected Mom to speak up, snap back at the cops "I work, too." She said nothing.

I felt bad for Ricky, sitting in a cold jail cell, his legs shackled to a big heavy ball to keep him from escaping. The police said he wasn't locked up. He sat in an office waiting for his mother. I asked what they were feeding him for dinner, and my parents told me to be quiet.

My older sister did her best to put up a tough front for the police, but I saw right through her. Clearly nervous, she fidgeted with the silk scarf wrapped over her head. She didn't like the area of questions the police arrived at.

"Did Ricky touch you? Did he try to kiss you?"

They wanted to know if Ricky was a sex maniac. While the police treated him nice right now, sitting in the chief's fancy office like a guest instead of a prisoner, his fortune would change if they found out Ricky picked up young girls and tried to touch them. People who touched young girls got locked up alongside the troublemakers who started fires or opened their pants in the park to show off their privates.

My older sister responded coyly, saying Ricky's romantic overtures were for her to know and them to find out.

The police asked Mom and Dad what they intended to do.

Dad knew what to say. "I'll tell you what, officers, it's going to be a long time before she has a day worth smiling about. I am going to make sure she understands how dangerous today was, not just to herself but to other people. And if she thinks she's going to get a reputation at school, fancy herself Bonnie Parker on the run with older boys, she's in for a big surprise. No one is going to be impressed she helped a poor, mentally retarded boy dig his own grave. The only thing she has to look forward to is a lengthy punishment."

Dad may have laid it on thick, but he wanted to be sure the police believed there would be repercussions, that she would be corrected at home, so they didn't have to punish her. I'd heard of girls my sister's age going to a children's jail. It could happen.

Finally, the leather notebook flipped shut and the police left.

Alone now, my older sister shrank into the couch. She looked as if wolves were descending on her.

"Can I go to bed now?"

Mom yanked the scarf off her head and long locks spilled over my older sister's face. Hair full of bounce, like it had recently been washed and blow-dried. It startled me to see her hair restored to full length. Mine had barely grown. You could still see my scalp.

Like a mouse caught in the kitchen, my older sister tried to make a run for it. She leapt off the couch and sprinted towards the stairs, but Mom grabbed her around the waist. She dragged my older sister back into the living room, who gasped as the long hair flew backwards into her mouth, choking her.

Mom pulled my older sister over her knee and brandished a pair of scissors. The big ones she used to cut open raw chicken. The scissors clanked, dropping long ropes of hair to the carpet. My older sister sobbed, her shoulders heaving.

"Stop it! Why can't you leave me alone?"

Not knowing what to do, I laid newspaper on the floor to catch my older sister's falling hair. Mustering the last of her strength, she tarred Mom and Dad with the most vile insult possible, the two-word expletive most often seen spray-painted on tunnel walls. Mom and Dad didn't even flinch. While Dad held her neck down, Mom ran the scissors all over her scalp. It turned out that particular curse word wasn't as shocking as we'd always imagined.

That night, Ms. Castle came knocking at the door. Mom didn't want to answer, afraid to face the woman.

In tears, Ms. Castle broke down on our doorstep. She begged forgiveness, pledging Ricky was a good boy and that she felt ashamed for what he'd done.

Mom opened the door and soon they were both hugging one another and sobbing. Two mothers who felt like failures in the wake of their rotten children's misdeeds.

Ricky didn't come the next day. His cookies stayed in the kitchen. The next time he knocked on the door, Mom spoke to him kindly, but firmly, explaining he couldn't see my older sister anymore.

"You two shared some good times, but now that's over."

My older sister watched their exchange from the top of the stairs, peering at her paramour through the banister rungs like a prisoner.

"Would you like some cookies before you go?" Mom asked.

Ricky shook his head. "You got a smoke?"

Mom flinched, surprised by the state of his voice. Strong. Coherent. She reached beneath the shoulder of her shirt and gave him the entire pack of cigarettes tucked beneath.

"I mean it, don't ever come back here," she said as he walked away.

A lot of windows were broken that night. Up and down the street, rocks sailed through glass. The ground was covered in shards, like the headlights from a hundred traffic accidents. Many houses were attacked. We had an assembly at school about it. The principal lectured as if every last one of us, right down to the kindergarteners, were accessories. We were ordered to bring any information to our teachers, who sat at the front of the gym like a jury, looking disgusted. Broken glass wasn't the worst part. A lot of pets had been hit with rocks. A dog's leg was broken and someone's cat had been smashed in the face, its eye crushed and its skull broken. They'd had to put it to sleep.

My older sister kept her hair short. She hadn't a choice in the matter. Once a week, Mom marched us into the bathroom for a checkup with the scissors.

"What's going to happen when the weather turns cold?" I asked.

"Better dig out your winter hats," Mom said.

My other younger sister still had her original long hair. Sometimes I saw my older sister staring at it enviously, like she wanted to pull out a bowie knife and scalp her.

Ricky disappeared from town without a word to anyone. Having reinvented himself, he must have desired new faces who knew nothing of his former life stumbling up and down the street, throwing pinecones at birds and whooping.

I saw Ms. Castle in the supermarket afterwards, looking lost. She reminded me of the grief-stricken birds who returned to shattered nests and dead babies. Was this karma? After ruining the lives of so many birds, had Ricky now done the same to his own mother? I braced myself for the morning we woke to the news that Ms. Castle's grief forced her to take a dive into the lake.

"No, darling," Dad said, popping the top on a fresh beer. "She would never do that, not while there's a chance Ricky might come back."

This soothed me some, but the next time I spotted Ms. Castle in the supermarket her face looked distraught, suggesting she believed her son was never coming back.

Surprisingly, my older sister wasn't bothered in the least by Ricky's flight from town. I would have thought her devastated, imagining her standing alone in the school parking lot, running a hand over her scratchy head, waiting for Ricky to pull up in one last stolen car, inviting her to hop in and join him on the road to freedom and adventure.

In honour of Ricky's memory, my older sister continued to hold after-school cookie parties in our bedroom. Privately, of course. I was never invited. She hadn't a key for the door but found she could use a hairpin to lock herself inside. She fired up the record player and set up the Monopoly board. Crouched with my ear to the door, I heard the stomping of her feet as she danced, all the while carrying on imaginary conversations with her vanished sweetheart, Ricky. Sometimes, I swore I heard someone in there with her for real, but when I tried peeking through the keyhole, I discovered that my older sister protected her privacy by jamming the lock with tissue paper.

SEVEN

The work at Stokes Seed factory drained Mom, which meant I'd been put in charge of getting my younger sisters off to school in the morning so she could sleep in. We always left the house late, running up the sidewalk with unlaced boots. While I struggled to zip-up my now bald, younger sister's jacket, my long-haired other younger sister took the opportunity to run into the widow Bruinanski's driveway and pop a piece of gravel into her mouth.

"Spit that out! Do you have any idea how filthy that is?"

My other younger sister wasn't concerned about the cleanliness of Mrs. Bruinanski's driveway gravel, clearly covered in car exhaust and dog piss.

"You're stealing. Mrs. Bruinanski paid a lot of money for a gravel driveway. What if everyone who walked by took a piece? There'd be nothing left and she would be very sad."

"I'm not stealing. I'll spit it back after school."

"Even still, it isn't right to borrow things without asking."

My other younger sister nodded, conceding my excellent point. "I'll knock and ask Mrs. Bruinanski for permission."

"Don't you dare!"

"I won't have to ask her every morning. Just once."

During school, my other younger sister sucked the gravel, flicking the stone with her tongue and rattling the wet lump against her teeth, making a sound like ice cubes in an empty glass. The noise drew attention and a note soon came home. The school expressed "concerns" and suggested counselling, assuming there were serious reasons as to why she sought security through a mouthful of gravel. Mom wasn't having any of that—no daughter of hers would be confessing anxiety to shrinks and getting filled up with pills.

Dad found her habit funny, calling her Rock Mouth and offering to rent her out to construction crews. "They can fill your mouth with stones and spin ya' around till you spit out cement."

"I'm willing to accept a bad habit," Mom said. "I just want it to be something that isn't going to break your teeth." My other younger sister was too young to start smoking, so Mom switched her to gum.

Hoping to pull the wool over the eyes of the school authorities, Mom filled an old pill bottle with Chiclets and instructed my other younger sister to tell her teachers the gum was medicinal.

"Take a piece in the morning and another one after lunch," Mom prescribed.

Our younger sisters' teacher, Mrs. Ramsey, wasn't fooled. School rules prohibited chewing gum. She didn't think it fair to the rest of the class for my other younger sister to sit chomping her jaw all day.

"You're like a cow with its cud," she said. The class laughed, but my other younger sister didn't feel embarrassed. She had confidence in herself.

Mom asked Dr. Janowski to write a note to the school, claiming the gum was necessary for my other younger sister's health but he refused to play along. "I don't want to encourage an unhealthy dependency on placebos."

My other younger sister hated gum anyways. She preferred the texture and flavour of junk found off the ground. The dirtier the better. She'd pop in coins, erasers, bits of plastic, anything her schoolmates dropped.

After Mom's chewing gum deceit, Mrs. Ramsey forever marked my other younger sister as a troublemaker, someone to keep an eye on. The oral tic disgusted her. What a nasty child. Believing Mom too lax in her parenting to fix the problem, Mrs. Ramsey decided the duty of correcting my other younger sister's behaviour fell to her.

"Get up here in front of the class."

Each morning, after the national anthem and the Lord's Prayer, Mrs. Ramsey inspected my other younger sister's mouth. She did this in front of the blackboard, beneath the portrait of the Queen. Mrs. Ramsey brought a small wooden box for my other younger sister to stand on, so even the kids at the back could see her disgusting mouth.

"Open wide."

Mrs. Ramsey went fishing inside, using two wooden sticks intended for head-lice inspection. Prodding the cheeks and lifting the tongue, Mrs. Ramsey never failed to find pay dirt.

"What do you have here?"

Mrs. Ramsey plucked out toy soldiers, marbles, pop can tabs, pieces of crayon... With each extraction, Mrs. Ramsey sneered, "Ewww!" and held up the item for the rest of the class to see, urging them to voice their disgust. Mrs. Ramsey didn't throw any of these things away but kept them in the bottom drawer of her desk. I think she planned to send them home to Mom in a bag, hoping the accumulation of chewed junk would shock her into taking action.

Mrs. Ramsey wiped my other younger sister's spit from her hands and warned, "Young lady, if you aren't careful, you'll wind up like one of those garbage sharks that swallows all the junk in the ocean. When they're caught and cut open, their bellies are full of licence plates and old fishing boots. Is that what you want? To grow up to be a garbage shark?"

I thought her teacher sounded stupid. Like, how was my sister going to grow up to be a shark? I suspect Mrs. Ramsey, cruel woman, hoped to pin a nickname on my other younger sister, but the ploy backfired. Due to her comical repetition of the phrase, the kids began calling the teacher Garbage Shark.

Deprived of the soothing objects inside her cheek, my other younger sister began filling her mouth with whatever she could scrounge up within the classroom. She stole pieces of chalk, caking the insides of her mouth with white paste. Garbage Shark caught on fast and branded her a thief, sending her home with a bill pinned to her dress, demanding fifty cents for the chalk. Still bitter over Garbage Shark's refusal of the chewing gum compromise, Mom dropped two quarters into my other younger sister's mouth, telling her, "Pay up."

During art period, Garbage Shark kept a close eye on my other younger sister, knowing crayons were liable to go right into her mouth. To combat this, Garbage Shark brought in a bottle of hot sauce and dipped her crayons into the spicy mix. Pretty smart. My other younger sister abhorred hot things. Unfortunately, Garbage Shark forgot about her tainted fingers and rubbed her own eye. The burning started at once, forcing the humiliated teacher to abandon the class and flush her eye in the children's bathroom, kneeling before a sink that hadn't been designed for someone her height. When she returned, all red and swollen, she could not disguise the naked hate she felt for my other younger sister.

"You are a rotten little girl!"

My other younger sister offered no resistance. She sat contentedly at her desk, mouth full of fresh chalk.

The hot sauce turned out to be the last straw for Garbage Shark. She wouldn't admit it but she felt defeated. To save face, she told my other younger sister, "I can no longer ask the rest of the class to put up with your distractions," before pulling her desk out of the aisle and butting it against the wall at the very back of the room. The janitor constructed a cardboard wall to seal her off from the other kids.

When Mom learned of the new seating arrangement, she said, "Good, I hope that's the last I'll have to hear from that ridiculous lady."

The cardboard barrier turned out to be yet another woeful lapse in judgement. Things were better for Garbage Shark when she could see my other younger sister. With her out of sight, Garbage Shark found herself unable to concentrate and stumbled through her lessons, too busy watching the cardboard barrier, imagining all the awful things her arch-nemesis got away with right under her nose. She thought about my other younger sister all day long. *What must she have in her mouth now?*

Before long, Garbage Shark called in sick, and a substitute teacher arrived to manage the class for the remainder of that tragically shortened year.

Vicious noises raged in the dark. Clicking and gnashing, like two rats trying to tear off one another's tail. Wild animals seemed to have invaded our bedroom, and I feared we'd be caught in the crossfire of their warring claws and pointed teeth.

My older sister threw on the light. My eyes stung, refusing to adapt to the sudden brightness.

The violence came from our younger sisters' bed. They wrestled face-to-face, taking turns on the bottom as they hit, scratched, and yowled. My younger sister grabbed a handful of my other younger sister's hair, trying to yank it out by the root. Since her opponent had no hair to grasp, my other younger sister spat into her older-by-five-minutes sister's face, painting it pink with the blood from her swollen gums.

"Dad! Help! Come quick!"

His crutches squeaked up the stairs and banged against the posts of our too-close-together beds.

"Jesus, what's going on here? Stop that!"

He tried separating our fighting sisters, but they chomped his wrist. Their bite went deep, raising a pink bracelet around Dad's arm. He lost his balance and fell back on my bed, his crutches clattering to the floor. Defeated, he pulled a cigarette from his shirt pocket and sat on the edge of the bed, looking deep in thought.

"Make them stop! They're killing each other!"

"Nah. Let 'em get it out of their system."

My older sister doused our feuding sisters with a pitcher of water, like they were two angry dogs. Soaked, our sisters continued fighting, but their strength had been exhausted.

Now, each swing of their fists carried less and less power until they were merely patting one another's face.

Finally, Dad pulled them apart. Thinking it best to keep them separated for the rest of the night, he placed my younger sister in bed with my older sister and my other younger sister in bed beside me. Before leaving the room, he pressed his fingers into their necks to check their pulse, and he nodded, satisfied. Their blood pressure must have been racing. Through her wet pyjamas, I felt my other younger sister's beating heart. The instinct to fight still possessed her. Any moment, the girls might leap from their separate beds and resume hostilities, this time using their teeth to finish things off.

The wall gurgled, reminding me of a fat man's stomach settling at the end of a long, heavy meal. I hoped to fall asleep before the maddening purring started up again.

Come morning, our younger sisters stood ankle-to-ankle at the bathroom sink, brushing their teeth and sharing cotton swabs of hydrogen peroxide they pressed to the wounds on their faces, wincing as the antiseptic fizzed. They seemed to be back on good terms.

"Maybe you ought to stay home today," Dad said. "It looks bad when an unemployed man sends his daughters to school with beaten up faces." He threw his recliner back, elevating his injured feet before directing our younger sisters to fetch him a beer from the kitchen.

"If they get to stay home from school, why shouldn't we?" my older sister demanded.

From his recliner, Dad motioned her to step closer, like a king asking a subject to approach the throne. He pressed his fingers to her throat, cocking his head while he appraised her pulse. "No bruises, no black eye. You're good."

I worried my older sister would take that as an invitation to run face-first into a door, giving herself a good marking, even chipping a tooth. "Am I bad enough to stay home now?" she'd ask.

"The twins can't look after you by themselves," I said,

stepping in to keep this brewing argument from turning into a full-fledged storm. "We better stay home to help them."

The look on my older sister's face let me know I'd said the wrong thing. Her lips turned into a perfect O, like Mom's when she blew smoke rings, and she stepped away from Dad's chair, not wanting to be anywhere in his vicinity when he blew up.

"Number one: you don't call your younger sisters that anymore."

"Sorry. I forgot."

"Number two: you aren't looking after anyone. Especially not me. The day I'm too busted up to function that I need my daughters to look after me is the day I'm led out to pasture and have a bullet put in my brain. Understand?"

He rose from the recliner, standing on his own two feet without the aid of his crutches for the first time since his accident. The veins in his legs swelled up; the pumping blood looked black as coffee. His temple twitched as he withstood the pain, which must have been tremendous. It took all my strength not to push him back into the chair. His kneecaps looked ready to burst from the pressure.

"I'm sorry," I said, but Dad continued to stand, showing off, pushing things too hard and long.

When he finally sat down, the cords in his legs made grinding noises, and the bones popped. My younger sisters returned with his beer, which he drained in a single, desperate gulp.

The unpleasantness passed. Dad smiled, back to his normal self, my insult forgotten.

"Number three: since your Mom is at work, I don't give a good goddam if you go to school. I'd be happier with you all here."

He shoved over, making room on the chair's armrests for our butts. My older sister and I clung to either side of him, while he hoisted our younger sisters in his lap. We remained that way, keeping Dad warm all through the Channel 11 Weekday Matinee, *Son of Frankenstein*, one of the good ones, the last time Boris Karloff played the monster.

The idyll of that final, perfect afternoon ended with a visit from Uncle Todd.

Unannounced, he marched up our steps, still carrying the empty pop bottle from his over-the-border church meeting, as though he intended to present the stupid thing to us a gift. Gee, thanks, Uncle Todd. How generous.

Dad met him at the front door, holding the screen shut, respectfully letting his brother-in-law know his offer of company, though appreciated, was not required.

"Fuck off, Todd."

Foolishly, Uncle Todd tried forcing his way in. He wrestled with the doorknob. Dad surprised him by pushing the door wide open. The metal screen bounced into Uncle Todd's chest and he stumbled backwards onto the lawn.

Although awkward with his crutches, Dad rolled up his sleeves and hobbled outside, anxious to squeeze in some fisticuffs before Mom returned. Too often, she stood between him and a good punching.

Uncle Todd took a pacifist stance, holding his arms behind his back to protect the bottle, instead of raising them over his face. "Would it make you feel better to hit me, Jack? Have at it, brother."

Dad threw three perfect jabs, BING BANG BOOM, right to the centre of Uncle Todd's face, hitting the nose, the eyes, and the mouth, which were known as the Triangle of Death, because internal injuries in that area spread infection into your brain that killed you.

My sisters and I watched from the doorway. We expected Uncle Todd's face to explode, painting his cheeks with blood and bits of nose cartilage, but he barely flinched. Dad's punches took no effect, landing dopey, as if his knuckles were made of marshmallow. He tried again. Round two. This time, he threw his entire shoulder into each punch, but his fists struck Uncle Todd's face with no more strength than the flap of a butterfly's wing. Incredibly, our younger sisters' lightweight fists inflicted more damage on each other last night. They must have used up the house's daily allowance of violence, the same way you could use up all the hot water, leaving nothing in the tank for Dad to throw at Uncle Todd.

Soon, Dad found himself hunched over, huffing and puffing. Cigarettes stole your breath, they taught us that in health class. Concerned, I once asked Dad why he didn't stop smoking. He said it took years for cigarettes to damage your lungs. By the time he got sick he'd be an old man and could buy a pair of robot lungs or whatever scientists had invented by the year 2000. I thought he placed an awful lot of faith in science and worried the year 2000 would leave him disappointed.

Dad lowered his head between his knees, trying to catch his breath. The sight of him penitent before Uncle Todd distressed my older sister and me. We both sensed the sinister thought running through Uncle Todd's head. He considered picking up a cinderblock from the side of the house and using it to smash Dad's head apart while he hunched over helpless, gasping for breath. Had they been somewhere private, I believe Uncle Todd would have done just that.

With the fight over, Dad touched his fingers to Uncle Todd's neck, pushing deep into the flesh beneath his stubbly chin. He nodded, seeming to say, *Very well then*, before slinking back into the house, trying to keep his face hidden from any neighbour who witnessed his humiliating failure to run Uncle Todd off his property.

Instead of taking his bottle and leaving us alone, Uncle Todd hopped around the lawn waving his arms, celebrating his victory. Really? What kind of boxer ever won without throwing a punch? Pathetic.

"Emery! Come over here!"

Uncle Todd waved to me. He thought he could fool me again. After the first kidnapping, I wouldn't so much as spit in his direction. I decided to show him.

Remembering a couple of squirrels I'd seen fighting, I dropped to my hands and knees and imitated their battle stance. I flared my nostrils and bared my teeth. I rolled my eyes until only the whites showed. I looked so fearsome I didn't have to make a move towards Uncle Todd. As soon as he saw my eyes all white, my fingernails digging into the porch boards, and heard me screeching like the devil's kettle, Uncle Todd scrambled for his truck. He fumbled with the door handle in pure panic. He almost jumped out of his shoes like in a Don Knotts movie. What a chicken!

Having bested Uncle Todd and restored Dad's honour, I crawled into the house on all fours, swaying my head and growling, wondering who else I could throw a fright into. My younger sisters barely looked up from their peanut butter and crackers. My older sister rolled her eyes, embarrassed for me.

Dad knew how to play along.

"Rebecca, run and fetch my silver hammer from the basement. There's a monster loose in the house."

I snarled, lowering a long strand of spit from my lips. Calling my bluff, my older sister hurried to fetch Dad's hammer, curious to see what he'd do with it. Dad pressed the end of the hammer into my forehead, right between the eyes, holding the silver circle there like a priest bestowing a blessing. Imitating a vampire, I made a sizzling sound effect and flipped onto my back, making my arms and legs spasm in a real good death rattle.

Dad nudged my belly with his foot. I kept my eyes shut tight and concentrated on breathing slowly to hide the rise and fall of my chest, expertly playing dead.

Always the spoilsport, my older sister said, "Let me tickle her."

Dad told her to stay back. "Monsters aren't like fish you throw back in the ocean. You first have to make sure they can't cause any more mischief and misery."

He stuck his fingers into my mouth, wedging them between my front teeth and pulling my jaw open. The claw end of the hammer, used for prying loose nails, forced its way into my mouth. The metal hit my front teeth and I felt reverberations along my jaw. The claw wedged itself against my bottom teeth.

"These teeth need to come out. Run and get me a pot to put 'em in."

The hammer claw scraped against my teeth, the taste of rust sending a chill down my spine. I could have ended the game by opening my eyes and giggling, but I wanted to see how far Dad would take it. I wanted him to be the one to cry "Uncle!" first.

Dad put more pressure on the hammer and I felt my teeth move. Only a millimetre, but for a tooth that's a great distance. Now I started to worry. Had Dad forgotten we were playing a game, and I wasn't really a tricky monster requiring their teeth yanked out?

Lucky for me, his fingers pressed into my neck. When he found my pulse, he angrily flung his hammer against the wall.

"Get up."

I tried smiling, to remind him what a fun game this started out as, but Dad would have none of it.

"I bet you think you're pretty smart, eh? Well, let me tell you something, it doesn't take a smart person to trick a fool." The lids below his bloodshot eyes trembled, making waves like a rough sea. Somehow, I'd shamed him.

"Wait, I'm sorry."

Dad huffed and puffed his way down to the basement. Soon after slamming the door, the hammering began, as he used nail after nail to barricade himself in.

Only Mom could lure Dad out from the basement, assuring him he didn't have to be afraid. It took ages for Dad to pry out the nails and open the door. Black electrical tape swaddled his hands, keeping his fingers bound tight. After the hammer incident, he no longer trusted himself not to hurt one of us accidentlly.

Mom yanked me into the bathroom. She turned the faucets on full blast, filling the tiny room with the rumble of Niagara Falls to drown out our conversation.

"I'd expect something like this from your older sister but not you, Emery."

Mom was past angry. She was disgusted with me. My actions had hurt Dad worse than a hundred tumbles off a roof.

Hurting a member of the family was the one thing Mom would never tolerate.

"Can't you see he's not getting the sleep he needs?"

Since his injury, Dad had grown impervious to sleep. No matter how many hours he got (Mom once counted him up to sixteen), he never felt rested. Some mornings, he looked at his eyes in the mirror and saw the irises expanding and contracting, like the mouths of hungry worms.

At night, Mom often awoke to find Dad standing over her, his fingers pressed into her throat. Dad confided in Mom shortly after the accident that he'd lost the ability to tell the difference between when he was sleeping and when he was awake. Sometimes, while watching us eat or waiting for us to come home from school, he would be gripped by an icy panic that all of this was a dream: the house, Mom, my sisters, and that at any moment he would awaken in a strange bed. Slowly, his real life would come back to him, and all of us would be forgotten forever. This fear paralyzed him.

Roman gave Dad his talisman. He said, "Did you ever notice the people in your dreams never have a pulse?"

It's true. Anyone can try it out. The next time you're having a dream, reach for the neck of someone and check for a pulse. No blood pumps, all you will feel is dead dream-flesh.

Roman touched Dad's neck and said, "I can feel your pulse, so I know I'm not dreaming right now." Dad felt silly at first, but he pressed two fingers beneath Roman's unshaven chin and learned to find comfort and confidence in the beating of a person's pulse, taking its rhythm as proof he was not dreaming.

Things might have turned out different had I taken Mom's scolding and promised to never again treat Dad so poorly, but instead I pushed back. Feeling it unfair for Mom to hold me accountable for Dad's mental state, I said, "Why aren't you doing something to help him?"

I might as well have poked out her eyes. Mom flinched, clearly stung by my accusation.

We'd let one another down. Mom went on the defensive.

"Young lady, you have no idea what I do to keep this family together."

My older sister showed me no mercy. In the night, she rolled into my bed, cupping an arm around my bruised side and whispering into my ear, "You know, Mom doesn't really work at the seed factory, right?"

How could that be? We'd all seen Mom off bright and early in the morning, wearing her factory overalls, the sleeves covered in white seed dust. Sometimes I worried about her breathing this dust in and having the seeds sprout in her lungs like tumours.

"Has she ever brought seeds home from work?"

No. She hadn't. Our own garden went barren; nothing but weeds and squirrel shit.

"Mom gives massages to men. That's why she's so tired when she comes home. But Dad doesn't know."

The national anthem ended hours ago, yet the TV remained on, tuned into the dancing static. I hated the aggressive grey of an empty TV set. The angry hissing made me think of a washing machine filled with bees.

A wall of beer cans sat along the armrest of Dad's chair. One beer remained in his loose grip. Half full, still fizzy. I wondered if right now, in his dreams, he pressed his finger to the necks of strangers, maybe even the Frankenstein monster, and failed to find a pulse.

I hoped he'd sleep a long time. Get the rest he needed so his pitiful legs and aching back could finally stitch themselves whole again.

The beer tasted organic, like cork or soft wood. The bubbles carried a pungent aroma into my sinuses, tickling my olfactory with a scent I'd never experienced before. Beer in the mouth smells different from beer in the air. I figured this must be why Dad drank so many beers one after another— he wanted to recapture his initial tasting. I knew my next beer wouldn't taste as good as this one, so I've never bothered drinking another.

Dad jerked in his sleep. His mouth half open, struggling to breathe.

The pulse in his neck raced. His heart must have been going two hundred beats a minute. No wonder he never felt rested; what a stress on the body. I dreaded to think what he must be dreaming of to raise such a pulse. Even worse, it seemed unlikely for Dad to carry this routine on for much longer.

Under the covers, praying my older sister was sound asleep, I ran my hand along the wall, making gentle waves back and forth, like you might pet a dog you aren't hundred percent sure isn't going to bite you.

My body rocked, feeling the dizziness of my first beer. Soon, the wall sparked to life and the familiar purring massaged my entire body, welcoming me back without judgement, the sensation spreading through me pure ecstasy.

I closed my eyes and committed wholeheartedly to stroking the wall. All the while I concentrated on Dad, imagining him once again healthy and strong.

EIGHT

For the first time in as long as I could remember, the TV wasn't on when I came downstairs in the morning to fix breakfast for my sisters. Someone had actually switched it off. Curious, I ran my hand along the dust slats at the back of the set. Stone cold. Incredible. The TV had been off for hours.

Dad's crutches lay across the arms of his empty recliner. I half expected to see his clothes lying there too; his dirty underwear all that remained of him after aliens had beamed him up. He came bounding from the bathroom wrapped in a towel, his skin beaded with water from the first shower he'd taken since the accident.

"Everyone into the kitchen!" he called. "Breakfast, breakfast!"

The stove burners were bright red. Dad sloshed sour milk and flour into the pan, whipping up sticky clumps of pancakes. He raced to mix his ingredients before they burned. My younger sisters set the table while my older sister dug up the bottle of syrup and used a butter knife to pry the lid off the hardened top.

"I'm ready to go back to work."

Mom didn't like this. She sat at the table in her work overalls, waving a lit match in front of her face, even though she hadn't a cigarette in her mouth. She stared into the flame, lost in thought. When she noticed me watching, she shook the match out, and tossed the blackened, smoking stick away, seemingly embarrassed to be caught.

"The doctor says you're not well enough," she said. "He won't sign a note authorizing your return to the job site."

Dad didn't care.

"Doctors don't know anything. The longer you're sick the more money they make."

Dad didn't need permission from the doctor to find employment. Any work crew would be happy to take him on and pay him under the table. Before we were done eating, Dad made a single phone call and got himself hired.

Dad pulled Mom's Stokes Seeds overalls right off her body, tossing the rags out the backdoor for some wandering hobo to find.

"Don't even waste time calling to let them know you're quitting," Dad said. Mom's working days were over. Bringing home the bacon was back under his domain.

A pickup truck chugged outside, the back full of men sitting on toolboxes and coils of wire. Dad pranced across the walkway while his coworkers clapped and cheered. Not only were they excited to see him after a long absence, his example filled them with hope. Why, if they got injured, they too could recover and work again—just look at Jack!

I felt proud watching him go, all the while keeping the terrible secret behind Dad's miraculous recovery between me and the wall.

After work, Dad sank into a scalding bath. Rather than soothe his pained joints, the water tortured him and he moaned, unashamed of his agony.

"Have you got this foolishness out of your system now?"

Dad pulled the stopper out of the tub. The filthy water sucked down the drain louder than a rocket ship.

"This is stupid," Mom said.

"I've got things under control," he said before falling asleep in the tub. Instead of waking him, Mom worked the faucets, keeping the water warm, guiding his dreams through the night.

Dad wasn't licked, not by one day. I made sure of that. In the middle of the night, while Dad slept dreamless in the tub, I put my hand to the wall and stroked, asking the vibrations to keep Dad healthy again.

Each morning, Dad awoke whistling a jaunty tune, his pain gone, his bones strong, and his muscles thirsty to exert themselves. With so much pent-up energy, Dad chased me and my sisters through the yard to keep himself from exploding.

"Clearly, my muscles needed to be used to heal. All those months sitting around the house feeling sorry for myself only made things worse. What a dope I am."

He showed off, piling all of us on the couch and raising the end like baby Superman lifting that car. He demonstrated his agility by walking up the stairs on his hands.

We barely saw him. At the crack of dawn, Dad leapt into the back of someone's pickup. He liked hauling bricks and cutting wood, lifting his hard hat to passing women and feeling eighteen years old again. At the end of a hard day's work, he'd follow the crew to some bar and they'd drink until their watches wound down. Mom hadn't the energy to wait up for him. She went to bed early, complaining of headaches and dizziness. Most mornings, she still slept when the work truck pulled up to collect Dad. Even on two hours sleep, he danced out the door, happier than he'd been in months.

My hand ached from touching the vibrations in the wall each night. At school, I switched to writing with my left hand, because my right had developed an involuntary twitch. Some nights, I held my hand beneath the cold-water faucet to numb the discomfort before falling asleep.

Still, I believed this was a small price to pay for keeping Dad happy and healthy.

A new sound filled our bedroom. A wet gurgle fouled the darkness. Hearing it gave you the urge to clear your throat.

"Do you hear that?"

"Hear it?" My older sister threw her covers to the floor. "I can smell it."

Using the flashlight my older sister kept under the pillow for her magazines, we followed the ugly rattle to its source, rising from the depths of our other younger sister's throat.

"Hey, are you asleep? Are you snoring?"

Her lungs heaved like a clogged drain. My older sister tipped the flashlight into her mouth, trying to peek down her throat. Given the frantic sounds emanating from there, I wouldn't have been surprised to see a drowning mouse.

I wondered if we should do like mothers in the arctic, who sucked the snot from the noses of their congested children? My older sister shuddered at the suggestion. "You want to suck goo out of her mouth, be my guest." We let our other younger sister be. If things continued to worsen, Mom would have to use the vacuum cleaner to clear out her throat.

Notes from school followed my other younger sister home, tattling on her for nodding off in class. Rather than show concern for her health, the tone of the notes was judgemental. The underlying message: *Please punish your daughter or we'll be forced to.*

Her oral tic grew worse. Now she carried gravel in her mouth nonstop. At dinner, she chewed her food with rocks still in her mouth. She even sucked them while she slept. The gravel wore grooves into her gums, like how Harry Houdini dug a deposit in his own cheek allowing him to stash tiny instruments needed to pick locks for his great escapes. The gravel fit snugly into the hole in her gums, in no danger of tumbling down her throat and choking her while she slept, but the grooves caused a steady trickle of blood to drool down her throat. Gargling blood in her sleep put a strain on her breathing. All night long, her heart pumped faster, until sleep became exhausting. She woke feeling worn out, her chest aching.

Shamefully, the idea of touching the wall to give her a better night's sleep wasn't even considered. I worried about my sore hand. I would endure pain for Dad, but my other younger sister, I left her to heal on her own.

My older sister soon caught on. I'd been foolish to expect her not to notice the nightly purring.

"I thought about it too," she told me.

Yeah, I bet she did, but decided regrowing her hair was more important than helping Dad out of the beer-soaked prison of his living room chair.

"It's only a matter of time before Mom figures out what you're doing. Trust me. She is going to be pissed."

Downstairs, Dad finally poured himself through the front door, his hair red with brick dust, his clothes reeking of the bar. Mom waited up for him, fortified by a pot of coffee and two packs of smokes.

Dad carried her into the bedroom, and together they moaned with a rhythm both gentle and loving. As I stroked the wall to replenish Dad's energy, I could barely hear the purring over the sound of their lovemaking.

Barely an hour later, the work crew sat in our driveway, hungover, waving their tools in the air and calling for Dad. *Move it along! Quit holding up the show!* Mom escorted Dad to the front door to send him off with a kiss. She was dressed only in one of his long shirts, and the men in the truck leered at her. Once they drove away, Mom stomped upstairs to our room, throwing on the light and shaking the mattresses.

"You better tell me what nonsense you girls have been up to."

She spoke to all of us, but her eyes laser-focused on my older sister.

"Oh, sure. Blame me for everything."

"Rebecca, you cannot keep doing this. After Ricky—"

"Why do you automatically assume everything is my fault?"

Mom snapped her fingers at me. "Take your sisters downstairs and get them their breakfast. Rebecca and I need to talk. Again."

Feeling guilty, I told myself I'd fix my younger sisters the best breakfast they'd have all week. I'd heap tablespoons of sugar over their cereal, just the way an older sister should. "Don't tell Mom," I'd whisper as I sweetened them up.

I didn't make it further than the bedroom door. My older sister grew tired of keeping my secret. "I'm not the one you need to talk to, Mom. So I think I'll take the girls downstairs for their breakfast."

Mom sat on the edge of my bed, placing her chin in her hands, and looking helpless. She expected trouble from my older sister. Mom had grown expert at putting out fires started by her firstborn. Me being the one out of line gave her pause. She wasn't ready for me to turn disobedient yet.

I lifted the hem of my nightgown, and dabbed the corners of her eyes where tears began to form.

"I'm sorry, Mom."

"Your poor father."

The light fixture overhead began to rattle, shaken by the purring coming from the wall, which made a rare early morning appearance, almost like it was boasting.

Mom squeezed my hand and I realized she was more heartbroken than angry. Given the choice, I would rather she be angry. Being spanked with a dozen leather belts would be easier punishment than knowing I'd filled Mom with such terrible sorrow.

"Come with me, honey. We have to talk."

We sequestered ourselves in the bathroom. Mom turned on the faucets to muffle the sound of our conversation, though from whom I'm not sure.

"When you touch the wall, not only do you get what you want, but the wall gets something it wants as well."

Mom opened an envelope filled with newspaper clippings. One by one she handed them to me, giving me time to scan each headline before the next. The smell of newsprint reminded me of the funny hats Dad used to fold for us.

A boy fell into the Welland Canal and drowned. A bus

on its way to the Toronto Zoo crashed into a guard rail, the metal bar impaling two men through the shoulder. An old woman's fire-trap-of-a-house burned to the ground in Niagara-on-the-Lake...

Some of the clippings included black-and-white photographs. A tearful woman watching as her life disappeared into smoke, a tourist speared to his seat like a shish kabob, a smiling boy missing two front teeth, now under the water.

"These terrible things probably were going to happen no matter what. Just like the half dozen awful things I could have clipped out of the paper last year when you weren't touching the wall."

A seventy-year-old man trimming branches fell off a ladder and nearly cut his own head off when the running chainsaw landed on his neck. Only his spine and tendons held his head in place. The doctors called his survival a miracle, though they cast doubts on whether he would speak again.

"But we'll never know for sure, will we? Which of these do you think was caused by you touching the wall? Which one of these do you think is fair trade for your father to be able to joke it up at the job site all day and drink all night 'til his lips fall off?"

A baby in their car seat was placed too close to a stove burner while its mother collected laundry from the backyard clothesline and the heat caused the carrier to ignite. While the toddler burned to death, his younger brother tried desperately to save him, but being only four years old he wasn't tall enough to reach his sibling.

"What if it's all of them?" Mom asked.

Feeling sick, I put the clippings down. I wanted to twist the pages into a black-and-white coil and shove them down the drain. The horrors they reported ought to be carried away with the sewer water.

"If you promise me you'll never touch the wall again, we can pretend it was none of them."

I nodded, eager to leave the bathroom and this awful conversation behind forever.

"What about Dad?"

Mom folded all the newspaper clippings together. She struck a match, and soon the newsprint made a bouquet of burning flowers.

"He'll go back to how he was before. After being so strong these last few days, he'll be devastated."

Water flowed from the tap but Mom didn't douse the fire. She stared into the flaming newsprint, allowing it to burn down to her fingers. I don't know if she was hypnotized, but the look in her eyes belonged to something far away. A dream or a hope. I saw the skin around her nails begin to blacken and I grabbed her hand and forced it under the water.

Mom sat down on the rim of the tub, tucking her burnt hand under her armpit. I opened the medicine cabinet to get the greasy tube of ointment.

"I don't know why, but when I see fire, I become... distracted."

I put a cigarette into her mouth. She closed her eyes while I lit it for her.

"You feel any better?"

She struggled to inhale.

"Don't even think about me. Your father is the one who is going to suffer."

Without me touching the wall, Dad's over-exerted body collapsed. His work crew hauled him home lying flat in the back of the pickup as though he were a pallet of cement bags. It took three men to carry him inside. They hoisted him over their heads, doing their best to keep his back and legs straight. Any stumble or bump on their part caused Dad to suffer an enormous belt of pain. His profane cries drew a few neighbours to their window in time to see Dad being carried into his house feet first.

Mom pushed everything off the kitchen table so Dad could be laid on a steady and flat surface. She gave nothing to the work crew, no beers, not even a thank you. They expressed their condolences and showed themselves out of the house.

My sisters and I ran to Dad and did a quick accounting of his limbs and digits. The job site is a dangerous place, with tools and bricks being tossed from worker to worker. Anyone not paying attention could get a face full of blunt iron. Safety commercials on TV showed horrifying accidents—workers stepping on nails or being buried alive by an avalanche of dirt. Dad promised those things could never happen to him, but his first accident already proved him to be fallible.

My older sister unlaced his knotted, tar-splattered work boots. Underneath, his toes poked through observation hatches in his socks.

I nuzzled my head into his chest, relieved to feel the beating of his heart.

With all four daughters holding onto him, he looked like a medieval painting I'd once seen of a knight lying on a church altar, dressed all in armour but for his gloves and boots, which had been pulled off to reveal the pink, vulnerable flesh beneath the iron. The painter spent a lot of detail illustrating the sunlight cascading onto the knight. There were four women in the painting. Fair maidens wearing conical hats dangling lacy trim removed the knight's armour to dress his wounds. The knight's face convulsed in agony. According to my older sister, the maidens were not attending to the knight but torturing him. She might have been right; her interpretation explained the maiden's clawed, bird-like hands.

I waited for Mom to kiss Dad on the forehead, like the prince did to Sleeping Beauty in the glass coffin surrounded by her forest pals. It would be a sweet moment. Once her lips touched his, all of us would be connected. Some sad families must go their whole life without being physically connected. Should lightening strike one of us, we would all go together.

But Mom did not kiss Dad. She kept her distance, looking down at Dad as though he were a tough chore.

Dad scowled back.

"You bitch."

My stomach lurched. Something fragile and irreplaceable had been dropped. Dad never spoke to Mom like that. He might yell at those bums on TV football or tell a cop issuing a speeding ticket to stick his ass down a toilet, but he never spoke foul to a woman. Not even one on TV. And certainly not in front of his daughters.

"You dirty bitch."

Mom took his abuse in stride. She pulled the tablecloth up to his chin, tucking him in nicely before turning to us and saying, "Your father needs some time to cool off."

By evening, Dad had left the table for his accustomed place in front of the TV, feet up, beer on his knee. Mom retrieved his crutches from where he had dumped them at the side of the house with the trash cans. He ignored our attempts to talk. He'd only say, "You're blocking the picture." He wasn't watching anything good, some black-and-white show from a hundred years ago that wasn't even funny, but each time the TV laughed Dad threw back his head and brayed like he had heard the most hilarious thing in the world.

Annoyed, I went into the bathroom and opened the window, which I discovered long ago messed with the TV reception.

"Janet!" I heard him call down below. "I need tin foil for the rabbit ears!"

A kitchen drawer slid open and a sheet of tin foil crinkled. Dad's way of asking Mom to be friends again.

Later that night, the moaning in Mom and Dad's bed started up, but this time, their coupling had changed. Their bedroom sounds were mechanical, forceful, and unrelenting. Dad grunted like he was enduring. Mom groaned like she was being punished. The sound drove my head under the pillow, and through the darkness, I felt my older sister's judgement.

"Listen to what you've done. This is all your fault."

Dad left his crutches downstairs, not wanting the squeak of their rubber stumps to give away his approach. He used his elbows to drag himself up the stairs. Our bedroom door creaked open and Dad crawled across the floor the way they taught us in school to do during a fire when the air was heavy with smoke.

I pulled the sheets over my face in a pathetic attempt to hide. I thought Dad must be furious. He resented my restoring his strength, reminding him of the glory of work, only to cruelly take it away. If he grabbed my hand and pressed it into the wall until my knuckles broke, I wouldn't utter a word of complaint. In fact, I'd only be surprised he waited this long to do so.

But I'd misjudged him. Dad hadn't come to make me break my promise to Mom. He crawled along the floor, over our dirty clothes. He stopped at each of my sister's beds, kissing their dangling hands. When he got to my bed, he grabbed hold of the mattress and hauled himself up, like a drowning sailor clinging to the side of a life raft too full to save him. He could only dangle off the side, half in the water until the sharks found his legs and pulled him under.

The bedroom shadows distorted Dad's face. He looked as though he wore a rubbery Halloween mask, one with dropping cheeks, crooked teeth, and black gaping holes where the eyes belonged. I wanted to tell him to take that ugly thing off, to stop trying to frighten us, but I knew from the rank sweat dribbling down his cheeks that he wore no mask. The distorted face hovering over my bed was made of Dad's true flesh.

"When two men are carrying a heavy pallet up several flights of stairs, a third man makes the job more strenuous and difficult. Two men can heft and manoeuvre easier than three. The best way for the third man to help is let go so the other two can finish the job faster and easier."

I wondered if that was true. Maybe the two men were a couple of show-offs, too proud to accept the help of the third man to get the job done.

Dad tapped a finger to the side of his head. "The sockets are loose. I gotta get them tightened up."

Down below, a car pulled up front. I recognized the motor running as belonging to Roman, the same chainsaw rumble that used to drop Dad off early Sunday morning in time for church.

Dad kissed my forehead. Sweat dripped from his brow into my eyes, blinding me. His oily sweat burned like chili powder.

"Once I'm out of the way, you girls will have more manoeuvrability. Don't worry, when I come back, you won't have to lift a thing. I'll carry this whole goddam household by myself. You'll see."

Still blind, I listened to Dad's jeans *zig-zag* as he slithered across the floor like a snake, winding himself down the stairs and out the front door where Roman stood, cigarette pasted to his lips, holding the car door open for Dad to crawl inside.

I spat on my hands and rubbed my eyes. Finally, my vision broke through the oily layer, but I was too late. The car door slammed and the tires squealed down the street, speeding away to wherever Dad hoped to get his sockets tightened.

"You're a liar."

My older sister wasn't angry. She'd barely paid any mind to my ludicrous report of Dad leaving in the night. She dressed and selected today's makeup from her little stash under the bed.

"What, you're so special he'd take time to say goodbye to you but ignore everyone else? What a narcissist."

Even my younger sisters looked skeptical, but the sight of the empty recliner in the living room soon garnered their concern.

"You were dreaming," my older sister said. "Dad'll probably be back before the end of the day."

I envied my sisters their hope, but I knew last night had been no dream. Before Dad left, I pressed two fingers beneath his chin, feeling his pulse beating erratic but very real, the way pulses never beat for people in dreams.

NINE

A letter from Auntie Linda always made Mom smile. Whenever one of those familiar blue envelopes landed in the mailbox, my sisters and I obeyed all our mother's demands. Dishes were scrubbed, leftovers made their way to the backyard, the lint trap got cleaned, and empty milk bags replaced. Mom strutted about the house while we toiled, teasing us by flapping the sealed envelope against her breast. We'd do anything to hear one of Auntie Linda's letters.

Auntie Linda always started off with a funny story. She lived without electricity, a lifestyle that lent itself to a never-ending barrage of new adventures. Auntie Linda had lots of boyfriends, numbers my older sister fantasized about. The boys lined up, competing to court her. Mom found her sister's polyamorous relationships unsuitable for her daughters' ears, so she composited all of Auntie Linda's men into a single character dubbed the New Bob, which led to the occasionally confusing sentence such as: *After lunch at the tree stump with the New Bob, we lingered too long lying low in the moss, hiding from the New Bob, who sounded angry, probably because we had borrowed Duke's blanket from the dog house to use as our tablecloth.*

Auntie Linda kept herself busy. One of the New Bobs was a veterinarian, who flew to isolated communities to neuter wild dogs. Auntie Linda assisted by sterilizing the equipment and making friends with the locals, some of whom were displeased with outsiders interfering with their animals. Auntie Linda knew how to make friends with everybody. The locals lent her snowshoes and took her for hikes. One time, in the middle of the lake, an enormous brown bear climbed onto the bow of her boat. Auntie Linda tried paddling to shore, thinking the bear would make a fine stew and a warm blanket, but every time she put her paddle in the water, the bear growled. Outweighed by over 300 pounds, Auntie Linda knew when she was beat, and allowed the current to carry her and the bear across the lake. The bear dunked its snout into the water, gobbling three large trout, bones and all, never offering so much as a whiff to his travelling companion. Auntie Linda didn't need to rely on the bear's fishing skills for survival. Trailing her fingers in the water, she collected enough minnows for a fresh fish lunch of her own. When the boat finally butted against shore, the bear dashed into the thick woods, grunting and snorting, letting his friends know he had returned. As Auntie Linda drifted away, an army of hairy eyes and black claws filled the tree line. She arrived back at the community just as the float plane loaded up. The New Bob told her she was lucky to make it, a few more minutes and she'd be a guest until the next month's plane brought the dentist. Auntie Linda explained how she'd been hijacked, and the locals all laughed, saying that was Bruin. Too lazy to swim across the lake on his own, Bruin often used boats to drift wherever he wanted. He growled something fearsome but no one thought Bruin would ever attack. The bear understood that the moment he spilled blood it would be his last ride. The locals would take to the lake with a lap full of buckshot and Bruin's hide would be stretched out tanning by the following afternoon.

Auntie Linda also met a writer, a young man who travelled all the way from Niagara to ask her questions about Uncle Todd. Auntie Linda admired the writer's scarf and the dimples on his young cheeks. She considered taking him on as a New Bob and suggested they go into town for lunch at the diner. If his newspaper could afford to send him up north, they must have given him pin money for expenses. She soured on him during their meal. He wouldn't put down the microphone attached to his tape recorder, eating with one hand, needing to capture every word out of her mouth. He even interrupted her, demanding she stop talking while he flipped the tape over. She didn't like his questions, which were nosy and implied she received money from Uncle Todd—as if there was something wrong with that! Each time the waitress passed their table, Auntie Linda flagged her down to add yet another addition to her order. *Bring an extra milkshake, honey. Oh sweetheart, I'll think I'll get a cheeseburger, with bacon and onions. Miss, sorry to trouble you, darling, but is the breakfast menu still offered? 'Cause I'd love a mushroom omelette to go with my pork chops.* She pushed the writer, seeing how much of a bill he'd allow her to run up. He didn't bat an eye, continuing to hold his microphone and ask his insulting questions while half the damn menu arrived at their table. The leftovers filled a dozen doggie bags which Auntie Linda brought home for the pigs and the New Bobs.

Mom folded the pages and tucked them into her shirt.

"Is that it?" I saw Auntie Linda wrote a lot more than that.

"Not everything is intended for children."

My older sister claimed she got a peek at the unabridged letter.

"Auntie Linda said she brought the writer home. She lit a hundred candles and they enjoyed a private romance."

That sounded gross to me, made worse by the way my older sister waggled her eyebrows.

"Auntie Linda said by the time she finished with him, her lip prints were seared into his neck. Permanently."

I took my older sister at her word. Mom read the rest of the letter in private, before tossing the pages into the washing machine where they dissolved and were sucked down the drain with the rest of the soapy water. Auntie Linda insisted Mom destroy her letters. She didn't want some jackal collecting them and publishing a book. Read back-to-back, the letters would have revealed too much about her.

"Auntie Linda told Mom we can identify troublemakers by lip prints on their neck," my older sister reported. "So distrust men wearing scarves."

The morning trek to school turned stressful. Already on guard against Uncle Todd popping out of nowhere to trick us into climbing into his truck, my younger sisters and I now had to worry about the appearance of men wearing scarves. All of them untrustworthy. Every last one suspect. The air turned chilled and our breath became visible, and men with scarves were everywhere.

I considered carrying a knife in my sleeve, one of the long sharp ones Dad and Roman threw at the dartboard they'd drawn on the garage wall, but I worried my younger sisters might cut themselves when reaching for my hand at the crosswalk.

My older sister continued to monopolize our bedroom. When the mood struck, she locked us out and turned the record player up until the music could be heard from outside the house. I pounded on the door but she never answered. She couldn't hear anything once she fortressed herself inside, or at least she pretended not to. Murder might happen in the front hall and she wouldn't so much as peek through the keyhole to see what was going on.

"Yes! Free Parking!"

My younger sisters and I set up the Monopoly board in the living room. Ordinarily, I refused to play with them. My younger sisters denied it but they played as a secret team, refusing to collect rent from one another and "gifting" properties to allow immediate house building. I'd never once beaten them. This time I joined the game, feeling bad for my other younger sister who was just getting over that awful phlegm infection that kept her from getting proper sleep. The black pouches under her eyes had receded and she wasn't spitting gunk up anymore.

Less than an hour into the game, my younger sisters' stronghold on the Utilities and the Railroads had me down to my last hundred dollars when footsteps sounded on the porch, followed by the confident knock of a man who expected to be greeted warmly.

He was handsome. Tall with blonde hair and a good, strong jaw. I imagined him riding a surfboard or driving with the top down. His good looks would have beguiled my older sister, and she would have ushered him into the hall immediately but my attuned nose detected a dangerous scent. Beneath our mystery caller's cologne and cigarettes was the smell of newsprint. I knew not to talk to him, even before I noticed the scarf Auntie Linda warned us about wrapped around his neck.

"Hello there, young lady."

A tape recorder hung from a strap over his shoulder. His fingers hit two buttons, setting the gears whirling, grinding like a misaligned bicycle tire.

"Do you like church? I bet you go to church, don't you?"

I considered yanking the scarf off his neck to reveal the markings Auntie Linda had left behind and let Lover Boy know I was onto his game.

He reached into his pocket and pulled out a picture of Uncle Todd. The photo looked blurry and Uncle Todd shimmered. It took me a moment to realize the picture had been snapped off a TV screen. The white halo above Uncle Todd's head was a reflection of the flash.

"Do you know who this is?"

Dad was the master at dealing with front-door pests. Whenever a door-to-door salesman or stranger passing out little booklets claiming the world was about to end in a holy nuclear war disturbed his nap, Dad put two fingers to his mouth and whistled loudly. "Bowser!" he'd call. "Here boy! Attack! Attack, boy!" Our imaginary guard dog always sent the bums running.

I bent down and patted my knees. Lover Boy extended his arm with the microphone, making sure he got all this good sound. The needle on his recorder spiked when I yelled, "Sic 'em!" down the empty hallway for our ferocious animal. I threw myself up against the wall as though I were making way for a dog the size of a bull who ate four cats a day and wore a spiked collar.

"Sic balls!" I shouted.

Lover Boy scrambled off the porch, jerking his limbs comically like in a Three Stooges movie when the film sped up. Not so macho now. I don't blame him for being afraid. Cracks and thumps emanated from the floorboards, sounding exactly like a large dog galloping to attack. You could even hear drool dripping off jagged fangs. Truth be told, the sounds frightened me for a moment. The growling sounded so convincing, I momentarily forgot we owned no dog. I'd known the walls could purr but this was the first time I'd heard them snarl.

The Monopoly board I returned to looked different from the one I left. New hotels sprouted along my properties and my meagre slush fund had quadrupled into a mess of orange bills.

I played on, accepting my younger sisters' pity. It mattered not. They trounced me in the end anyway.

"Who was at the door?"

Mom sat in the kitchen. One of Dad's beers was open on the counter. She wasn't drinking it but the faint sound of its bubbles fizzing to the surface reminded her of his company. There were flat beers opened all over the house. Several sat along the rim of the bathtub like candles.

"A man with a tape recorder. He had a picture of Uncle Todd."

One of the stove burners blazed bright red, heating the kitchen. Mom got up from the table and touched a cigarette to the stove to light it. She'd got rid of all her lighters and matches, no longer trusting herself around flames.

"He wants to write an article about your uncle. Something to make him look bad, I'm sure. Embarrass the people who give him money. Good thing I didn't answer the door. I'm feeling foul so I might have talked, told him all kinds of stories that'd make Todd look like the bum of the world."

Her cigarette caught. The stove burner was covered in black marks from the lighting of multiple smokes.

"I shouldn't say that. It doesn't matter how much I loathe that ridiculous show Todd puts on for suckers. You never, I mean *ever*, intentionally harm family. Remember that, Emery."

Above our heads, the music went quiet as my older sister switched one record out for another. In the brief silence, we heard the purring of the vibrating wall. Then the music resumed. My older sister was trying to cover up the noise the same way Dad lit matches to cover up the smell of the bathroom; unsuccessfully.

Mom lost her balance. I grabbed hold of her waist and jerked her away from the stove before she fell face-first on the red burner.

"I don't think I can get much worse," Mom said. She smiled and poked me in the belly. "Which means I can only start getting better. It's a law of nature."

I took the cigarette out of her mouth to tap the ash. I appreciate her trying to protect me, but I was too old to believe her lie. No one is entitled to good health and Mom had no idea just how much worse she could feel.

TEN

Mom reached her breaking point at the most inconvenient location—in the middle of the preserves aisle at Miracle Mart.

"I don't feel good."

The jar of pickles slipped from her convulsing fingers, hitting the marble-patterned linoleum so hard the freshness seal audibly popped. Mom's jaw quivered and from deep in her throat came a series of jibbers and squeaks. People looked at us.

I tried to save her from collapsing but she flattened me, sending us both crashing into the shelves of canned fruit. Mom sank to the floor, the hem of her skirt ripping as her legs spread too far apart.

Her brain scramble took only a moment to do its dirty work. Mom shook her head, collected her scattered wits, and struggled to get to her feet, looking angry and embarrassed. Two Miracle Mart employees in white butcher smocks came running. One took Mom's arm to keep her steady while the other picked up the fallen pickle jar and examined it for cracks before gently placing it in our shopping cart.

With slurred words, Mom ordered me to round up my younger sisters from the cereal aisle.

"We have to go. Now."

The Miracle Mart manager took Mom by the arm, trying to drag her to his office to make her sit down for a few minutes.

Mom knew he was stalling for time while someone called an ambulance. The only thing stores hated more than shoplifters were people injuring themselves. Both represented loss of profits. Mom abandoned our cart and, over the objections of the manager, scuttled through the automatic doors to the parking lot.

Once outside, away from the prying eyes of Miracle Mart customers and employees, Mom fell apart, letting the full extent of her ailment hang out, like a man who'd been sucking in his gut at the swimming pool. Before my eyes, her back hunched, her hands withered into claws, and the skin under her eyes drooped. She pushed her purse into my hands.

"Get my keys out. You're going to have to drive."

My younger sisters buckled themselves in. The keys fumbled out of my hand as I tried sticking them in the ignition. The pressure of sitting in the driver's seat overwhelmed me. Mom adjusted the rearview mirror, which was a joke as I barely sat tall enough to see over the steering wheel.

"This is as good a time as any to pick up some driving basics," Mom said, slumping into the dashboard. "You never know when there's going to be an emergency and you'll have to drive for real."

Alternating between stomping the gas and brake pedals, I jerked through the parking lot, moving in fits and starts. One of the Miracle Mart employees saw me driving the car and chased after us, waving his hands and hollering to stop, but I made it onto the main road before he caught up with us.

Mom focused on the positives.

"You're doing good, honey. Keep those hands at ten and two."

Back home, we called for our older sister to help us get Mom out of the car. The four of us struggled to carry Mom across the lawn. We lifted her arms and legs but her butt dragged along the ground, getting grass stains and hitting each step of the porch with a THUMP THUMP THUMP.

Even with sleep and orange-flavoured aspirins, Mom's health did not return. She stopped sleeping in her bedroom, unable to muster the strength to get off the couch.

"The worst part is the boredom."

Mom had never been confined to a single room like a prisoner. She tried composing a new letter to Auntie Linda, but barely scrawled more than a few words before exhaustion overtook her and she needed another nap.

"You can dictate to one of us," we offered.

"It's bad enough you listen in on my phone calls. I don't need you prying into my private correspondences too."

Mom sent us to the store to buy diapers. Grown-up diapers, intended for old people who had outlived the warranty on their plumbing. Mom's pain was so bad she'd rather pee into a diaper than get up and struggle to the bathroom.

"What are you crying about?" my older sister asked me in bed.

"Mom's sick."

"We know."

"Really sick."

I understood Mom could die. The graveyard is full of dead moms, and dead dads, dead brothers, dead sisters... Our family had yet to plant a member in Victoria Lawn but such a blessing seemed unlikely to last forever. Death must be due to swoop in and take one of us. Selfishly, I hoped it wouldn't be me. Given the choice between dying and grieving, I'd choose grief. Nothing unusual about that. Choosing grief is the key to mankind's survival.

My older sister told me I was wrong—death had not passed our family over.

"Grandpa's dead. And as far as we know, Dad's mom and dad are dead too."

"I don't think they count. They were all gone long before we got here."

The coughing and retching coming from Mom's sickbed comforted me. So long as she groaned and hacked, I knew she was still alive. I dreaded the coming silence, which would signify Death had finally taken Mom by the hand and dragged her into the blackness.

The laundry became increasingly bloody. Mom's pillowcases were covered in brown stains. I don't know if the blood leaked from her gums or if she coughed it up in the night, but the blotches got bigger and darker. Soon, the stains would be as thick as scabs.

I showed the worrisome sheets to my older sister.

"Ew. When you do laundry, you put the wash on and keep your mouth shut. Respect people's privacy. You'll want the same when you start staining your sheets."

I did as she said. Each day, the soiled sheets went into the washer. I looked away as I loaded the machine. My hand brushed over the hard, crusted stains, but I didn't know if they were vomit or blood. I respected Mom's privacy.

Dad needed to be here. He'd make damn sure Mom got well, even if it meant breaking down the doctor's doors and busting some noses. Where could he be?

Mom feigned optimism but none of us believed her story about Dad's disappearance, that he and Roman were off on one of their fishing trips. According to her, the boys were having a great time, caught up in the excitement, enjoying good food and good drink and the company of beautiful women (whom Dad only looked at, never touched unless they were dancing). Like all fishing trips, he'd return with a pocketful of money and an armload of gifts.

"Don't be so dramatic, you gloomy faces. Your father deserves a break. He'll be back before you know it."

"What if he's dead?" I pictured him lying in a ditch. Somewhere dark and barren.

Mom laughed. "I haven't given him permission for something like that."

According to her, the squeak of Dad's crutches would come thumping through the front door any day, carrying a million stories of his adventures.

None of us were fooled. Least of all Mom. We heard her crying whenever she thought we weren't around.

I'd given the matter serious thought.

"I'm going to quit school to stay home and look after

you." I felt old enough. Fifty years ago, by this age I would have been pulled out of school to help on the farm and raise the babies.

In my mind, my altruistic declaration made Mom burst into tears of appreciation. Instead, my older sister giggled and Mom groaned.

"If I can't survive the few hours you guys are at school, then there isn't much hope in me ever getting better." Mom planned to spend her days sleeping, and she enjoyed the quiet. If I wanted to be Florence Nightingale so damn badly, I could fluff her pillow and empty the coffee cup she'd been using as an ashtray.

Cracks appeared in Mom's tough facade. At first, she'd fooled us, and maybe even fooled herself that her illness had abated and she was on the road to recovery, but as her health became dire she finally dropped the act and asked for assistance. She didn't want to, but her frail body and pained joints left her no choice.

"Emery, I need you to take me to the bathroom."

"Sure thing."

Mom wrapped her arms over my shoulders, almost like a piggyback ride, only Mom's feet dragged across the floor as I hauled her into the bathroom. The ease with which I carried Mom was alarming. Her body had grown so frail I wore her on my back like a silk gown. Right before our eyes, Mom was vanishing on us.

I expected to drop Mom off at the bathroom door and return five or so minutes later after she'd done her business but Mom still required assistance. After holding her bowels for so long, she could no longer hold on to her pride.

"Pull up my nightie and remove the diaper. I can't bend to reach."

This was more than I'd signed up for. Holding my eyes shut and turning my head away, I tugged off Mom's wet diaper, ripping the fastening tape slowly, like opening an unwanted Christmas gift.

Mom plopped onto the toilet. I tried to rush out but she wouldn't let me go. Mom needed me to massage her stomach to break up the impacted material. I knelt beside the toilet, putting both hands on Mom's swollen belly and rubbing the skin vigorously.

Mom suffered the humiliation. She'd tried her best to hide her bodily functions, wanting to spare her children, but how long could that go on for? The best years of her life were spent diapering and washing up after us, yet when her time of need came, we responded with disgust and revulsion. I should have done more to put her at ease.

I helped Mom off the toilet and leaned her over the sink to wipe her ass. After carrying her back to the couch, outfitted in a fresh diaper, I went upstairs and collapsed on my bed, shell-shocked.

"Next time is your guys' turn. I can't do that again."

My younger sisters shrugged their shoulders. "How are we supposed to carry Mom anywhere?"

"Figure it out."

"I'm going to try taking a bath."

We drew water and added bubbles, hoping to make Mom's soak luxurious, but her skin was too sensitive. The washcloth scratched like sandpaper and the fluoride in the water broke her skin out in rashes. Steam wafted from the tub, turning the bathroom white and misty as a sauna, yet Mom's teeth chattered. Hours after her bath she still shivered. My younger sisters rubbed her all over, trying to restore warmth. After massaging Mom their hands felt numb, like they had been packing snowballs.

Mom spat up so much phlegm I worried she'd choke in her sleep. She filled tissues with thick, runny gunk. Her snot smelled terrible, like rotting meat. Mom never got used to the taste of the river of slime bubbling up through her mouth. She gagged and retched. Sometimes the strands were too long for her to spit up and she stuck a fork down her throat to dredge up the blockage. It looked like green egg yolk. My older sister hated when Mom did that, saying the fork tines might scratch her throat and give her an infection. These ropes of phlegm stretched all the way down her into her lungs. Sometimes, halfway through extraction, the strands broke and slurped down her throat like she was sucking up spaghetti.

A postcard from Auntie Linda arrived. She'd got wind of Mom's ailments and suggested a couple home remedies of hot soup and relaxing mud treatments. According to Auntie Linda, a woman's feet were the hub of all good energy flowing through her body, so she recommended Mom mix dirt with hot water and use her toes to claw through the mud.

Practice this regiment twice daily using the dirt in your basement, which is sure to be full of good nutrients.

I read the postcard to Mom, who told me to throw it away.

"Your Aunt's head is full of good nutrients."

Grandma visited often, always reeking of perfume. She doused herself to mask Mom's foul smell, which my sisters and I learned to tolerate, but it clung to our clothes and made us even bigger pariahs at school.

Grandma brought soup but Mom refused to eat.

"Come on, dear. You need your nourishment."

"If I want soup, I'll get the girls to dig some up."

"You're being ridiculous."

"I'm not eating anything unless I know exactly where it came from."

Grandma snuggled me on her lap. She always brought donuts or fried chicken. Our house had become gloomy in the shadow of Mom's illness, but Grandma filled our living room with light and positive energy. She joked with us, laughing so much I believed Mom would soon be well again. Grandma's levity assured us we needn't be concerned. What kind of monster laughed at her daughter's deathbed?

Not everyone enjoyed Grandma's company. My older sister fled to the bedroom, locking the door and playing records. Loud. Grandma wasn't hurt by the rejection. She only sighed and remarked wistfully on how quickly time passed.

"The little ones grow into surly teenagers, wanting nothing to do with the old folk. Don't worry. One day, all children recognize the wisdom of their elders. They return."

Mom unclogged her throat and struggled to sit up. "To this day, I still wouldn't rely on your wisdom for so much as how to change a fuse."

Grandma nodded, continuing to smile, running a hand through the bristles on top of my head. "Oh, this is coming in fine. Soon you'll be beautiful and long-haired again."

A familiar rumble started up in the basement. Dad's table saw let out a high-pitched squeal as it tore into a plank of wood. Dad was back! Hiding out in the basement until Grandma left, no doubt dreading her lecture on leaving his family out to dry without so much as a note or a phone call.

I jumped from Grandma's lap and raced to the basement. Skipping half the stairs, I ran barefoot across the dirt floor, holding my arms spread wide in anticipation of Dad's enormous bear hug, only to meet disappointment. Operating the table saw was not Dad, but my older sister.

"What do you think you're doing?"

The table saw had the power to take our fingers off. Dad didn't like us fooling around with his dangerous tools. He'd be furious once he found out. My older sister looked oblivious to the depth of her trespass. Wearing a pair of Dad's old glasses for protection against splinters, she dropped another plank onto the machine and pushed the wood through the spinning blade.

I stomped back to the living room and informed everyone we were wasting our smiles. It was only my older sister fooling around with the table saw. We'd got our hopes up for nothing.

Grandma stood up. "Jack is letting Rebecca cut wood?" Alarmed her granddaughter was using dangerous machinery, she rolled up her sleeve, ready to charge down into the basement and give Dad a little lecture on safety.

"Oh Mum, she's old enough. Jack is supervising her. It's fine. The girls take woodworking class at school these days."

I bunched up my fists and shouted, "Dad is not supervising her! He still isn't back!" I broke into tears.

Grandma patted my back. "What's the matter? Where is your father?"

"I don't know." Dad had been missing for weeks. Maybe a month.

"Janet, is Jack gone? Where is he?"

Mom shook her head and tried to force a laugh. "Oh Mum, she's making up stories. Emery, don't tease your old grandmother like that; it isn't nice."

After Grandma left, my older sister waited for me in the hall, furious that I'd exposed her ruse. She grabbed my arms and slammed me into the wall. Her angry dragon breath scorched my neck.

"You and your stupid, big mouth. I ought to drag you down there and run your empty head through that saw."

"Rebecca, stop it! She didn't know, honey."

Mom and my older sister had been in conspiracy together, creating the illusion Dad still lived in our house. Each time Grandma visited, my older sister scattered empty beer cans on the coffee table and the arm of Dad's chair. Grandma always collected the empties and threw them in the kitchen garbage, muttering, "If that man is going to make a mess while you're sick, the least his majesty can do is pick up after himself."

"We'll lock the door," my older sister said. "The next time the old woman comes, we'll lock the door and tell her she has to leave."

Mom shook her head. "Oh Rebecca, no matter what happens, you have to remember she is still your grandmother."

Grandma returned before the end of the day. She slipped through the front door as Mom slept, her clogged throat still rattling and wheezing.

"Girls! Come here," Grandma called.

My younger sisters and I attended to her arrival. My older sister stayed upstairs in the bedroom, hiding.

"Would you two be good girls and bring in Grandma's belongings from the car?" My younger sisters returned with two suitcases, each big enough for them to lie inside and be zippered shut.

"Guess what? Grandma is going to be staying for the next little while. You'll get to see me every day. I'll fix you breakfast in the morning and tuck you into bed each night. Isn't this going to be a good time?"

She wheeled her suitcases into Mom and Dad's bedroom to unpack, filling the closet from end to end with blouses and dresses, packed as tightly as spines on a bookshelf. How long was she planning to stay?

Mom awoke to the sight of her mother in an apron, dusting the windowsills, pulling up clumps of spiderwebs full of dead bugs and cigarette ash, her hips bouncing back and forth to the old timey songs she hummed. Mom looked unhappy but she bit her lip and said nothing more than:

"Well, if this is how it's to be."

Having taken command of the household, Grandma implemented a few changes.

"It's silly for growing girls to be crammed into one stuffy bedroom like fruit pickers in a bunkhouse."

With a hammer, she busted the locks off our bedroom doors. Dad would be furious when he saw the damage done. Grandma expected us to be jubilant at the return of our bedrooms, which she unsealed like the exquisite burial chambers of the pharaohs. Our toys and clothing and privacy returned to us.

"Well, what are you guys waiting for? Go on in. Don't tell me you've outgrown everything in there."

I expected my older sister to be ecstatic with the return of her vanity mirror. She wouldn't have to lock herself in the bathroom anymore. She wouldn't have to lock us out of our room anymore. I was flabbergasted when she turned her nose up at her old room. She preferred her current sleeping arrangements.

"Let Emery move in there. I'm staying here."

Happy to have everything settled, Grandma patted her knees. "Who wants to help cook dinner?"

The sight of our barren fridge made Grandma shake her head.

"It looks like a robbed grave in there."

She dropped the box of baking soda into the trash, where it belched a cloud of powdery blue mould. A case of Dad's favourite brew chilled inside the fridge. We formed a fire line and Grandma passed the bottles one by one to my younger sisters who passed them to me to be popped open and handed to my older sister to pour down the sink. Each time Grandma had her back turned, my older sister guzzled from the bottle. She tried to drink more than she poured, puffing her cheeks and coming close to shooting foam out her nose.

With the fridge empty and scrubbed out, Grandma said, "Looks like we need to go shopping. What shall we have for dinner? Roast beef? Lamb? Please don't say boring old boiled hot dogs. I want to fix us something special."

"We have lots of food."

Grandma opened the empty freezer and peeked inside our crumb covered pantry. "I don't see anything to eat. Where are you keeping it all hidden?"

We led Grandma to the backyard. Before her illness, Mom took care of burying the groceries and marking the plots carefully. She had a good system. She staked the ground with a stick and a bit of cloth, labelled M for Meat and V for Vegetables. She also wrote a date, so she knew to dig up 9/12 before 9/17.

We grabbed shovels and turned over the yard. My younger sisters struck pay dirt first, finding a section of pork shoulder. Grandma was disgusted, barely willing to touch the meat, as if my younger sisters had hauled up the severed head of a pirate. The pork looked fine to me. Sometime the meat you dug up was riddled with little white worms, but this had been well protected in tin foil.

"Ugh, throw that nasty thing away."

Grandma ordered the rest of us to keep digging. She wanted to see everything we kept down there in the cool earth.

We piled our bounty high. Ground beef and bananas, zucchini and head cheese, lettuce and tubes of liverwurst and bags of walnuts. Every so often, my older sister found a thick juicy worm and laid it on my shoulder and laughed. Drunk on Dad's beer, she leaned on her shovel to keep from falling over. In addition to perishables, I also found a stock of cans. We dug up enough tomato soup to fill the bathtub and drown a horse.

We carried the excavated groceries inside and laid them on the dining room table for Grandma to sift through like Halloween candy. The vegetables were squeezed and sniffed to determine their freshness.

"The plastic bags probably kept them clean from the dirt," Grandma said.

"What's the matter?" I asked. "Don't vegetables grow in the dirt to begin with?"

The meat was given no chance to plead a case. It all went directly into the trash. Seeing our garbage can burping over with good food pained me. I thought of the starving babies with their pregnant stomachs who would weep and curse us for such waste. The vegetables were handed to us one at a time to be placed in the fridge, Grandma telling us over and over, "Food is kept in the refrigerator. That's what it's for. The fridge keeps the food fresh until you are ready to eat it." At first, I didn't think there would be room enough for all our carrots and celery and peppers, but the fridge had a drawer at the bottom, just like a desk, and everything fit neatly inside.

"From now on, we're going to keep our food in the fridge, not the backyard."

I giggled, imagining Dad coming home and opening the refrigerator for a beer only to find it stuffed full of carrots and lettuce. Boy, would he laugh. He'd shake his head and say to Mom, "Do you know what your mother did?"

Grandma found the scissors, which had been tucked beneath the couch cushions Mom slept on, like a hidden weapon for stabbing late-night intruders. What Grandma was doing snooping under Mom's sleeping body I have no idea.

"Let's do something about that hair," Grandma said to my other younger sister, taking hold of her hand and leading her to the bathroom, where in record time she emerged with hair as short and scraggly as her older-by-five-minutes sister.

At the sight of her youngest daughter's new haircut, Mom lit a cigarette, took a single drag, then mashed the burning end into the wall, where it joined a pattern of other black ash marks.

"They look so much better matched, don't you think?" Grandma said, pushing my younger sisters together and patting the tops of their heads as though they were a pair of cute salt 'n' pepper shakers. "Twins once again."

Grandma wasn't lying. Already, I could barely tell which younger sister was which.

Mom didn't say anything but her displeasure was evident. She scrunched her face, strained, and soon urine poured off the edge of the cushions, hitting the newspaper on the floor with an angry *trat-trat-trat*.

Still smiling, Grandma sent us off while she attended to Mom's wet spot.

Bedtime was chaotic. We filled the hall with our bedding and belongings, trying to sort out our rooms. When the smoke cleared, my younger sisters returned to the captain's bed in their old room, I moved into my older sister's room, and she luxuriated in the large room all by herself.

"There's going to be some changes around here," Grandma said. "Your Mom and Dad loved you and did the best they could, but you're in need of some civilizing. Maybe in the old days it was acceptable for kids to run around with snotty noses and dirty knees, but this is the modern era. We need to be the best we can. As strong as we can. It's time to learn a different way of doing things."

"Like keeping food in the refrigerator?" the twins asked.

"Among other things."

Grandma and Mom fought at night. They hushed their voices, trying to avoid detection, but the heating ducts carried their conversation directly into our ears. Mom pleaded with Grandma to leave.

"Let Jack and me raise the girls the way we've decided best."

"Oh Janet, this foolishness has gone on far too long. Look at you. Look at your children. Land's sake, look at what's become of your husband. For all you know he's dead drunk under a sombrero somewhere in Mexico."

Grandma refused to leave while Mom was in this condition. Grandma needed to take care of everyone.

"I'll not allow my granddaughters to starve in filth because you're too proud to let your own mother look after you. If disobeying your wishes and making you angry is what it takes to protect them, then tough titty."

Maybe Mom knew she was licked. Maybe Mom was formulating a plan. Maybe Mom was so doggone tired she couldn't keep her head up for another go around. As she conceded to Grandma's occupation of the house, she said, "Just promise me you aren't going to bring Todd here."

"Oh Janet, isn't it time you let this silly grudge against your brother go?"

"Promise me you will not let Todd in this house."

"Fine. I will not bring Todd into this house."

Instead, Grandma brought strange men.

The dark hairs on my arm stood up and danced to the vibrations of the wall. I lay my face at my elbow to watch them up close. The hairs wiggled like bugs. They looked alive. I feared my hairs would soon tire of dancing and, with tiny little mouths, would begin eating my skin, nibbling me down to white bone.

"Rebecca!" I shouted. "Turn the music down!"

She was locked upstairs in the bedroom, playing her records. Quiet at first, but as the hours went by the volume knob kept inching closer and closer to maximum. Her dancing excited the wall, which purred in appreciation. The vibrations ran all the way down into the living room. The words in my book became blurry. A smouldering cigarette at Mom's couch-side rolled out of the ashtray. I pounced to pick it up before the whole carpet caught fire. Grandma often warned Mom her carelessness was going to burn down the whole city one of these days.

"There's no need to shout," Grandma said. She placed her hand on the wall and smiled. "Everything is fine."

Heavy feet pounded up the porch steps. I knew very well the steps of the mailman and the paperboy, and this was neither of them. For a moment, I thought it was the man with the tape recorder Auntie Linda had marked on the neck with her lips, coming back to give digging up dirt on Uncle Todd a second shot. I soon realized it couldn't be him either. There were too many feet drumming the boards of the porch. Unless our visitor was a centipede. A whole mob had descended on us, like the ones with pitchforks and torches who were always chasing the Frankenstein monster.

The front door swung open and a group of men, maybe as many as six, invaded the house. They didn't knock. None of them even took off their white sneakers. They scuffed dirt onto the rug as they marched into the living room.

I jumped to my feet and threw my book at them. Without even looking, one of the men raised his hand to swat the book away. He did this with such grace and precision, he must have got books thrown at him regularly. I hope some got through and hit him hard.

Ridiculously, I made my hands into puny fists, as though I had any hope of fighting off a gang of grown men. My heartbeat was still normal. Things were happening so fast my nerves barely had a chance to keep up.

Grandma showed no sign of alarm at the men's arrival. She continued smiling, with her hands clasped together. I thought she might offer them lemonade. She walked over to the couch, where Mom wheezed and gagged while she slept, with one arm slung over her eyes and a hundred balls of snotty tissues dotting the blankets. Grandma knelt, picked up one of the tissues, and wiped Mom's drooling mouth before kissing her on the cheek.

The men nodded. They advanced towards the couch.

"Stop it! Don't touch her!" I shouted. There was no weapon within reach. Dad had taken his crutches when he left, otherwise they would have been resting against his vacant easy chair. I could see nothing within reach that could be used to hit or stab.

The men surrounded the couch. One of them grabbed Mom's wrists and yanked her arms above her head. Another grabbed her legs and pinned them together. They pulled her at each end, making her body stiff as a board as they lifted her off the couch. The way the blanket dangled over her stomach made me think of the trick where a magician made a lady rise off a table. Another man wound the blanket around Mom tight, even covering her face. Together, they lay her across their shoulders and carried her out of the house like an old rug.

Grandma did nothing. She stood watching while her daughter got taken away, smiling like someone had just answered all her prayers.

If someone comes into your house and carries away the TV, you'd call the police immediately. "There's robbers in the house!" you'd say. A person is a hell of a lot more valuable than a TV, right? So I ran for the phone but one of the white sneaker men grabbed me. "Calm down," he commanded, as though being a grown man was all the authority he needed.

Outside, a van idled in the driveway. The men had painted the vehicle white so people would mistake it for an ambulance. The side door slid open and Mom got tossed inside without any care. Even if they were dropping her onto a soft surface with no risk of injury, it pained me to see her treated like something disposable.

I kept fighting, reaching for the phone, but the man still had his arms wrapped around me, making me still. He leaned back and my feet left the floor. The only part of me free was my mouth, so I produced a loud, piercing shriek. I wanted the man's ears to feel like they were being stabbed.

He clamped a filthy paw over my mouth. I tried biting him but his skin was calloused and leathery, probably strengthened by all the women who had bitten him over the years. He shoved me as he let me go, and I tumbled into the corner of the room.

The white van had no sirens. Once Mom was loaded inside, the men jumped aboard and the van pulled out into the road. It moved silent as a shark, giving no hint as to the prisoner strapped in its belly.

My shriek and the commotion summoned my sisters. The sight of the empty couch made them halt in their tracks. Mom's blankets were jumbled on the floor, looking like dead bodies thrown from a car crash.

The front door remained wide open. Grandma gently closed it, turning the lock. The click echoed through the house, which had never sounded so empty before. I'd never realized how lively both Mom and Dad made the house. With them gone, the house felt bigger and unfamiliar.

Grandma opened her arms wide, beckoning me and my three sisters towards her.

"Come here, my sweet girls. I need some hugs."

ELEVEN

"When's Mom coming back?"

My younger sisters were the first to ask.

The three of us stood at the sink, using new toothbrushes Grandma had pulled out of her suitcase. Our old brushes had been worn flat, the bristles turned green, so for the longest time we'd cleaned our teeth with a dab of toothpaste on our fingertip. I didn't like the stiff white brush in my mouth. It seemed unsanitary. I mean, you can't wash your toothbrush, can you? The bristles must be coated in germs. As far as I was concerned, using the same toothbrush day after day was like using the same Kleenex over and over.

Grandma closed the toilet lid to sit down and drew my younger sisters close to her. She fed us a story mundane enough to pass as the truth.

"Your mother has a terrible sickness. One buried so deep in her bones none of the doctor's needles or X-rays can find it. She hasn't been acting like herself lately, has she?"

What did Grandma know about the way Mom's been acting? Sure, she got tired a lot, but who wouldn't after working nights to take care of four daughters and a wound-ed husband?

"Your mother feels sad, even when good things happen, like you hug her and tell her you love her. It's exhausting to feel sad all the time. Your muscles ache and your bones feel brittle and you can't catch your breath. All she can do is sleep on the couch. She can't wash herself or use the bathroom or, worst of all, take care of you girls."

"Mom isn't like that all the time."

My older sister appeared in the bathroom doorway. Her eyes were red and puffy. She said, "If Mom needed to go to the hospital, Dad would have taken her long ago. He would have picked her up and carried her."

Grandma sighed. "Your father suffers a sickness very similar to your mother's. Only his is self-inflicted. We all ignore it, hoping one day he'll wake up and cure himself, but if he had the strength to stop, he would have a long time ago. But he didn't. He left."

My older sister retreated to the bedroom. She slammed the door, turned the lock using her hairpin, and blasted music from the record player, creating a wall of sound to keep Grandma at bay. Grandma had said bad things about Dad many times before, but never to our faces, never asking us to agree with her.

Next, Grandma dropped my younger sisters into the tub. She claimed regular bathing was an important part of a healthy life, like brushing our teeth or going to bed early. Right now, we looked about as clean as jungle missionaries, leaving muddy imprints of our behinds wherever we sat. "When was the last time you girls had a bath?"

Hard to say. Mom wasn't fanatical about bathing. As long as we kept the major areas clean, our faces and our hands, she seemed happy to let the occasional rainstorm take care of the rest of us.

Grandma was horrified.

"That is an absolute disgrace. Imagine, a house where the cutlery is cleaner than the people."

She picked me up and dropped me into the tub between my younger sisters, which was a tight fit. The water turned the colour of pencil lead. Grandma scrubbed us with a cake of foul-smelling Ivory. My younger sisters splashed around like happy puppies, until Grandma pulled the plug, revealing a thick river of mud blackening the slope to the drain. After cleaning the tub, she turned the faucets back on and washed us again.

The only pleasurable part of the bath was at the end, when Grandma waved the warm hair dryer over us as we towelled off. She sprinkled baby powder on our skin to help pull our arms and legs through the sleeves of our new pyjamas. The white dust looked like icing sugar, but I knew better than to taste it.

"There, doesn't that feel wonderful, to be so clean?"

Cleanliness was okay. I could take it or leave it. A bath certainly wasn't worth the investment of time that could have been spent reading or watching TV.

Not done with us yet, Grandma ran a flat brush over our heads, painfully combing the scalp. My skin burned.

"Brushing is very important," Grandma said. "Hair loves attention. The more you brush, the faster it grows. That's why dogs and cats have so much hair. All that stroking and petting keeps their hair growing thick and strong. Mice have short hair, never having got petted. Otherwise, you would see some pretty hairy mice."

She brushed our scalps raw, ignoring our cries of pain, promising we wouldn't hurt as much next time. She told us if we kept brushing, we'd have heads of long hair the entire neighbourhood would envy. I didn't disbelieve her, but wondered why she'd just yesterday sheared the pleasant, healthy locks from my youngest sister's head. She already had perfect hair and now she had to start again all over.

"It's special to be twins, so why not look that way? Better their hair grows together, always matched. I'm not going to try and hide you away like your mom. I want you girls to look your best, to be attractive to all the positive energy in this world."

"Mom told us we aren't allowed to call our younger sisters 'twins' anymore," my older sister reminded her.

"Well, your mother isn't here now, is she? Look at the

twins." She stood them side-by- side in front of the bathroom mirror. "Why, I can barely tell them apart."

"When can we visit Mom?"

During dinner (lamb shanks from the A&P butcher counter, not the backyard), I suggested a trip. Just because Mom was in the hospital didn't mean no one could see her. Even ladies with fresh babies got visits, exposing them and the newborn to all kinds of germs.

Grandma wasn't very enthused by my idea. "Your mother's in a different kind of hospital, for people sick in the mind."

"An insane asylum?" I pictured Mom locked in a padded room, trussed up in a jacket with no holes in the sleeves, just like that movie about the lady who chopped people's heads off with an axe.

Grandma laughed. "Oh honey, such places haven't existed for years. We live in the civilized age."

The way Grandma told it, Mom's hospital stay was a vacation. She had a fancy, clean room with a comfortable bed and her own colour TV. Instead of slaving away vacuuming the house, Mom strolled through the hospital's lush garden before retiring to the atrium for tea and all the tobacco she could smoke.

"They don't just take anyone as a patient. It's very expensive."

"Then why can't we go see her? Even prisoners are allowed visitors."

Grandma looked cross for the first time. "Your mother is not a prisoner. She doesn't want you girls missing school. Wait until the weekend. I'll take you then."

Grandma parked her Chevy on the street outside the hospital, far from the front doors. Instead of the regular part of the hospital, where people with broken bones and pneumonia sought treatment, the doctors kept Mom on the other side, in the Norse Wing.

That ancient, unfriendly name made me shudder. No matter how much Grandma assured us the nurses pampered

Mom like an Egyptian princess, I couldn't forget the stories I'd heard at school about the Norse Wing. The Norse Wing was where the police had hauled Robbie Clattenberg's father after he hosed himself down with gasoline and threatened to set himself on fire. Mom shouldn't have to live amongst self-destructive maniacs reeking of gas. She didn't have a dangerous bone in her body.

"Wait here. I'll be back in a few minutes."

According to Grandma, the Norse Wing had a rigid visiting system. People weren't allowed to walk in unannounced. When patients were ready to receive visitors, they wrote their name down in a big ledger in the lobby. Grandma went inside and returned a few minutes later, shaking her head and saying the doctors looked, but Mom did not write her name in the ledger. She wasn't ready to see anyone today.

"Let me look," my older sister said. "Maybe Mom wrote down her maiden name. Did they check carefully?"

"I'm sorry, honey. I looked myself. There isn't a trace of your mother's handwriting. Maybe she's still sleeping or forgot what day it is. The rules are the rules. We'll have to try again some other time."

Before bed, Grandma threw me and the twins back in the tub for another round of washing. Again? I questioned this excessive bathing. Washing yourself every night seemed like overkill. My fingers wrinkled and I didn't want the rest of my body withering in the hot water. After too many baths, the skin would fall off my bones like tender meat from steamed ribs.

The twins were less concerned. They happily splashed one another while Grandma scrubbed them.

"Shall I draw a tub for you once these three are put to bed?" Grandma offered my older sister.

"No. I feel clean enough."

My older sister was too big for Grandma to dunk in the tub like a muddy puppy, so she tried to entice her.

"Why don't you take a good book and crawl under the hot bubbles for a while? I can think of no better way to unwind than a good hour in the tub. Sometimes I enjoy a nice glass of wine." She said this with a conspiratorial wink, letting my older sister know the privilege of grown-up libations were hers for the asking, all she needed to do was slip into the tub.

My older sister didn't take the bait. "I worked up a good sweat this afternoon. That likely trickled away all the dirt." She peeked down the front of her dress. "Yep. I'm pink clean."

"Sweat is filthy," Grandma said. "It's like peeing all over yourself." She raised a hand and scratched the back of my older sister's neck. My older sister recoiled; it looked like it hurt. Grandma showed us her hand. The bottom of her fingernails were filled with a dark, gummy substance, all my older sister's dead skin. Disgusting.

"You don't want to go to school painted black with grime. What will your friends think?"

My older sister scowled at her. "Let me scratch the back of your neck. Let's see how clean you are."

The chattering of my own teeth woke me up. I groped through the dark, still unfamiliar in my older sister's bed, looking for my covers. Then it hit me. I wasn't cold. If anything, I needed a fan. Sweat poured off my forehead, filling my ears. Beside me, the wall purred strong enough to rattle the bed and knock my teeth together. The slats holding my mattress rubbed the frame, the friction liable to start a fire.

In my old bedroom, my older sister set the record player's volume to MAX. Each pop in the vinyl crackled like grease in the frying pan. The music summoned Grandma, who banged on the bedroom door, ordering my older sister to cut this nonsense out and go to sleep before the neighbours started complaining. My older sister ignored her, pretended she didn't hear.

Calmly, Grandma plucked a hairpin from her head and inserted it into the lock. She smiled to herself, thinking she'd outsmarted her rebellious granddaughter. She tried turning the hairpin but it wouldn't move. Turns out my older sister was the one who'd outsmarted Grandma by stuffing tissue paper into the keyhole, preventing the hairpin from turning the tumbler and opening the door.

Defeated, Grandma resorted to threats.

"If you don't open this door, I'll come back with an axe and chop it right off its hinges!"

My older sister ignored her, keeping the record player spinning and her feet dancing across the floor until we all heard a bang at the side of the house. Grandma placed a ladder against the bedroom window and climbed up for a peek inside. She and my older sister locked eyes. In one raised hand, Grandma held a rock wrapped in a pillowcase.

You wouldn't dare, my older sister thought.

The sound of breaking glass filled my head, so loud I thought my skull had burst apart and a million shards of bone were piercing my brain. Grandma crawled through the broken window, like an intruder set to do us great harm.

The commotion behind the bedroom door sounded like a wrestling match. My older sister and Grandma grappled across the bed before tumbling onto the floor. They sounded like wild animals gnawing each other to death. A tiger against a monkey, or an elephant against a lion.

I knew my older sister had lost the fight when she began crying. Now, I'd heard her cry a million times before, tears were her way of pouting. She cried if she couldn't watch her TV show; she cried if Mom wanted her to fill the dishwasher. But these tears were fresh territory. This new crying signalled an admission of defeat and humiliation. I'd say this was the first time I heard my sister cry for real.

Through the door, I heard the tearing of my older sister's dignity, or maybe it was her clothing. Grandma had her pinned somewhere, maybe over the bed, maybe against the wall.

"Why are there so many markings on your body?"

"LET GO OF ME!"

"Look at your neck. And your stomach."

Grandma dragged my older sister into the hall by her ankles. She was completely undressed, her desperate fingernails raking the wood floor. In the bathroom, Grandma threw open the faucets and they poured thick torrents of hot water into the tub. Grandma pushed my older sister inside, forcing her at last to bathe. Water gushed over the rim, flooding the bathroom floor while Grandma rolled up her sleeves and scrubbed my older sister clean.

"Act like a baby, get treated like one," Grandma said.

Seeing Grandma toss my older sister about no better than the hospital men had treated Mom horrified me. I couldn't watch. I left the bathroom doorway but could still hear the splashing and the crying, and Grandma's cold, foul voice. Wanting to get away, I went into my older sister's bedroom to survey the damage.

The record reached the end and the needle drifted aimlessly inside the label. Wind rushed through the punctured window, lifting the pages of scattered magazines and sent a lipstick tube rolling across the floor like a spent shotgun shell.

In the darkness at the very back of the room, a small red circle floated, seeming to wave at me. The orb grew larger and brighter. I was looking at the end of someone's burning cigarette. They inhaled, briefly illuminating their face before blowing a cloud of cigarette smoke in my direction. Frightened, I ran back to bed, abandoning my older sister to Grandma's wrath.

My older sister turned her bathwater into a grey soup. Month's worth of dirt and dead skin made the water as thick as gravy. Eventually, she stopped crying, conceding Grandma had won.

But Grandma wasn't through yet.

"Now drink."

Grandma's command didn't need repeating. My older sister cupped her hands, raised the murky swill to her mouth and guzzled it down. Something, perhaps the taste, made her retch and Grandma told her to drink again.

"From now on, I expect you to keep yourself clean. The next time I have to put you in this tub, your sisters are all going to drink the water too, so if you have any respect for them, you'll see that you're clean."

My older sister was not allowed to return to her bedroom. For now, Grandma decided, they would sleep downstairs together. "Until I can trust you again."

The drama between Grandma and my older sister ended once they settled down to sleep, but the house was not yet quiet. Footsteps came from the empty bedroom, walking down the hall to my room. The mattress shifted as someone lay their heavy weight alongside me.

"Emery," a familiar voice whispered.

I was in no mood to entertain, so I feigned sleep, hearing only the crackle of my bedmate's burning tobacco. Their hand ran across my back, patting my shoulder blades as if to say everything would be alright. They were familiar hands, powerful ones I knew could throw a pinecone and hit a bird's nest with deadly accuracy.

TWELVE

The lone good thing about Mom being locked up in the Norse Wing was at least we knew where she was. She may have been gone, but she hadn't vanished. That kept us hopeful.

Dad's whereabouts were completely unknown. My sisters and I wanted nothing more than for him to return home, grab Grandma by the scruff of the neck, and throw her out of the house. But how could we wish for him to return when we didn't even know where he needed to return from?

We speculated where Dad could be.

"Dad must be in jail. The only reason he's been gone so long is 'cause he's locked up. It's the only thing that makes sense."

My older sister's jailbird theory gained support from a newspaper clipping Robbie Clattenberg showed me at school, about two men robbing a camera store in the Falls. They used chains to pull the front door right off its hinges and filled the car with expensive lenses before racing to the Peace Bridge, where they were apprehended.

"This is your dad," Robbie Clattenberg told me.

No names were mentioned in the article but Robbie pointed to a line: "One of the men attempted to flee on foot but was apprehended by border guards." According to Robbie, this obviously referred to Dad.

"The thief couldn't run away because he was a cripple on crutches."

I told Robbie that the thief was probably an arthritic old fart, since Dad could move faster than any man, even on crutches.

At home, I wasn't as confident. Grandma ran our newspaper past a pair of scissors, snipping out certain articles for some mysterious reason. News of Dad's capture?

My older sister laughed. "If the old woman thought Dad was in jail, she'd dance an Irish jig. You know what she cuts out of the paper? Scary movie ads and sexy letters to Ann Landers."

The twins' theories about Dad were downright vicious. According to them, Dad's car ran out of gas, forcing him to set out for home on foot. The sky was clear, so he followed the stars, knowing the tail of the Big Dipper hung over the QEW highway. Unfortunately, Dad wandered into the Black Tricky Forest. The tree branches reached into the sky and rearranged the stars, fooling Dad into walking in the wrong direction, deeper into the woods.

Each morning, the twins changed their story. At first, Dad crawled into a cave, needing sleep, but the soft, warm pillow he nestled his weary head on was actually the belly of a ferocious lion who chased him up a tree. The lion wanted to eat Dad and thought if he waited long enough Dad would fall asleep and tumble out of the tree. Dad outsmarted the lion by threading his belt around the branches. Day and night, the lion waited below for Dad. Soon, the lion's patience would run out, and he would begin gnawing the bottom of the tree like a beaver. When that day arrived, Dad would snap off the thickest branch and chew the end into a spear. After slaying the lion, Dad would use sharp rocks to skin the beast's fur for a coat for Mom and assemble the bones into bracelets for his daughters. Only then would he return home.

"Lions live in the jungle," I said. "Not in the woods around here."

The twins didn't know what to tell me. "Maybe the lion escaped from a circus?"

The next day, the twins forgot about lions. According to them, Dad found a cabin owned by an old hermit. Our starving father guzzled three bowls of the hermit's stew before the poisonous mushrooms within knocked him unconscious. He awoke chained to the floor. The lonely hermit wanted company. Afraid Dad would talk his way free, the hermit took a jagged rock and cut Dad's tongue out. Each night while the hermit slept, Dad tugged on the nub of his tongue, slowly forcing a new one to grow. Once Dad had a new tongue, he would sweet-talk the hermit into releasing him. A tongue grew at the same rate as fingernails, so we had to be patient. Only then would Dad return home.

Robbie Clattenberg showed me a new article. In Port Dalhousie, a burglar got attacked by a homeowner's Doberman pinscher, and had three of his fingers bitten off. The animal was taken to the vets to have its stomach pumped, but the digits were too mangled and digested for police to take prints. Authorities kept an eye on the hospital emergency rooms since "an injury of this severity would require medical assistance."

"This is your dad."

Nonsense. All dogs recognized Dad as a champion stick thrower and belly scratcher. I'd never seen a dog so much as bark at Dad. Mom said he should have been a mailman, his rapport with dogs was so strong.

According to the twins, all of Dad's fingers were intact, it was his feet that were chewed off, courtesy of a pair of bear cubs. Once they began gnawing on his feet, Dad was helpless to stop them, knowing if he so much as touched the cubs, momma bear would come to the rescue and he'd stand no chance against a seven-foot-tall grizzly. Once the cubs' bellies were full, Dad tied rocks to his stumps, new granite feet, but they were heavy and made walking slower.

On the bright side, he was never cold at night, needing only to click his heels together to spark fire into a pile of kindling.

*

"I want to sleep in my own room."

"Rebecca, it's a privilege to share my bed." Sleeping with Grandma meant my older sister got to stay up late and watch Johnny Carson on the old black-and-white set in Mom and Dad's (former) room, a real treat.

"Why can't you let me sleep alone?"

"I thought some time together would give us the chance to become friends again. I miss you, sweetie."

The disappearance of my older sister from her bedroom angered Ricky. At night, I heard him pacing, muttering angrily to himself, striking matches to light his cigarettes. When he gave up waiting for her, he came down the hall into my room, as though it were my responsibility to keep him entertained. He liked to wake me up by kicking the bottom of my bed. The mattress lifted, and I was startled awake.

I told him to go downstairs and snuggle between my older sister and Grandma while they yukked it up watching Johnny Carson. Let me have my rest. He laughed, but not like I'd said something clever. He laughed like he'd watched me trip and hurt myself.

That's when I knew Ricky wasn't leaving me alone anytime soon.

The closet door creaked open and Ricky glided into the room. His bare feet slid across the floor like they were wheeled. Before I could tell him to go away, he wedged himself between my sheets, stinking of cigarettes.

My bed used to feel large, but now Ricky crowded me. I had no trouble sleeping with any of my sisters. When we shared a mattress, we snapped naturally into comfortable positions like pieces of a jigsaw puzzle. Ricky felt like a stolon, a clump of roots growing off me, sapping my restful sleep. He took up the lion's share of the bed, nearly pushing me onto the floor. He spent the entire night, leaving only when Grandma called us to rise for school.

I hated rolling over in the night to feel Ricky's cold drool soaked into the pillow, so I crowded the bed with dolls and stuffed animals. My soft bears and plush seals left no room for anyone else. Dozens of button eyes kept watch over me.

Let's see him get in now, I thought, proud of my cleverness. I almost couldn't wait to see the look on Ricky's face when he discovered there was no room in the bed. I just hoped he wouldn't start crying. I wanted him to leave me alone, but I didn't want to be mean about it.

I underestimated him. He grabbed the animals by their ears and flung them to the floor. He didn't even look annoyed. He thought I hadn't put my toys away.

I became a hostile bedmate. I kicked. I dragged my toe-nails along his legs, gouging his skin. Blood squished between my toes, but he slept like a hibernating bear.

"You're starting to look like a raccoon," Grandma said at breakfast. "You better start going to bed earlier."

I choked on my cereal, spitting milk across the table. Going to bed early meant spending longer pressed next to Ricky and his stinky cigarettes. Each time he struck a match against the wall next to my head, I wanted to slap him. How dare he smoke in my bed. Did he want to burn the whole house down?

As if Ricky sucking on cigarette butts weren't bad enough, I also heard the twins whispering in their room. Their voices carried through the heating ducts, coming up with the latest instalment of "What Happened to Dad."

According to the twins, Dad met other men in the Black Tricky Forest. He discovered a village of lost travellers, confused by the nightly rearranging of the stars. Some of them had lived in the woods for years, growing beards long enough to cover their shame. Winter and rain had rotted their clothes away. The men never went hungry. Nightly, they roasted lions and bear cubs captured from caves. In the winter, when the animals hibernated, the men would roast one of their own, but Dad refused to wait around for that to happen. He made himself king, ordering the men to sharpen their lion bones into spears.

They would escape the woods by tunnelling underground. In the darkness of the Earth, the men couldn't be fooled by the moving stars. Only then would Dad return home.

I'd had enough of the twins' childish bullshit. I banged on the wall.

"You two shut up! No one wants to hear your lies!"

The twins went quiet. Not because I'd yelled at them, but because they'd finished saying all they wanted and now wished to sleep.

Robbie Clattenberg showed me a new article. In Font Hill, a man had climbed one of the electrical towers. At the top, he'd lost his grip and fallen between two wires that zapped him to a crisp. The power got knocked out at the Can-View Drive-In, the screens going black, prompting the audience to honk their horns before driving to the candlelit ticket booth to demand a refund. Most customers felt bad the next day when they learned a man's death was responsible for the blackout. They would have demanded their refunds more respectfully had they known.

"This is your dad."

"Let me get this straight. After robbing a store and having his hand eaten by dogs, my dad climbed a tower and electrocuted himself?"

Robbie Clattenberg nodded. "Oh, he did a lot of other things too. I have the articles saved. Come over some time and I'll show you."

I built an obstacle course of sharp toys across my bedroom floor. Green army men, shards of broken doll faces, and the spiky ends of pickup sticks I hoped would stab Ricky's bare feet. In preparation, I snuck a towel under my pillow to mop up his blood.

The closet door opened. Ricky deftly navigated my ersatz booby traps. He swung his hips, sliding around each danger spot with the practised grace of a dancer. He might have been showing off. My bladder squeezed as Ricky lay on top of me, but I didn't dare get out of bed until sunrise. I didn't remember where all the danger zones were. Trapped by my own cleverness. I could just imagine how my older sister would roll her eyes at that one.

"Get out of here."

Ricky played deaf, ignoring me as he lit another cigarette.

"Are you listening to me? Get out of my bed."

A solution burst into my head, one so obvious I couldn't believe the thought hadn't occurred to me earlier. Before, whenever Ricky lumbered up and down the sidewalk, killing baby birds and whooping like a steam whistle, any adult could chase him away by invoking the name of the one God he feared.

"Ricky, your mother wouldn't be very happy to hear about this," they would say. Threatening to disturb his mother with reports of wrongdoing always sent Ricky scampering off in a blind panic. Once, he ran jabbering through Mr. Popowitz's clothesline, a white sheet plastered across his face like wet wallpaper and a red rope burn line seared across his throat. This was all long before Ricky found self-confidence and took up smoking, but I was sure it would still work. After all, the Frankenstein monster never mastered its fear of fire—why would Ricky be any different?

I cleared my throat and announced, "Ricky Castle, if you don't get out of this bed right now, I am going to call your mother."

He stubbed his cigarette butt into the headboard. Pieces of glowing tobacco rained onto my face, burning my cheeks and forehead like firefly bites. Well, now I had his attention.

Ricky grabbed my side. His tight grip re-flamed the pain of my old bruises from the Pincher. He lifted me by my ribs and tossed me out of bed like an unwanted teddy bear. I crashed amid the toys laid over the floor, crushing plastic tea cups and stabbing my calf on the twisted end of a broken Slinky.

For a moment, my pain was lesser than my sense of outrage. How dare he throw me out of my bed? I lunged at the mattress, ripping the sheets and flinging the spread into the air. The pillows went flying. My swinging arm knocked over the lamp and the bulb shattered against the floor. I jumped up and down on the bed, trying to break the support beams. The slats held up, refusing to crack (built by Dad), so I pulled my underwear down and pissed all over the wounded bedding. Let's see Ricky sleep in my damp filth.

"Get out of here! Go back to your own home! This isn't your goddamn bed!"

All my rumbling and thrashing woke Grandma. She pushed the door open and peered inside, looking more alarmed than upset. She wasn't here to yell at me for making a ruckus. She was worried about me. I felt a little better, knowing someone wanted to protect me.

My older sister stood alongside Grandma. The smell of the smouldering cigarette butt burning out on the floor angered her. She recognized Ricky's brand. She knew he'd been here.

Grandma knelt to lift me off the floor. She rubbed my cold arms. "Oh baby. Did you have a dream?"

Too frazzled to be comforted, I chattered like a spooked squirrel until Grandma backed away. Even my older sister knew to keep her distance. My aching side made me bushy and feral, unable to distinguish between friend and foe. If Dad had come back at that moment and swooped in for a hug, I would have ripped his nose from his face.

Grandma wanted to know what happened. My ribs ached from Ricky's clutch. Uncertain how to explain Ricky Castle was hiding inside our house, only coming out at night, I told her I must have fallen out of bed.

She looked at me, but threw her voice over her shoulder, clearly speaking for the benefit of my older sister. "You know what I think? I think some young ladies have been fooling around, putting funny ideas into the heads of boys. Do we know anybody like that around here?"

My older sister took advantage of Grandma's turned back. She snatched Ricky's cigarette off the floor, hiding it beneath her nightie. As soon as she was alone, she'd put it in her mouth, tasting where his lips had been.

"Go back to bed, Rebecca, I'll be there in a moment."

My older sister left the room slowly. Her eyes shifted back and forth, looking for other signs of Ricky. She hoped to spot him hiding somewhere. This could be their chance to knock Grandma over the head, steal the keys to her car, and take off together on a permanent adventure.

It took a few minutes to put my bed back in order. The piss-covered sheets were tossed into the hall. I fixed the askew mattress while Grandma fetched fresh linen. It felt good to escape the smell of Ricky, both his smoke and his drool. I pulled the sheets around me tight, covering my entire body, even my face. The sheets may provide lousy protection, but they were all I had.

Grandma sat on the edge of the mattress. She peeled the covering away from my eyes, and for the first time, looking up at her, I noticed how deep the resemblance between her and Mom ran. Grandma may have been much bigger, but the way her legs spread and her back slouched was identical to the position Mom took every time she sat down. I could also see Mom in Grandma's face. That was exactly how Mom would look when she was older. It was how I would look when I was older. Grandma's face was a mirror into the future.

"When I was a little girl, my mother put me to bed with the covers pulled tight up to my neck. I had to sleep with my hands above the covers. If she ever came in and caught them under the sheets—WHACK!"

I flinched.

"See, that's the way my grandmother raised her. She wanted to make my mother feel guilty. You don't have to worry Emery. You have nothing to feel guilty about."

She reached beneath the covers, lifting one hand, then the other, arranging my arms along the bedspread. Beside me, faint purring came from the wall, like it too had been roused from sleep, and wanted someone to comfort it, just as Grandma had comforted me.

"Goodnight," Grandma whispered as she left the room. "Remember, there's nothing wrong with what you're doing."

Once she'd gone, I slid my hands back under the covers. The wall took offence. The purring came at me in short, angry beats. First Ricky, now the wall, felt like it was entitled to my attention. I wondered at what point I would no longer have to do what others demanded of me.

I rolled onto my side and tucked my hands between my legs. I squeezed the muscles hard, until my hands flattened, and I could feel the blood pushing to the tips of my fingers. My hands would be secure there. I could fall asleep and know they wouldn't cause any trouble.

I stood in the kitchen pouring a bowl of cereal when my older sister pressed into me from behind, pinning me against the counter. The tip of her nose grazed the back of my neck, and I anticipated the warmth of her arms wrapping around me in a protective hug.

"If you ever try and hurt Ricky again, there is going to be big trouble."

Last night, when my older sister came into my room, I thought she'd throw up her fists, prepared to save me from Ricky's harassment. He betrayed her friendship doing these horrible things to her little sister. His actions were unforgivable, I would have thought. Instead, the fight brewing in her eyes wasn't for Ricky, but directed at me.

"I am not going to let you spoil the one good thing in my life."

Being snapped at when you're expecting a hug drains you of all hope. Standing up for yourself becomes impossible. You feel stranded. Incredibly, in a fight between me and Ricky, my older sister had chosen him.

"I'm not doing anything to keep Ricky from you. Take him back. Take him away so I never have to see him again."

I lifted the hem of my nightgown, thrusting my side out so she could take a good look at the bruises Ricky imprinted on me when he picked me up to throw me out of bed. My fragile rib ached. If I went to the doctors, they'd probably tell me it was crushed.

My older sister pretended not to see. She snatched the bowl of cereal I'd prepared, and said, "Grow up," before leaving me alone in the kitchen. I kept my nightgown pulled up, continuing to air Ricky's bruises, which were indistinguishable from the ones given to me by the Pincher, in what now felt like an entirely different lifetime.

That night, the twins concocted the final story about Dad.

Through the heating duct, I heard them say Dad and Roman got together and went out driving. Usually, they went into a part of town pulsing with excitement and danger, but that night they parked alongside the lake, drinking from a shopping bag of beer cans, staring at the sky and saying nothing, not because they were deep in thought, but because nothing rolled around in their empty heads worth verbalizing. Yawning and farting, they drank and stared at the black lake, wishing the water was desert sand they could walk across and disappear. The boredom made them nasty, and they spoke thoughts better kept private.

"I used to have this girl," Dad said. "Sometimes I think she was *the* girl, y'know. Hips for boys. Strong boys. Not like those troublemakers roosting back home. Sometimes I think about looking for her. She'd be easy to find, every now and then I catch a whiff of her scent. I got the bloodhound nose. I could track her down. There would be a man in her life, no doubt about that. Some soft loser she made second best."

Dad thought he could knock on the door of his old flame and when her man answered he would be no match for Dad. Even with crutches. This girl's man hadn't worked as hard as Dad had, never developed those muscles. He also wouldn't be as desperate as Dad was. Desperate men fought viciously.

"I'll put a finger in each eye and my thumb in his mouth, like a bowling ball. Let him bite it off; I don't care. I'll grow a new one. Let's see him grow a new head after I tear his off. I'll rip out the jaw and throw the rest so far no one'll ever find it. Before his lights blink out, I'll tell him, *She's still mine, I'm taking her back.*"

Dad's old flame would have children, each of whom Dad would swing by the ankles and dash their heads against the rocks. The house would be empty now, just Dad and his flame, the way things were supposed to be. She'd be afraid of him at first. How could she not, covered in the gore of her husband and children? That was okay. Dad understood their reunion would take time. He'd be gentle, never yelling or threatening, allowing her the time needed to forget her old life. She was *the* girl for him, and Dad would wait patiently until she remembered.

"Then we'll make boys of our own. Strong boys, not like those troublemakers roosting back home."

I heard every filthy word and hated the twins for making up lies about Dad. I didn't care that it was just a story. My mouth could never pass such vile words, even in jest. The idea Dad mistrusted us, resented our sex, and would throw Mom away so casually was obscene. No one who spent five seconds with Mom and Dad doubted the depth of their love. If they were lost at sea, dehydrating in the punishing sun, Dad would slice his wrist for Mom to drink, giving his own life for hers, and Mom would spit the blood back into his mouth, unwilling to go on without him. They would be found in each other's arms, having died lip to lip, sharing one another's fluid. It was the most devoutly romantic thing I could imagine.

Fed up, I kicked the twins' bedroom door open, catching them huddled together, weaving their lies. I didn't know which one of them had been telling the story, so I advanced on the one closest and socked her right in the eye. The bottom flap puffed out as blood filled the whites of her socket. She had a surprised look on her face, like she'd expected us to talk about this first.

"Keep your shit mouths shut!" I said before storming back to bed. My sister didn't cry. The house kept dead silent, as if afraid of setting me off again. For once, Ricky didn't dare come visit.

Sleep found me, and in my dreams, the story of Dad's disappearance reached its conclusion.

I saw Dad crumple his beer can and toss it into the lake, saying, "Fuck it" to his fantasy of snatching his old flame back. "What am I talking about? I'll never get her. Too much time has passed. I'm too old to make a new life for myself."

Roman, Dad's most trusted advisor, slung an arm around his shoulder. "You may think you're old now, but in ten years, you'll be even older, and you'll look back on yourself now as a young man and feel like you'd been wrong, that there was still time, and you'll regret doing nothing and letting this girl slip out of your life for the second time."

"You're probably right, but I'm drunk and overestimating my own strength."

He started running himself down, claiming to be weak, past his prime. Dad could easily dispatch his flame's husband, but he wouldn't have the juice left for their boys. After the death of their father, these strong boys would spill out of the house and take Dad apart limb by limb. "They'll mount my head on a pike made outta my own bones," he said.

Roman asked, "Why kill the boys in the first place?"

"I can't have two sets of children."

"Why not kill the girls then? It would be easier."

Roman's cleverness filled Dad with awe. "While those boys are only getting stronger, my girls have as much fight in them now as they ever will." Dad said this as if it were something he had been considering for a long time.

In the end, Dad got up on shaky, beer-filled legs and climbed into the lake. "Keep an eye on me," he told Roman before disappearing under the black water, but Roman did not stand guard. He got into the car and drove away. The lake became much bigger once Dad was in it, the bottom seemingly on the other side of the world. Dad sank for weeks before coming to rest amongst the piles of bones belonging to thousands of grieving, suicide birds.

I felt vile for having put Dad through this disgusting play, making him speak those obscenities. I kept my sick vision to myself. Not one of my sisters would ever hear it.

No one was proud of what I'd done.

My younger sister's (or my other younger sister's) eye

looked like a gunshot wound. Twitching, all red and purple. Grandma made a big fuss and wrapped ice in a sock to press against the injury. She refused to listen to more than two words of justification, leaving me to stew in the irony of having avenged Dad's honour by attacking the thing most precious to him—his family.

Grandma was duty-bound to punish me.

"Do you feel remorse for what you've done?"

More than could be expressed. I couldn't stomach the sight of my poor sister.

"How do you feel seeing your sister's eye?"

Sickened. Ashamed. I wanted to bow at her feet and beg for her forgiveness. Most of all, I wanted to know which sister she was.

What Grandma said next both confused and horrified me.

"You deserve to feel the guilt not once, but twice as hard. So raise your fist and let's see how much you enjoy hitting her this time."

"You want me to hit her again?" A second punch would pop my sister's eye like a blister.

"She's suffered enough." Instead, Grandma offered me the clean face of the injured girl's twin sister. "She won't mind. She's willing to help teach her big, bad sister a lesson, isn't she?"

My new punching bag wore a complacent look on her face, as though she had come to accept this was happening and she might as well save her pleading and tears for a situation where they might do some good.

I begged Grandma not to make me go through with it but she only mocked me. "Who's that crying? It couldn't be the big tough girl with the dynamite fists. Well, come on, big shot. Show us how tough you are."

I shouldn't have held back. My first punch bounced off my sister's cheekbone with a weak splat like the opening move in a game of patty-cake.

Grandma slapped me across the face. "Again!"

Shocked, I hit my sister a second time. Still not hard enough.

"Again!"

Each time I landed a soft tap onto my sister's face, Grandma slapped me harder. My cheek burned like fire ants swarmed the skin. My vision disappeared; there were too many tears to see through. If I could have traded, I would have let Ricky and the Pincher lay their hands all over me for hours rather than punch again.

My sacrificial sister reached out and took my hand. She squeezed gently, signalling, *It's alright, just do it.* I forced my hatred of Grandma into my shoulder and threw a strong punch into my sister's eye. Her head snapped back and an enormous tooth flew from her mouth and skidded across the kitchen floor. I wiped my eyes and saw the flying object wasn't a tooth, but a piece of gravel. It was my other younger sister I had just punched. It was my youngest of all my sisters whose eye now filled with blood, until once again the twins were identical.

Grandma smiled like Johnny Carson coming back from commercial break, giving no inkling of the depravity that went on when the cameras weren't running. "Good. Now this unpleasantness is behind us, who wants some breakfast?"

At school, I kept my head down on my desk all day. The lips of my eyes burned from the salt of my tears. Robbie Clattenburg came by with another newspaper clipping, but I ignored him. For the first time since Dad left, I hoped he wasn't coming home soon. I couldn't take his heartbreak upon seeing what I'd done to his two beautiful daughters' faces.

How long did it take for gruesome eyes to heal? The encyclopedias in the school library wouldn't say. I suppose it didn't matter. When we got home, we discovered Grandma had broken her final promise to Mom and allowed Uncle Todd to move into the house.

THIRTEEN

Uncle Todd climbed the porch steps and came through our front door with confidence, arriving as neither an intruder nor a guest, but a man returning to where he has always belonged. He'd grown much heavier since our trip across the border, and a jolliness permeated his walk, like he was auditioning for Santa Claus.

Neither Mom nor Dad would have approved. Practically the last thing both of them said was: *Keep Uncle Todd out of the house*. I reminded Grandma of their wishes.

"Doesn't he have his own house to live in?"

"Emery, I asked your uncle to help me out. I hate to tell you this but taking care of four rambunctious princesses has taken a toll on my bones. Besides, every house needs the balance of a man. Nothing but women knocking around is liable to tip it over."

Grandma ordered me and my older sister to carry Uncle Todd's suitcases into the house, just as the twins had done for her own bags. I thought of vampires, who according to the movies Dad watched, needed to be invited in before they set foot in a person's house. We fetched the suitcases from his truck, and I took the opportunity to open the driver's door, hoping the keys had been left in the ignition. If they were, I'd have put Mom's supermarket crash course to use and driven the pair of us out of there, searching for Dad.

We set the heavy suitcases at his feet. So many of them; how long did he intend to stay?

The first thing Uncle Todd unpacked was the empty pop bottle from our trip across the border. Seriously? He still had that sticky thing? I hoped he'd washed the insides, otherwise it might start drawing ants.

To thank us for our service, Uncle Todd gave us the phony, exaggerated grin grown-ups wore when talking down to children and idiots.

"How's your boyfriend?" he asked my older sister.

"I don't have a boyfriend."

Uncle Todd waggled a finger. "I see those love bruises on your neck. You didn't get those swatting mosquitoes." He took a Bruce Lee stance. "Invite buddy over for supper, maybe I'll show him my karate moves."

The arrival of Uncle Todd forced a change in the sleeping arrangements. Grandma moved to the living room couch, giving him the master bedroom. My older sister perked up, figuring she'd be allowed to return to the big bedroom upstairs and Ricky's company. Not so fast. Grandma wasn't ready to give up her bedmate. They would continue sleeping together.

"There isn't room on the couch for the both of us. Am I supposed to sleep on the floor?"

"Until you've earned your trust back, I need to know where you are at all times. If I can't feel you in the night, I'm not doing my duty."

"God! Why don't you tie my wrist to yours?"

"Oh, Rebecca. You're not being tied up like a dog. Don't be ridiculous."

Since Grandma kept my older sister under close watch, I took the opportunity to sneak into my former bedroom. I felt I had the right to be in there. The room felt colder than I remembered, and so much larger now that my sisters weren't filling the beds with their snores and body heat.

Cigarette butts littered the sheets. I shook the fibreglass stubs to the floor and stuck my face in the blankets, inhaling deeply. My older sister's scent dominated. I recognized the tomato soup aroma from her sweaty armpits. I also smelled boy in the sheets. Motor oil and playground dirt.

No one hid under the bed, which was a relief. If I crouched down there and found myself face-to-face with Ricky, surely I'd give myself the fright of my life. My scream would die in my throat, and Ricky would grab me by my cheeks, pulling me beneath with him. Holding me prisoner amongst the dust and my older sister's dirty clothes. I might never be found.

Uncle Todd poked his head in the door. "Whatcha doing?"

I jumped back, looking guilty, like he'd caught me trying to steal. To appear casual, I scooped up one of my older sister's magazines and hopped on the bed. See? I'm just doing a little relaxed reading.

Uncle Todd examined the broken window. Grandma hadn't fixed it yet, only taped black garbage bags over the hole in the glass. When a breeze shot past the house, the black plastic puffed in and out like a cancerous lung.

"Grandma broke the window," I said.

Uncle Todd didn't seem to care. He moved along to the record player. He shook his head as he used his feet to sift through the stack of records spilled over the floor. Most of them weren't even in their sleeves. No wonder the music filled with cracks and pops.

"I can't listen to any of this," he said. "Trash."

"Those are Dad's records." You could still smell his spilled beer on the album covers.

Uncle Todd switched the record player on. Jackie Wilson's voice lifted higher and higher, cutting off when Uncle Todd lifted the needle. He placed his empty Coke bottle on the middle of the record, in the red label, butting against the spindle. The glass bottle pirouetted, catching the rays of the setting sun and projecting them across the walls.

"Revolutions are special," Uncle Todd said, and he didn't mean what The Beatles sang about. "Did you know if you took two clocks with the same time, and put one on the shelf and left the other spinning on your record player, the one on the record player will start to lose time?"

He pressed his thumb to the edge of the turntable, slowing down the bottle's revolutions. Dad would have given him a whack if he'd caught Uncle Todd fooling around with his equipment like that.

"Not much at first, only seconds, but the longer you leave the clock turning, the slower the time goes until finally, after years, it just... stops."

Losing interest in the record player, he started peeking in the closet, knocking our dresses off the hangers and not bothering to put them back up. Broken glass crunched under his feet. I began to sense the two of us were looking for the same thing.

"Do you have funny dreams in the night?" He sat on the edge of the bed, right beside my crossed legs. I worried about him reaching over and tickling my feet. I didn't want Uncle Todd trying to make me laugh. He wasn't Dad, and he hadn't earned the right.

"Do you ever wake up 'cause you hear noises... or think you see someone?"

I played dumb. I threw the magazine to the floor and jumped up, bouncing on the mattress and singing, "Four little monkeys jumping on the bed!"

"Okay, enough. You're gonna hurt yourself. Get down."

Like the twins would have, I continued bouncing until Uncle Todd lifted me by under the arms and set me on the floor. He patted my head. *Good, he thinks I'm a moron.* That might be beneficial. My older sister was already openly hostile to Uncle Todd, so she could never fool him. But so long as he considered himself smarter than me, I'd have a chance at putting one over on him.

"I'll be fixing things up around here. Getting this house nice and clean."

My older sister lurked in the hallway, unseen by Uncle Todd. I knew by the sight of her scrunched eyebrows that it concerned her to see the two of us alone, speaking so civilly. We must have looked like we were colluding together.

A wet smack hit the hallway floor. My older sister returned

downstairs, leaving a puddle of spit behind for Uncle Todd to slip in. I'd have to speak with her fast, make her understand that I wasn't consorting with the enemy.

Uncle Todd didn't go to sleep that night. Instead of using the room Grandma vacated for him, he sat upstairs all night in the room with the broken window. He sat on the edge of the bed, a sheet cloaking his body from head to toe like a monk's robe. He played Dad's records over and over, so I guess the music wasn't trash after all.

He reminded me of a picture from a cowboy storybook, showing a cattle herder on night watch, sitting by the fire, a gun across his lap, keeping an eye out for rustlers. Dad read this book to me dozens of times and, when I outgrew it, I read it to the twins, who noticed a few details that had escaped me. The campfire cast light over the vigilant cowboy's face, which I mistook for his eyes being open. As the twins observed, his eyes were shut. You could see the near microscopic curls of his eyelashes along the closed lids. The twins also saw into the darkness behind the cowboy. Over the years, the jet-black ink had begun to fade, revealing a person squatting in a patch of cactus. You couldn't see if it was a cowboy or an Indian, just an ear and the curve of his arm jutting from the spiked plants. In his hand was a long white knife carved out of bone or maybe elephant tusk. Once the twins pointed him out I couldn't unsee him and I was always in a rush to turn the page before the man pounced and opened the sleeping cowboy's neck with his knife bone. If the rustler snapped a twig, the cowboy might awaken in time and spin around, momentarily lighting up the camp with a blast from his shotgun, but the cowboy looked fatigued, deeply asleep, and I didn't hold out much hope for him.

Uncle Todd didn't have a weapon. He trusted his silver tongue and Bruce Lee hands to rid us of any unwanted guests. He waited in the dark until he could barely keep his eyes open, unaware that Ricky had been sitting behind him for hours.

Drowsiness overtook Uncle Todd. His head dipped down, and Ricky seized the moment, lifting the sheet over Uncle Todd's face and pulling it tight, like a hangman necking the noose. Uncle Todd struggled to stand up while Ricky tied the ends of the sheet into intricate knots, preventing him from wiggling free. The sheet became a straightjacket; hang him upside down and it would be a trick fit for Houdini. Uncle Todd crashed to the floor, where he wiggled violently, like a caterpillar too weak to break out of its cocoon.

Ricky picked up a heavy book from the shelf and smashed Uncle Todd in the face. He snarled as he lifted the book over his head again and again. Uncle Todd lay on the floor unconscious, snoring through his bloody nose.

I would have rooted for Uncle Todd harder had I known once he was incapacitated, Ricky would celebrate his victory by crawling beneath my covers and laying his filthy body against mine. Pink insulation fibres from inside the wall covered Ricky's legs and chest. Who could sleep with such a mess in your bed?

Ricky loved the scent behind my ears. He planted his nose there, moving around in the slick of my sweat like a kitten groping for momma cat's nipple. I kept my nightgown bunched into the band of my underpants, puffing out the front like a boy. Ricky unhinged his mouth like a snake swallowing a rabbit. Without removing his nose from my ear, his bottom jaw elongated, and he tugged the hem of my nightgown from my underpants with his teeth. The warm fabric pulling away from my skin made a cooling sensation, and I hummed pleasantly. Ricky took this as encouragement and pressed his hand against the softest part of me. Instinctively, my legs bucked powerful as an angry horse, knocking him out of the bed.

Downstairs in the living room, I made the phone call I should have ages ago. After twenty rings, Ms. Castle's confused voice came on the line. "Hello?"

"Your son is here. You need to come and get him."

"What?"

"Ricky. He's in our house and we don't want him here anymore."

Ms. Castle sounded like she was half dreaming. She spoke slowly, as though forming her sentences by pulling tiles out of a Scrabble bag. "Who... are... you... talking... about?"

"Ricky is here. He was friends with my sister but now he won't leave. Please come and get him."

"It's... too... late... for... jokes."

"He's lonely. He misses you." Ms. Castle let out an anguished sob. I felt terrible for her; all alone in her house, no one to comfort her, her son's room empty.

A dial tone took over the line. I thought Ms. Castle hung up, not believing me, but Uncle Todd stood at my side. Awake now from his knockout, he pressed the buttons in the cradle before taking the receiver out of my hands and hanging up. His bloody face poked through a tear in the sheet. Without a word, he pointed upstairs, sending me back to bed.

In the morning, a naked spot occupied the table where the phone used to rest.

"Unnecessary gadget," Uncle Todd said, his eyes blackened, and lips so swollen they looked about to burst and spray blood everywhere. "We have no desire to talk to anyone who might be calling us. Any important news will reach us by mail."

He wouldn't go to the hospital for his injuries. Grandma visited the pharmacy and used butterfly stitches to close the crack in his forehead. Uncle Todd poured hydrogen peroxide over his face the way boxers splashed themselves with water, making his cuts fizz.

It pleased me to see him suffer. In a fight between Uncle Todd and Ricky, the only outcome to root for was mutually assured destruction.

Uncle Todd picked us up after school. He parked obnoxiously at the edge of the asphalt lot, engine running, two wheels resting on the road. Traffic swerved around him and drivers angrily honked their horns, but Uncle Todd did not care. He wanted to make sure we got home from school safe instead of wandering off and getting trapped in the Black Tricky Forest like Dad.

Driving home, Uncle Todd idled longer than necessary at a stop sign. Traffic built up behind us. I knew he was up to something.

"Oh, look," he pointed out the window. "Who's this fella?"

Before anyone could answer, Uncle Todd leapt out of the truck and jogged across the street to someone's front lawn. A small white dog lay beneath a tree, a collar tethering him to the porch. Uncle Todd petted the dog, who jumped up, wagging his stubby tail, happy to meet a new friend. After stealing a glance at the house, Uncle Todd undid the dog's collar, letting it fall onto the well-maintained lawn. Before anyone from the house spotted him, he tucked the little dog under his arm and skipped back to the truck, dumping the animal into our laps and speeding away.

"Hey!" What did Uncle Todd think he was doing? He couldn't steal a family's dog.

"He's a stray," Uncle Todd said. "The dog catcher would have snatched him up and stuck him in a cage." He spoke gravely to the twins, like he wanted to give them nightmares. "If the dog catcher gets him, he'll get a big needle and be killed. We don't want that to happen, do we?"

Once the little dog was inside our house, his tail no longer wagged. His shoulders slouched and he kept his head close to the floor. He didn't like being with us, regretted his friendliness. He wanted to go back to his yard; he was missing his family. When he started to whimper, I considered opening the front door and setting him free. I trusted him to find his way back home. Some animals are reported to have travelled great distances.

Before I could release him, Uncle Todd nudged him down the basement stairs. The dog's well-groomed coat wouldn't be white much longer. In the basement he was certain to get dirty.

A terrible sight awaited us. Grandma had been busy during our school day. Dad's easy chair, the anchor of the living room, no longer sat in its comfortable spot before the TV screen. Dad had been relaxing in that chair since before I was born. I doubt even my older sister remembered a time before the chair. The leather seat still carried the depression of Dad's body. The smell of his smokes and his beers might never scrub out of the armrests, but more importantly, the smell of his love remained. My sisters and I had all taken a good sniff of that chair since Dad's disappearance. Scent is a powerful memory enhancer. It kept us going to breathe in a little bit of Dad.

The living room without Dad's chair came as a shock. Someone should have warned us. Even at hospitals with an injured loved one, the doctors are careful to pull you aside before you go into the room so you can emotionally prepare yourself. *"We had to amputate both legs and most of the right arm, but he's resting comfortably now, perusing catalogues of the latest artificial legs."*

"You'll have to put that back," I said. Boy, was Dad going to blow his stack when he returned. No beer, his chair gone, Uncle Todd sleeping in his bed... He'd be stumbling into some terrible version of Goldilocks and the Three Bears.

The missing chair freed up a lot of space. The newly exposed section of wall behind it gave the appearance of missing a door. The empty area needed a painting or a window. I didn't like seeing so much naked wall. It felt imposing, like a giant wave about to crash and sweep us out into the cold, black sea.

"Stand over there," Uncle Todd said, pointing to the wall. "I want you all to see me good."

We could see him fine. Uncle Todd's flashy clothing always drew eyes to him.

"Now, I'm not going to be like your parents and drag you to church. That's a decision you have to make for yourselves. All I ask is that we spend some time together. You can worship God without going to church."

One time, during Dad's beloved matinee movie, I asked him if there really was a God or not. I trusted Dad to have the correct answer.

Dad sipped his beer, giving himself time to think. After collecting his wisdom, he said, "All the evidence in the world says there is no God; however, we still have to contend with the fact that there's existence." He patted his face; he patted the arm of his chair. "All this... stuff. What is it, atoms and shit? Just coming from nothing, forming into these intricate systems like plants and rocks and TV shows. Sometimes I think we ought to be running around in a state of constant awe, amazed that all this stuff is *just here*. It's incredible." His movie came back from commercial, putting an end to our theological discussion.

Incredibly, the twins seemed to miss church, because they immediately took advantage of Uncle Todd's spiritual knowledge. They had questions.

For example, the twins wanted to understand a passing statement made by the gargoyle church minister about how our faith taught there were no such things as ghosts.

Their interest pleased Uncle Todd. While Dad enjoyed needling him with nuisance questions (like: where did Cain's wife come from?), it delighted Uncle Todd to discuss honest matters of a spiritual nature with his nieces.

"No ghosts. After death there is only oblivion. The soul goes to sleep, to be awakened on Judgement Day."

"When we die, we'll become nothing?" This bleak outlook disappointed them.

Uncle Todd shrugged like it was no big deal. "Just the same as before you were born."

I shuddered. What an awful thought, to become nothing after you died. Being nothing before you were born was no big deal as you could always read about the things you missed before you were alive, but who wants to miss out on all the interesting things that will happen between your death and the end of time?

Uncle Todd had a more positive outlook. "You should rejoice, for the dead are unaware of the passage of time. To them, death is like blinking, a millisecond passing between their final breath and opening their eyes on the Resurrection."

Soon, my older sister jumped into the conversation, raising her own doubts on the possibility of an afterlife.

"Your brain is an organ, the same as your heart or your lungs, capable of being injured. What about people like Ricky Castle, who get injured in the womb and aren't born with healthy minds? How would he awaken during the Resurrection? Back to normal? Your mind can't travel to the afterlife if it's capable of breaking."

She mentioned Ricky specifically to taunt Uncle Todd, reminding him of who pounded his face raw, but Uncle Todd didn't rise to my older sister's provocation.

"Oh, Rebecca. What makes you think your consciousness survives death? Only the soul is eternal."

This sudden fixation on death and the mystery of the afterlife concerned Grandma, who didn't consider this appropriate conversation for the twins. To change the subject, she cupped a hand to her ear and said, "Do you hear that? Sounds like someone is crying."

We didn't hear anything but Grandma must have. I suppose being older and having spent so much of her life as a caregiver made her more attuned to suffering. She went into the basement, and when she returned, she held the small white dog in her arms. The animal lay limp, boneless like a furry jelly fish, his body starting to slide through the gaps in Grandma's arms.

Uncle Todd looked neither surprised nor alarmed at the injured animal. *You did this*, I wanted to say. He must have hidden something nasty in the basement, knowing he'd be bringing an extra, four-legged passenger home with us. I pictured a plastic dog dish slathered in chocolate, which dogs found poisonous. Maybe grapes, which were so populous in the region we'd been taught at school never to feed to dogs or they'd go into shock and die. Or maybe Uncle Todd set out nothing more elaborate than a piece of meat doused in rat poison.

"Poor little guy," Uncle Todd said, lifting the animal's ear, flopping the thin fold back and forth. Animals don't like people messing around with their ears, doing so is the best way to get nipped, yet the little dog didn't protest the rough handling. He lay flat on the floor where Grandma placed him, his stomach rising up and down irregularly, seeming to only take every second or third breath.

Bring him home, I wanted to say. *Bring him to his family. If he's going to die, let him see them one last time.*

Kneeling over the dog, placing his head against the animal's side to listen to his heart, Uncle Todd slapped his hands together, like a brilliant idea had suddenly hit him. "I think he needs some loving energy. Let's all bow our heads and think about him."

Behind us, the living room wall began to purr.

My hand itched, wanting to touch the wall, but not in front of my older sister. I had to set a better example, for both her and the twins. I crushed my hand between my legs, holding it tight so it didn't develop a mind of its own and wander to the wall. I squeezed my knees until the joints cracked. Everyone must have thought I badly needed a pee.

"Hold hands," Uncle Todd urged us. "I think his spirit is coming back. You getting better, boy?"

Uncle Todd grabbed the dog by his ears and yanked his head up. The dog's eyes opened. They looked red and unfocused. The mouth parted and a pitiful growl emerged.

"How's the boy feeling?"

Uncle Todd jerked the dog's head back and forth. I wouldn't treat an old stuffed animal that way. The dog whimpered.

"Come on, boy, quit playing around. Stop faking."

Before I could say anything to stop him, Uncle Todd placed one knee on the dog's hind leg and twisted the body. There was a crack, and the leg stretched into a long tube of empty skin between the two broken bones. The dog tried to howl but the weakest of sounds came from his throat. His backside unleashed a torrent of shit onto the rug, splattering Uncle Todd's knees.

I couldn't hold out any longer. My hand slid across the wall, delving deep into the purring. During the whole experience I bit down on my tongue, filling my mouth with the penny taste of blood and jackhammering my senses with self-inflicted pain, anything to distract from the pleasure of stroking the wall. I didn't touch for selfish reasons.

Almost immediately, the dog sprang to life. He lunged at Uncle Todd's face, his teeth just missing the tip of his nose. The animal landed on four strong paws and scrambled into the dining room to hide under the table. You could see the broken leg had mended, perhaps sturdier than before.

"Will you look at that," Uncle Todd said, rubbing the spit from the tip of his nose. "What a faker. Just looking for attention." He smiled at me and winked, as though we shared a secret.

I expected my older sister to razz me for touching the wall after promising Mom I wouldn't, but she turned out to be more understanding than anticipated. "I was about to touch the wall myself," she whispered. "Even though that's what Uncle Todd wanted, to know how we do it."

Not to say she was completely devoid of criticism.

"Only I was going to put the dog to sleep. You didn't do him any favours sparing his life. Now he has a chance for even more awful things to happen to him."

We weren't through yet. Immediately after reviving the dog, before the vibrations and purring ceased, Uncle Todd backed me up against the wall and handed me the empty pop bottle. He did not smile. He loomed over me as though I were a wretched sinner and he had the hotline to God's ear. One word from Uncle Todd to the almighty determined my fate— either salvation or holy wrath.

"Let's try this again. This time, do what comes naturally."

For a moment, I thought "do what comes naturally" meant he wanted me to squat over the bottle and pee inside. One look at the tiny opening in the mouth convinced me there's no way I wouldn't have messed all over the floor. I was about to ask Grandma to lay down newspapers.

"Hold on tight."

I gripped the bottle by the neck, squeezing until my knuckles turned white and threatened to break through the skin. I wanted Uncle Todd to see I had strength and things would turn out bad for him if only I could wrap my hands around his throat.

"Now use your other hand and touch the wall again."

I wouldn't. Not again. I wished I was tall enough to smash the bottle over Uncle Todd's head. While he knelt dribbling blood on the floor, before he could regain his senses, I'd use the other half of the broken bottle to stab my palms, slice away all the skin. A painful sacrifice, but necessary. I recalled hearing an old expression once, something about it being better to lose your hand than your whole self. Something like that.

When it became obvious I wouldn't cooperate, Uncle Todd took a knee, bringing himself down to my level, but not for negotiations. He went straight to threats.

"Come here, girls," he called the twins. He spread his arms, beckoning them closer for a hug. He dared me to disobey him with my younger sisters in his grasp. Imagine their tiny legs stepped on and their bones shattered.

The empty pop bottle took on weight. I gripped it with both hands, struggling to keep it aloft. My arms shook. Uncle Todd rested his hands over the twins' heads, rubbing the bristles of their matching close crops. He didn't touch them gently. Both girls' eyes squinted into tight slits from the pressure of his "healing hands." The *britz*-ing of their stubble rubbing against his palms sounded like zippers and I pictured the skin from the top of their skulls to the bottom of their chins parting to reveal the bloody bone and muscles underneath. Having their skulls exposed to the air would sting, and without skin to hold them in place their eyeballs would pop out of their sockets and roll across the floor.

My arms became light. Before I knew what had happened, my older sister stepped forward and relieved me of my burden, taking the pop bottle from me.

"She can't do it twice in a row. You'll exhaust her."

I stepped away from the wall. I grabbed hold of her arm, begging her to be my protector.

Holding the bottle with one hand, my older sister pressed the other against the wall. Her hand lay flat and she stroked in tiny circles. She lifted her palm every now and then, grazing her fingertips against the surface in a tickling motion.

Behind us, the wall purred, setting off vibrations of such intensity the hem of our skirts lifted, as though we were catching a strong breeze. Seeing Uncle Todd keep a straight face, pretending he didn't notice the sudden activity swirling within the wall, impressed me. Beneath his cool demeanour, Uncle Todd longed to fall to his knees and smush his face against the faded wallpaper. It must have tortured him to stand there and pretend nothing special occurred, yet he managed to restrain himself.

Something in the wall boomed, like a bolt of lightning, coming without warning and startling the four of us. Together, we leapt into the air as if we'd been prodded with sharp sticks. Even the twins blurted out words I'd never heard from their mouths before. It was an elegant use of profanity. They seemed mature to have a vocabulary so polished.

The bottle fell to the floor with a clatter, spinning around, the hollow mouth making a *whoo-whoo-whoo* sound. Uncle Todd scooped the bottle up and threaded on the cap. Sandwiching the top and bottom between his palms, he raised the centre of the bottle to his eyeline, as though peering inside at an imprisoned insect.

Grandma looked too, but when Uncle Todd offered her the bottle, she stepped away as if touching it would burn her hands.

"It's so much heavier," Uncle Todd said before shaking the bottle next to his ear. "I can definitely feel something."

The bottle looked empty to me. I don't know what the pair of them were so excited about. Tears ran down Grandma's cheeks. For a moment, I expected them both to fall to their knees and begin worshipping the mighty pop bottle.

"Excuse me a moment," Uncle Todd said. "I'm going to take this in my office."

Behind the bathroom door, Uncle Todd laughed. When he came out, he ripped the bandages from his face and we saw all of the cuts and bruises that Ricky inflicted were gone. He stuck a finger into his mouth to count his teeth. The missing pieces from the bar fights and car crashes of his youth had been filled in. I wanted to run my fingers through his hair, check and see if the scars on his scalp had vanished as well.

The empty pop bottle rested in the crook of his arm. From now on, he'd be carrying that thing everywhere he went.

Alone, in my older sister's bedroom, I got on my knees, closed my eyes, and held my hands together. I wasn't praying, as my message was not intended to be heard by God. I was apologizing to whatever random person would be struck down by a terrible dose of bad luck resulting from me touching the wall.

I didn't want to. Uncle Todd tricked me. I had to stop him from hurting that dog.

I pictured orphan children being pallbearers, struggling to carry the coffins of both their parents. Would my apology mean anything or only enrage them further? *A dog? You made this happen to save a dog?* They'd be well within their rights to be outraged. When a dog and a person were drowning in the ocean and you could only save one, you saved the person, even if they were a complete asshole. Everyone knew that.

I abruptly ceased my apology-prayer.

Once again, the sheets rustled as my bed was invaded. For a brief moment, I was willing to accept this as punishment for what I'd done. I soon changed my mind when the thing in bed dived between my legs, wedging them apart and snuggling into the warmth between. This couldn't be Ricky unless he'd shrunk. Whoever had snuck into my bed was heavy, but tiny.

The small white dog had come to see me, perhaps expecting us to be friends now. I couldn't bring myself to kick him out of bed, but I wouldn't pet him or name him. I wouldn't bond with an animal whose very sight filled me with feelings of shame and disappointment.

Sorry, but I should have let you die.

Wisps of music came from the big bedroom. For fear of waking others, my older sister didn't play her record at full volume. She didn't even have the player turned on. Instead, she used her finger to spin the record beneath the needle. The music seemed to play hundred miles away, and the speed alternated between too slow and too fast, but my older sister still managed to summon Ricky.

Without the music blaring, I heard each sound between the two of them as clear as if I were in the room watching. Their lips pressed together, the slick insides making smacks that turned my stomach. Ricky's rough hands ran up and down my older sister's nightgown until the threads ripped. Soon, I heard the sound of skin on skin. My older sister moaned across a spectrum of sensations. Over the course of one long breath, she sounded afraid, then pained, then relieved, then insatiable.

The little white dog growled. He should have done so when Uncle Todd first approached, instead of stupidly wagging his tail and acting friendly. The little dog had learned from his mistake. He wasn't trusting any new men.

Using his freshly healed leg, the little dog leapt to the floor and sailed towards my old bedroom, moving through the hall as swiftly as a torpedo. He barked in rapid succession, leaving not a millisecond of rest between each snap of his jaw. *RafRafRafRafRafRafRafRaf!*

The barking awoke both Uncle Todd and Grandma, who arrived in time to see the little white dog chase Ricky around the room before he scooted under the bed and disappeared. I thought Uncle Todd would have been disappointed to not get his hands on Ricky and toss him out the front door, but he was too delighted by Ricky's fear. In this moment, the pugilistic Ricky revealed his true, cowardly self.

"Alright, boy! Look at you!" Uncle Todd said, bending down to praise the little white dog, who continued to run in circles, still going *RafRafRafRafRafRafRaf!* Something had changed within the dog. After coming from generations of domesticated animals, the human bond had broken and the little white dog reverted to feral instincts. The damn thing had lost its mind. Couldn't Uncle Todd see that?

Apparently not. He tried picking the little white dog up, only to be immediately bitten. He let the dog go and it went scrambling down the stairs, looking for a lair to hide in.

Grandma turned her attention to my older sister, who tried hiding behind the door. She'd successfully snuck away from the couch she shared with the old woman, and now she would be made to pay.

Together, Grandma and Uncle Todd seized my older sister by the arms. Painfully twisting her elbows, they bum-rushed her into the bathroom.

My older sister found herself tossed into the tub. Her head banged against the enamel floor. While she was disoriented, they flipped her over. Uncle Todd gripped both her wrists, pinning her arms above her head. Grandma removed my older sister's nightgown. She wasn't gentle. I heard the fabric rip from her body. The tearing sounded like a tooth being wrenched out of your mouth.

Once they had her completely undressed, Uncle Todd and Grandma gasped at the multitude of marks all over my older sister's body. Red hickeys formed a winding trail from her neck to her stomach. Others pointed down between her legs.

The sound of her cries chilled me. Her humiliation woke the twins, who pushed against me, wrapping their arms around my legs, seeking comfort. Every light in the house dimmed, seemingly out of consideration for my older sister's modesty.

Grandma's voice boomed, carried by the heating ducts into every room of the house. Her voice must have even gone into the walls. "Why are there so many marks all over your body? All over your inside body?"

While Uncle Todd held my older sister down, Grandma pushed her legs open wide. The sight devastated Grandma, who alternated between pounding the rim of the tub, and smacking my older sister about the face.

After each *whack!* my older sister laughed. Her laughter

was born in despair, bitter enough to wilt flowers. The more Grandma whacked her, the stronger my older sister's laughter became, until it sounded like she had regained control.

Grandma threw open the faucets, attempting to drown my older sister's taunting laugh. She fought against the rising water, lifting her head and spitting out the cold brine, taking full advantage of the bathroom acoustics to broadcast her laughter, which now sounded unmistakably victorious.

FOURTEEN

Encouraged by the little white dog's success chasing Ricky off, Uncle Todd opened his arms to any lonely, hungry looking animal unfortunate enough to cross his path.

"I knew that dog was smart. He'll be good to keep away burglars. Intruders don't belong here, right, Emery?"

Uncle Todd filled the house with stray cats. Unfriendly, matted beasts who hid during the day, only coming out at night to look for food. These cats had no interest in people and refused to let us pet them. Any names we tried to apply were shaken off like so many drowned fleas. Three cats teamed up to take down the wild rabbit Uncle Todd found along the escarpment. The poor floppy-eared thing looked terrified to be inside a house. Its nose twitched neurotically and its eyes watered, surely smelling the piss of the hiding cats. We found the rabbit on the kitchen floor one morning, the meat on its back stripped to the spine. Such a waste; the cats barely ate him. At least the rabbit got one act of revenge in before the hunt, chewing through the TV's electrical cord, knocking the set out of commission. Uncle Todd didn't have it fixed. He said, "Just as well, nothing on but junky distractions." I bet he didn't even know how to fix the TV. Dad would have sliced a cord off an old lamp, threaded the wires together, and had the set good as new faster than it took to change a light bulb.

Grandma exhausted herself, fighting to keep the house clean against the tide of Uncle Todd's animals. She vacuumed the rugs, scrubbed the piss puddles, and scooped up their poop. She was always on her knees, looking tired and old. Despite what she had done to Mom, I felt sorry for her and offered to help clean.

Grandma smiled, the last genuine smile she ever gave me. She refused my help, saying, "This is your time to be young, free from sickness and worry and responsibility."

Whenever Grandma cleaned up an animal carcass, she breathed a sigh of relief, as if each corpse represented the lightening of her load.

Uncle Todd promised me and the twins exciting days ahead.

"Don't tell your teachers, but you'll probably miss a lot of school. Boy, are your friends going to be jealous when they see what we're all up to."

I kept my expression placid, telling myself, *Humour him, just humour him.* One of his stray animals darted beneath the dinner table, its rough fur grazing my shin, and I lifted my legs to avoid being bitten. We were all out of Band-Aids and hydrogen peroxide.

Uncle Todd did not make the same promise to my older sister. On his orders, she'd been excommunicated from the family. Much to her delight.

"It's going to be a beautiful day," Grandma said. "We ought to visit the botanical gardens in the Falls."

Skipping school to check out greenhouse flowers was not my idea of a fun afternoon. Grandma may as well have suggested we look at carpet samples. Still, the twins and I climbed into her little Chevy and drove to the glass building adjacent to the waterfall. The windowpanes were bright blue from reflecting the clear sky. Once inside, our attitudes changed. Grandma had chosen a glorious time to visit. Within the greenhouse's artificial climate, exotic flowers that would have withered and died the moment you took them outside stood in full bloom.

The twins and I enjoyed an immature moment, giggling at the white marble fountain whose centrepiece featured a young boy peeing a stream of water from his ivory privates. Grandma gave us each a penny to throw into the fountain and make a wish. I can't remember what I wished for, but I remember being mesmerized by the beauty of the flowers. In room after room, petals unfolded, displaying intricate designs and shades of colour I'd never seen before.

I wondered if people were buried in the greenhouse, for I would love to be put to rest in this rich soil and have these glorious flowers rise out of my bones year after year. It pleased Grandma to see us enjoy ourselves. We felt serene, perhaps even hopeful that we might be able to put the recent nastiness behind us and feel loved again.

Grandma whispered, "The air inside the greenhouse is special. Can you tell? Take a deep breath."

We breathed in. My head began to swim. Grandma was right—something intoxicating enriched the air.

"This is new air, my darlings, as clean and pure as a baby. You see, plants feed on the waste our lungs expel and transform it back into precious oxygen. This is how the world works. When you feed natural things, you are rewarded in return."

In the lushest part of the greenhouse, mist settled on our cheeks, making them sparkle. The twins, in particular, reminded me of fairies, and I imagined wings sprouting from their backs and the pair of them soaring high to the skylights. Plant leaves as heavy as elephant ears draped over our shoulders. Grandma squatted on her tired, cracking knees, drawing us close and whispering family secrets.

"You girls are going to do something wonderful for your uncle. Your parents are stubborn. They want to deny you all the rewards the world has to offer. Your uncle is the one keeping this family blessed. Not only today, but generation after generation, long after all of us and our children are dust."

The plants began to purr, massaging our shoulders while the branches bounced playfully through the swirls of fresh oxygen, tickling the tip of our noses with their sprouting buds.

"You girls are very special. From time to time, someone ought to treat you that way."

We baked a mountain of desserts. Crisp cookies with golden brown edges and chunks of soft chocolate, plump date squares dusted with oats and brown sugar. Grandma stood out of the way, content to watch us sift the flour and roll the dough. The delicious smells wafting out of the oven caught the attention of our stray animals and they flooded the kitchen, always getting underfoot. One yelped when I stepped on its paw, but I didn't care.

The Sunday morning church bells of our old gargoyle church sounded. Uncle Todd stayed out of the kitchen, preferring to spend his morning pacing back and forth in the hallway, watching the street through the front door. The weight of the world pressed on his shoulders. Relief did not come until a long black vehicle, something between a limousine and a hearse, pulled up out front.

The Party Women exited the car and strutted single file onto our porch, wearing fancy church hats and carrying identical black purses. These women went everyplace together. Some of them still had husbands; others buried theirs long ago. Uncle Todd welcomed them graciously, ushering them into the living room and sitting them down on Mom's sick couch, which Grandma spent all night cleaning the snot and animal fur from.

The Party Women intrigued me. Watching the order in which they sat down, I easily figured out the role each woman played in the group: who was the leader, who was the diplomat, who was the one with no idea the others spoke badly behind her back...

Anyone paying attention to the newspapers recognized the Party Women, who were photographed often, usually with stern, warrior-like expressions on their faces. They took a close interest in the region, making their opinion heard on all matters, from getting a new incubator for the hospital, to approving the new shield design on our police cars. They lobbied against bringing back hanging and toiled restlessly to abolish the gambling some churches hosted under the guise of Bingo.

Two summers back, the Party Women held an enormous gathering at the Port Dalhousie beach, with a big band, a million fireworks, and passionate speeches about how filthy the water had become. Very soon we wouldn't be able to swim in it. The fight against pollution had been lost. Man's short-sightedness and greed had vanquished reason and fairness. Soon, the lifeguard towers were replaced with metal signs WARNING WATER IN THIS AREA IS NOT SAFE FOR SWIMMING OR BATHING. You won't see those signs today, not because the water has improved, but because the warning became unnecessary. Everyone knows to stay out of the water by looking at it, too contaminated with a poison far worse than the bones of grieving birds.

The Party Women gifted the city with a final outing at the beach, kicking off their shoes and dancing into the surf. There is a picture, the lake as black as oil, reflecting the bloom of fireworks, and the Party Women standing in a chorus line, lifting the hem of their dresses as their bare legs kick and splash. It may be the only picture where they are smiling. You won't find another. Today, most of the Party Women's public pictures have been mysteriously redacted. Hundreds of negatives disappeared from the archives. You can go to the library and look at the microfilm newspapers, but they have been tampered with too. The articles are still there. You can read the Party Women's names and speak them aloud if you like, but nearly every photo has been scratched off the plastic film. Whoever did it must have used a microscope and a pin. I wonder if they missed the beach photo by accident or if it was the lone image the Party Women wished to remain as their epitaph; dancing together in the water, arm in arm, looking happy.

The Party Women weren't randomly stopping at our house for a neighbourly chitchat. Uncle Todd must have worked on the invite for weeks. If suitably impressed, the

Party Women had the means to elevate Uncle Todd to a grander church, not only by fishing those impressive cheque books out of their handbags, but by whispering into the ears of the right people, making the introductions Uncle Todd couldn't create on his own.

I looked forward to seeing him fall flat on his face. Maybe the suckers who watched him push people down on TV fell for his Saccharin-sweet veneer but the Party Women, I'm sure, were more sophisticated when it came to dealing with hucksters. They ought to chew him up and spit him out in five seconds.

"Good morning," Uncle Todd addressed his small but regal congregation, happy to be speaking publicly after his temporary retirement. He told the Party Women he didn't spend those months in the dark, licking his wounds, no sir. He had been lifting weights and eating a good diet. Building up spiritual strength, even greater than what he had before.

"Yes," one of the Party Women said. "Some people believe you have a gift."

I saw the empty pop bottle, held discreetly behind his back.

Grandma cleared her throat, the signal for my sisters and me to serve coffee and dessert. I felt too nervous to smile in front of them. They looked so stern, faces like shields. The skin around their lips and eyes stretched tight, looking on the verge of tearing. I wondered if they were sisters, for they had identical noses. Long pointed beaks. Dad would have called them "hatchet faced" and Mom would have bopped him one, demanding he set a better example for us children.

One of the Party Women ran her hand over my head. "Is it cooler in the summertime?"

"No," I replied. "The summertime is always much hotter." I figured she came from one of those countries where the weather was upside down and they had cold summers and hot winters.

She grunted, disapproving of my answer, but one of the other Party Women hatched a wheezy rumble that may have been a laugh.

Uncle Todd beamed, pleased to have his audience with the Party Women at last.

He jumped right into his sales pitch. Probably practised his words for weeks. "I want to tell you ladies about my vision. Every night, I have the same dream. I see a tent. The lone bright object in a field of black, like a ship on the ocean. People come from miles around, pouring inside, out of the darkness into the light."

According to Uncle Todd, there had once been a Golden Age for faith healing. He spoke the names of forgotten men: Kenneth Hagan, T.L. Osborne, A.A. Allan, Jack Cole. These preachers didn't confine themselves to churches. They raised tents and they laid their hands on the sick, and the sick were cured.

"When the doctor or surgery could do nothing and someone was told to go home and wait to die, people didn't give up. They knew there was someplace they could go and find a miracle."

These tent meetings were massively popular. A small tent might draw 5,000 people. On the same night, another tent would draw 10,000. A fellow named Oral Roberts owned the largest tent in America. His meetings drew 20,000, even 30,000 people.

"Back in those days, people had a hunger for spiritual things. When they saw a miracle happen, you better believe word spread."

These old-time healers meant business. When you went to one of their meetings you wouldn't see just one person get out of a wheelchair, you would see a hundred stand up. Eyeballs grew back, legs grew out, you'd hear bones crack and twisted arms unravel. There was power at that time.

The glory days went on throughout the 50s and early 60s, but man's heart became competitive and jealous. The healing movement was now about who brought in the most money. One healer would buy a piece of canvas to make his structure two feet bigger and boast he had the biggest tent. Then another healer would go out and buy a piece of canvas so he could claim *he* had the biggest, and so these two fools would escalate back and forth, adding sections and poles, each trying to be the biggest. Others turned to vandalism. During service, a competitive preacher would tie one end of the tent to their car and speed away, ripping down a whole section. Or they resorted to setting fire to their competitor's tent. People got trampled, a few burned up.

"And the Lord punished them by shutting the entire movement down. He turned off the tap and there were no more miracles. Any man claiming to be a healer was a liar, because the Lord took His blessings away."

"What are we to make of your claims of healing, then?" one of the Party Women asked. "That you're a liar?"

"Take me as a sign that the Lord is ready to allow the miracle of healing once again. He wants me to lead the movement, to start erecting those giant tents."

"Amen!" Grandma shouted.

Uncle Todd lowered his voice, speaking confidentially. "In fact, ladies, I sense an illness amongst you."

The Party Women remained silent. No one fessed up to being sick. They weren't falling for an easy trick. If the Lord truly had his ear, he should know which of them needed a miracle.

Uncle Todd wiped the empty pop bottle across his forehead. Drops of condensation clung to the glass, putting a shine on Uncle Todd's skin. He held the bottle between his palms and closed his eyes.

Everything darkened. A cloud the size of a continent passed over the sun, casting the living room into a blue murk like an underwater cave. Uncle Todd began to hum, for no practical reason, I'm sure, other than to build up drama.

He placed his hand on the stomach of one of the Party Women, kneading the skin, gauging the illness underneath.

"I sense you are in great discomfort."

She rose to her feet, astonished to have been called out by Uncle Todd.

Big deal. Any jackass didn't need God's help telling them she was sick. Her body had betrayed her. Unlike the other

Party Women, she didn't eat any sweets or even drink the coffee. She looked yellow and gaunt, and the smell wafting from her, like the IV Man, was unmistakable.

"Let me heal you."

Uncle Todd shook his face, making his cheeks jiggle. Sloppy grunting noises shot out of his nose. It was all I could do not to laugh. He sounded like a drunk imitating a pig.

The rest of the Party Women shifted awkwardly in their chairs. A couple looked down at their laps, embarrassed. I saw the big cheque Uncle Todd hungered for flying out the door.

"*Hukkkkk!*"

Disgusting. He spat on her. A finely moulded wad of white phlegm hit dead centre in her belly. She couldn't have looked more surprised if she'd been shot. Uncle Todd's juice oozed down the elegant fabric of her Sunday best, thick as raw egg. I'm sure the stain would never come out.

Clutching the bottle with one hand, Uncle Todd pressed his fingers into her stomach, digging into the skin and twisting. The wall came to life, purring loudly for the Party Women, showing off how hard the vibrations could make the coffee in their saucers dance.

He blew into her face and she toppled over, just like a tree felled by beavers. Timber! I didn't understand how a woman with so much life experience could be duped by Uncle Todd's fancy routine. That's what Dad called "the power of suggestion." Some folks wanted to believe in Uncle Todd so bad they made themselves fall over when he touched them. They were too embarrassed not to.

Grandma couldn't contain her excitement. She clapped her hands and whooped.

The other Party Women were stunned, regarding Uncle Todd with a mix of fascination and fear. He could back up his bluster, he'd demonstrated that.

Helping the fallen Party Woman to her feet, her knees knocking together like a newborn foal taking its first step, Uncle Todd said, "I want you to go to your doctor and watch the stupefied look of amazement on his face when he proclaims you to be, beyond all rational explanation, fully cured. Miraculously cured."

"Amen!" Grandma proclaimed.

"You're not cured," I said, forgetting my place. I didn't care if I embarrassed Uncle Todd and Grandma, and I didn't care what they would do to punish me once the Party Women left.

Touching the wall once hadn't restored Dad's strength indefinitely. Each day, I had to touch the wall for him anew, arousing the purring and causing who knows how many tragedies across the city. Unless Uncle Todd visited the old woman every day to touch her with the bottle, her disease would grow back and she wouldn't last until the year's end.

"Your pain might have gone away, but not forever. You're still going to die."

The purring in the wall subdued. A worrisome idea crossed my mind as painfully as a razor slicing over my eyes. What if Uncle Todd did intend to heal her every time her illness returned?

He chuckled. *Oh, ye of little faith.* He wouldn't argue with me. The proof was in the pudding. Now that he'd proclaimed the Party Woman cured, only a funeral would provide evidence to the contrary.

To the Party Women, I looked like some brat with no hair and a disrespectful spirit. The sun emerged from the clouds, filling the living room with radiant light. Our gathering continued undisturbed. Uncle Todd told the Party Women more about his vision and what resources he'd need from them to accomplish what the Lord wanted.

"Erect a tent, fill it with thousands of people, and I'll deliver the kind of miracles no one's seen since the old days. The Lord wants me to heal everyone."

Thousands of miracles.

Thousands of drawings from the wall.

Thousands of terrible things.

FIFTEEN

The animals fought through the night.

The sounds of slaughter reigned supreme. Blood and hair swirled in the air like dust mites, filling my mouth with a dirty taste.

In the morning, the losers littered the battlefield. Strewn from the kitchen to the living room were dozens of twisted, bloody corpses. None killed for food. The necks and faces were chewed up but all the meat left intact. Amongst the massacred, I recognized the little white dog Uncle Todd had stolen from its front lawn. The dog's family had made MISSING posters and hung them on trees along our path to school. I wanted to rip them down, let the family know to quit searching. Juju (as the poster identified her) was not coming home.

The survivors crossed all lines of species. Both felines and rodents shared the victory. Former predator and prey snoozed side-by-side, their snouts smeared with blood and bits of fur stuck between their teeth. They respected one another, putting aside natural aggression, all having proved themselves as the toughest of the lot. Uncle Todd congratulated them. Impressed by their might, he fed them choice scraps from the garbage.

The task of cleaning up fell solely on my older sister. Grandma decided it was no longer her time to be young, free from sickness and worry and responsibility. She could get on her knees and dirty her hands. Outfitted with rubber gloves, a mop, and a box lined with newspaper to catch the drippings, my older sister collected the furry lumps and wiped away their blood stains. The water in the bucket soon turned red, clogged with whiskers and fur.

I snuck into the backyard, where my older sister emptied the red water and animals into a mass grave. This disgusted me. We were supposed to keep our food there. What happened if Mom and Dad came back and dug for groceries only to find a pit of bones?

My older sister pulled a cigarette and a book of matches from her dress. She exhaled smoke leisurely, enjoying her private moment of respite after a long morning of physical labour. She clenched the cigarette between her knuckles, her fingertips too muddy and bloody to touch the paper. Noticing me in the weeds, she looked around to make sure we were alone, no Grandma peeking at us, and held out the cigarette, offering me a puff. I hated the smell of smoke, how it rotted in Mom and Dad's mouth, giving a fecal taste to their kisses, but I would have taken my older sister's extended hand had she offered me death. I joined her at the animal's grave, gamely taking a puff, filling my mouth with smoke and making my eyes water. I passed the cigarette back. It was nice to touch my older sister's hand again.

Motioning to the pile of animals in the ground, my older sister said, "This isn't the only thing that happened last night."

"I know. I can smell it."

"Go into the street. You can see soot in the gutters."

I looked at the sky. Even the clouds were stained with char. The whole city knew what happened. No one needed to wait for their morning paper to find out the General Hospital had burned down.

Hours after Uncle Todd "cured" the Party Woman, the same building where Grandma had Mom hidden away from us began to glow orange and belch smoke over the city. When I closed my eyes, I could vividly see the conflagration at its apex; flames dancing on the roof, making maniacal faces. I heard inmates trapped in the Norse Wing, screaming from third story windows until they were forced by the flames to jump, rolling on the grass with broken legs, trying to smother the fire eating up their gowns.

In the chaos, many inmates escaped, eluding the line of police and firemen, scuttling off into the night. For days after, vans patrolled the streets. People locked their doors and called the police to report jabbering madmen taking refuge in their garden sheds or under their porches, their clothing still smouldering. It's doubtful the Norse Wing rounded up all of the escapees. I'm sure a few wander the streets to this day, wearing clothes stolen off clotheslines, cupping water from back-alley puddles to balm their cooked skin.

Such a destructive fire had been set deliberately. Someone wanted to burn and had no reservations about taking everyone else with them. Only dumb luck allowed the long arcs of water shooting from the fire trucks to quell the blaze before it spread to the main parts of the hospital. People comforted themselves by saying it was only the Norse Wing that had burned, as if the souls of those patients were all forfeit anyway.

The nurses in the Norse Wing had the duty of making sure none of their patients got hold of anything deadly. Most inmates had been confined there for trying to hurt themselves or others, so there were no tines on the forks, just blunt spoons, too thick to stab with. Before bed, each patient stood under the shower for a thorough scrubbing. If a patient got hold of a match, no matter where they hid it, behind the ear, in between their toes, the water disarmed it.

The Norse Wing fire started as an ember from a single cigarette. Of that, I'm positive. I can even smell the brand: Export 'A' Light. Whoever lit that fatal cigarette couldn't imagine the length and breadth it would burn. They were probably shooting past the hospital in a car, unaware a red spark of tobacco broke off and went drifting through the air like a dandelion seed. The ember was tiny but had the strength of the sun, capable of glowing for billions of years.

I wondered which patient caught the ember. Perhaps it

was Robbie Clattenberg's father, who already expressed an interest in setting things, including himself, on fire. Boy, wouldn't that serve justice right, allowing me to come into school with articles about the fire, letting Robbie Clattenberg know "This is your dad."

More likely, the ember drifted into the hands of a long-time inmate. One who had been in the Norse Wing long enough for the colour of their hair to change. One who had been there since coming back from the war, and I don't mean Vietnam. Whoever it was, they managed to pluck the little ember from the courtyard breeze, where inmates were encouraged to visit during pleasant weather. The nurses locked the doors when the inmates went out for peace and quiet. The nurses took this time to catch up on their TV stories or to steal a nap in the inmates' empty beds. To keep the inmates from pounding on the door, trying to get back inside, the nurses left chessboards in the courtyard but it was difficult to play because the cardboard pieces kept blowing over in the wind. The inmates couldn't be trusted with stone Queens capable of being swallowed or pressed into someone's eye.

Alone in the courtyard, no one saw the inmate catch the ember. He hid the red dot in the dirt under his fingernail, where the nurses couldn't see and the shower pressure couldn't reach.

He kept the ember for days, hidden under his pillow. When he slept, the ember warmed his ear. He blew on the ember every now and then, giving it lots of oxygen to keep going. At night, his room glowed red. He worried one of the nurses would discover the ember and snuff it out, but the ember survived each room inspection. In the bright sunlight, the tiny ember became invisible, easy for the nurses to miss. The nurses never inspected the rooms at night, knowing the moon filled the inmate's heads with bad dreams and made them dangerous.

His breath fed the ember, making it bigger. First the size of an apple seed, then the size of a dime. In another week it would be a baseball. He kept the ember hidden in his slipper, ignoring the pain like the Yogi on TV who walked over hot coals. The nurses noticed him limping and he knew soon they would be coming to cleanse his room with the fire hose. Every inmate's room had a drain, remnants of a darker era when inmates were beaten and their blood sluiced into the floor.

Working fast, he chewed strips from his bedsheet. He laid the ember in the nest of shredded cloth, which began to smoke and then spark and then burn. The rest of the sheet he stuffed under the door crack, making the room airtight. As the flame fed on the limited oxygen he began to feel light-headed, but he was not afraid. Before long one of the nurses smelled smoke. When she opened the door the sudden influx of oxygen swelled the fire to the ceiling. The nurse got blown right out of her little white shoes. The other nurses screamed and ran to pull the alarm, but it was too late, everything was already burning.

"No," my older sister interrupted. "That's not what happened at all." Taking a final puff on her cigarette, she tossed the stub into the open grave and whispered: "It was Mom. Mom started the fire."

My older sister dismissed my story of the Ember Man as nonsense, because every Norse Wing patient had access to fire.

"Everyone smokes in the hospital. Cigarettes are good for crazy people. Smoke is medicine for their brains."

"I don't feel good after smoking."

"You weren't smoking. You barely had a puff. I feel great."

According to my older sister, Mom simply filched a wooden match and set fire to her mattress. It wasn't any more complicated than that.

"Or maybe she set fire to her gown. Or maybe she set fire to another woman who ran down the hall screaming. Who knows what the fire investigators will find out?"

"Why would Mom start a fire?" She'd never done anything like that before. Mom was different from the other madmen, who hurt animals and pulled up women's skirts in Woolco, and did all kinds of disgusting things.

My older sister shovelled dirt over the animals. Inside the

jumble, a paw twitched, I looked away, hoping it was only wind ruffling the fur.

"Grandma isn't lying about everything. Mom is sick. That part's true." Just as Grandma told us, Mom suffered from an illness in the brain. Dark thoughts invaded her mind, and neither her love for her daughters nor her husband could dilute them.

While my older sister shovelled, I grabbed handfuls of dirt to throw over the animals. It hurt to look at them.

"Mom promised us she was getting better," I said. "Every day, she expected to get off the couch, good as new."

"When people get cancer or MS, they think it's bad luck or God's angry at them, but sometimes there's cause and effect. I remember when Mom first got sick. I saw the pattern."

Grandma called from the window, interrupting our secret discussion of Mom's illness.

"Emery, get out of that dirt! Those chores are for your older sister. Don't let her bully you into helping."

My older sister nodded, letting me know she understood. We'd continue talking later.

Inside the house, Grandma made me wash my hands over and over. She didn't want to see a speck of dirt on me anywhere. Her hands clasping my shoulders, Grandma reminded me that this was my time to be young. Free from sickness and worry and responsibility. "Leave the toil to your sister. Never forget, she chose to get her hands dirty."

The twins followed me along the sidewalk, sitting in their red wagon, each with a leg slung over the side to propel themselves. I wanted this to be a private trip. I told them to go home, but I'm sure you can guess how well they listened.

After several blocks, I came to an empty driveway covered in fresh oil spills. The house gave off the aura of being vacant, no parents around. The twins parked in the overgrown grass along the boulevard, while I climbed the steps to ring the doorbell.

Robbie's copper head peered through the window. He smiled and opened the door.

"Hi Emery, come on in."

I took a deep breath and flashed a secret signal to the twins: *If I don't come back, get help.* At school, Robbie always acted intense, like he was on the verge of either kissing or stabbing me. In private, he might behave worse, but what choice did I have other than to smile and follow him inside.

Robbie's bedroom stank of newsprint and dust. All at once my nose began to run. Newspapers surrounded Robbie's bed. A dozen towers, each nearly as tall as him. How could he sleep in such a fire hazard? A single stray spark from his mom's cigarette would send the whole house blazing worse than the Norse Wing.

This newspaper collection filled Robbie with pride, both as a curator and a scavenger.

"The corner stores throw away the copies that don't sell. Sometimes I find magazines too, but the covers are always torn off."

The papers smelled like trash. An off-putting mix of soda and rotten pizza.

"One time I found a gun."

"Liar."

"I'm going to bring it on the last day of school and scare the shit out of Mrs. Schneider."

Robbie dropped to the floor and groped under his bed, where I would never dare stick my hand. Countless gross things found in corner store alleyways were hidden under there; some of which would snare your hand like a bear trap.

He emerged with a bundle of newspaper clippings. Saved especially for me. I expected more lurid headlines about Dad (HEAD HALF CUT OFF BY SAW, MAN SURVIVES BY 'MIRACLE'... MOLESTER FLEES TERRIBLE TOTS... 3 HEARTS BEAT IN MAN IN ONE DAY...) but the newspaper clippings Robbie produced showed the burning Norse Wing moments before the walls tumbled to the ground. Robbie had retrieved today's paper just for me.

"Let me see."

I reached for the clippings too fast, too eager. My fingertips grazed the edges before Robbie jerked the papers away, holding them above his head like mistletoe.

"What will you give me for them?"

I knew he didn't want money. The alleyways provided Robbie with everything he wanted; money held no value for him. Whatever I offered for the papers would have to be priceless.

Seeing I was open to negotiations, Robbie closed his bedroom door, even though no one else was in the house to disturb his privacy. When he turned around, he unbuttoned the top of his shirt and puckered his lips like an orangutan. I relaxed. Robbie wasn't interested in my affection, just my humiliation.

I played along, giving Robbie the illusion of his total control over me. When he'd had enough, I took the clippings and ran out of the house. I made sure Robbie saw me scurry, knowing he'd like that, believing he'd frightened and confused me.

The twins waited for me in their wagon. Their faces lit up, delighted to see me emerge from the bear's cave with a few scratches but otherwise fine. They appreciated what I'd done, and insisted I sit in the wagon while they pushed me all the way home.

The Standard had a long tradition of upsetting readers with gory front-page photographs. Today's edition was no exception. The largest photo showed police dragging a body across the hospital lawn, both officers ducking to pass under the arcs of water shooting from the firemen's hoses. The pressure in those streams was powerful enough to take a dog's head off. Another photo captured the police in silhouette, either rescuing a survivor or retrieving a corpse (the caption didn't say). It chilled me to look at the burning hospital behind them, knowing inmates were trapped in the flames, many strapped to their beds, no chance of saving themselves. The worst photo showed a squadron of black leather bags. An accommodating police officer held one open for the photographer, giving us a glimpse of the blackened limbs inside. The bodies would have to be identified by their teeth.

The photographs made me cry. "What if Mom's in there?"

My older sister retrieved a shot glass from the kitchen.

Turned upside down over the newsprint, the bottom of the glass acted as a lens, magnifying the crowd pictures. With one eye over the cup, my older sister and I took turns scanning the blurry ink dots for Mom's face.

We failed to find her.

"Thank God."

"Exactly. Mom wouldn't stand in front of the hospital waiting to be locked up again."

"She'd run out of there as soon as she could."

"Her absence from the photos proves she escaped!"

For the first time that day, we felt hopeful. Chances were Mom was closer to us now than she had been the night before. She could be hiding anywhere in the neighbourhood.

Still, we needed to proceed cautiously.

"Is Mom going to be arrested?" Starting a fire was serious business, especially when people died.

"I doubt it. Nobody knows Mom started the fire except for us. There's no proof. Besides, even if Mom confessed, how good could her word be? She was in the nuthouse."

The police came. Grandma and Uncle Todd sent us away so they could speak to the officers privately. One of them was the same cop who'd brought my older sister home after she'd been in Ricky's stolen car. He noticed her and me listening at the top of the stairs but didn't say anything to give our presence away.

Although none of the burnt bodies were identified as Mom, the police said they continued to search the wreckage and expected to find her within the next few days. On the very minor chance Mom returned home, we were to call them immediately, as Mom would be confused, perhaps terribly injured. In a disoriented state she'd be dangerous. The nurses from the Norse Wing marked her files: "Aggressive."

My older sister shook her head, like the police were complete buffoons. "Mom won't come back here. She knows it isn't safe. She knows what the old woman will do."

"You're right," I said. "Grandma won't let Mom back here. She'll send her away."

"Oh, she'll do worse than that."

The hospital fire offered the perfect alibi. If Mom came home for a glimpse of her beloved children, Grandma would seize the opportunity. The official story would be Mom's bones remained unrecovered in the fire, and Grandma would be free to look after us forever. My older sister and I could run all over town, telling people Grandma welcomed Mom home, clutching a dagger behind her back. We'd be witness to the most horrible betrayal: a mother against her child. We'd beg people to come and search the freshly turned dirt in our backyard for Mom's mutilated body, but no one would believe us. We would be branded as "imaginative children in denial about their fire-bug mother," a polite way of calling us liars.

"Her and Uncle Todd together. They'll murder her."

Grandma's voice boomed from the kitchen: "Rebecca! You haven't started dinner. Get in here."

As part of her punishment for giving into temptation with Ricky, my older sister acted as our scullery maid. She ate in the kitchen, separate from the rest of us.

"Watch out," she warned. "Grandma and Uncle Todd will be keeping a closer eye on you now. I can't do any miracles now, not with my *dirty hands*."

She reached for the wall. Instinctively, I tried to stop her, like you would smack away the hands of a child reaching for a burning iron. I couldn't take the sound of the purring, not right now. Ignoring me, my older sister swept her hand across the wallpaper, massaging the pattern, beckoning whatever vibrated beneath the plaster to come to the surface for the attention it so craved.

However, the same as when the IV Man pressed himself into the wall, my older sister's touch stirred nothing. The wall remained dead silent. She rubbed until the skin on her palm turned flush, trying to rekindle the flame, but the power that had once flowed so freely to bestow favours was shut off. She might as well have petted a cold tombstone. The wall had turned its back on her.

I was astounded. My older sister smiled, looking at peace with the loss of her ability to touch the wall.

"I'm free, Emery."

SIXTEEN

The wall had brought our family nothing but pain. From swallowing New Kitten, to corrupting Ricky, to tempting Grandma and Uncle Todd into evil, to running off Dad, and, finally, nearly killing Mom. Before the vibrations and the purring, we did a great job of loving one another. Sure, there were squabbles and Mom yelled a lot. Grandma considered Dad a loser, but they could share a holiday meal with civility. From the moment New Kitten slipped into the wall, all of our comfort and sense of protection had been stolen from us. For the rest of my life, I will dream of growing up in a house without walls or floors, just a frame. Animals may wander through, and there'd be no protection from winter wind, but I would rather freeze to death than see our family destroyed.

Still, my older sister wanted credit for being the first to discover the energy in the wall, as though her natural curiosity made her clever.

Maybe her arrogance protected her. Without it, the guilt would torture her beyond all sorrow.

According to my older sister, she drew energy from the wall responsibly.

"I didn't ask for much. Only little things. I didn't even touch with my whole hand, just my fingertip. A little scratch."

To demonstrate, she tickled her finger under my chin, like you would twirl a dandelion to see if someone liked butter.

"Just wait until you start high school. Appearance is so important. So when I touched the wall and the purring erased the pimples on the end of my nose, what was I supposed to do? I could have asked for a million dollars. Instead, I appreciated little things, like soothing my cramps, and removing that black mole on the back of my leg that grew back no matter how many times I scratched it off..."

As she recited the litany of her blessings, I wondered how a girl capable of willing up anything she desired could be unhappy so much of the time.

"Eventually, I discovered the energy in the wall could be directed the opposite way. Not to heal, but to hurt." She shook her head, still bitter. "It's all the fault of that blonde, scheming bitch."

She referred to a girl at school, one of the adored elite, who'd noticed my older sister's poor dress and shabby hygiene and said something she thought was funny about it. A lot of other people thought so too and laughed. They laughed so hard that other people wanted to hear what had been said, and the Funny Girl repeated her joke over and over to an ever-widening audience.

"I didn't intend to go overboard. I only used one finger on the wall for her. Guess which one?"

My older sister expected light retribution, nothing lethal. Perhaps the Funny Girl would bleed at an inopportune moment on white jean day and she would feel the same humiliation her joke bestowed on my older sister. Maybe the Funny Girl would be tormented by nightmares, frightening visions that would deny her sleep, making her dull and unpleasant, and her circle of friends would drift away.

"I watched her closely for days but it sure didn't look like the wall did anything to her. So I kept trying."

Unbeknownst to my older sister, revenge had already taken root inside the mouth of the Funny Girl. The pleasure receptors in her tongue went to sleep, making lunch time a messy chore. Without the sense of taste, the act of eating became repulsive. The Funny Girl's mouth worked like a cement mixer, turning over the bread and meat of her sandwich into a tasteless, wet mass. Meals were thrown out barely eaten, only a few bites taken. The Funny Girl tried to shock her taste buds back into operation, buying ice cream to fill her mouth with sweetness, but each lick tasted like cold paint. Eventually, her entire mouth went to sleep and the Funny Girl didn't realize the tough hunk of roast beef she strained to chew through was actually her own tongue. Her friends didn't laugh anymore. They shrieked at the blood spilling from her mouth onto the lunch table. When the Funny Girl tried to speak, hunks of her tattered tongue flopped out. The torn flaps of meat dangled all the way to her chin. An ambulance came, and luckily for her, the doctor who stitched her up was adept at jigsaw puzzles. It took skill to fit her jagged strips of flesh back into a flat tongue. The feeling in her mouth returned shortly after, so she tasted the scabs and the black thread of her stitches. Her tongue swelled as it healed, making her talk like a cartoon character. Any further funny remarks about my older sister, or anyone else, were kept to herself.

"Where did all your makeup come from?" I asked, curious, since the wall wasn't like a genie who could summon physical objects.

"I took it from the store."

"You shoplifted?"

"Not really. Shoplifting means sticking it under your dress and sneaking out the door. Whenever I told the wall I wanted new lipstick, the clerk at Drug Mart would get a bad headache. She'd lay her head on the counter and cry. She'd be in so much pain I'd say, 'Hey, can I have this?' and she'd say to take whatever I want and just leave her alone."

I felt sorry for the clerk, who'd probably been visiting the doctor for X-rays, afraid of brain tumours.

"I'm pretty sure that's still shoplifting."

"God, I don't do it anymore."

I thought of the mountain of makeup stacked inside her

closet. I didn't dare ask how many times she *did* do it.

"You were right—we shouldn't have been touching the wall." It pained my older sister to concede her mistake, that I'd been the wise one after all. She didn't go so far as to apologize to me, but I sensed she regretted ignoring my warnings. She didn't linger on her mistake, quickly moving on to what was truly important.

"After you started touching the wall for Dad, I noticed things. Like how every time you drew from the wall, Mom got sick."

Every time *I* drew from the wall. Notice how she ignored any of the bad things caused by all *her* touching.

I remember Mom's sickness started small. Coughing at breakfast, her stomach bug making her smell up the bathroom... But the symptoms my older sister recalled were much more severe, having to do with the disease in Mom's mind.

"At night, she asked me to hide her matches and pull the knobs off the stove. She didn't care about hurting herself but she was terrified of doing something to us."

No matter what precautions my older sister took, they were never enough. Each night, Mom rose in a somnambulistic trance and wandered out of the house and into the road, nearly run over by the wheels of a car like a dumb cat.

I thought of the black bile Mom had vomited in the orchard after I'd touched the wall to get back at the Pincher, and her disturbing habit of staring into flames, her mind completely disassociated from our presence. "So we hadn't only been causing all those tragedies in the newspaper, we'd been poisoning our own family."

My older sister nodded.

I closed my eyes tight. How does one atone for such a terrible trespass? Perhaps for things this wicked, atonement is impossible.

"Now Uncle Todd thinks he can fill his bottle up anytime he wants and be all, *Look at me, I'm the miracle worker.* He's going to make you draw from the wall until the wheels come off."

"We'll refuse. We'll let the twins know what's happened."

My older sister shook her head. Nice idea, but too late in coming.

"He's still got healing in that bottle. When he uses it, Mom will feel it hard. Do you know what happens when a person is allergic to bee stings? They swell up like a balloon and their skin fills with poison. Each time they get stung, the reaction becomes worse and worse until finally they die. How many stings has Mom endured from the wall already? The last time Uncle Todd used the energy in the bottle Mom set the goddam hospital on fire. How much worse do you think it'll be next time?"

Her question frightened me. I imagined Mom in her allergic madness, setting fire to everything around us, drowning the entire city in a tidal wave of flames.

My older sister's prediction sounded no less apocalyptic.

"Mom will die. She'll close her eyes, forget everything, and never remember again."

I stopped breathing. Hearing her speak of Mom's death with such certainty made spots appear before my eyes. The wall began to purr, eager to dispense more sickness and tragedy.

"Leave us alone!" I flung a heavy book at the wall. The spine broke and the pages lay spread on the floor, like a bird that had flown into a skyscraper window.

My older sister put her arms around me. "There's something you have to do tonight. Something that helps Mom for real."

I felt more than up to the task. My older sister gave me something to rage against, and with her confidence in me, I could barely wait for night to fall.

"This'll make Mom all better?"

My older sister bit her lip. "Well, it'll help protect her from getting stung again."

Creeping down the stairs late that night, I stayed close to the wall. Dad taught us burglars liked to walk on the very edge of the steps because they were used less and wouldn't creak. I wondered if Dad ever burgled a stranger's house to know this. For my mission to be successful, I needed to move through the house silently. Not waking Grandma or Uncle Todd was key, but I also didn't want to wake the twins. My task would be dangerous. Better they not follow me into the lion's den.

I made it to the front hall without making a sound, only for the floor to crack like lake ice. I wished for a pair of snowshoes to spread out my weight and allow me to walk softly. Why could I just not glide over the floor?

On the couch, my older sister pretended to sleep beside Grandma. Should the old woman wake up, we decided, my older sister had a better chance of physically subduing her than I did. She cuddled close to Grandma, like there was still love between them. She gave me a thumbs up as I passed, undertaking the riskier part of her plan.

"You're so brave, Emery," my older sister mouthed. "I'm proud of you."

Grandma snored. Her grotty breath sawed the air rhythmically. I fell in time with her snores and took three long strides across the creaky floor, then waited fifteen seconds for the next wave of strangled breathing to cover my footsteps.

Surprisingly, none of the stray animals came out of the dark to nip my ankles. The beasts must be around somewhere. Maybe after gobbling one another up, the sole survivors were too fat to move, all belly and dulled claws now.

Mom and Dad hadn't allowed us in their bedroom. They'd given us the whole house to play in, but their bedroom remained a sacred space. They demanded we respect its sanctity. This prohibition, of course, made their bedroom tantalizing to us, and we'd looked for all kinds of loopholes that would permit us entrance. Mom couldn't figure out what made her bedroom so dad-blasted interesting. She never understood her messy nightstand with its sexy novels and desiccated apple cores revealed more to us than any diary she might have kept. Her bedroom unlocked a glimpse of the life she lived long before becoming our mother, an identity beyond her maternal role.

Yet there was no thrill in my trespass now. Rooms never have personalities of their own, only what's rubbed off from the people who live in them. With Mom and Dad gone, the bedroom ceased to be theirs, so all its mystery and magic disappeared.

I crawled on my stomach, using my elbows to pull myself forward. From the floor, I saw Uncle Todd crashed out on the bed, the centre mound of his stomach rising and falling with mechanical regularity. Once I reached the side of the bed I held my breath, not wanting him to awaken. If he reached over the side and swatted my head with his healing hand, my brains would smash against my skull, mixing up like egg yolk. A divine lobotomy.

So long as Uncle Todd slept, I'd be safe.

Where did he keep his bottle? My older sister offered no guide, just told me to sneak in the bedroom. She trusted me to figure out his hiding place. I ran my hands over the nightstand, clear now of Mom's fossils, covered instead with Uncle Todd's pocket change and sweat bands. The bottle was too precious for Uncle Todd to leave out of his sight. He must sleep with the damn thing tucked under his arm like a teddy bear. I grimaced at the thought of having to crawl beneath the covers like Ricky. I'd rather lay down with a man-eating tiger. Mustering up courage, I snaked my hand under the sheet, groping across a mattress warmed by Uncle Todd's body heat, searching for the bottle.

I had my arm buried up to the elbow in Uncle Todd's sheets when a loud creak sounded through the house, rippling for several seconds like a sustained fart. I froze. A second creak followed, running from the front hall to the foot of the stairs. I slowly withdrew my arm before Uncle Todd could open his eyes and seize me.

My older sister, *goddam her*. She'd left her position on the couch beside Grandma and was running up the stairs, not even using the edges to lessen her footsteps. She stomped like she wanted to wake the whole house up. I waited for Grandma's voice, stirred awake and angry, yelling for my older sister to get back, but her snoring continued uninterrupted, the same steady pattern.

Something soft and mushy on the bedroom carpet smeared across my hand. From one of the animals, no doubt, but in the dark I couldn't tell if it came out of the mouth or the back end. Uncle Todd had better put his socks on first thing in the morning or else he'd step in quite the mess. I wiped my hand clean and knew immediately I was in trouble. Hot breath hit my wrist. Hot breath from multiple mouths, all of them hiding under the bed. The surviving animals slept there, as many as a dozen, and I'd awakened them.

Keep still, I told myself. Most animal's vision depends on movement. Anything quick begs to be pounced on. That's why you never run. You can fool animals by backing up slowly, no faster than the hands on a clock.

One by one, the animals emerged from their lair, claws scratching the carpet. Not wanting to move, I remained crouched at their eye level, face-to-face. Showing no fear, they climbed over my hands. First the tickle of fur, then the prick of their nails. I kept my mouth locked. When the inevitable bites came, I couldn't scream. I would have to endure. The animals would bite me, I knew, because that's what wild animals did. They weren't pets. All had refused names. Each had earned their place by devouring the weaker.

While I did my best to be small and hold any noises, my older sister clunked around overhead. Her footsteps moved from the top of the stairs to our old communal bedroom. Uncle Todd and Grandma continued to snore, even when my older sister dropped the record needle and scratchy music began to flow from the speakers.

Animals surrounded me. Growls vibrated in their throats, as threatening as any rumble coming from the walls. The first nails dug into my back, and I moaned softly as one of the heavy animals struggled to climb aboard. I hoped it to be a fat, football-shaped cat, but the scent suggested a bigger, more dangerous animal. A raccoon or a skunk. Hot breath blasted from its snout onto the back of my neck, then wetness hit my skin. A

231

drop of drool. I twisted my back, trying to cast him off before I felt teeth pierce my skin. More animals circled me, their fur brushing my arms and legs. They squatted on my hands, butted their heads into my side. I was being detained.

A second animal tore my nightgown when it climbed on my back. Balanced on my spine, the two animals snarled, each attempting to establish dominance, too preoccupied to notice a third beast climbing onto my shoulder, his long tail dangling against my lips. Did the animals plan to continue piling on until I buckled beneath their weight, pinned to the floor? Smart creatures. I hoped their bellies had the patience to hold me until morning. Remembering the vicious way they fought one another, I feared Uncle Todd would awake to find nothing left of me but a tattered nightgown and gnarled bones surrounded by his animals, sleeping fat and contented.

My older sister's feet pounded on the ceiling, giving herself over to the music and dancing. Did she have her old wig on? Was she watching herself in the mirror?

A smaller creature, a squirrel I think, dug its nails into my cheeks and crawled up my face. The claws were tiny and stung like paper cuts. If I got out of this, I'd have to splash hydrogen peroxide all over my body. Every claw must be diseased, covered in filth and death. While the squirrel dangled from my forehead, I bit his tail. Beneath the fluffy hairs it felt thin and tough, like a strip of licorice. The squirrel went wild, digging its claws into my scalp. Since it was the only part of my body I could move, I jerked my head, sending the squirrel flying across the room and crashing into the sharp edge of the dresser. It took several rapid breaths before lying still, the mob reduced by one.

Before I could spit the disgusting tail hair out of my mouth, the rest of the animals charged, working together to bring me down. The heaviest perched on my neck while the smallest nibbled my elbows. Why had I come in here alone? I should have dragged a length of dental floss with me, tying one end to my wrist and leaving the other with my older sister, like an air hose running from a deep-sea diver's helmet that could be given three sharp tugs to alert the boat above of danger. But I had foolishly dived into this black ocean without a tether or a diving helmet or even a compass to point the way back to the boat. I didn't have air in my lungs for bubbles to guide me to the surface. My heavy body would soon settle to the ocean floor, amongst the shark bones, before I closed my eyes and forgot everything and never remembered.

The weight of the animals broke me. My stomach pressed against the rug and the animals crowded around, forcing their long, bushy tails into my mouth, making it impossible to call for help. One long tail entered my throat, trying to make me gag. I choked on my own sick. Spitting up was impossible. My mouth and nose were so backed up with hair I felt tufts coming from behind my eyes.

New feet entered the bedroom and I sighed, relieved the worse was over.

As soon as I smelled the cigarette smoke, I knew I was wrong.

I was not rescued by Ricky any more than a mouse in a glue trap is rescued by the cat that devours it. He picked the animals off me without regard for my comfort. Teeth and nails ripped from my skin as his rotten cigarette ash rained down on my face. The animals put up no fight, scampering away. Some protectors they turned out to be. All teeth and no real bite.

Ricky yanked the final tail out of my mouth. My throat remained clogged with fur, like I'd swallowed a mink coat. I worried about my injuries. Did I have rabies? Would I transform like Dad's beloved Wolf Man into a half girl/half squirrel whenever the moon is nut shaped? I hadn't much time to collect myself before the full weight of Ricky landed on my back. Those long, dusty arms that once held my older sister while they danced now hooked under my arm pits, immobilizing me, preventing any chance I had of fighting back. I couldn't grab for anything, not even Uncle Todd's big toe hanging off the side of the bed. Ricky pressed one hand against my bare head, pinning my chin to my chest while his other hand clamped over my mouth. Ricky lifted me onto my knees with such precision I felt like we'd been practising this moment for ages.

More than fear, more than pain, the sensation enveloping me was familiarity, as though I'd experienced being held this way before, as a prisoner in a man's arms, across a multitude of different locations and times.

I smelled forest and the green scent of leaves while my knees pressed into soft moss. Then I shifted, my knees now feeling the hardness of stone, then the coolness of marble, and then the grittiness of sand. My memory filled with many scents (hay, smoke, animals) and sounds (music, lowing, laughing). They merged into a feeling of unity. All around me, I heard the whispers of every woman before me who had been forced onto her knees with a man on her back. If I listened closely, I could parse the collective and identify individual women. Would I find Grandma on her knees? Mom? My older sister? I began to weep, not with sadness, but gratitude that I was not on my knees alone. All of the women who had come before me were here, experiencing my suffering as I experienced theirs. I remembered Mom once saying, "Many hands make the load light."

Ricky used his thumb and forefinger to pinch my nostrils shut. The smells of the past, of all those women's strength, disappeared, and my lungs heaved against my chest, begging for oxygen. *How odd,* I thought as my eyes began to darken on all sides. *This must be what it feels like to drown underwater.* All my senses shrank, like an iris closing. Soon I'd pass out, unable to put up a struggle. Already, I felt Ricky using his hips to lift the hem of my nightgown.

Two black eyes appeared in the doorway. I recognized them well, as my fist had created both of them. The twins turned out to be the best listeners in the house. They alone had heard my struggle.

One of them spat at Ricky. A large grey stone dripping blood from her leaky gums struck him in the centre of the forehead. He didn't topple over like Goliath, that would have been too easy. He maintained his grip over my mouth and nose, starving me of oxygen. Towards the twins, he hissed like a snake. *Get out of here! You're spoiling things!* His mouth sounded full of venom. I hoped my younger sisters had the sense to keep their distance.

The twins would not back down. They stood close together, heads touching. The wallpaper in Mom and Dad's bedroom puffed up, hinting at the shape of whatever lurked on the other side. Vibrations crossed from one corner of the room to the next. Through his pants, I felt Ricky's wicked instinct diminish.

Ricky cast me aside before scurrying like a lizard along the floorboards. His fingernails raked the wood, looking for an opening. Once he found one, he slithered away to his hiding place.

Above us, the music changed. With a new song came new footsteps. Now two people were dancing. My older sister in a loving embrace with the boy who'd attacked me. Between the two of us, she chose him.

The bloody stone spat at Ricky lay beside my head. My other younger sister picked it up and placed it back into her gums. I closed my eyes and passed out. The last sound I heard were the joyful dance steps of the reunited Ricky and my older sister, so I didn't care if I ever woke up.

SEVENTEEN

I woke in the bath, water up to my chin. Baking soda clotted my wounds. The twins sat on the tub's rim, their feet dipping in the water as they shampooed my scalp, plucking all the loose whiskers and nail clippings clinging to my skin. They found an embedded tooth, which landed in the suds with a loud PLINK.

My mind took a little longer to catch up to my body in awakening. For a brief moment I didn't think about who I was or what had happened. Only when my hand grazed the rug burns on my knees did everything come back and I began to shiver and sob.

The twins took turns holding me while the other washed. They rubbed me gently in the places I hurt; on my back, my shoulders, my face. Their tiny hands and thin arms treated me precious.

"He was right," the twins said.

"Who?"

"Uncle Todd. The dead are oblivious. Not in Heaven. Not ghosts, just nothing."

The twins spoke softly, barely moving their lips. Most of the words snuck out on the breath from their noses. I leaned closer to better hear their discoveries about the nature of the dead. My younger sisters sounded apologetic. They wanted to wait until I was mature enough to hear of these things, but we'd run out of time, so they did their best to explain in a way I could understand.

Initially, the idea that there were no ghosts shocked the twins. That must be incorrect. If the dead had no consciousness, like the church insisted, then to whom did the voices in the wall belong?

"When did you hear voices in the wall?"

The twins said they'd listened longer than they could remember, since infancy. The voices in the wall spoke low, without vowels, communicating by purring. Some nights the voices argued, each trying to make their viewpoint heard with so much passion the walls shook. Because the twins shared the same bed, they discovered the pair of them made a fine receiver, absorbing the signal broadcasting out of the wall. Pressed together, with their jaws touching, the purring from the wall danced across their teeth, tickling the enamel and wiggling the loose babies. The hollow of their throats became amplifiers, like the horns on old phonographs. When the girls slept cheek-to-cheek, they heard everything.

At first, the voices struggled for clarity. Late at night the voices attempted to build a collective language. Each voice had its own ideas about how many syllables and what pronunciation should be used to express ideas. One at a time, new words were tossed up for the voices to consider. The process was slow, every voice allowed a chance to give its opinion. By the time a decision was reached, a new multitude of voices had joined the collective, forcing them to go back to the beginning and start over.

Progress on building the language came slow, but by the time the twins started kindergarten, they heard the voices all the time, whether they were in the house or not. During nap time on the school's vinyl mats, the twins pressed their heads together and tuned in the squabbles they had come to think of as "our stories."

Eventually, the voices realized the twins were listening. One night, a voice happened to make a little joke, and my younger sisters giggled. This distressed the voices. They hadn't meant to garner a reaction. The building of their language halted and the voices went into protective mode, speaking all at once until their words (many of them still not approved) stitched a wall of sound. No gaps for syllables or rises in inflection. The twins could no more find meaning in the chaos of voices than they could pluck a single raindrop from a block of ice. By becoming loud, the voices silenced themselves, perfectly protected against the twin's eavesdropping.

This frenzied babble overwhelmed the twins. They no longer needed to press their heads together to receive the signal; the voices roared all day long in the hollow of their right ear, like tinnitus.

Reaction between the twins was split.

My younger sister found she quite liked the babble. It relaxed her, allowing her to feel private in public. Whenever she wanted to disengage, she turned her attention over to the constant stream purring in her ear, like slipping on a pair of Walkman headphones.

My other younger sister detested the constant sound. Couldn't they give her ears a rest for one minute? Luckily, she'd discovered a way of blocking the signal. A good-sized object (a rock worked best but in a pinch anything would do) absorbed the vibrations. It played hell on her gums and her teeth, but it stopped the babble from reaching her ear.

"If I press my head against you, will I hear the voices rattling around in there?" I asked.

My other younger sister spat the piece of gravel into her hand and immediately winced as the babble filled her ear. She made a face like she was itchy.

"Go ahead, but... how do you know the voices won't stay in your head? Maybe they'll be stuck in your ear forever, like us."

I didn't take such a warning lightly. I decided not to press my head against hers, trusting she spoke the truth.

The twins had discussed the voices at great length. Initially, they were certain the babble belonged to the dead. The voices in the wall were legion, their numbers equal to the grains of sand at Port Dalhousie, but they couldn't represent the voices of ALL the dead. There had to be other collectives, in other walls, having different conversations, building languages of their own.

So the twins put their theory to a scientific test.

Late at night, when even the man in the moon had dozed off, the twins left the house, carrying a suitcase they'd packed with equipment, and visited places where the dead were sure to congregate. At Victoria Lawn, they sat in the oldest part of the graveyard, where the white tombstones had eroded like salt licks. A century of rain had smoothed away the carved names. These were anonymous graves.

Sitting in the neatly trimmed grass, the twins unpacked an old telephone from their suitcase. They slid an old photograph under the base of the phone. The picture came from Dad's collection of antique photos he'd found at flea markets and garage sales. I knew immediately which picture my younger sisters had chosen—the one of a lynched man. The body hung from a tree, the ash of a fire beneath him. Only his head and torso remained, the appendages were burned away by fire. You could see the stumps of bone, white sticks protruding from his charred body. This wasn't one of those postcard reproductions that had been popular back in the day, sold for a penny apiece, but the original picture from some terrible family's album. Mom hated knowing the picture was in the house. She'd felt we had a duty to burn the photo and bury the ashes. Dad said we had a duty to preserve the picture for its historical significance.

Next, the twins poured wine over the grave. An offering. While the red libation soaked into the grass, the twins took turns lifting the receiver and asking to speak to whoever might be out there. They had many questions about the Land of the Dead. They focused on older tombstones, believing that to learn about being dead, they needed to speak to someone who had been dead a long time. Dead for so long, the voice likely had questions of their own. What year was it? Had the war ended? The twins thought they might tell the voice that mankind had travelled to the moon and expected to be laughed at—who would believe such nonsense?

The phone line remained silent. From grave to grave, nothing responded.

Failure did not deter their efforts. The twins were determined to prove the dead did not sleep in oblivion, but swam underground in a strong current, and if you stooped low and listened hard enough, you'd hear what they had to say.

So they experimented, using their telephone ritual to listen wherever the Dead might be. They tried the churchyard. Not a whisper was to be found amongst the rocks in the escarpment or the trees in the woods or from the depth of the lakes. Every place they listened was silent, even the sooty bricks of the burnt hospital.

The twins accepted their conclusion reluctantly; Uncle Todd, goddam him, was right.

The Dead are mute. They know nothing and haven't lips or breath to speak.

"Whatever the purring babble in the wall is, it does not belong to the Dead," the twins assured me. "Anyone claiming otherwise is a liar."

My older sister never returned to her place beside Grandma on the couch.

We found her sleeping in the upstairs bedroom, stretched luxuriously across the mattress, the soft sheet woven around her body like ivy, cupping her private areas but leaving most of her skin exposed. Her arms and shoulders were covered with goose bumps, less from the breeze through the broken window than from intimate satisfaction. She smiled, off in the land of good dreams, no doubt. The record player spun in the corner, the needle lazily drifting back and forth, scratching the same rhythm as her gentle snores.

Emotionally, Grandma cut my older sister loose. She wasn't worth the energy to punish. Let the lost child sleep her life away.

"Your sister could have done so much, such opportunity,

and now it's gone. Not even mature and already she's as use-less as her mother, or me."

The twins dressed me in long sleeves to cover the scratches on my arms but could do nothing about the marks the an-imals left on my face. Grandma held me by the chin as she brushed my stubble hair, promising me it would soon be long and feminine again. "You want great things for your uncle, don't you? You're not shortsighted like your sister, who gave everything away. And for what? To roll around on some bed your mother couldn't be bothered to change the sheets on. It's filthy." Her face lit up at the thought of a wonderful af-ternoon. "Let's take the sheets and burn them. We'll go shop-ping for new ones and we'll make up all the beds real nice. Things will be pretty around here once again."

The school day went by in a puff. I clutched my pencil but didn't lift it all day, returning my ditto sheets virginal. Robbie Clattenberg came at me during lunch hour, asking if I wanted to buy more newspaper clippings; he'd give me a good price, eager to get me back in his bedroom. Still holding my pen-cil—nails biting into the yellow paint—I considered stabbing Robbie. Poking out his eyes like a crow.

The end-of-day bell didn't register with me, I only no-ticed the other kids slamming the lids of their desks and racing into the halls, otherwise I might have sat there till the janitor came and swept me up with his long broom pushing lemon-scented sawdust.

My older sister lay in bed, wearing that ratty wig of our scalped hair. The cut locks had grown longer, reaching all the way to her ankles. The record player filled the room with ugly notes. Having finished dancing, her chest rose and fell rapidly as she caught her breath. I wrapped my arms around the re-cord player and lifted it, summoning strength I didn't know I had. The speaker cords ripped out with an electric crack. The record continued to spin, music rising wispily from the needle. I carried the record player into the hall and flung it down the stairs. The casing broke open and pieces of plastic scattered. The record shattered into a dozen black shards and the turntable spun like a dropped dime. I wanted to dance on the debris, crushing it beyond repair. The record player's siren call to Ricky would be silent now.

My older sister looked upon the wreckage but did not despair. Getting angry would only escalate the fight. She stood composed, waiting for the two of us to catch our breath, hoping I would feel silly, deciding I'd overreacted.

"Feel better now?"

She must have been out of her mind to think I'd grovel and apologize to her.

My crashing the record player down the stairs stirred Grandma.

"Emery! Rebecca! What are you girls up to?"

"Keep it down!" Uncle Todd called. He had serious work to do and couldn't be disturbed by our foolishness.

I grabbed my older sister by the throat, pushing her into the bedroom. I closed the door and made her lock it with her hairpin so we could speak in private. She smirked, dutifully locking the door with exaggerated ceremony. My sore eyes filled with tears. After what she had done, how could she mock me?

She wasn't ashamed.

"Come on, don't pretend it was so bad." She put her hands on her hips, trying to look like Mom. I hated her for posing that way. Blasphemy.

There would be no apology. My older sister wouldn't hear of Ricky's animal breath slobbering on my neck or his crushing weight on my back. She stood stubborn, betraying no emotion as I described his hands over my mouth to silence me.

"Instead of pouting you ought to be thanking me."

I lunged for her. Nails out, looking to draw blood. My agony made me clumsy, so my older sister swatted me aside. I tumbled out of her way as though I had no weight, like a doll made of balloons.

"I was trying to help you. You want Uncle Todd to make you draw from the wall again? That doesn't have to happen. Mom's safe from me. She can be safe from both of us."

I moved to the other side of the room. My entire life I'd looked for ways to be closer to my older sister. I envied her knowledge and her experiences. I'd considered her a better version of me. Because she would always be older, always a step ahead of me, I'd aspired to be like her my entire life. Now I could barely look at her. She would never have my trust.

She gave me time to myself. She picked through the records on the floor, brushing away Ricky's cigarette ashes before filing them back into their sleeves. Since the record player's corpse lay at the bottom of the stairs, she wouldn't be playing them anytime soon.

"If neither of us can draw from the wall, what remains in the bottle is all Uncle Todd will have left. And after we steal that, he'll be left with nothing."

I choose to believe my older sister forced herself to act cruel. She ignored my tears and pushed for me to suffer not because she was inhumane, but afraid. She wanted to protect me as well as Mom, but didn't have the luxury of time. My heart pitied her, as I could not imagine what it must be like to go through life capable only of making terrible decisions.

Outside the room, Grandma's feet tread over the guts of the record player and soon she pounded on the locked door, demanding to be let in. The plastic bags taped over the window reminded us she made no idle threats. My older sister couldn't afford to waste time now our privacy had come to an end, and she made her final point with anger, the most effective of all shortcuts.

"You want Mom to die? Because she will. Stop being so goddam selfish. You aren't special."

The door jamb cracked, courtesy of a good kick from Uncle Todd. They rushed into the room, relieved to find just the two of us and no one else. Grandma latched onto my arm and yanked me to her breast. She wiped the tears pouring down my face and glowered at my older sister.

"What cruel game are you playing on your little sister?"

Uncle Todd stepped forward, valiantly making himself a barrier between me and my older sister. He would keep me safe, protect me like his little glass bottle, aware of my fragility and how dangerously close I was to being irreparably damaged.

That night, the twins and I met in secret. We grabbed a book from the shelf and tore out the blank end page.

"What should we write to Auntie Linda?" I asked, counting on my younger sisters to help me compose the letter we desperately needed to send.

The twins deliberated briefly. "Everything?"

I needed to tear out more paper.

We were still writing at the break of dawn, our wrists and fingers sore, the smelly blue ink staining our fingers. We didn't dare not finish the letter. We couldn't risk Grandma finding it.

The twins struggled to write. The babble in their ears distracted them. I could tell by the way their jaws twitched the voices grew louder and more aggressive. I wanted to bandage their heads tight before they cracked open.

"That'll have to do," I said, putting down our pens. We opened the window and flung the letter into the wind, just as Mom always did, trusting our words would find their way to Auntie Linda's mailbox.

EIGHTEEN

Leading up to the Great Catastrophe, a stark line drawing of a circus tent appeared in *The Standard* each day. The ad ran silent, with no words indicating what the dark outline of canvas and dangling ropes advertised. A curlicue number in the tent doorway counted down the days.

Kids at school speculated the circus was coming to town. Shame they were wrong, as the circus would have provided the perfect means of escape for me and the twins. We'd stowaway in one of the animal cars, leaving behind Grandma and Uncle Todd and our older sister forever. We'd have to earn our keep, so the twins would paint their faces and join the clowns, while I'd stick my head in the lion's mouth, showing the audience I had no fear.

"This is your uncle," Robbie Clattenberg told me, handing over yet another clipping.

The same newspaper ad now included Uncle Todd's face, floating above the tent like a beaming star, or a guillotined head catapulted through the air.

There were no more numbers in the countdown. Instead, big block letters proclaimed: TOMORROW NIGHT!

A match flared outside my bedroom. Tendrils of cigarette smoke wafted through the darkness, searching for me. I cursed Ricky's presence.

The arsenal of weapons I'd assembled lay under my bed, in easy reach. I both dreaded and desired the chance to test their effectiveness. A cup of bleach, a handful of lye, and Dad's rusty axe. I slept with the axe under my pillow, even though I feared knocking into it in the night and cutting myself.

Ricky's footsteps approached. I prepared to attack. I filled my cheeks with bleach and slipped out of bed. The plan was to allow him close enough to wrap his strong, muscular arms around me and then I'd hiss like a cobra, spraying a blinding mist into his eyes. When he bent doubled in pain, I'd grab the axe. I practised cutting cords of wood in the backyard, imagining they were Ricky's skull as I split them.

A red cigarette tip floated in the darkness. The embers grew brighter as the smoker inhaled, illuminating a familiar pair of cheeks. Cheeks that were smooth, not sandpaper rough. My older sister blasted twin plumes of smoke from her nose, watching me with great suspicion.

"What do you think you're up to?"

I spat the bleach onto the floor. The fumes burned my throat like Halls cough drops.

"Not up to nothing."

"Have you ever heard the house so quiet?"

My older sister was right—the silence made a difference. Without her record player constantly spinning, the house felt hollow, as if the floors were made of eggshells and, if we weren't careful, we'd crack right through.

She hummed to herself.

"Come sing with me, Emery. You have a lovely voice. We'll sound pretty together." She began singing that song about prayer and being halfway there, holding the notes open, giving me a place to join in. She flattered me; I sang nowhere as nicely as her.

Without the music from her record player, she couldn't summon Ricky from wherever he hid. She missed dancing with him. Good. I didn't care if her bed felt lonely. He'd never lift my cover again. As soon as he tried, I'd bury my axe in his chest.

"Please, Emery. Sing for Ricky. I promise I won't be

jealous. I'll sit at the back of the room to give you privacy."

I stood mute. After awhile, she gave up with a shrug and walked back to her empty bed, trailing smoke.

Grandma threw me and the twins in the tub until we were scrubbed and fresh. Uncle Todd's big tent night had arrived. All were welcome.

Well, almost all.

My older sister loomed in the doorway, watching us splash around in the bath. She loosened her top.

"Maybe I ought to hop in to save water."

"There isn't room," Grandma said. "You can bathe after we leave."

The twins and I towelled off, crowding the bath mat while Grandma dashed out of the room.

"You stay right there. I have something special for you girls."

A patch of goose bumps spread down my arm, making my skin look tough, almost reptilian. The twins pressed their chests against the sink, leaning forward to reach the medicine cabinet where they found one of Dad's old blue razors. We had all played with them before. Whenever Dad slathered a shaving cream beard on his face, ho-ho-ho-ing like Santa Claus, he dabbed some foam on our chin and let us clean it off with the blunt end of his razor. One of the twins (it was currently impossible to tell my younger sisters apart) pulled the plastic open and removed the folded blade.

"Be careful with that—"

Before I could say anything, she swiped the blade across her forehead. The razor flicked quickly, looking at first like it didn't touch the skin, but a second later, a pink line formed over her brow. It turned longer and darker as more blood pushed its way to the surface. The blood grew thick as a caterpillar. The bleeding twin looked at herself in the mirror and smiled as a few drops hit her cheek.

Grandma scrambled to clot the wound with toilet paper, pinching the slit between her fingers and blowing in a futile attempt to stem the flow of blood.

"Oh, honey, your beautiful face! Rebecca, how could you let this happen?"

My older sister ignored the medical crisis. She stepped out of her clothes and lowered herself into the cool remains of our bath water. She splashed about, pouring the grey soup over her face and into her hair, happily bathing in our filth.

Grandma picked up the razor. She spat on the tip and rubbed it clean against her blouse, which I don't think is the way they sterilize equipment in the hospital. Grandma pushed the twins' heads together, examining their faces side-by-side. Using the first twin's forehead as a guide, Grandma drew the razor across the other's brow, making a cut of equal length, copying even the little curve at the wound's bottom. Once again, the twins were indistinguishable from one another.

"There," Grandma said. "Don't the two of you look perfect."

Happy again, Grandma presented the twins and me with her surprise—new dresses. They were light and airy, draping over us like togas.

"These will keep you cool. It's going to be a long night, and it's going to get hot."

She spoke like we ought to be excited but I doubted Grandma's idea of a fun night was similar to Dad's, who loved piling us into the car for a surprise drive-in movie. He'd wrap a bundle of hotdogs in tin foil and set them on the engine block before pointing in the direction of the Can-View Drive-In. Whizzing down country roads, the smell of franks wafted from the air vents. When we arrived, Dad popped the hood and ripped open the steaming foil to reveal cooked, plumped wieners. Engine cooking always disgusted Mom, but us girls gobbled them down. To this day, every time I eat a hotdog, I think of the smell of motor oil.

After rising from the tub, my older sister draped her arms over my shoulders, sending dirty water running down my sides. Her touch disgusted me and I moved away, but she held me tight, as possessive as her lover Ricky. She whispered in my ear: "Get the bottle before Uncle Todd uses it. Then run home and let Ricky do what needs to be done."

She kissed my cheek, smearing me with her fecal, cigarette breath. Her lips felt corrosive against my skin.

Uncle Todd proudly showed off his pickup. He'd swiped some of Dad's paint from the basement and stencilled flaming crosses on the side of the truck.

We squeezed inside the vehicle while my older sister stood on the porch. She folded her arms across her chest, watching us go. Being deemed unworthy of Uncle Todd's tent meeting complimented her, like getting a gold star. She looked forward to revelling in her wickedness while we were gone.

Along the drive, we passed a familiar copper head, Robbie Clattenberg, ambling down the street, lugging a stack of discarded newspapers fresh from the alleyway. He spotted me and waved. For the first time, his offer of friendship looked genuine.

I so badly wanted to join him, to leap out of the truck and abandon this sinking ship, but I needed to keep an eye on my younger sisters. It was still my responsibility to make sure they came home safe.

Uncle Todd slowed down, urging Robbie to climb in the back and join us. We were off to somewhere spectacular. Robbie laughed and continued on his way. I was proud of him. Uncle Todd shook his head as he turned the wheel, saying, "Woe to he that hears the call of the Lord and does not answer."

The tent was a mutt.

Erected in the parking lot of the Fairview Mall, the healing tent fell short of the majesty of Uncle Todd's vision. Anyone bringing the newspaper ad along was liable to holler "False Advertising!" The canvas walls were pieced together from different sources; one section white and the next beige and the third blue. The tent looked more like a serving of Neapolitan ice cream than part of the Lord's divine vision. The 127th Scout Troop assisted Uncle Todd's crew with the erection, because after all, who had more experience raising tents? The

Scouts exchanged their service for merit badges and seats near the front for the evening show.

Wood chips covered the floor inside the tent. A carelessly dropped cigarette butt would send the whole thing up. I saw that in a book once, about a circus. Hundreds of families and animals and acrobats burnt to a black paste. The exits in Uncle Todd's tent were few and inaccessible. In the event of a fire, there would be few survivors.

The crowds arrived, filling the plastic chairs, and forking over a quarter apiece for a hand fan with a picture of Jesus on one side and *John 3:16* on the other. My older sister would have scoffed. "The amount of energy it takes to wave that fan heats your body more than the breeze being generated cools it. You might as well drink salt water."

Or drawing from the wall, I thought, *which generates a larger unit of sickness than it heals.*

Seats were reserved for our family up front. Grandma held the twins on her lap, clenching their tiny hands in hers. The injured twins kept picking at the cuts along their foreheads.

"It's hot in here," I complained, causing Grandma to laugh.

"You think this is hot now? Pretty soon you won't have the room to move. Wait and see how hot it gets. You'll sweat that dress right off."

People continued to fill the tent. You could tell pretty quickly who'd been drawn out of curiosity and who'd been driven by desperation. So many wheelchairs. I wouldn't have thought we had so many cripples in the whole city; they must have bussed some in from Thorold. The wheelchairs got bogged down in the wood chips, so I did my best to help. I took the handles of a chair belonging to an older woman with frizzy grey hair. She looked back at me and smiled. As I pushed her through the wood chips, I leaned forward and whispered, "You should go home. Only terrible things will happen here."

The infirm showed up in droves, coming through the tent flaps on crutches, their skin jaundice yellow, some of them so withered you saw every bump and crevice of their skull. Some were walking skeletons. I took their arm, giving a warm shoulder of support as I led them to their seats. I took this opportunity to whisper in their ears, letting them know my mother was sick too, why should they be healed at her expense? Most took offence, calling for an usher to eject this rude girl clearly intent on causing trouble. Others took a gentler tact, telling me God's grace wasn't like a cup of sugar that got all used up. They said healing was for everyone; it didn't come at the expense of others. I shook my head, marvelling over how little some people knew and how proud of this fact they were.

Men with cameras staked out a corner of the tent to capture the miraculous feats Uncle Todd promised. Some came from Uncle Todd's church, recording for his silly TV show he had to pay the TV station to air, but I also saw people from the newspaper like Lover Boy, still running his tape recorder and wearing his scarf to hide Auntie Linda's warning marks. On the off-chance these images wound up on a TV where Dad might see them, I made sure to smile and wave whenever a camera pointed in my direction, mouthing the words over and over: *We miss you we love you.*

The heat under the tent grew oppressive. I flapped my dress, trying to get a good airflow going. Grandma chided me for "showing off my legs." This gave me an idea. I looked through the crowd for boys and invited them to come follow me into the parking lot.

Hidden on the other side of the canvas, I kissed them. Real kisses, with my mouth open and our tongues pressing together. I kept tally of the flavours of gum I tasted; counting two mint, one watermelon, one grape, one vending-machine pink, and two cherry.

Some boys broke our kiss and scuttled back inside the tent. Others tried prolonging our lip-lock. I had to stand on tiptoe to reach many of the boys' mouths. Only one required me to bend down to reach his tiny lips.

The kisses did nothing for me. I felt no excitement, not even a sense of superiority over my older sister, as I finally lived her fantasy of having all the boys line up to be with her. I hoped if I rubbed lips with enough boys, the wall would judge me as dirty and worthless as my older sister. I wouldn't allow Ricky to violate me, but I pushed my lips into as many boys as I could. It was worth a shot.

"Do you only kiss little boys?"

Roman stood outside the tent, peering from behind one of the metal poles holding up the canopy. His spying gave me hope that he was still in communication with Dad and I waved him over.

"Where's Dad?" Surely, old buddy Roman had been last to see him.

Roman lit a cigarette and told me he had been sworn to secrecy, but if I let him whisper into my ear, he would tell me.

I put both hands on Roman's chest and pushed him back. No way I'd let any man get too close again. Ricky's big trick was always pretending he had something quiet to say but, really, he wanted to get close so he could pervert-slobber all over me.

Roman told me Dad wanted to take a breather, so he asked Roman to truss him up in heavy chains before padding him into a steamer trunk, just like Houdini. Roman dragged the trunk to the railway station and tossed it onto a passing train, chugging to who knows where. Once Dad worked his way through the locks, he would make his grand escape and rejoin us, full of hugs and gifts and stories. Roman spun his tale with confidence, but I didn't believe a word of it. Living with Uncle Todd made me an expert at spotting liars.

Grandma came around the side of the tent. Roman jumped back to his hiding place behind the pole.

"What have you been doing? Your uncle is ready to start."

Respectful applause greeted Uncle Todd as he took to the sparsely dressed stage. The empty pop bottle rested on a wooden podium. Finally, his lucky charm had come out of hiding. Grandma had gussied it up something pretty, gluing crepe paper around the body and affixing little gold crosses.

The original bottle had looked cheap and ugly, so Uncle Todd wanted something majestic, like a finely designed Easter egg those Ukrainian women spent weeks decorating. He doted on that bottle like it was the Holy Grail, but to me it looked gaudy, like a cheap piñata.

He surveyed the impressive crowd inside his tent, waiting for the pre-show chatter to die down. People found a tent less threatening than a church, more inviting. Why, I bet if I hadn't known who Uncle Todd was, I would have been drawn in by the tent, which gave off the aura of excitement. A few hundred people fanned their sweaty faces with *John 3:16* paddles, flapping like a flock of birds. In the old days, before air conditioning, they used to haul huge blocks of ice as big as coffins into the tent to cool off. Must have made a terrible muddy mess by the end. I imagined women arriving in their Sunday best, with hats and pearls, getting touched by the preacher and falling to the ground, covering themselves head to toe in black mud, looking like coal miners, only their eyes and teeth visible.

A couple police officers poked their heads into the tent, making sure everything looked on the up and up, that we weren't going to be drinking poisoned Kool-Aid or taking our clothes off and dancing lasciviously.

Uncle Todd quickly silenced the chatter and commanded all eyes on him by declaring: "I am a false prophet!"

A few people gasped but not me. I knew Uncle Todd's declaration would soon be qualified with an "if" or a "but".

It was an If.

"I am a false prophet IF I don't heal the first five people to come to the front of this tent. It doesn't matter how severe your ailment is. If you have a visible tumour, if you are missing a limb, if you are blind, I promise the Lord will heal you tonight or I will give up the ministry. I will stop preaching."

It was a bold statement. I thought Uncle Todd's ego had finally got the better of him with this foolish challenge but he had things carefully under control. A few people made their way to the front of the stage but none of them were missing limbs. These were people with things wrong INSIDE of them, naturally. The ushers stood blocking the aisles, preventing anyone in a wheelchair from making first call. The cripples were all stuck in the back, mired in wood chips. Uncle Todd pointed and told them to relax. He would get there in time.

The first woman to walk the plank onto the stage looked great-grandmotherly, old and spindly, with hair as white and puffy as a poodle. Her crooked fingers formed an arthritic claw but it was her vision that troubled her. Uncle Todd pressed his hands on either side of her head and squeezed, as though he were preparing to lift her.

He promised the woman she would see clearly again only if the Lord felt her faith.

Sure, make it her fault if you fail.

While Uncle Todd manhandled the old woman, I turned my attention to the bottle. This was the moment I'd been waiting for. The source of Uncle Todd's power to harm Mom rested unattended, not twenty feet from where I stood. The pressure was on to come up with a plan.

Pop bottles do not break easily. On the schoolyard, I once saw Robbie Clattenberg conk Josh Gander over the head with a Dr. Pepper bottle, and you better believe it was Josh Gander's head that cracked open and spewed blood all over the asphalt. I approached the edge of the stage, thinking I could snatch the bottle and drop it to the hard ground, but the wood chips covering the floor were a million soft pillows that would cushion its fall.

The twins looked at me, wondering why I didn't smash the damn thing already. Give me a second, guys! Let me think.

On stage, Uncle Todd's hands shook and his throat made an ugly *EH-EH-EH-EH* sound like a stalled truck. He prayed loudly, beseeching the Lord to heal this woman, but you heard the first sprouts of panic in his voice. He started to sound desperate. Something wasn't working the way he expected. Uncle Todd laid his "healing hands" on the great-grandmother's head but her eyes remained cloudy. Like a teaspoon of cream in black coffee.

Time passed slowly. The crowd grew bored, talking amongst themselves; a few laughs here and there. Uncle Todd's arms shook and sweat dribbled into his eyes but he couldn't release the great-grandmother's head without looking like a failure. He had no exit strategy.

Of course, this was part of his showmanship. The pretend failure. He let go and backed away from her, waving his hands to signify this was too much; he couldn't do it. He turned around and gave the bottle a quick squeeze. Before my very eyes, the bottle vibrated. The glass changed shape as something transferred into his hands.

He grabbed the great-grandmother's head again. More forcefully, confident. This time, she yelped, more in surprise than pain. All at once, Uncle Todd had people's attention. They shut up and watched, half of them wondering if he might kill her.

Uncle Todd hawked from deep in his throat and PTU! Spat in her cloudy eye. She recoiled as if she had been hit with snake venom. His spit sizzled and bubbled, dribbling down her face in a steamy trail. She pulled her hand away, and I expected to see melted eyes oozing down her cheek. Nope. Her eyes were not only intact but clearer than when she arrived.

"How many fingers am I holding up?" Uncle Todd asked. He repeated her correct answer into the microphone and proclaimed her cured. A miracle! The tent applauded and praised the Lord.

The moment I climbed on stage my balance shifted and I tumbled hard to the ground. Thank goodness for those wood chips. Somewhere, I sensed Mom, and the first wave of pain unfolding in her stomach, preparing to shoot into her veins and poison her entire body. The awful effects of our drawing from the wall to fill his stupid bottle.

Now that the seal had been broken, Uncle Todd worked at a faster pace, waving a whole line of folk on stage to be healed. I watched him grab a man's arm, twisting the elbow to an angle it was clearly not meant to bend. The gruesome spectacle made the crowd groan. Some averted their eyes. While the man cried out, Uncle Todd squeezed the arm between his knees. I waited for the sound of bone shattering, but the man laughed. Someone tossed a baseball on stage and the man demonstrated his miraculous recovery by pitching the ball over the head of the crowd, out the door of the tent, and sailing across the parking lot, landing who knows where. Maybe it flew all the way to the lake. Uncle Todd punched another man in his bad heart, blew on a deaf woman's ear, grabbed another man in a chokehold and wrestled him to the ground until his face turned red and beads of blood sweated from his forehead. People cheered like the crowd at WrestleMania. I expected Uncle Todd to climb one of the tent poles and perform a leg drop on someone's windpipe.

The cameras captured every moment of the excitement, but I wondered, were the violent theatrics necessary? With the bottle by his side, Uncle Todd could have healed just as efficiently with a lift of his pinky finger, or a soft-blown kiss, even a raised eyebrow. He wasn't doing anything. But he knew miracles were quiet, unnoticeable things and did not make good television. A miracle needed to be dressed up with a lot of ritualistic preamble. It reminded me of the weightlifting I saw during the Olympics. Dad said the athletes could lift those weights as easily as I could lift a broomstick. They only did all that straining and grunting, pretending they could barely pull the weight so the event looked more exciting on television.

"It's no fun watching people do things easy."

You'd think all the bloody, spit-flying, wham-bam-slamming would make people think twice about asking for their miracle, yet the sick kept approaching. The line of hunched over, pain-wracked bodies never diminished as more and more stepped in to fill the vacant spots. I was dumbfounded at their eagerness to be mauled. And the rougher Uncle Todd treated them the happier they were. The person blown on was jealous of the person spat on. The person spat on was jealous of the person punched in the mouth.

All the while, Uncle Todd grinned maniacally, enjoying himself, basking in all the applauses and AMENS!

With each healing, I sensed Mom more clearly, lost in the outskirts of the city, climbing the escarpment, her mind a feverish mess. Self-destructive thoughts raged within her. I didn't see how Mom could survive this incredible amount of energy Uncle Todd drew. Already, he must have expended more than me and my older sister combined.

Everyone hushed up when Uncle Todd got to the two women holding a baby. The raucous excitement in the tent quieted down. The child was yellow. Not a pretty yellow, like Tweety Bird, but a dark shade closer to green. An unripe banana in diapers. No hair on his head, not even eyebrows. Where the baby's eyes should have been were dark pockets, the eyes buried by swollen cheeks. Not healthy baby fat, but skin full of poisonous bile. Uncle Todd conversed with the two women, a mother and grandmother, repeating their responses into the microphone for all to hear.

"He has a liver disease?... The doctors have given up all hope?... So if he doesn't get a miracle, he won't survive?"

The women nodded, keeping one hand on the baby and the other wiping away their copious tears. Uncle Todd tickled the baby beneath its chin and the child looked around, bewildered. The little yellow fellow glowed underneath the stage lights. Uncle Todd prayed, asking for the Lord to heal the child, to fix his liver, make the impurities leave his body. The tent went silent, even the flapping of the *John 3:16* fans held off. The train had unexpectedly run out of tracks. Everyone having such a good time sobered up as the sight of the yellow, struggling infant brought their secret doubt in miracles to the surface. The yellow infant might sleep peacefully tonight, may even return to his natural colour, but he wouldn't be entering kindergarten. He would never finger paint a Christmas card, never get to say, "I love you, mommy." Uncle Todd sensed the shift in the crowd and he distanced himself from the yellow child. He blew into the infant's face, gently said "Amen," and turned his back on the women and the dying baby to walk to the other side of the stage.

I hoped the tent meeting would come to a natural end, but Uncle Todd reeled the crowd back in. I was foolish to have doubted his charm. A consummate showman, he'd no doubt come back from worse bombs.

He asked everyone to reach into their pockets. "Some of you have received miracles. Ask yourself, what's a miracle worth? When the time comes to make an offering, what is fair to give? Half of what's in your pocket? Everything that's in your pocket? Take your money out and hold it up, let the Lord see what you are willing to give."

A rustle of movement swept through the tent as purses snapped open and men groped tight pants for wallets and money clips. Fathers passed dollar bills to their children and one old woman tugged a ring off her finger. Across the tent, money waved overhead, a sea of green and orange bills, a few patches of purple, and one weeping man fanned several reds.

Goddamn, he was good.

The sky turned red. The setting sun bled its dark colours into the clouds. Fortified by the lips of nearly every young boy in the tent, I prepared to end things.

No one noticed me at first. According to those watching, I seemed to materialize out of thin air at the back of the stage. I crawled lithely, my shoulders and hips swaying like a great jungle cat. With a flash of my claws, I snatched the bottle. The cheap crosses glued to the outside tore off.

On stage, I made an alarming sight. Taking a knee, I bludgeoned the bottle against the floor. *Whack! Whack! Whack!* A hollow thud shook the stage planks, but like the bottle Robbie Clattenberg once wielded on the schoolyard, this glass was too thick to shatter.

Uncle Todd turned around. He would be on me soon, tearing the bottle from my grasp. Before the tent's stunned eyes, I pulled the sweaty dress over my head. Clad now only in sneakers and underpants, I leapt off the stage. The boys I'd kissed were terrified. The seductress who lured them into impure thoughts and actions now stood disrobed before everyone, about to publicly expose their sin. Some boys averted their eyes, frightened by my body. I couldn't afford a moment for modesty. I wrapped the bottle in my dress and began swinging it overhead like a sling. The bottle spun fast as a helicopter blade. You heard it whistle inside my dress.

People tried to grab me but failed. I charged down the aisle, targeting the main pole holding the tent roof. I swung the bottle at the metal support beam, hitting my target dead on. It exploded into a million little pieces, glass shards shooting out of the sleeve of my dress and sprinkling the tent. The flying glass struck people's arms and faces. The tent pole shook, the clamps holding it in place snapping, and the canvas roof tumbled, smothering us all. The heavy fabric covered everyone and the weight pushed us to our stomachs, pinning us face down in the wood chips, sawdust shooting up our noses. People screamed. Frightened. Injured.

The palms of many men lifted the heavy canvas, creating a tunnel for us to crawl out into the cool twilight like penitent sinners seeking forgiveness under the Lord's starry night. Right then, the drive-in movies would be starting. Oh, how I wished we'd gone there instead, munching on Dad's engine-cooked hot dogs, cheering the shootouts and covering our eyes for the monsters.

The flattened tent looked like an amoeba, spitting people out one at a time.

No one liked seeing the evening come to an end the way it had. After so much joy, the collapse of the tent violated everyone's sense of peace. The crowd lingered on the asphalt, trading stories, brushing each other off, a few waiting for the ambulances we already heard wailing in the distance. One man held his tiny daughter in his arms, trying to comfort her. She had been lashed across the face by a snapped rope. Her lip swelled up like two giant worms. Her skin split and blood sprayed out.

Uncle Todd went to the girl. I believe his intentions were compassionate. Even the hardest of hearts could be softened by a child suffering. He pressed his hand to her face and blew gently, but unlike the miracles in the tent, nothing happened.

Blood continued to pour from her lips, messing up his hands and legs. He couldn't help her. The crowd still collected their wits, calling for loved ones trapped inside the tent. No one watched Uncle Todd, so his failure to heal went unnoticed.

I watched intently, waiting for Uncle Todd's face to fall. His magic feather had been pulverized and Jezebel, not Samson, had pulled the temple down upon his head. This had to be the final blow to his self-confidence. The longer the girl cried, the more people would see him to be as he confessed at the beginning of the tent meeting, a false prophet, worthy only of their derision.

"Look! Everyone, look!" I cried, wanting all eyes on his moment of failure. He had no place to hide.

The little girl's anguish, my cause for celebration, concerned the twins. Maybe if the child had been older her pain would have seemed unremarkable, but my younger sisters' sympathy overrode their better judgement.

My other younger sister reached into her mouth and removed the stone from her gums. Her eyes strained as the multitude of babbling voices filled her head. She was clearly in torment.

The twins put their heads together, temple-to-temple. In their matching dresses, with the same sheared hair and identical cuts on their faces, you'd swear you were looking at one person leaning against a mirror.

Emergency vehicles drove into the parking lot, flashing their lights and wailing their sirens. Even over the noise, I felt vibrations in the ground beneath the twins' feet. From their open mouths came the familiar purring I was used to hearing come from the wall. It terrified me to see them filled with this energy, even for a brief moment.

The little girl stopped crying. My other younger sister placed the stone back into her gums. The purring and the vibrations abruptly ceased.

The injured girl's lips returned to normal and she offered a big smile to her daddy, who lifted her into the air and hurried her away from this place.

Uncle Todd held on to the twins by their shoulders. He wouldn't let go. His knuckles turned white from the intensity of his grip. His thoughts were obvious. He knew he needn't bother with that asinine pop bottle anymore. No need to waste time with a middleman when the twins could harness this miracle energy directly.

I saw the Scouts mourning the collapse of the tent, assuming their inexperience was to blame. I didn't want them to feel bad, so I saluted as they filed past.

You can bet I didn't ride home in the front of Uncle Todd's truck. He lay the twins on the seat and stretched both seat belts across their bodies. Already, they were nodding off. They were exhausted, nothing unusual about that. At the drive-in, they always fell asleep during the first movie, leaving me and my older sister to later act out the end of the picture for them; usually to great improvement (to this day, they believe *Star Wars* ends with Princess Leia cutting Darth Vader's head off with his own lightsaber).

At home, Uncle Todd carried the twins inside. Instead of putting them in their room upstairs, he brought the sleeping girls to his bed. I followed but he and Grandma slammed the door in my face.

I stood alone in the kitchen. None of the lights were on. Out of the darkness, the remaining animals emerged from their hiding places. They squatted in front of the door, on guard for Uncle Todd's precious bounty. They exposed their teeth, a warning to anyone who thought they might snatch the two little girls and smash them like empty pop bottles.

Left behind, I tried to keep my eyes open, certain if I went to sleep I would awake to an empty house; all the furniture gone, the house sold to strangers who'd chase me out the back door. I'd be forced to live under the porch, subsisting on mice and whatever scraps I found in the garbage.

Outside, the final symptoms of Mom's illness rushed into the air, creating black clouds that approached silently from the north, like grim Zeppelins fated to crash and rain fire over the entire neighbourhood.

NINETEEN

Fingers traced my neck, sliding along my windpipe, searching for a pulse.

Dad!

I expected to open my eyes and discover the last few months had all been a fever dream. Dad would be home, Mom would be well, and Grandma and Uncle Todd would be out of the house. I reached for Dad, eager to run my hands along his rough, workshop skin. Instead, I felt only the disappointment of my older sister's soft, lady flesh.

Shit.

My older sister shared my disappointment.

"I thought I might be dreaming," she said. My pulse shattered her last hope. I'd failed her by not being a dream.

My bedsheets were heavy with dampness, like a bear had stumbled into the house and pissed all over me while I slept. I kicked the icky things to the floor. My bare feet burned against the hardwood. A concerning amount of heat rose from the floor. It felt like hot sand at the beach. I skipped to the window and beheld the frightening vision outside.

A volcanic Aurora Borealis coloured the night sky. Dark clouds blanketed our street, soaking up orange light and reflecting the burning escarpment. Miles of flame roared in the distance. The moist forest trees whistled as they were consumed. On the wall behind us, our shadows danced in the flickering light. A black stench flooded through the curtains, choking us. The smoke smelled of burnt trees and tires and animals. A smell that would never wash out. Not even acid could eat this smell.

My older sister stood frozen in horror by the flames circling us. For once, she hadn't a bit of cleverness up her sleeve. We were witnessing the full effect of Uncle Todd drawing massive amounts of healing from the wall. This catastrophic fire was unstoppable.

With The End staring us in the face, my older sister took my hand, counting on me to forgive her so we could spend our final moments amicably.

In the distance, as faint as the sound of humming mosquitoes, came sirens. The fire brigades from each county teamed up to fight the wild blaze eating its way down the escarpment. Despite the approaching wall of flames—several stories tall in some areas—I dropped my older sister's hand. She needed to earn this.

"Trucks won't be enough," she said. "The fire is too big. And how are they going to share one little fire hydrant?"

"Planes will drop water. I bet the mayor calls in the army too."

"What's the army supposed to do? Bomb the fire?"

"They'll have bulldozers."

My older sister, in a perverse display of optimism, said, "At least we know Mom is still alive. She was well enough to set the fire."

Uncle Todd's tomfoolery, his greedy hands scooping gallons of water from the treacherous stream flowing through our walls, had inflamed Mom's insanity even worse than her stay in hospital. I imagined her wandering the woods, confused, hungry. She dug in the ground for roots to eat and ran her dirty fingers over the trees, combing the trunks of mighty oaks for a pulse to confirm whether she was dreaming. In her travels, she'd discovered the camp of men living in the woods and searched for Dad among them, grabbing fistfuls of their burr-clogged beards, looking for Dad's hidden face. When she didn't find him, the men made trouble, trying to force Mom to her knees. Fearless now, she stuck her hands in the fire, turning her fingernails into candles. She touched dozens of tree roots, trusting the small fires to meet, making a single blaze as long and tall as the skyline. A fire so hot, the rock of the escarpment would melt, flooding the streets with red lava.

My older sister stared out the window. The heat tanned her cheeks. "Before they die, I hope Uncle Todd and the old woman know they're at fault."

Downstairs, Uncle Todd and Grandma took precautions, covering the twins' and their own mouths with damp towels to filter the air. The smoke was surely death to breathe. Everyone heard the stories of chemical drums buried atop the escarpment by cheap, shortsighted businessmen. Poisoned fish, their bodies plumped full of cancer, were reeled out of ponds. When you snapped a plant's stem for a taste of milky sap, your tongue burned. The fire consumed this poison, blowing it straight into our lungs.

Our street was positioned like a canal—collecting everything pouring off the escarpment. There was no escape from the toxic cloud. You could only crawl on the floor while the good air lasted, hoping the cavalry would stem the blaze before an avalanche of fire swept down, burying our neighbourhood like a snow drift.

A few neighbours tried running but none made it past their front lawns. The smoke and the orange heat were too thick. Those attempting to escape collapsed face down in the grass. A desperate, panicked plan. Even if you made it to the car, you wouldn't get far. All the tires went soft, melted like fresh chewing gum.

Other neighbours threw open their faucets, overflowing sinks and bathtubs, thinking their houses might be saved if the floors were flooded. I tried to open the window to yell at them, explain this strain on the water supply would sap the pressure of the firemen's hoses, but the metal window handle seared my fingertips. Forget the neighbours; let them figure things out for themselves.

The pollution turned the moon blood-red, an ominous sign. In the Bible, it says the sun will turn into a sackcloth and the moon will turn to blood during Judgement Day and all the oblivious dead will awaken, but that was superstitious nonsense. The moon didn't really turn red. If you climbed into a rocket ship and flew past all the filth in the atmosphere, you'd see the moon was still her pretty, pale self.

Neither Uncle Todd nor Grandma made any effort to rescue me and my older sister from the choking smoke. They didn't want us in their lifeboat. We pounded on the bedroom door, begging to be let in. They didn't budge. They had the windows sealed tight and weren't wasting good oxygen on the likes of us dirty girls.

All around us, Uncle Todd's animal protectors began to succumb, filling the hall with their death rattles. They died hard. The dogs went first, hiding under the couch, huffing and puffing, trying to cool down but gasping only brought smoke into their lungs faster, blackening the pink tissue. They closed their eyes and bit through their tongues and finished in anguish. The cats crouched and hacked, like they had one mammoth hair ball to spit up. They coughed until their throats ripped and they asphyxiated on their own blood. The snake got cocky, confident he could withstand the heat until his skin began sticking to the floor. He crisped up nicely, like a worm in a dried mud puddle. The squirrels scurried into the basement, exiting through gaps around the storm window. The brightness of the fire blinded them and they died on their backs in the brown grass.

My eyes stung. Rubbing them with my smoke-stained fingers only irritated them worse.

My older sister pounded on the locked door. I refused to join her, my days of asking Grandma for anything were long over.

"Let us in!"

Dream on. I pressed my back against the door and slid down until I sat on the floor. "It's a real shame Dad isn't here."

"Grandma!"

"He'd pull a screwdriver from behind his ear and have the door hinges stripped off lickety-split."

"Don't you dare leave us out here!"

"Then he'd blow on the door like the big bad wolf. He'd huff and he'd puff. He'd gobble Grandma and Uncle Todd right down."

"Aw, shit on you!"

I wasn't sure if she was talking to me or Grandma. We couldn't pound on the door all night. Having snuffed out the animals, the black smoke came for us next. I began to choke.

Common sense dictated we stay low. The best chance for survival would be crawling into the cool embrace of the basement, but my older sister padded up the stairs, ignoring her entire childhood worth of fire safety instructions. The first thing they told you was NEVER go upstairs.

I called for her to come back, warning she was climbing to her doom. Only the basement could save us.

"I'd rather be on top of a burning house than under one!" she yelled back.

That sounded logical, smart even. Who wants tons of burning wood collapsing on them? So I followed behind her, up the stairs and into our old playroom. The scattered Barbies wore soot on their cheeks like blush, and the tipped over doll houses were empty, even the toy families had evacuated.

My older sister attacked the wall, slamming her shoulder and beating her fists along the floorboard. She searched for the hollow *thud* behind the drywall. This was where Dad made the hole to retrieve New Kitten. I admired his craftsmanship. The pattern of the wallpaper lined up precisely along the seams, hiding his work as effectively as a stitch sewn from the inside.

"Don't just stand there, HELP ME!"

My older sister kicked the wall with the point of her toe. I thought her bones would shatter.

"Careful."

She kicked again, focusing all her strength on the end of her foot. This time, the wallpaper cracked. Encouraged, she dropped to her knees and punched. White dust puffed from the breaking drywall. I knelt beside her and pounded on the wall but I didn't have much strength. The smoke made me woozy. My older sister pummelled the wall with the stamina of a boxer. All those cigarettes she puffed had fortified her lungs and made her better prepared to withstand the smoke. I wish I'd smoked more when she'd offered.

Pieces of skin broke off her knuckle, sticking to the bloodied wall. Each time she struck, the drywall weakened, caving in on itself. Finally, her arm broke through, disappearing inside up to her elbow. A cold blast of fresh air shot into the playroom, lifting the dresses of the scattered dolls. The two of us pushed our faces to the gap. Kneeling cheek-to-cheek, we sucked down the cool, refreshing air. Our breath made white clouds. The hole grew larger as the rest of the drywall crumbled under our weight. Soon we could rest our chins on the edge of the hole, and next we could grip it with our hands. Once the drywall collapsed completely, we crawled into the wall.

I took a moment to rest while I coughed up terrible things. Thick, black phlegm shot from my throat. I also coughed up solid bits, maybe pieces of lung. The coolness inside the wall invited me to wrap my arms around myself. I wished for a thick quilt so I could curl up and go to sleep.

"What are you doing?" my older sister said. "Get up."

"Forget it. You'll have to drag me."

An angry boom erupted outside the house. The floor rattled and dust rained on our heads. It sounded like the army.

"They're dropping bombs!"

Another boom echoed across the street. My older sister smacked my shoulder. Those weren't bombs.

"Barbeque tanks are exploding."

Wonderful. More fire.

Break time was over. My older sister pushed her shoulders into my rear, and we began crawling through the wall. A tight squeeze. My knees picked up dozens of slivers but the air remained clean and cool so I kept moving. Any direction must be better than the way we came. Unfortunately, we hadn't far to travel before we'd be forced to turn around and come back. The playroom window looked out on the backyard, a distance of ten, maybe fifteen feet. My older sister encouraged me to keep crawling, and soon we'd covered twice that distance, continuing to move well past where we should have reached a dead end.

After a few minutes, we reached a wall of pink cotton-candy insulation. I didn't want to touch it, knowing the material was super itchy, like poison ivy—get it on your skin and you'd be scratching like a monkey for days. Besides, there wouldn't be anything on the other side, only the end of the house.

"What are you waiting for? Go!"

My hand sank into the soft cloud, pushing the pink fibres apart, discovering yet another pathway waiting for us on the other side.

Over my shoulder, I heard the wall creak. The beams shrank, the wood closing in on us. I panicked. What if the drywall healed over and trapped us inside?

"What difference does it make?" my older sister said. "Keep moving."

We trudged on, scratching and thumping through the wall like nesting squirrels. The narrow path inside the wall grew colder as we travelled deeper. My nose ran and my throat went numb. Whenever I tried turning around my older sister refused to budge.

"We're sharks. We can't stop moving or we'll die."

The floor inside the wall began to slope. I lost my balance and slid headfirst down an incline I could not see the bottom of. The quality of the air changed, filling our nostrils with a wet stench, like clogged drains, or dirty dishrags.

"There's a big hole. Which way do we go now?"

My older sister was resolute. "Down."

We became lost explorers, crawling down the centre of a mountain with no idea if the bottom offered a way out. We only knew death waited behind us. With no place to go but into the mysterious, never-ending darkness, I moved slowly, fighting to keep my balance. The slope dropped so severely I nearly tumbled ass-over-teakettle.

Behind me, my older sister turned chatty. "If I still had my record player, we'd have Ricky with us. He'd make Uncle Todd open the door, that's for sure."

I ignored her.

"I'm just saying."

At the bottom of the long slope, my hand sank into a soft mess. Something with the consistency of a rotting pumpkin, the surface dotted with little bumps and hairs. I first thought a field of mushrooms sprouted in the dark, surviving on water dripping from our pipes. I continued feeling, and my hand ran across a familiar pattern—ladder rungs made out of bone. Not mushrooms I touched, but flesh. My hands pressed against someone's rib cage.

"Rebecca, back up."

The chest inflated, its owner drawing a deep breath, wheezy and painful. I screamed and tried to climb over my older sister, but she pushed me and I fell to the damp floor alongside the mystery person. Their exhaled breath blew across my chin. I lay with my face inches from this invisible body, our lips close enough to kiss.

Using leaky lungs and split lips, the person in the wall struggled to pronounce my older sister's name.

"Becca..."

We used our fingers to trace his body. First, we felt his shin, where the skin clung tight to the bone. The leg smooth, no hair. We felt his sunken stomach and knotted chest, our fingers making plunking sounds over his ribs, like a stick dragged across a picket fence. His ears were stumps, barely more than two holes in the side of his head, the skin and cartilage either withered or gnawed away. Even through all this deformity, he felt familiar to my older sister. She recognized her old friend.

I tried saying his name but my voice came out as a whimper. My older sister abruptly hushed me. "Don't make things worse for him."

Moving around in this enclosed pit was awkward, but my older sister managed to slide her arm behind the lame figure's shoulders and sit him up. He weighed nothing. She glided her palm over the dimples in his bald head. He relaxed, his sick breath coming out gently now. His terrors were over. She pressed her cheek against his, her nose nuzzling into the rotted bulb of his own, a gaping hole trailing a moustache of crusted snot across his lip. She wiped his face clean and whispered into his ear holes. The body in her arms felt both familiar and foreign.

"Oh, Ricky. I'm so sorry, buddy."

Curious, I touched his arms. Despite the dead skin and cold rot clinging to his bones, I recognized immediately these were not the hands that had seized my ribs to throw me out of bed. These were not the hands that pressed my softness under the covers, or clamped my mouth shut so I couldn't scream, or forced me to my knees. These dying arms overflowed with gentleness, posing a danger to no one except some noisy, germ carrying birds. I sniffed his fingertips, which smelled only of the cookies used to lure him into our house, no trace of the thousand cigarettes "Ricky" consumed in my bed.

The moment of the switch seems obvious in retrospect. This Ricky, our Ricky, never mastered speech or learned to drive or took up smoking. This Ricky ran home to his mother each day, expertly avoiding my older sister's attempts to kiss him.

The smell of the imposter's cigarette butts were so distinctive I couldn't believe I failed to recognize them earlier in the healing tent, when I had pushed Roman away as he tried leaning close to whisper in my ear.

"Oh no."

Ricky's body felt in danger of breaking apart. I didn't dare hug him. I felt shame for every time I cursed his name. All along, he hadn't been in my bed, but stuck in the wall, his agony more prolonged than New Kitten's. I couldn't bear to count the months. Worse, he couldn't understand what imprisoned him in the dark. Did he think he was being punished? Had he done something wrong? He must have cried endlessly for his mother. Would it be cruel to tell him how sad she was without him? She missed him terribly, thinking of nothing but her lost little boy.

Ricky didn't deserve this misery. Rotting inside the walls.

"We can't leave him here," my older sister said. Neither of us would crawl an inch further without Ricky. We couldn't abandon him.

Being moved caused Ricky tremendous pain. We tore strips from our gowns and tied him to our ankles to drag behind us, over rivets and through the insulation. In a breaking voice, my older sister sang to him. She tried songs from the record player, but he didn't recognize them. He hadn't heard that music. The only song he seemed to know was "Do You Believe In Magic?" from the McDonalds commercial, so we sang the jingle over and over during our long slog through the walls of the house.

Our path narrowed. We went from our knees to our stomachs, inching along like a couple of worms. The house pressed down on my head and we became wedged too tight to turn around. The space between the floor and the ceiling cracked our ribs. The only hope keeping us going was a tiny dot of light in the distance. Our North Star. Though for all we knew, this promise of escape was as far away as the end of the galaxy. Maybe we crawled towards a light that had died millions of years ago. I reached for that speck, wanting to plug my finger inside the twinkling, white circle and stretch it wide.

"I smell smoke," my older sister said. "We're going to make it."

We tumbled through the basement ceiling, out the hole Dad ripped beneath the dishwasher, in a rain of missing marbles and mice skeletons. Ricky didn't survive the fall. He transitioned to peace the moment he reached the other side of the wall. The light went out of him and he no longer looked like a real person, but a crude approximation my older sister and I hastily constructed out of papier-mâché, a Halloween decoration to sit on the porch.

My older sister kissed his forehead, not like a lover, but like a sister, the way she should have to begin with. "Poor Ricky."

We folded his arms over his chest and tucked him into the dirt floor, trusting he would be embraced by whoever else was buried down there.

Ricky's funeral rites were brief, lasting as long as it took for sweat to re-form on our brows. The fire had not abated, only drawn closer. More booms echoed from neighbouring houses. Instead of exploding barbeque tanks, this time the noise came from hunting rifles pulled off the rack and loaded one last time to save wives and children from the suffering of burning alive.

"Let's crawl into the dryer. Maybe the steel walls will protect us from the heat and the lint trap will filter the smoke."

My bright idea only infuriated her.

"Goddamn you, Em. Are you going to live in a fantasy world forever? Only little babies believe stories instead of the way things really are."

"Who's a baby? Dancing in your make-believe wig, kissing and rubbing against your make-believe boyfriend... Talk about believing stories."

There was no time to argue with her. The smoke clouds grew bigger and orange light poured through the storm window as the flames approached. The fire engines had gone silent long ago, no doubt melted like tin soldiers. With no one left, the fire would blaze all the way to the Great Lakes. Soon we'd be consumed, just black bones that would scatter to ash in the morning breeze.

Facing a tragic death didn't make us special. Every person on Earth will one day find themselves finished. Only the lucky ones leave behind corpses in bed. Innocents like Ricky are forever denied that final blessing. My older sister and I still had a choice in how we spent our final moments, something Fate denied most of human history.

"Let's go upstairs, get under the covers, and fall asleep for the last time," I said. "We don't have to be alone; we can lie down together." Maybe it won't be so bad. Maybe we'll remember some things after all.

The floor above our head creaked. Heavy feet stomped

down the hallway, clunking like the Frankenstein monster. The front door opened, filling our house with the smoke of burning trees and homes and people.

"Let's see who that is," my older sister said, denying me permission to lie down just yet.

In the hallway, the wallpaper melted right off the wall, landing on the floor in big sticky sheets. Underneath, you saw the original colour. Faint markings in black chalk were doodled all over. Symbols and words I couldn't make out through the smoke. Latin? Hieroglyphics? Before I could look closer, a rush of hot air blasted through the hall, lifting the hem of my tattered dress and spitting red embers into my face. They burnt little pockmarks all over my skin.

Both the front door and the door to Mom and Dad's bedroom stood open, creating a searing wind tunnel. Outside, at the end of our walkway, came the shouts of a crazed man who believed himself to be on a heroic mission. His last follower, a ratty old woman, cheered him on. Neither could catch their breath in the boiling air.

When Uncle Todd first locked himself behind the bedroom door, he believed he could ride Mom's firestorm out and emerge from his bunker as a living testament to the Lord's mercy. As the temperature grew more destructive, Uncle Todd decided he would be better served by taking action. If he stayed hidden in the bedroom, he would be finished. Deciding martyrs didn't leave behind cowering bones, he kicked open the door and charged into the street.

Carrying the twins like a shield, Uncle Todd endured the heat. Standing across the melted yellow lines of the road, he faced the approaching wall of flames, pelting them with prayer and commands to abate. Where the fire engines and the army failed, Uncle Todd believed his "healing hands" would prevail. What a horse's ass. He looked mighty foolish. What did he think he was going to do? I mean, how does one "heal" a fire?

I nudged my older sister with my elbow, urging her to get a load of Uncle Todd. He pushed the twins' heads together, trying to get them to draw for him. My older sister grabbed my hand. She pled for my help.

"Sing with me, Emery. He's close by, I can tell."

"Who?"

"I don't have my records but if we sing together, he'll come."

She wanted to summon Roman. The idea of revenge excited me. That disgusting creep. He took my older sister by deceit; tried taking me by force. He must be nearby, hiding behind a bush or squatting in the gutter, spying as he always had.

Roman would pay for fooling all of us, fooling Dad even, pretending to be his friend all these years then swiping his daughters as easily as he might swipe the last beer out of the fridge. In my anger, I became barbaric.

"What will we do? Trip him on the stairs and pour lye in his eyes? Use the garden trowel to stab his face apart?" I swore before I died, I'd splash his blood on my body.

My older sister rolled her eyes. Boy, was I stupid. She said, "Let Roman go to the twins."

"And do what?"

"Make them unable to draw from the wall."

I ran for the house. I'd dive under the covers and wait for the flames to surround me. The flames would make me forget all of this. If the twins turned out to be mistaken about oblivion after death, and Mom and Dad managed to join us in the afterlife, I'd tell them nothing about how their eldest daughter spent her final breath calling for the rape of her youngest sisters. Her baby sisters.

I couldn't run fast enough to escape my older sister. My legs were too sore from crawling through the wall. She tackled me from behind, wrapping her arms around my waist and pushing me to the ground. Fireflies from the burning grass landed on my face.

"Emery, listen. Once the twins can't use the wall again, Mom can't be hurt ever. It'll be safe for her to come home. Dad too. Don't you want that?"

I struggled to throw her off my back. Was she insane? What could possibly be left for Mom and Dad to come back to? A smouldering heap? No way to know the difference between the bones of their children and the bones of stray animals?

"What if Mom and Dad left on purpose?" My older sister kept me pinned to the ground. "What if they wanted this to happen, for us to be protected from Uncle Todd. Maybe Roman didn't betray Dad. Maybe he's only doing what Dad commanded."

For the first time in my life, I hoped Mom was dead. I wanted her in the gentle embrace of eternal oblivion, protected from this total fracturing of her once beautiful family.

My older sister sang. Her voice sounded beautiful, the part of her I would always envy. She laid kisses on my neck, encouraging me to join in, lift up my voice and summon the one person who could keep the twins from hurting Mom.

While I lay in the grass, watching my fingernails turn black in the scorching heat, my mind returned to the halcyon days spent hiding from Uncle Todd within the gargoyle church. In particular, I recalled the minister's boring sermon about Sodom and Gomorrah, that sinful city visited by beautiful angels. When the degenerate citizens learned the angels were hiding in Lot's house, they pounded on the door, demanding the angels come out so they could violate them, which I took to mean force them on their knees. Lot tried to mollify the mob by offering his daughters instead to satisfy their perversity.

The minister paused the narrative, saying nonbelievers liked to use this story as an example of the Bible's barbarism. A man offering his own daughters to be torn apart in a pack of lust? Disgraceful. The minister said those people missed the point. Lot was not gleeful to offer up his daughters. Surely his heart was heavy but under the circumstances, what else could be done? "There is beauty in a man who loves the Lord so much he is willing to give up the purity and maybe even the life of his own precious daughters."

I'll never forget Dad's reaction. He jeered the minister worse than he would an outfielder who let an easy ball roll between his legs. "I missed the part where dandy-boy Lot offered himself to the mob first!" Dad didn't care how badly Lot felt afterwards. The guy was a bum, below contempt. My older sister was wrong. Dad would never have agreed, let alone orchestrated for any of his daughters to be sacrificed.

My older sister was making a terrible mistake.

The smell of Roman's cigarettes flooded my nostrils, and I saw piles of his butts littering the lawn. My older sister's voice lured him this far and soon she would sic him on the twins like a ravenous dog.

At last, I managed to struggle from beneath her. Casting her aside, I ran down the street, small stones piercing my feet, leaving a trail of bloody footprints. I'd never run so fast before. I needed to get to the twins before Roman.

Blind to any other option, I raced to my sisters who dangled from Uncle Todd's arms. The worst part of that moment was how they smiled, happy to see me, as if I came to protect them.

In a way, I did.

For the last time, no one could tell the twins apart. I lifted the tiny hand closest to me and bit through her fingers. Flesh and bone cleaved evenly with one savage chomp. Her nails cut my throat and her knuckles blocked my windpipe. Let's see Uncle Todd work any magic with them now. Nearly blacking out, my ears filled with my baby sister's agonizing screams as I collapsed to the soft blacktop, my face splashed with her blood, and feeling more wicked than old Lot.

IN THE WALL

Police searched the neighbourhood for days, only to find the identical, eerie scene at every house. Announcing themselves with a shout and a knock, the police entered, guns drawn, and began the long task of making the houses silent by turning off all the faucets, switching off the TVs, unplugging the automatic can openers whirling in the kitchen, and dumping food into bowls for dogs who were no longer there.

Later, some officers anonymously shared their observations on talk radio. One spoke of ashtrays full of cigarettes burned down to the filter, another reported seeing empty bird cages and aquariums, and several mentioned turntables left spinning. The most common record playing? *Saturday Night Fever*. One officer alleged all the clocks had stopped. An astute radio host asked if the stopped clocks all shared the same time but the caller didn't remember. Every police officer agreed on one thing: there wasn't a single person anywhere.

At first.

The search quickly became demoralizing, the repetition mind-numbing. Knock on the door, enter, find no one inside. In desperation, the police lifted basement dryers and knocked on the walls, looking for secret panels homeowners might be hiding behind. Each house left the police shaking their head, feeling defeated, and moving onto the next.

The houses in our neighbourhood remain unoccupied to this day. The once vibrant community where you couldn't throw a rock without hitting a barbeque or a garage sale has become a ghost town, like the abandoned cities in the shadow of Chernobyl. For years, grieving family members tended the lawns, raising cardboard placards bearing the names of the deceased—tombstones in the style of election signs. Photographs of the lost were stapled to boarded up doors and windows. Many people left flowers. For houses with children, the lost nieces and grandsons, stuffed teddy bears and favourite Transformer toys were left behind. As the years rolled by, the memorials were updated less frequently, only on holidays and anniversaries. Nowadays, they're all neglected, their keepers passed on. From our front porch, we can see the remains of these rotted shrines.

To aid the search, the police borrowed search-and-rescue dogs from the big city. Now they expected to get somewhere. Trained to sniff out corpses, the dogs went right for the walls, scratching and pawing. Police crawled beneath the porches, finding their way into the foundations, and looking up between the walls with flashlights. From then on, whichever wall the dogs pawed and howled at was smashed open with picks and hammers. The former owners were entombed inside, their withered bodies sunken into the pink insulation. Messy work. In old pictures of the police crews, their uniforms looked like they were covered in volcanic ash but it was actually plaster. Breaking open the walls took time. Eventually, the police were forced to accept civilian volunteers, the only way to complete the task in a reasonable amount of time.

The crews worked all through the night, removing bodies and carrying them to the front lawn. By morning, they had recovered nearly four hundred and no one had an idea of how many houses were left to go. Every police officer asked the same terrifying question: How long did the lane of ghost houses stretch? How many walls must they split open like piñatas, spilling these gruesome prizes into the grass?

The lengthy operation resulted in the near collapse of the region's emergency departments, seeing a mass exodus of police, firemen, and ambulance workers. Old timers on the force weren't surprised by the quitting. According to the salty dogs, most officers had the mental strength to handle a finite number of dead bodies. It differed from man to man, maybe one hundred, maybe two. Under ordinary circumstances, this threshold took the course of a career to reach, not a single exhaustive weekend. Half of the total dead were children. This had been a family neighbourhood after all.

Outside the city, the Niagara tragedy found what can only be called "popularity," aided by a morbid fascination with the iconic photos showing the thousands of recovered bodies laid out across the city. People still travel to look at our house. The real pushy ones knock on the door, thinking we'll be so excited for company we'll invite them in for cookies and coffee. *We drove all the way from Saskatoon,* they say. My sisters and I treat them like Jehovah's Witnesses, no reason to let them get a foot in the door. I look forward to the day this fascination with my sisters ends.

"Do they hate us?" I often wonder about the locals, who never give visitors directions to the house. "Do they wish we'd moved someplace else?"

My sisters find the question confusing. "Where else are we supposed to live? This is our home. All of our stuff is here."

We might have followed Auntie Linda's example and found new lives in places far away, where we'd have to communicate by mail. One of us could brave Toronto, another could move to Regina... My sisters have no interest in entertaining the idea, not even in a "What If" scenario. Besides, what was the point now? The time to move would have been decades ago when we still had the possibility of new lives ahead of us.

Halfway to being old bags now, my sisters and I are comfortable together. Old age has been a great equalizer. We're balanced now. No one thinks of us as the younger girls and the older girls any longer. We're just four, reclusive, despised old women.

*

My sister ran across the burning street, through flickering orange light, clutching her hand to her chest, the blood streaking faster than her tears. The pain left her in hysterics. I'd never seen her so unhinged. She spent her entire life quietly watching, as if she already knew better than anyone in the room, be it older siblings, teachers, or minister. Now my actions caused her suffering. She must have felt as betrayed as I had when my older sister offered me up to Roman.

Her bitten off fingers still pulsed with life. The orphaned digits clawed inside my stomach, trying to dig free, knowing every moment inside me diminished their chance of being reattached. They tickled, trying to make me vomit. I flexed my tummy muscles, trying to drown her fingers in a wave of digestive acid.

My sister's blood sizzled on the hot asphalt. Her stains lasted for years. The sight of her running down the street, terrified, a great fire behind her, reminded me of a similar picture I saw of a village girl caught in a war. I regretted what I'd done. History would judge me as harshly.

Uncle Todd lifted his remaining niece above his head and shook her like a rag doll, as if her mere presence would hold back the dragon's breath rolling off the escarpment. No longer in tandem, the ability of my younger sisters to draw good fortune for Uncle Todd, be it with miraculous healing or holding back the flames, was nonexistent.

While Uncle Todd stared into the advancing fire, Grandma collapsed on the road. She had been cheering him on, shouting *Amen!* Until the very end, she counted on her darling boy to put out the fire and save us all. She grabbed her chest, keeping her pounding heart from breaking its way through her chest bones.

Neither Uncle Todd nor Grandma noticed Roman walking amongst us, still wearing his Ricky disguise. He hummed my older sister's song. A cigarette popped into his mouth, self-ignited in the burning air.

My bleeding sister barrelled right into Roman's waist, knocking herself backwards. Her head hit the road, but the blacktop had melted soft, protecting her from the slightest bruise.

I tried to yell at Roman to get away from her. Only black smoke coughed from my mouth.

My bleeding sister was ripe fruit on a sagging branch, so easily plucked. Roman grabbed her wrist. At first, I thought he was going to sling her over his shoulder and carry her away, but he only examined her wounded hand. He blew smoke, dismissive, moving on, leaving her crying and bleeding in the street. No longer identical to her sister, she ceased to interest him.

Roman walked past me, pushing his way into the house, probably to root through the fridge looking for free beer. All Roman did was take. It never occurred to him people might want to keep the things that belonged to them.

Grandma could no longer breathe. The corners of her mouth turned black with soot. The smoke and the heat overwhelmed her preexisting medical conditions and knocked her down for the count. One side of her face slacked, the other twitched as blood vessels spasmed. She pointed a finger at me, holding her mouth open wide, but the words died on her swollen tongue. I could have dragged her inside, given her water, allowed her to die in a bed instead of in the same street where cats got run down by cars, but my compassion was at an end. I'd already harmed family, good family. I wasn't going to redeem myself with her.

My older sister waited in the front hall, arms crossed, unimpressed with my solution to the twins.

"You thought that was better than a moment with Roman? Scarring her for life?"

I brushed her aside, climbing the stairs to the old playroom. A low purr, operating on a frequency only dogs and the wicked could hear, came from the wall. Instead of strength or menace, the low purr sounded weak, wounded, like the last flutters of a dying beetle's wings.

Standing before the wall, I wondered, was this victory? Soon I would be dead, the edge of my mouth covered in soot like Grandma, but the fire would also consume the entire house. Whatever lurked in the walls would be naked. Exposed. Perhaps it couldn't survive on the other side of the wall. Perhaps it too would burn.

Using the back of my hand, I swatted the wall. A final display of contempt. I hoped I survived long enough to watch the first flames singe the wallpaper.

A force emerged from the wall and seized hold of my wrist, squeezing until my knuckles cracked and the fingernails felt about to pop off. I kicked my feet against the wall, trying to back up, but the hold on me was too strong. My hand disappeared into the wall. Whatever resided on the other side pulled me in deeper and deeper, demanding another Ricky or New Kitten, something new and warm to hold against its belly and fall asleep with. Soon my chin sank into the wall; it was about to swallow my entire face.

My older sister had followed me up the stairs. At the first sight of me being pulled into the wall, Rebecca charged into the room. She wrapped her arms around my waist and held on, digging her heels into the floor, doing her best to be my anchor.

Her effort made no difference— the wall continued sucking me further inside. The smell of damp and rot filled my nose, the cool air nearly too foul to breathe. I braced myself for Rebecca to let go, but she held on, refusing to give me up, even as her own hands were sucked into the wall.

I didn't care what the thing looked like, so I closed my eyes. The vibrations washed over my face, rubbing my pupils, using phosphenes to sketch its shape, making me "see" it. I believe the technical term for what was happening is "prisoner's cinema". Behind me, Rebecca screamed when her face entered the wall. She saw it too.

The shape took the form of a massive tree. Hundreds of shoots and trunks branched out in all directions. The leafy canopies recalled our trip to the greenhouse with Grandma, where the plants couldn't keep their hands off us, stroking our bodies the way we stroked the wall. It would take a greenhouse the size of a city to contain the multitudes inside the walls.

A new sound entered the playroom; the *thump-thump-thumping* of blood spilling from Mary's blunted fingers. Her blood solidified the moment it hit the scalding floor, gasping like a dying ghost. Mary linked her arms around Rebecca's waist. Her blood leaked over both our legs. She was so tiny; how could she bleed so large? I worried she'd soon be empty.

"She's coming now too," Mary said.

Somehow, Uncle Todd's grip loosened, perhaps to lie beside his dying mother, and he released our other younger sister, Shelley. She joined us in the playroom in time to see me disappear into the wall fully, with Rebecca and Mary following close behind.

Understandably, Shelley hesitated. She knew what needed to be done, and that it would be the worst pain she would ever endure. Hard to rush into.

Shelley knew the easiest way to perform the necessary operation. She selected the largest and heaviest of our wooden dollhouses. Lifting with her back, she lifted the flat, heavy base and wedged her fingers underneath. She pinned the same three fingers missing from her older-by-five-minutes sister's hand, laying the wood right along the knuckles. She placed one foot on the back of her hand, and the other on the first floor of the open-faced dollhouse. Once she had her hand immobile, Shelley used all her strength to bend her fingers in the opposite direction. Brave girl, she did it on the first jerk. It sounded like three fistfuls of spaghetti being snapped in half.

Her fingers now pointed in impossible directions, looking like full cigarettes stuffed out into an ashtray. During the whole process, she was quiet. She kept her agony to herself.

And she was nowhere near through yet. She crammed her broken, floppy fingers into her mouth and bit down.

Until my dying day, I will continue to be astounded that she didn't pass out. Seeing her three sisters being pulled into the wall made her determined to keep biting, no matter the pain. She later described her fingers as having the texture of squid;

plump and rubbery. The whole thing would be much easier if only she had time to file her teeth, to make the edges sharper.

She twisted her head back and forth as she gnawed through her flesh. Under this extra tension, the meat tore. She yanked her hand from her mouth, revealing three shredded stumps, with protruding white bone. She joined Mary, wrapping her arms around Rebecca's waist before she disappeared behind me completely into the wall.

I felt shameful that Rebecca and I behaved like Lot, offering our young daughters up to the mob before we first offered ourselves. Shelley didn't force one of her sisters to suffer. Instead of choosing one of us to sacrifice, she sacrificed herself.

Using her functioning hand, Shelley reached into her mouth and removed the piece of gravel from her gums. This time, when she leaned against her twin sister, temple-to-temple, the babble speaking away inside her head passed through both Rebecca and me. Together, the four of us listened to the cacophony of ancient, angry voices. The sensation was unbearable.

This, I'm sure, is what Mom and Dad feared the most, the powerful twins touching the wall together. Looking back, bad haircuts and different birthdays were a small price to pay for security.

Mary and Shelley gained strength. They pulled backwards, extracting first Rebecca, and then me from the dank void on the other side of the wall.

Standing together, we all thought the same thing. *Be quiet!* We didn't want the eternal babble running through our heads. *Be quiet forever!*

The house went dark. The flickering orange light disappeared as flames slithered into the ground. I listened for whoops of celebration—the firemen honking their horns and flashing their sirens, mocking the fiery foe they assumed had been subdued by the strength of their hoses.

They made not a sound.

If not the firemen, I listened for the boastful praises of Uncle Todd. Surely, he'd be kicking up cartwheels, dancing in the street, believing he had put the fire out with his "healing hands." I'm sure he was already dreaming of the next natural disaster he'd vanquish—shushing a hurricane, singing an earthquake to sleep with a lullaby...

He made not a sound.

My sisters and I stepped back. The once malleable walls were now cracked slabs, as cold and dull as tombstones. We felt our way through the pitch-black house, making our way down the stairs onto the porch to investigate the new neighbourhood. There wasn't a sound to be heard across the barren landscape, not the chirping of a cricket or the wings of a moth. Even the grass had no more breath, not a single blade made a rustle.

Shelley had sacrificed others after all, sacrificed who knows how many hundreds of households across the city, just to save us, her unworthy sisters.

Rebecca and I took both girls into the bathroom, sitting them together on the same toilet where we used to undergo our horrendous haircuts together. "Let me dress your wounds," we said, dipping their finger stumps in bleach and dampening toilet paper to mould a cast. I felt awkward handling Mary's injury even as I continued to digest her missing fingers, but she put on a good face, telling me she would be alright. She was confident she'd grow up to roll her own cigarettes one-handed.

I retrieved the piece of gravel from the playroom floor. After brushing the soot away, I offered the stone to Shelley, assuming she wanted her talisman back in its familiar groove.

She tossed the bloody lump away. "I don't need it anymore. The babble is quiet now." Without asking, I knew she meant for good.

*

By the time the police made their way to our house, they were loopy with weariness, driven half mad by the repetition of empty houses followed by bodies in the wall. They weren't excited to see us, keeping their distance at first, suspicious. We were the only survivors they had seen in a week. Only Mary and Shelley, feverishly convulsing on the floor from infection, broke the spell and their rescue training kicked in, prompting one of the officers to whisper into his radio for an ambulance.

Coming in behind the police was Auntie Linda, who persevered to the end, finally completing her journey back to us. Instead of rushing to cover us in hugs and kisses, her face crumbled under the weight of sorrow. She shook her head, seeming to think she had failed us by not arriving sooner.

We told Auntie Linda we were fine, upright and pink, our bellies all grumbling 'cause dying folk got no appetite. We told her to get the police to unblock the street before Mom and Dad made their way home. Any moment now, they would walk through the door hand-in-hand and scoop us up. We'd laugh as Dad's long beard tickled our faces, and we'd groom him, plucking the twigs and stones from his whiskers and braiding a loop under his chin. Mom hated a beard and couldn't wait for Dad to hack his off with an axe. Reunited, Dad would declare it was time for us to take a vacation, claiming he had a little more "roughing it" to get out of his system. We'd go into the woods, where the animals retained their natural fear of people, hiding whenever we got close. A beautiful hut awaited us, constructed by Dad out of twigs and mud, based on building skills he learned from observing the beavers. We would sleep comfortably, because it was a hut built in the spirit of optimism. Knowing his whole family would be joining him, Dad built it big. We'd fish from the lake, so plentiful with salmon I'd dare my older sister to wade in on all fours like a bear and snatch one with her mouth. She would show me up, dunking her head into the rushing water and tossing on shore enough fish for the whole family. We'd have big fires at night, our camp as bright as if we had the sun in our laps. The smoke trail so tall it could be seen all the way from the city. Dad would carve new fingers for my sisters out of rock, giving them a grip so strong they could crack raw chestnuts for us to roast over the fire. Mom would tut, saying we'd have to see a doctor about those missing fingers when we came home, but Dad would laugh and say that could wait, it was only a scratch. At night, Mom and Dad would lie in each other's arms and my older sister and I would giggle before burying our heads under a blanket of leaves to give them privacy. It would be the greatest summer ever, surpassed only by the following summer, and then the one after that and then the one after that...

Auntie Linda pressed her hand to her heart, trying to hold its broken pieces together. The police dogs growled, straining against their leashes. Slipping out of the policemen's hands, the dogs raced across the living room, sniffing and barking at the wall. Shaken from their spell, the men advanced, wielding hammers and picks covered in the dusty drywall of a hundred previous homes. Sore and weary, they began smashing through the wall and pulling out the bodies.

ACKNOWLEDGEMENTS

As well as Adam Dale, to whom the book is dedicated, I give great thanks to Shannon Lotecki, who was not only the first reader of this book, but of each of my previous attempts at writing novels. I don't know if I would have continued to develop as a writer without the generous gift Adam and Shannon gave of their time to be an audience. As well as your feedback, you made the work feel worthwhile.

Thanks to my parents for years of support. And to my older brother Jonathan, and younger sister Amy, who together made me understand the benefits and cons of being a middle-child.

Thanks to Shanta Rangaratnam for her tireless cheerleading, and insightful suggestions.

Writing fiction is both reporting and imagination. I fondly recall my high school drama classes, which I realize now were also group exercises in storytelling. I believe the many hours spent honing these skills contributed to my growth as a writer, and feel thankful to my many collaborators, such as Bryden Dunn, Jeff Rogers, Adam Forrester, Paula Korince, Jane Mitchell, Michelle Duguay, Jenn Ajandi, Morgan Walker, Uke Bosse, and others.

Thanks to Conan Tobias and Taddle Creek, who published my first story, and went on to provide both friendship and recommendations for grants that kept me working on other projects.

In 2005 I collaborated with filmmaker Chris Triffo on a documentary titled *Circus Of God* about tent revivals, which gave me insight into the world of charismatic preachers that aided in the writing of this book.

The first draft of *Sacrifice of the Sisters Lot* was written over a period of three months within the Mansion House, St. Catharines oldest tavern, where the dark wooden interior gave off a nautical vibe. This was like being gifted with a second high school experience, where I was supported and encouraged by the likes of Jay Kline, Vicki Smith, Bruce Bellows, RJ Jackson, Pige, and others.

Small passages from this book appeared in different form as parts of short stories published in *Freefall Magazine* and *The Feathertale Review*.

Thanks to Aimée Parent Dunn and Palimpsest Press for publishing this story I've spent many years crafting. And finally, thank you to all the readers, without whom, a writer's work only feels half-done.

Chris Kuriata lives in and often writes about the Niagara Region. His short fiction has appeared in magazines in Canada, the US, the UK, Australia, Ireland, South Africa, and Japan. *Sacrifice of the Sisters Lot* is his first novel.